A Classic Collection
of Haunting
Ghost Stories

Selected by
Marvin Kaye

With
Saralee Kaye

LITTLE, BROWN AND COMPANY

A *Little, Brown* Book

First published in The United States by
Doubleday under the title *Ghosts* in 1981
This edition published by Little, Brown in 1993

A CIP catalogue record for this book
is available from the British Library

Printed in England by Clays Ltd, St Ives plc

ISBN 0 316 90565 8

Little, Brown and Company (UK) Limited
165 Great Dover Street
London SE1 4YA

CONTENTS

ACKNOWLEDGEMENTS

"Minuke" copyright © 1950 by Nigel Kneale. Reprinted from *Tomato Cain and Other Stories* by permission of the author.

"Legal Rites" copyright © 1950 by *Weird Tales;* renewed 1977 by Isaac Asimov and Frederik Pohl. Reprinted by permission of Issac Asimov.

"A Quartet of Strange Things": "The Vampire of Croglin Grange," "The Old Man in Yellow," "The Glowing Maggot of Doom" copyright © Bernhardt J. Hurwood 1971; "Corpse at the Inn" copyright © Bernhardt J. Hurwood 1965. Reprinted by permission of the author.

"The Lady of Finnigan's Hearth" copyright © 1977 by Parke Godwin. All rights reserved. Reprinted from *Fantastic Stories* magazine by permission of the author.

English versions of "The Fisherman's Story" and "The Ghost of the Capuchins" copyright © 1981 by Faith Lancereau and Marvin Kaye, and reprinted by permission of the adapters.

"Who Rides with Santa Anna?" copyright © 1958 by Columbia Publications, Inc. Reprinted by permission of the author.

"Jane" copyright © 1981 by Barbara Gallow. Permission granted by the author.

"Doorslammer" copyright © 1969 by Donald A. Wollheim. From *Two Dozen Dragon Eggs*, by arrangement with the author.

"A Gathering of Ghosts" copyright © 1981 by Craig Shaw Gardner. Permission granted by the author.

"21 Main Street No." copyright © 1981 by Ila Jerom. Permission granted by the author.

"Four Ghosts in Hamlet" copyright © 1965 by Mercury Press, Inc. Reprinted by permission of Robert P. Mills, Ltd., literary representative of the author.

"The Ghost of Sailboat Fred" copyright © 1981 by Saralee Terry. Permission granted by the author.

"The Haunting of Y-12" copyright 1981 by Al Sarrantonio. Permission granted by the author.

"Blind Man's Buff" copyright 1929 D. Appleton & Co., renewed 1957 by H. Russell Wakefield. Permission granted by Arkham House Publishers Inc., Sauk City, Wis.

"Money Talks" copyright © 1981 by Dick Baldwin. Permission granted by the author.

"How Fear Departed From the Long Gallery" reprinted by permission of the Estate of E. F. Benson.

Thanks to my wife, Saralee, for handling all the basic negotiations and technical demands of shaping this huge volume in a tiny amount of time.

My gratitude to Kit MacDonald and Bernhardt J. Hurwood for making available certain valuable works of ghost literature and folklore.

—M.K.

WARNING TO THE READER

Tales rich in atmosphere may please in moderation but—just as sweet-meats cloy if eaten wholesale—will lose luster if read overabundantly at a single sitting. The stories and verses in these pages vary greatly in mood, style, and impact, but for best effect, they ought to be consumed like chocolate marshmallow fudge: a little at a time.

For best results, take one or two just before bedtime, preferably on the stroke of twelve and with the rain slashing at the panes, the lightning splitting the firmament, and soft music on the FM interrupted by storm reports that all nearby bridges have been washed out. Taken neat under those conditions, the doses herein contained ought to have optimum results, especially if there is no one else in the house, for many occultists believe that if one thinks profoundly enough upon the spectral, some itinerant phantom will look upon that state of mind as an invitation to come in through the wall and enjoy a midnightcap. . . .

Enjoy, enjoy! And I hope you make it to daybreak.

—M.K.

INTRODUCTION

Why Are Ghosts Coming Back to Life?

When I was a boy, I whiled away many lonely hours shivering with the latest issue of *Weird Tales* and other macabre magazines and comic books. Saturdays were reserved for going to the movie house across the street, where I squirmed impatiently through the latest rubber-stamped Western in order to see the featured event of the week, Universal's most recent *Frankenstein, Dracula,* or *Wolfman* film.

My taste for the ghastly did not please my family, and at school my closest friends were those who shared a similar predilection. Easily cowed then, I accepted the attitude of relatives and teachers as accurate: Fantasy fiction was not really respectable, and I would probably outgrow it.

Then one day I bought an early paper edition of *Dracula* and discovered, to my astonishment, that Bram Stoker's classic graveyard thriller was a smashing success in England and America when it appeared in print in 1897.

I wondered what was wrong with people at the turn of the century.

Today I know the people weren't at fault, the culprit was American pragmatism in the 1940s. As long as man could transfer concept into symbol, weird fiction has flourished. Yet several generations of Americans tried to turn their backs on past superstitions; where could ghosts lurk in a world flooded with fluorescence—lightning—lit by the atom?

But there was still a trickle of fantasy magazines and books being published in the mid-40s. The night side of human nature found other devious channels of expression; science-fiction soon came of age; radio thrillers stressed the unknown and inexplicable; in Hollywood, horror films were big business, and we were not far away from the advent of television, many early shows of which were supernatural in character.

Yet ghostly tales were rare in literature, and the idea of an occult novel achieving best-seller status was ludicrous as America moved into the 1950s. (Shirley Jackson's *The Haunting of Hill House* was not printed till late 1959, and one might well argue that even it is really a psychological suspense tale.)

The era of best-seller horror novels did not occur until nearly a decade later—significantly, after the assassinations of John F. and Robert Kennedy.

The funereal weekend following November 22, 1963, ushered in a new era of American national awareness. Tragedy, confrontation, and strife distinguished the presidencies of Lyndon B. Johnson and Richard Nixon.

At the same time, the spiritual conflict that spawned agnosticism, atheism, irrelevationism, and other humanistic philosophies began to work surprising face-lifts in many organized religions. Age-old canons began to become modified to contemporary needs; the form of services saw sea-changes in a desperate effort to keep straying youth in the bosom of traditional Church.

Crime, too, changed in character. It escalated, became commonplace in overcrowded cities, and organized crime assumed a quasi-respectable profile. Morality began to develop an unhealthy relativistic appearance.

America was ripe—spiritually and practically—for a rebirth of faith and its "flip side," superstition. An explosion of fundamentalism, back-to-Jesus movements, Hari Krishna, and Reverend Moon demagoguery was matched by a new interest in vampirism, satanism, demonic possession.

Why is today's crazy quilt of faiths a logical adjunct to the sudden popularity of supernatural literature?

America is no longer adolescent. The bright dreams of the Industrial Revolution and the counterthrust of labor unionism are both tarnished; our invincibility abroad has been challenged at the same time that our international and domestic motives became gravely suspect. As our country emerged from the blood-spattered '60s, the common citizen dimly began to perceive man's age-old dilemma: that we seem to be lost in a void with no guide star. Even as scientists probe beyond the old limits set on human knowledge by orthodoxy, a backlash of superstition grips Americans. Frightened youth of all ages cast about for faiths that will not crumble overnight.

The idea of an afterlife, even a hellish one, has the roots of permanency in it. It suggests a plan, an order to life; ultimately it lets believers avoid the heavy weight of self-responsibility.

In a recent interview in the Sunday magazine section of the New York *Times,* filmmaker Stanley Kubrick put it succinctly: ghost stories, no matter how dreadful, still are ultimately optimistic: they promise shape beyond Self.

For Ghosts Only

I admit to feeling mystified at the success of much of today's supernatural literature. Witchcraft, vampirism, demonic possession seem to me, at best, impossibly dated themes, incapable of making me look over my shoulder; at worst, they excuse the sociopath his culpability. The thing that really frightens me, for instance, about Blatty's priest-despoiling imp in *The Exorcist*—other than the critical acclaim accorded his embarrassingly purple prose—is that it is a premise which attempts to excuse human nature for its bloodiest actions, shunting aside guilt onto the scapegoat of the Medieval painted devil.

Ghosts alone retain their ability to make me uneasy, largely because it is not necessary to accept any concomitant religious system to believe the possibility of their existence. If man passes to another plane, it may only be because there are more aspects to our puzzle-box universe than we originally realized. Or parapsychologists may be right when they suggest that violent emotions leave an energy residue in "haunted" houses, an ash that manifests itself as magic-lantern shows of the mind.

Eyewitness accounts of meetings with ghosts abound throughout history. Even discounting the ephemera, the magnitude is remarkable. Personally, I have experienced a few odd things in my life, things which further persuade me to keep an open mind on the topic of the spectral. (See Appendix A.)

By personal preference, then, I have excluded from this collection all miscellaneous demons, witches, elder gods, invisible damned things and the like. Only ghosts appear (and vanish) in these pages . . . though an occasional Hell-sent phantom may flit by, and a pair of vampires did manage to creep past Charon. But, remember, vampires are, technically, reanimated corpses, and I have nothing against *revenants,* other than their compelling need for deodorant and dentifrice.

The stories and poems I picked represent a great variety of style, theme, and mood. I tried to choose selections that embody many viewpoints of the spectral. (One might call it a relativistic anthology aimed at defining the state of ghosthood, though that smacks of pedantry and, after all, the underlying reason for any ghost compendium is to raise goosebumps.)

A few principles guided the final choice: limitation of each author to a single story; preference given lesser-known works over familiar tales; inclusion of a few "true" accounts and occasional stories that, despite literary merit, depict some classic aspect of the folklore of ghostly behavior. Finally, I commissioned a few new stories specially for this volume.

Those who wish to continue their midnight reading, but don't know where to find first-rate ghost tales and novels, may consult Appendix D for a representative sampling of some of my personal favorites that length or familiarity excluded.

Those hardy souls who yearn to confront a spook face-to-sheet will do well to read the advice of Appendix B, and before starting out, check Appendix C, which lists the sites of more than fifty allegedly haunted houses and spots throughout nineteen American states, as well as the District of Columbia. Many of the places named are open to the public.

Now it is time to dim the lights and embark on a journey into night. But first, be sure to stop at the Prologue and read a few choice epitaphs. Since the Other World is usually reached by way of the cemetery, it is appropriate, I feel, to peruse a sampling of tombstones. For is it not written that the paths of gory lead through the grave?

MARVIN KAYE,
Manhattan, 1980.

A PROLOGUE OF LAST WORDS

Bon mots at the time of death are probably few—though H. G. Wells is reported to have snapped at an overly fussy nurse, "Get away, woman! Can't you see I'm busy dying?"—but those who survive often cannot resist a final joke at the expense of the deceased.

Here are a few of the more inventive epitaphs and parting shots I have gleaned from the annals of humorous verse and transcriptions of actual gravestone markers. (The last and longest entry was really copied from a tomb in Penobscot, Maine.)

*   *   *

Hurrah! my boys, at the Parson's fall,
For if he'd lived he'd a buried us all.

*   *   *

Within this grave doth lie
Back to back, my wife and I.
When the Last Trump the air shall fill,
If she gets up, I'll just lie still.

*   *   *

Here lies father and mother and sister and I,
We all died within one short year.
They all be buried at Wimble, except I,
For I be buried here.

*   *   *

This is the grave of Mike O'Day
Who died maintaining his right of way.
His right was clear, his will was strong,
But he's just as dead if he'd been wrong.

*   *   *

Here lies old John Porter,
Who was both 'ale and stout.
Death laid him on a bitter bier
And in Hell he hops about.

*   *   *

Here lies John Bun

Who was killed by a gun.
(His name wasn't Bun, it was Wood,
But Wood wouldn't rhyme with gun, but Bun would.)

     *   *   *

Beneath this clay
Lies Arabella Young.
On the 24th of May
She finally held her tongue.

     *   *   *

Here lies the body of Mary Anne Beltzer,
Who burst while drinking an Alka-Seltzer.
Called from this wide world too soon, no doubt;
She should have waited till it all fizzed out.

     *   *   *

Little Willie from his mirror
Licked the mercury right off,
Thinking in his childish error,
It would cure the whooping cough.
At the funeral, his mother smartly said to Mrs. Brown:
" 'Twas a chilly day for Willie when the mercury went down!"

     *   *   *

Beneath this stone, a lump of clay,
Lies Uncle Peter Daniels,
Who too early in the month of May
Took off his winter flannels.

     *   *   *

Beneath these stones repose the bones
of Theodosius Grimm;
He took his beer from year to year,
and then the bier took him.

     *   *   *

Here lies a poor woman,
Who always was tired;
She lived in a house,
Where help was not hired;
Her last words on earth were,
"Dear friends, I am going;
Where washing ain't done,
Nor sweeping nor sewing;
But everything there is exact to my wishes.

For where they don't eat,
There's no washing dishes;
    I'll be where loud anthems will always be ringing,
But having no voice, I'll be clear of the singing;
    Don't mourn for me now, don't mourn for me never,
I'm going to do nothing forever and ever."

*   *   *

But death is not always such a lark. Beethoven is said to have died shaking his fists at the lightning-split skies, Abraham Lincoln is rumored to walk the corridors of the White House whenever the country is troubled. (When does he *ever* rest?) And one obscure political terrorist in the sixteenth century penned what may be the most moving final words in English . . .

I sought for death and I found it in the womb,
    I lookt for life and saw it was a shade,
I trod the earth and knew it was my tomb,
    And now I die, and now I was but made;
My glass is full, and now my glass is run,
And now I live, and now my life is done.

The grave gapes, the earth yawns and the hosts of night bid you welcome. The comedy is ended.

"Minuke" is an ugly house that one would do well to avoid. This gripping story is taken from Tomato Cain, *the first collection of tales by* Nigel Kneale, *one of England's finer writers. Born in 1922 in Lancashire, Kneale studied law, changed allegiance to the theatre, acted for two years at Stratford-on-Avon and wrote in his spare time. In 1949, the British theatre was not healthy, and Kneale was advised to try writing full time. Soon after,* Tomato Cain *appeared in Great Britain and America. Science-fiction buffs know Kneale as the creator of the* "Quatermass" *series, the scripts of which are available in Penguin paper editions. The first of the trilogy was filmed as* The Creeping Unknown, *starring Brian Donleavy as Quatermass. It is still being shown today.*

"Minuke"
by Nigel Kneale

The estate agent kept an uncomfortable silence until we reached his car. "Frankly, I wish you hadn't got wind of that," he said. "Don't know how you did: I thought I had the whole thing carefully disposed of. Oh, please get in."

He pulled his door shut and frowned. "It puts me in a rather awkward spot. I suppose I'd better tell you all I know about that case, or you'd be suspecting me of heaven-knows-what kinds of chicanery in your own."

As we set off to see the property I was interested in, he shifted the cigarette to the side of his mouth.

"It's quite a distance, so I can tell you on the way there," he said. "We'll pass the very spot, as a matter of fact, and you can see it for yourself. Such as there is to see."

It was away back before the war (said the estate agent). At the height of the building boom. You remember how it was: ribbon development in full blast everywhere; speculative builders sticking things up almost overnight. Though at least you could get a house when you wanted it in those days.

I've always been careful in what I handle—I want you to understand that. Then one day I was handed a packet of coast-road bungalows, for letting. Put up by one of these gone-tomorrow firms, and bought by a local man. I can't say I exactly jumped for joy, but for once the things looked all right, and—business is inclined to be business.

The desirable residence you heard about stood at the end of the row. Actually, it seemed to have the best site. On a sort of natural platform, as it were, raised above road level and looking straight out over the sea. Like all the rest, it had a simple two-bedroom, lounge, living-room, kitchen, bathroom layout. Red-tiled roof, roughcast walls. Ornamental portico, garden strip all round. Sufficiently far from town, but with all conveniences.

It was taken by a man named Pritchard. Cinema projectionist, I think he was. Wife, a boy of ten or so, and a rather young daughter. Oh—and dog, one of those black, lop-eared animals. They christened the place "Minuke," M-I-N-U-K-E. My Nook. Yes, that's what I said too. And not even the miserable excuse of its being phonetically correct. Still, hardly worse than most.

Well, at the start everything seemed quite jolly. The Pritchards settled in and busied themselves with rearing a privet hedge and shoving flowers in. They'd paid the first quarter in advance, and as far as I was concerned, were out of the picture for a bit.

Then, about a fortnight after they'd moved in, I had a telephone call from Mrs. P. to say there was something odd about the kitchen tap. Apparently the thing had happened twice. The first time was when her sister was visiting them, and tried to fill the kettle: no water would come through for a long time, then suddenly squirted violently and almost soaked the woman. I gather the Pritchards hadn't really believed this—thought she was trying to find fault with their little nest—it had never happened before, and she couldn't make it happen again. Then, about a week later, it did; with Mrs. Pritchard this time. After her husband had examined the tap and could find nothing wrong with it, he decided the water supply must be faulty. So they got on to me.

I went round personally, as it was the first complaint from any of these bungalows. The tap seemed normal, and I remember asking if the schoolboy son could have been experimenting with the main stop, when Mrs. Pritchard, who had been fiddling with the tap, suddenly said: "Quick, look at this! It's off now!" They were quite cocky about its happening when I was there.

It really was odd. I turned the tap to the limit, but—not a drop! Not even the sort of gasping gurgle you hear when the supply is turned off at the main. After a couple of minutes, though, it came on. Water shot out with, I should say, about ten times normal force, as if it had been held under pressure. Then gradually it died down and ran steadily.

Both children were in the room with us until we all dodged out of the door to escape a soaking—it had splashed all over the ceiling—so they couldn't have been up to any tricks. I promised the Pritchards to have the pipes checked. Before returning to town, I called at the next two bungalows in the row: neither of the tenants had had any trouble at all with the water. I thought, well, that localized it at least.

When I reached my office there was a telephone message waiting, from Pritchard. I rang him back and he was obviously annoyed. "Look here," he said, "not ten minutes after you left, we've had something else happen! The wall of the large bedroom's cracked from top to bottom. Big pieces of plaster fell, and the bed's in a terrible mess." And then he said: "You wouldn't have got me in a jerry-built place like this if I'd known!"

I had plasterers on the job next morning, and the whole water supply to "Minuke" under examination. For about three days there was peace. The tap behaved itself, and absolutely nothing was found to be wrong. I was annoyed at what seemed to have been unnecessary expenditure. It looked as if the Pritchards were going to be difficult—and I've had my share of that type; fault-finding cranks occasionally carry eccentricity to the extent of a little private destruction, to prove their points. I was on the watch from now on.

Then it came again.

Pritchard rang me at my home, before nine in the morning. His voice sounded a bit off. Shaky.

"For God's sake can you come round here right away," he said. "Tell you about it when you get here." And then he said, almost fiercely, but quietly and close up to the mouthpiece: "There's something damned queer about this place!" Dramatizing is a typical feature of all cranks, I thought, but particularly the little mousy kind, like Pritchard.

I went to "Minuke" and found that Mrs. Pritchard was in bed, in a state of collapse. The doctor had given her a sleeping dose.

Pritchard told me a tale that was chiefly remarkable for the expression on his face as he told it.

I don't know if you're familiar with the layout of that type of bungalow? The living-room is in the front of the house, with the kitchen behind it. To get from one to the other you have to use the little hallway, through two doors. But for convenience at mealtimes, there's a serving-hatch in the wall between these rooms. A small wooden door slides up and down over the hatch-opening.

"The wife was just passing a big plate of bacon and eggs through from the kitchen," Pritchard told me, "when the hatch door came down on her wrists. I saw it and I heard her yell. I thought the cord must've snapped, so I said: 'All right, all right!' and went to pull it up because it's only a light wooden frame."

Pritchard was a funny colour, and as far as I could judge, it was genuine.

"Do you know, it wouldn't come! I got my fingers under it and heaved, but it might have weighed two hundredweight. Once it gave an inch or so, and then pressed harder. That was it—it was *pressing* down! I heard the wife groan. I said: 'Hold on!' and nipped round through the hall. When I got into the kitchen she was on the floor, fainted. And the hatch-door was hitched up as right as ninepence. That gave me a turn!" He sat down, quite deflated: it didn't appear to be put on. Still, ordinary neurotics can be almost as troublesome as out-and-out cranks.

I tested the hatch, gingerly; and, of course, the cords were sound and it ran easily.

"Possibly a bit stiff at times, being new," I said. "They're apt to jam if you're rough with them." And then: "By the way, just what were you hinting on the phone?"

He looked at me. It was warm sunlight outside, with a bus passing. Normal enough to take the mike out of Frankenstein's monster. "Never mind," he said, and gave a sheepish half-grin. "Bit of—well, funny construction in this house, though, eh?"

I'm afraid I was rather outspoken with him.

Let alone any twaddle about a month-old bungalow being haunted, I was determined to clamp down on this "jerry-building" talk. Perhaps I was beginning to have doubts myself.

I wrote straight off to the building company when I'd managed to trace them, busy developing an arterial road about three counties away. I daresay my letter was on the insinuating side: I think I asked if they had any record of difficulties in the construction of this bungalow. At any rate I got a sniffy reply by return, stating that the matter was out of their hands; in addition, their records were not available for discussion. Blind alley.

In the meantime, things at "Minuke" had worsened to a really frightening degree. I dreaded the phone ringing. One morning the two Pritchards senior awoke to find that nearly all the furniture in their bedroom had been moved about, including the bed they had been sleeping in; they had felt absolutely nothing. Food became suddenly and revoltingly decomposed. All the chimney pots had come down, not just into the garden, but to the far side of the high road, except one which appeared, pulverized, on the living-room floor. The obvious attempts of the Pritchards to keep a rational outlook had put "paid" to most of my suspicions by this time.

I managed to locate a local man who had been employed during the erection of the bungalows, as an extra hand. He had worked only on the foundations of "Minuke," but what he had to say was interesting.

They had found the going slow because of striking a layer of enormous flat stones, apparently trimmed slate, but as the site was otherwise excellent, they pressed on, using the stone as foundation where it fitted in with the plan, and laying down rubble where it didn't. The concrete skin over the rubble—my ears burned when I heard about that, I can tell you—this wretched so-called concrete had cracked, or shattered, several times. Which wasn't entirely surprising, if it had been laid as he described. The flat stones, he said, had not been seriously disturbed. A workmate had referred to them as "a giant's grave," so it was possibly an old burial mound. Norse, perhaps—those are fairly common along this coast—or even very much older.

Apart from this—I'm no diehard sceptic; I may as well confess I was beginning to admit modest theories about a poltergeist, in spite of a lack of corroborative knockings and ornament-throwing. There were two young children in the house, and the lore has it that they're often unconsciously connected with phenomena of that sort, though usually adolescents. Still, in the real-estate profession you have to be careful, and if I could see the Pritchards safely off the premises without airing these possibilities, it might be kindest to the bungalow's future.

I went to "Minuke" that afternoon.

It was certainly turning out an odd nook. I found a departing policeman on the doorstep. That morning the back door had been burst in by a hundredweight or so of soil, and Mrs. Pritchard was trying to convince herself that a practical joker had it in for them. The policeman had taken some notes, and was giving vague advice about "civil action" which showed that he was out of his depth.

Pritchard looked very tired, almost ill. "I've got leave from my job, to look after them," he said, when we were alone. I thought he was wise. He had given his wife's illness as the reason, and I was glad of that.

"I don't believe in—unnatural happenings," he said.

I agreed with him, noncommittally.

"But I'm afraid of what ideas the kids might get. They're both at impressionable ages, y'know."

I recognized the symptoms without disappointment. "You mean, you'd rather move elsewhere," I said.

He nodded. "I like the district, mind you. But what I—"

There was a report like a gun in the very room.

I found myself with both arms up to cover my face. There were tiny splinters everywhere, and a dust of fibre in the air. The door had exploded. Literally.

To hark back to constructional details, it was one of those light, hollow frame-and-plywood jobs. As you'll know, it takes considerable force to splinter plywood. Well, this was in tiny fragments. And the oddest thing was that we had felt no blast effect.

In the next room I heard their dog howling. Pritchard was as stiff as a poker.

"I felt it!" he said. "I felt this lot coming. I've got to knowing when something's likely to happen. It's all round!" Of course I began to imagine I'd sensed something too, but I doubt if I had really; my shock came with the crash. Mrs. Pritchard was in the doorway by this time with the kids behind her. He motioned them out and grabbed my arm.

"The thing is," he whispered, "I can still feel it! Stronger than ever, by God! Look, will you stay at home tonight, in case I need—well, in case things get worse? I can phone you."

On my way back I called at the town library and managed to get hold of a volume on supernatural possession and what-not. Yes, I was committed now. But the library didn't specialize in that line, and when I opened the book at home, I found it was very little help. "Vampires of southeastern Europe" type of stuff. I came across references to something the jargon called an "elemental," which I took to be a good deal more vicious and destructive than any poltergeist. A thoroughly nasty form of manifestation, if it existed. Those Norse gravestones were fitting into the picture uncomfortably well; it was fashionable in those days to be buried with all the trimmings, human sacrifice and even more unmentionable attractions.

But I read on. After half a chapter on zombies and Rumanian werewolves, the whole thing began to seem so fantastic that I turned seriously to working out methods of exploding somebody's door as a practical joke. Even a totally certifiable joker would be likelier than vampires. In no time I'd settled down with a whisky, doodling wiring diagrams, and only occasionally—like twinges of conscience—speculating on contacting the psychic investigation people.

When the phone rang I was hardly prepared for it.

It was a confused, distant voice, gabbling desperately, but I recognized it as Pritchard. "For God's sake, don't lose a second! Get here—it's all hell on earth! Can't you hear it? My God, I'm going crazy!" And in the background I thought I was able to hear something. A sort of bubbling, shushing "wah-wah" noise. Indescribable. But you hear some odd sounds on telephones at any time.

"Yes," I said, "I'll come immediately. Why don't you all leave—" But the line had gone dead.

Probably I've never moved faster. I scrambled out to the car with untied shoes flopping, though I remembered to grab a heavy stick in the hall—whatever use it was to be. I drove like fury, heart belting, straight to "Minuke," expecting to see heaven knows what.

But everything looked still and normal there. The moon was up and I could see the whole place clearly. Curtained lights in the windows. Not a sound.

I rang. After a moment Pritchard opened the door. He was quiet and seemed almost surprised to see me.

I pushed inside. "Well?" I said. "What's happened?"

"Not a thing, so far," he said. "That's why I didn't expect—"

I felt suddenly angry. "Look here," I said, "what are you playing at? Seems to me that any hoaxing round here begins a lot nearer home than you'd have me believe!" Then the penny dropped. I saw by the fright in his face that he knew something had gone wrong. That was the most horrible, sickening moment of the whole affair for me.

"Didn't you ring?" I said.

And he shook his head.

I've been in some tight spots. But there was always some concrete, actual business in hand to screw the mind safely down to. I suppose panic is when the subconscious breaks loose and everything in your head dashes screaming out. It was only just in time that I found a touch of the concrete and actual. A kiddie's paintbox on the floor, very watery.

"The children," I said. "Where are they?"

"Wife's just putting the little 'un to bed. She's been restless tonight: just wouldn't go, crying and difficult. Arthur's in the bathroom. Look here, what's happened?"

I told him, making it as short and matter-of-fact as I could. He turned ghastly.

"Better get them dressed and out of here right away," I said. "Make some excuse, not to alarm them." He'd gone before I finished speaking.

I smoked hard, trying to build up the idea of "Hoax! Hoax!" in my mind. After all, it could have been. But I knew it wasn't.

Everything looked cosy and normal. Clock ticking. Fire red and mellow. Half-empty cocoa mug on the table. The sound of the sea from beyond the road. I went through to the kitchen. The dog was there, looking up from its sleeping-basket under the sink. "Good dog," I said, and it wriggled its tail.

Pritchard came in from the hall. He jumped when he saw me.

"Getting nervy!" he said. "They won't be long. I don't know where we can go if we—well, if we have to—to leave tonight—"

"My car's outside," I told him. "I'll fix you up. Look here, did you ever 'hear things'? Odd noises?" I hadn't told him that part of the telephone call.

He looked at me so oddly I thought he was going to collapse.

"I don't know," he said. "Can you?"

"At this moment?"

I listened.

"No," I said. "The clock on the shelf. The sea. Nothing else. No."

"The sea," he said, barely whispering. "But you can't hear the sea in this kitchen!"

He was close to me in an instant. Absolutely terrified. "Yes, I have heard this before! I think we all have. I said it was the sea, so as not to frighten them. But it isn't! And I recognized it when I came in here just now. That's what made me start. It's getting louder; it does that."

He was right. Like slow breathing. It seemed to emanate from inside the walls, not at a particular spot, but everywhere. We went into the hall, then the front room; it was the same there. Mixed with it now was a sort of thin crying.

"That's Nellie," Pritchard said. "The dog: she always whimpers when it's on—too scared to howl. My God, I've never heard it as loud as this before!"

"Hurry them up, will you!" I almost shouted. He went.

The "breathing" was ghastly. Slobbering. Stertorous, I think the term is. And faster. Oh, yes, I recognized it. The background music to the phone message. My skin was pure ice.

"Come along!" I yelled. I switched on the little radio to drown the noise. The old National Programme, as it was in those days, for late dance music. Believe it or not, what came through that loudspeaker was the same vile, sighing noise, at double the volume. And when I tried to switch off, it stayed the same.

The whole bungalow was trembling. The Pritchards came running in, she carrying the little girl. "Get them into the car," I shouted. We heard glass smashing somewhere.

Above our heads there was an almighty thump. Plaster showered down.

Halfway out of the door the little girl screamed, "Nellie! Where's Nellie? Nellie, Nellie!"

"The dog!" Pritchard moaned. "Oh, curse it!" He dragged them outside. I dived for the kitchen, where I'd seen the animal, feeling a lunatic for doing it. Plaster was springing out of the walls in painful showers.

In the kitchen I found water everywhere. One tap was squirting like a fire hose. The other was missing, water belching across the window from a torn end of pipe.

"Nellie!" I called.

Then I saw the dog. It was lying near the oven, quite stiff. Round its neck was twisted a piece of painted piping with the other tap on the end.

Sheer funk got me then. The ground was moving under me. I bolted down the hall, nearly bumped into Pritchard. I yelled and shoved. I could actually feel the house at my back.

We got outside. The noise was like a dreadful snoring, with rumbles and crashes thrown in. One of the lights went out. "Nellie's run away," I said, and we all got into the car, the kids bawling. I started up. People were coming out of the other bungalows—they're pretty far apart and the din was just beginning to make itself felt. Pritchard mumbled: "We can stop now. Think it'd be safe to go back and grab some of the furniture?" As if he was at a fire; but I don't think he knew what he was doing.

"Daddy—look!" screeched the boy.

We saw it. The chimney of "Minuke" was going up in a horrible way. In the moonlight it seemed to grow, quite slowly, to about sixty feet, like a giant crooked finger. And then—burst. I heard bricks thumping down. Somewhere somebody screamed.

There was a glare like an ungodly great lightning flash. It lasted for a second or so.

Of course we were dazzled, but I thought I saw the whole of "Minuke" fall suddenly and instantaneously flat, like a swatted fly. I probably did, because that's what happened, anyway.

There isn't much more to tell.

Nobody was really hurt, and we were able to put down the whole thing to a serious electrical fault. Main fuses had blown throughout the whole district, which helped this theory out. Perhaps it was unfortunate in another respect, because a lot of people changed over to gas. And the local rag still ran a leader about "lost standards in the building trade."

There wasn't much recognizably left of "Minuke." But some of the bits were rather unusual. Knots in pipes, for instance—I buried what was left of the dog myself. Wood and brick cleanly sliced. Small quantities of completely powdered metal. The bath had been squashed flat, like tinfoil. In fact, Pritchard was lucky to land the insurance money for his furniture.

My professional problem, of course, remained. The plot where the wretched place had stood. I managed to persuade the owner it wasn't ideal for building on. Incidentally, lifting those stones might reveal something to somebody some day—but not to me, thank you!

I think my eventual solution showed a touch of wit: I let it very cheaply as a scrap-metal dump.

Well? I know I've never been able to make any sense out of it. I hate telling you all this stuff, because it must make me seem either a simpleton or a charlatan. In so far as there's any circumstantial evidence in looking at the place, you can see it in a moment or two. Here's the coast road. . . .

The car pulled up at a bare spot beyond a sparse line of bungalows. The space was marked by a straggling, tufty square of privet bushes. Inside I could see a tangle of rusting iron: springs, a car chassis, oil drums.

"The hedge keeps it from being too unsightly," said the estate agent, as we crossed to it. "See—the remains of the gate."

A few half-rotten slats dangled from an upright. One still bore part of a chrome-plated name. "MI——" and, a little farther on, "K."

"Nothing worth seeing now," he said. I peered inside. "Not that there ever was much— Look out!" I felt a violent push. In the same instant something zipped past my head and crashed against the car behind. "My God! Went right at you!" gasped the agent.

It had shattered a window of the car and gone through the open door opposite. We found it in the road beyond, sizzling on the tarmac. A heavy steel nut, white-hot.

"I don't know about you," the estate agent said, "but I'm rather in favour of getting out of here."

And we did. Quickly.

ISAAC ASIMOV *is one of the eight wonders of the world. Born in Russia in 1920, his first story appeared in 1939; since then, he has written well over two hundred books, most of them brilliant popularizations of contemporary scientific data and methodology. He has tried his hand at widely diverse subjects—from* The Bible *through Shakespeare through the risibly bawdy. But he is best known as a science fiction writer whose output includes the* Foundation *trilogy and perhaps the most astonishing tour de force in all SF,* The Naked Sun, *in which Asimov concocts an ingenious murder mystery that could only occur on an alien world, yet also manages to say quite a bit about contemporary society. (No one told him it couldn't be done.) The one type of story Asimov has eschewed is the traditional supernatural tale . . . but editor Frederik Pohl once suggested such a clever idea for a ghost story that Dr. A. succumbed. The result:* "Legal Rites," *as untraditional a ghost story as ever hath been wrought!*

Legal Rites
by Isaac Asimov and Frederik Pohl

I

Already the stars were out, though the sun had just dipped under the horizon, and the sky of the west was a blood-stuck gold behind the Sierra Nevadas.

"Hey!" squawked Russell Harley. "Come back!"

But the one-lunged motor of the old Ford was making too much noise; the driver didn't hear him. Harley cursed as he watched the old car careen along the sandy ruts on its half-flat tires. Its taillight was saying a red *no* to him. *No,* you can't get away tonight; *no,* you'll have to stay here and fight it out.

Harley grunted and climbed back up the porch stairs of the old wooden house. It was well made, anyhow. The stairs, though half a century old, neither creaked beneath him nor showed cracks.

Harley picked up the bags he'd dropped when he experienced his abrupt change of mind—fake leather and worn out, they were—and carted them into the house. He dumped them on a dust-jacketed sofa and looked around.

It was stifling hot, and the smell of the desert outside had permeated the room. Harley sneezed.

"Water," he said out loud. "That's what I need."

He'd prowled through every room on the ground floor before he stopped still and smote his head. Plumbing—naturally there'd be no plumbing in this hole eight miles out on the desert! A well was the best he could hope for—

If that.

It was getting dark. No electric lights either, of course. He blundered irritatedly through the dusky rooms to the back of the house. The screen door shrieked metallically as he opened it. A bucket hung by the door. He picked it up, tipped it, shook the loose sand out of it. He looked over the "back yard"—about thirty thousand visible acres of hilly sand, rock and patches of sage and flame-tipped ocotillo.

No well.

The old fool got water from somewhere, he thought savagely. Obstinately he climbed down the back steps and wandered out into the desert. Overhead the stars were blinding, a million billion of them, but the sunset was over already and he could see only hazily. The silence was murderous. Only a faint whisper of breeze over the sand, and the slither of his shoes.

He caught a glimmer of starlight from the nearest clump of sage and walked to it. There was a pool of water, caught in the angle of two enormous boulders. He stared at it doubtfully, then shrugged. It was water. It was better than nothing. He dipped the bucket in the little pool. Knowing nothing of the procedure, he filled it with a quart of loose sand as he scooped it along the bottom. When he lifted it, brimful, to his lips, he spat out the first mouthful and swore violently.

Then he used his head. He set the bucket down, waited a second for the sand grains to settle, cupped water in his hands, lifted it to his lips. . . .

Pat. HISS. Pat. HISS. Pat. HISS—

"What the hell!" Harley stood up, looked around in abrupt puzzlement. It sounded like water dripping from somewhere, onto a red-hot stove, flashing into sizzling steam. He saw nothing, only the sand and the sage and the pool of tepid, sickly water.

Pat. HISS—

Then he saw it, and his eyes bulged. Out of nowhere it was dripping, a drop a second, a sticky, dark drop that was thicker than water, that fell to the ground lazily, in slow defiance of gravity. And when it struck each drop sizzled and skittered about, and vanished. It was perhaps eight feet from him, just visible in the starlight.

And then, "Get off my land!" said the voice from nowhere.

Harley got. By the time he got to Rebel Butte three hours later, he was barely managing to walk, wishing desperately that he'd delayed long enough for one more good drink of water, despite all the fiends of hell. But he'd run the first three miles. He'd had plenty of encouragement. He remembered with a shudder how the clear desert air had taken milky shape around the incredible trickle of dampness and had advanced on him threateningly.

And when he got to the first kerosene-lighted saloon of Rebel Butte, and staggered inside, the saloonkeeper's fascinated stare at the front of his shoddy coat showed him strong evidence that he hadn't been suddenly taken with insanity, or drunk on the unaccustomed sensation of fresh desert air. All down the front of him it was, and the harder he rubbed the harder it stayed, the stickier it got. Blood!

"Whiskey!" he said in a strangled voice, tottering to the bar. He pulled a threadbare dollar bill from his pocket, flapped it onto the mahogany.

The blackjack game at the back of the room had stopped. Harley was acutely conscious of the eyes of the players, the bartender and the tall, lean man leaning on the bar. All were watching him.

The bartender broke the spell. He reached for a bottle behind him without looking at it, placed it on the counter before Harley. He poured a glass of water from a jug, set it down with a shot glass beside the bottle.

"I could of told you that would happen," he said cautiously. "Only you wouldn't of believed me. You had to meet Hank for yourself before you'd believe he was there."

Harley remembered his thirst and drained the glass of water, then poured himself a shot of the whiskey and swallowed it without waiting for the chaser to be refilled. The whiskey felt good going down, almost good enough to stop his internal shakes.

"What are you talking about?" he said finally. He twisted his body and leaned forward across the bar to partly hide the stains on his coat. The saloonkeeper laughed.

"Old Hank," he said. "I knowed who you was right away, even before Tom came back and told me where he'd took you. I knowed you was Zeb Harley's no-good nephew, come to take Harley Hall an' sell it before he was cold in the grave."

The blackjack players were still watching him, Russell Harley saw. Only the lean man farther along the bar seemed to have dismissed him. He was pouring himself another drink, quite occupied with his task.

Harley flushed. "Listen," he said, "I didn't come in here for advice. I wanted a drink. I'm paying for it. Keep your mouth out of this."

The saloonkeeper shrugged. He turned his back and walked away to the blackjack table. After a couple of seconds one of the players turned, too, and threw a card down. The others followed suit.

Harley was just getting set to swallow his pride and talk to the saloonkeeper again—he seemed to know something about what Harley'd been through, and might be helpful—when the lean man tapped his shoulder. Harley whirled and almost dropped his glass. Absorbed and jumpy, he hadn't seen him come up.

"Young man," said the lean one, "my name's Nicholls. Come along with me, sir, and we'll talk this thing over. I think we may be of service to each other."

Even the twelve-cylinder car Nicholls drove jounced like a hay-wagon over the sandy ruts leading to the place old Zeb had—laughingly —named "Harley Hall."

Russell Harley twisted his neck and stared at the heap of paraphernalia in the open rumble seat. "I don't like it," he complained. "I never had anything to do with ghosts. How do I know this stuff'll work?"

Nicholls smiled, "You'll have to take my word for it. I've had dealings with ghosts before. You could say that I might qualify as a ghost exterminator, if I chose."

Harley growled. "I still don't like it."

Nicholls turned a sharp look on him. "You like the prospect of owning Harley Hall, don't you? And looking for all the money your late uncle is supposed to have hidden around somewhere?" Harley shrugged. "Certainly you do," said Nicholls, returning his eyes to the road. "And with good reason. The local reports put the figure pretty high, young man."

"That's where you come in, I guess," Harley said sullenly. "I find the money—that I own anyhow—and give some of it to you. How much?"

"We'll discuss that later," Nicholls said. He smiled absently as he looked ahead.

"We'll discuss it right now!"

The smile faded from Nicholls' face. "No," he said. "We won't. I'm doing you a favor, young Harley. Remember that. In return—you'll do as I say, all the way!"

Harley digested that carefully, and it was not a pleasant meal. He waited a couple of seconds before he changed the subject.

"I was out here once when the old man was alive," he said. "He didn't say nothing about any ghost."

"Perhaps he felt you might think him—well, peculiar," Nicholls said. "And perhaps you would have. When were you here?"

"Oh, a long time ago," Harley said evasively. "But I was here a whole day, and part of the night. The old man was crazy as a coot, but he didn't keep any ghosts in the attic."

"This ghost was a friend of his," Nicholls said. "The gentleman in charge of the bar told you that, surely. Your late uncle was something of a recluse. He lived in this house a dozen miles from nowhere, came into town hardly ever, wouldn't let anyone get friendly with him. But he wasn't exactly a hermit. He had Hank for company."

"Fine company."

Nicholls inclined his head seriously. "Oh, I don't know," he said. "From all accounts, they got on well together. They played pinochle and chess—Hank's supposed to have been a great pinochle player. He was killed that way, according to the local reports. Caught somebody dealing from the bottom and shot it out with him. He lost. A bullet pierced his throat and he died quite bloodily." He turned the wheel, putting his weight into the effort, and succeeded in twisting the car out of the ruts of the "road," sent it jouncing across unmarked sand to the old frame house to which they were going.

"That," he finished as he pulled up before the porch, "accounts for the blood that accompanies his apparition."

Harley opened the door slowly and got out, looking uneasily at the battered old house. Nicholls cut the motor, got out and walked at once to the back of the car.

"Come on," he said, dragging things out of the compartment. "Give me a hand with this. I'm not going to carry this stuff all by myself."

Harley came around reluctantly, regarded the curious assortment of bundles of dried faggots, lengths of colored cord, chalk pencils, ugly little bunches of wilted weeds, bleached bones of small animals and a couple of less pleasant things without pleasure.

Pat. HISS. Pat. HISS—

"He's here!" Harley yelped. "Listen! He's someplace around here watching us."

"Ha!"

The laugh was deep, unpleasant and—bodiless. Harley looked around desperately for the tell-tale trickle of blood. And he found it; from the air it issued, just beside the car, sinking gracefully to the ground and sizzling, vanishing there.

"I'm watching you, all right," the voice said grimly. "Russell, you worthless piece of corruption, I've got no more use for you than you used to have for me. Dead or alive, this is my land! I shared it with your uncle, you young scalawag, but I won't share it with you. Get out!"

Harley's knees weakened and he tottered dizzily to the rear bumper, sat on it. "Nicholls—" he said confusedly.

"Oh, brace up," Nicholls said with irritation. He tossed a ball of gaudy twine, red and green, with curious knots tied along it, to Harley. Then he confronted the trickle of blood and made a few brisk passes in the air before it. His lips were moving silently, Harley saw, but no words came out.

There was a gasp and a chopped-off squawk from the source of the blood drops. Nicholls clapped his hands sharply, then turned to young Harley.

"Take that cord you have in your hands and stretch it around the house," he said. "All the way around, and make sure it goes right across the middle of the doors and windows. It isn't much, but it'll hold him till we can get the good stuff set up."

Harley nodded, then pointed a rigid finger at the drops of blood, now sizzling and fuming more angrily than before. "What about *that?*" he managed to get out.

Nicholls grinned complacently. "I'll hold him here till the cows come home," he said. "Get moving!"

Harley inadvertently inhaled a lungful of noxious white smoke and coughed till the tears rolled down his cheeks. When he recovered he looked at Nicholls, who was reading silently from a green leather book with dog-eared pages. He said, "Can I stop stirring this now?"

Nicholls grimaced angrily and shook his head without looking at him. He went on reading, his lips contorting over syllables that were not in any language Harley had ever heard, then snapped the book shut and wiped his brow.

"Fine," he said. "So far, so good." He stepped over to windward of the boiling pot Harley was stirring on the hob over the fireplace, peered down into it cautiously.

"That's about done," he said. "Take it off the fire and let it cool a bit."

Harley lifted it down, then squeezed his aching biceps with his left hand. The stuff was the consistency of sickly green fudge.

"Now what?" he asked.

Nicholls didn't answer. He looked up in mild surprise at the sudden squawk of triumph from outside, followed by the howling of a chill wind.

"Hank must be loose," he said casually. "He can't do us any harm, I think, but we'd better get a move on." He rummaged in the dwindled pile of junk he'd brought from the car, extracted a paintbrush. "Smear this stuff around all the windows and doors. All but the front door. For that I have something else." He pointed to what seemed to be the front axle of an old Model-T. "Leave that on the doorsill. Cold iron. You can just step over it, but Hank won't be able to pass it. It's been properly treated already with the very best thaumaturgy."

"Step over it," Harley repeated. "What would I want to step over it for? *He's* out there."

"He won't hurt you," said Nicholls. "You will carry an amulet with you—that one, there—that will keep him away. Probably he couldn't really hurt you anyhow, being a low-order ghost who can't materialize to any greater density. But just to take no chances, carry the amulet and don't stay out too long. It won't hold him off forever, not for more than half an hour. If you ever have to go out and stay for any length of time, tie that bundle of herbs around your neck." Nicholls smiled. "That's only for emergencies, though. It works on the asafoetida principle. Ghosts can't come anywhere near it—but you won't like it much yourself. It has—ah—a rather definite odor."

He leaned gingerly over the pot again, sniffing. He sneezed.

"Well, that's cool enough," he said. "Before it hardens, get moving. Start spreading the stuff upstairs—and make sure you don't miss any windows."

"What are you going to do?"

"I," said Nicholls sharply, "will be here. Start."

But he wasn't. When Harley finished his disagreeable task and came down, he called Nicholls' name, but the man was gone. Harley stepped to the door and looked out; the car was gone, too.

He shrugged. "Oh, well," he said, and began taking the dust-cloths off the furniture.

II

Somewhere within the cold, legal mind of Lawyer Turnbull, he weighed the comparative likeness of nightmare and insanity.

He stared at the plush chair facing him, noted with distinct uneasiness how the strangely weightless, strangely sourceless trickle of redness disappeared as it hit the floor, but left long, mud-ochre streaks matted on the upholstery. The sound was unpleasant, too; *Pat. HISS. Pat. HISS—*

The voice continued impatiently, "Damn your human stupidity! I may be a ghost, but heaven knows I'm not trying to haunt you. Friend, you're not that important to me. Get this—I'm here on business."

Turnbull learned that you cannot wet dry lips with a dehydrated tongue. "Legal business?"

"Sure. The fact that I was once killed by violence, and have to continue my existence on the astral plane, doesn't mean I've lost my legal rights. Does it?"

The lawyer shook his head in bafflement. He said, "This would be easier on me if you weren't invisible. Can't you do something about it?"

There was a short pause. "Well, I could materialize for a minute," the voice said. "It's hard work—damn hard, for me. There are a lot of us astral entities that can do it easy as falling out of bed, but—Well, if I have to I shall try to do it once."

There was a shimmering in the air above the armchair, and a milky, thin smoke condensed into an intangible seated figure. Turnbull took no delight in noting that, through the figure, the outlines of the chair were still hazily visible. The figure thickened. Just as the features took form— just as Turnbull's bulging eyes made out a prominent hooked nose and a crisp beard—it thinned and exploded with a soft pop.

The voice said weakly, "I didn't think I was that bad. I'm way out of practice. I guess that's the first daylight materialization I've made in seventy-five years."

The lawyer adjusted his rimless glasses and coughed. *Hell's binges,* he thought, *the worst thing about this is that I'm believing it!*

"Oh, well," he said aloud. Then he hurried on before the visitor could take offense: "Just what did you want? I'm just a small-town lawyer, you know. My business is fairly routine—"

"I know all about your business," the voice said. "You can handle my case—it's a land affair. I want to sue Russell Harley."

"Harley?" Turnbull fingered his cheek. "Any relation to Zeb Harley?"

"His nephew—and his heir, too."

Turnbull nodded. "Yes, I remember now. My wife's folks live in Rebel Butte, and I've been there. Quite a coincidence you should come to me—"

The voice laughed. "It was no coincidence," it said softly.

"Oh." Turnbull was silent for a second. Then, "I see," he said. He cast a shrewd glance at the chair. "Lawsuits cost money, Mr.—I don't think you mentioned your name?"

"Hank Jenkins," the voice prompted. "I know that. Would—let's see. Would six hundred and fifty dollars be sufficient?"

Turnbull swallowed. "I think so," he said in a relatively unemotional tone—relative to what he was thinking.

"Then suppose we call that your retainer. I happen to have cached a considerable sum of gold when I was—that is to say, before I became an astral entity. I'm quite certain it hasn't been disturbed. You will have to call it treasure trove, I guess, and give half of it to the state, but there's thirteen hundred dollars altogether."

Turnbull nodded judiciously. "Assuming we can locate your trove," he said, "I think that would be quite satisfactory." He leaned back in his chair and looked legal. His aplomb had returned.

And half an hour later he said slowly, "I'll take your case."

Judge Lawrence Gimbel had always liked his job before. But his thirteen honorable years on the bench lost their flavor for him as he grimaced wearily and reached for his gavel. This case was far too confusing for his taste.

The clerk made his speech, and the packed courtroom sat down en masse. Gimbel held a hand briefly to his eyes before he spoke.

"Is the counsel for the plaintiff ready?"

"I am, your honor." Turnbull, alone at his table, rose and bowed.

"The counsel for the defendant?"

"Ready, your honor!" Fred Wilson snapped. He looked with a hard flicker of interest at Turnbull and his solitary table, then leaned over and whispered in Russell Harley's ear. The youth nodded glumly, then shrugged.

Gimbel said, "I understand the attorneys for both sides have waived jury trial in this case of Henry Jenkins versus Russell Joseph Harley."

Both lawyers nodded. Gimbel continued, "In view of the unusual nature of this case, I imagine it will prove necessary to conduct it with a certain amount of informality. The sole purpose of this court is to arrive at the true facts at issue, and deliver a verdict in accord with the laws pertaining to these facts. I will not stand on ceremony. Nevertheless, I will not tolerate any disturbances or unnecessary irregularities. The spectators will kindly remember that they are here on privilege. Any demonstration will result in the clearing of the court."

He looked severely at the white faces that gleamed unintelligently up at him. He suppressed a sigh and he said, "The counsel for the plaintiff will begin."

Turnbull rose quickly to his feet, faced the judge.

"Your honor," he said, "we propose to show that my client, Henry Jenkins, has been deprived of his just rights by the defendant. Mr. Jenkins, by virtue of a sustained residence of more than twenty years in the house located on Route 22, eight miles north of the town of Rebel Butte, with the full knowledge of its legal owner, has acquired certain rights. In legal terminology we define these as the rights of adverse possession. The layman would call them common-law rights—squatters' rights."

Gimbel folded his hands and tried to relax. Squatters' rights—for a ghost! He sighed, but listened attentively as Turnbull went on.

"Upon the death of Zebulon Harley, the owner of the house involved —it is better known, perhaps, as Harley Hall—the defendant inherited title to the property. We do not question his right to it. But my client has an equity in Harley Hall; the right to free and full existence. The defendant has forcefully evicted my client, by means which have caused my client great mental distress, and have even endangered his very existence."

Gimbel nodded. If the case only had a precedent somewhere. . . . But it hadn't; he remembered grimly the hours he'd spent thumbing through all sorts of unlikely law books, looking for anything that might bear on the case. It had been his better judgment that he throw the case out of court outright—a judge couldn't afford to have himself laughed at, not if he were ambitious. And public laughter was about the only certainty there was to this case. But Wilson had put up such a fight that the judge's temper had taken over. He never did like Wilson, anyhow.

"You may proceed with your witnesses," he said.

Turnbull nodded. To the clerk he said, "Call Henry Jenkins to the stand."

Wilson was on his feet before the clerk opened his mouth.

"Objection!" he bellowed. "The so-called Henry Jenkins cannot qualify as a witness!"

"Why not?" demanded Turnbull.

"Because he's dead!"

The judge clutched his gavel with one hand, forehead with the other. He banged on the desk to quiet the courtroom.

Turnbull stood there, smiling. "Naturally," he said, "you'll have proof of that statement."

Wilson snarled. "Certainly." He referred to his brief. "The so-called Henry Jenkins is the ghost, spirit or specter of one Hank Jenkins, who prospected for gold in this territory a century ago. He was killed by a bullet through the throat from the gun of one Long Tom Cooper, and was declared legally dead on September 14, 1850. Cooper was hanged for his murder. No matter what hocus-pocus you produce for evidence to the contrary now, that status of legal death remains completely valid."

"What evidence have you of the identity of my client with this Hank Jenkins?" Turnbull asked grimly.

"Do you deny it?"

Turnbull shrugged. "I deny nothing. I'm not being cross-examined. Furthermore, the sole prerequisite of a witness is that he understand the value of an oath. Henry Jenkins was tested by John Quincy Fitzjames, professor of psychology at the University of Southern California. The results—I have Dr. Fitzjames' sworn statement of them here, which I will introduce as an exhibit—show clearly that my client's intelligence quotient is well above normal, and that a psychiatric examination discloses no important aberrations which would injure his validity as a witness. I insist that my client be allowed to testify on his own behalf."

"But he's dead!" squawked Wilson. "He's invisible right now!"

"My client," said Turnbull stiffly, "is not present just now. Undoubtedly that accounts for what you term his invisibility." He paused for the appreciative murmur that swept through the court. Things were breaking perfectly, he thought, smiling. "I have here another affidavit," he said. "It is signed by Elihu James and Terence MacRae, who respectively head the departments of physics and biology at the same university. It states that my client exhibits all the vital phenomena of life. I am prepared to call all three of my expert witnesses to the stand, if necessary."

Wilson scowled but said nothing. Judge Gimbel leaned forward.

"I don't see how it is possible for me to refuse the plaintiff the right to testify," he said. "If the three experts who prepared these reports will testify on the stand to the facts contained in them, Henry Jenkins may then take the stand."

Wilson sat down heavily. The three experts spoke briefly—and dryly. Wilson put them through only the most formal of cross-examinations.

The judge declared a brief recess. In the corridor outside, Wilson and his client lit cigarettes and looked unsympathetically at each other.

"I feel like a fool," said Russell Harley. "Bringing suit against a ghost."

"The ghost brought the suit," Wilson reminded him. "If only we'd been able to hold fire for a couple more weeks, till another judge came on the bench, I could've got this thing thrown right out of court."

"Well, why couldn't we wait?"

"Because you were in such a damn hurry!" Wilson said. "You and that idiot Nicholls—so confident that it never would come to trial."

Harley shrugged, and thought unhappily of their failure in completely exorcising the ghost of Hank Jenkins. That had been a mess. Jenkins had somehow escaped from the charmed circle they'd drawn around him, in which they'd hoped to keep him till the trial was forfeited by non-appearance.

"That's another thing," said Wilson. "Where is Nicholls?"

Harley shrugged again. "I dunno. The last I saw of him was in your office. He came around to see me right after the deputy slapped the show-cause order on me at the house. He brought me down to you—said you'd been recommended to him. Then you and him and I talked about the case for a while. He went out, after he lent me a little money to help meet your retainer. Haven't seen him since."

"I'd like to know who recommended me to him," Wilson said grimly. "I don't think he'd ever recommend anybody else. I don't like this case —and I don't much like you."

Harley growled but said nothing. He flung his cigarette away. It tasted of the garbage that hung around his neck—everything did. Nicholls had told no lies when he said Harley wouldn't much like the bundle of herbs that would ward off the ghost of old Jenkins. They smelled.

The court clerk was in the corridor, bawling something, and people were beginning to trickle back in. Harley and his attorney went with them.

When the trial had been resumed, the clerk said, "Henry Jenkins!"

Wilson was on his feet at once. He opened the door of the judge's chamber, said something in a low tone. Then he stepped back, as if to let someone through.

Pat. HISS. Pat. HISS—

There was a concerted gasp from the spectators as the weirdly appearing trickle of blood moved slowly across the open space to the witness chair. This was the ghost—the plaintiff in the most eminently absurd case in the history of jurisprudence.

"All right, Hank," Turnbull whispered. "You'll have to materialize long enough to let the clerk swear you in."

The clerk drew back nervously at the pillar of milky fog that appeared before him, vaguely humanoid in shape. A phantom hand, half transparent, reached out to touch the Bible. The clerk's voice shook as he administered the oath, and heard the response come from the heart of the cloudpillar.

The haze drifted into the witness chair, bent curiously at about hip-height, and popped into nothingness.

The judge banged his gavel wildly. The buzz of alarm that had arisen from the spectators died out.

"I'll warn you again," he declared, "that unruliness will not be tolerated. The counsel for the plaintiff may proceed."

Turnbull walked to the witness chair and addressed its emptiness.

"Your name?"

"My name is Henry Jenkins."

"Your occupation?"

There was a slight pause. "I have none. I guess you'd say I'm retired."

"Mr. Jenkins, just what connection have you with the building referred to as Harley Hall?"

"I have occupied it for ninety years."

"During this time, did you come to know the late Zebulon Harley, owner of the Hall?"

"I knew Zeb quite well."

Turnbull nodded. "When did you make his acquaintance?" he asked.

"In the spring of 1907. Zeb had just lost his wife. After that, you see, he made Harley Hall his year-round home. He became—well, more or less of a hermit. Before that we had never met, since he was only seldom at the Hall. But we became friendly then."

"How long did this friendship last?"

"Until he died last fall. I was with him when he died. I still have a few keepsakes he left me then." There was a distinct nostalgic sigh from the witness chair, which by now was literally spattered with muddy red liquid. The falling drops seemed to hesitate for a second, and their sizzling noise was muted as with a strong emotion.

Turnbull went on, "Your relations with him were good, then?"

"I'd call them excellent," the emptiness replied firmly. "Every night we sat up together. When we didn't play pinochle or chess or cribbage, we just sat and talked over the news of the day. I still have the book we used to keep records of the chess and pinochle games. Zeb made the entries himself, in his own handwriting."

Turnbull abandoned the witness for a moment. He faced the judge with a smile. "I offer in evidence," he said, "the book mentioned. Also a ring given to the plaintiff by the late Mr. Harley, and a copy of the plays of Gilbert and Sullivan. On the flyleaf of this book is inscribed, 'To Old Hank,' in Harley's own hand."

He turned again to the empty, blood-leaking witness chair.

He said, "In all your years of association, did Zebulon Harley ever ask you to leave, or to pay rent?"

"Of course not. Not Zeb!"

Turnbull nodded. "Very good," he said. "Now, just one or two more questions. Will you tell in your own words what occurred after the death of Zebulon Harley, that caused you to bring this suit?"

"Well, in January young Harley—"

"You mean Russell Joseph Harley, the defendant?"

"Yes. He arrived at Harley Hall on January fifth. I asked him to leave, which he did. On the next day he returned with another man. They placed a talisman upon the threshold of the main entrance, and soon after sealed every threshold and windowsill in the Hall with a substance which is noxious to me. These activities were accompanied by several of the most deadly spells in the Ars Magicorum. He further added an Exclusion Circle with a radius of a little over a mile, entirely surrounding the Hall."

"I see," the lawyer said. "Will you explain to the court the effects of these activities?"

"Well," the voice said thoughtfully, "it's a little hard to put in words.

I can't pass the Circle without a great expenditure of energy. Even if I did I couldn't enter the building because of the talisman and the seals."

"Could you enter by air? Through a chimney, perhaps?"

"No. The Exclusion Circle is really a sphere. I'm pretty sure the effort would destroy me."

"In effect, then, you are entirely barred from the house you have occupied for ninety years, due to the wilful acts of Russell Joseph Harley, the defendant, and an unnamed accomplice of his."

"That is correct."

Turnbull beamed. "Thank you. That's all."

He turned to Wilson, whose face had been a study in dourness throughout the entire examination. "Your witness," he said.

Wilson snapped to his feet and strode to the witness chair.

He said belligerently, "You say your name is Henry Jenkins?"

"Yes."

"That is your name now, you mean to say. What was your name before?"

"Before?" There was surprise in the voice that emanated from above the trickling blood-drops. "Before when?"

Wilson scowled. "Don't pretend ignorance," he said sharply. "Before you *died,* of course."

"Objection!" Turnbull was on his feet, glaring at Wilson. "The counsel for the defense has no right to speak of some hypothetical death of my client!"

Gimbel raised a hand wearily and cut off the words that were forming on Wilson's lips. "Objection sustained," he said. "No evidence has been presented to identify the plaintiff as the prospector who was killed in 1850—or anyone else."

Wilson's mouth twisted into a sour grimace. He continued on a lower key.

"You say, Mr. Jenkins, that you occupied Harley Hall for ninety years."

"Ninety-two years next month. The Hall wasn't built—in its present form, anyhow—until 1876, but I occupied the house that stood on the site previously."

"What did you do before then?"

"Before then?" The voice paused, then said doubtfully, "I don't remember."

"You're under oath!" Wilson flared.

The voice got firmer. "Ninety years is a long time," it said. "I don't remember."

"Let's see if I can't refresh your memory. Is it true that ninety-one years ago, in the very year in which you claim to have begun your occupancy of Harley Hall, Hank Jenkins was killed in a gun duel?"

"That may be true, if you say so. I don't remember."

"Do you remember that the shooting occurred not fifty feet from the present site of Harley Hall?"

"It may be."

"Well, then," Wilson thundered, "is it not a fact that when Hank Jenkins died by violence his ghost assumed existence? That it was then doomed to haunt the site of its slaying throughout eternity?"

The voice said evenly, "I have no knowledge of that."

"Do you deny that it is well known throughout that section that the ghost of Hank Jenkins haunts Harley Hall?"

"Objection!" shouted Turnbull. "Popular opinion is not evidence."

"Objection sustained. Strike the question from the record."

Wilson, badgered, lost his control. In a dangerously uneven voice, he said, "Perjury is a criminal offense. Mr. Jenkins, do you deny that you are the ghost of Hank Jenkins?"

The tone was surprised. "Why, certainly."

"You *are* a ghost, aren't you?"

Stiffly, "I'm an entity on the astral plane."

"That, I believe, is what is called a ghost?"

"I can't help what it's called. I've heard you called a lot of things. Is that proof?"

There was a surge of laughter from the audience. Gimbel slammed his gavel down on the bench.

"The witness," he said, "will confine himself to answering questions."

Wilson bellowed, "In spite of what you say, it's true, isn't it, that you are merely the spirit of a human being who had died through violence?"

The voice from above the blood drops retorted, "I repeat that I am an entity of the astral plane. I am not aware that I was ever a human being."

The lawyer turned an exasperated face to the bench.

"Your honor," he said, "I ask that you instruct the witness to cease playing verbal hide-and-seek. It is quite evident that the witness is a ghost, and that he is therefore the relict of some human being, ipso facto. Circumstantial evidence is strong that he is the ghost of the Hank Jenkins who was killed in 1850. But this is a non-essential point. What is definite is that he is the ghost of someone who is dead, and hence is unqualified to act as witness! I demand his testimony be stricken from the record!"

Turnbull spoke up at once. "Will the counsel for the defense quote his authority for branding my client a ghost—in the face of my client's repeated declaration that he is an entity of the astral plane? What is the legal definition of a ghost?"

Judge Gimbel smiled. "Counsel for the defense will proceed with the cross-examination," he said.

Wilson's face flushed dark purple. He mopped his brow with a large bandanna, then glared at the dropping, sizzling trickle of blood.

"Whatever you are," he said, "answer me this question. Can you pass through a wall?"

"Why, yes. Certainly." There was a definite note of surprise in the voice from nowhere. "But it isn't as easy as some people think. It definitely requires a lot of effort."

"Never mind that. You can do it?"

"Yes."

"Could you be bound by any physical means? Would handcuffs hold you? Or ropes, chains, prison walls, a hermetically sealed steel chest?"

Jenkins had no chance to answer. Turnbull, scenting danger, cut in hastily. "I object to this line of questioning. It is entirely irrelevant."

"On the contrary," Wilson cried loudly, "it bears strongly on the qualifications of the so-called Henry Jenkins as a witness! I demand that he answer the question."

Judge Gimbel said, "Objection overruled. Witness will answer the question."

The voice from the chair said superciliously, "I don't mind answering. Physical barriers mean nothing to me, by and large."

The counsel for the defense drew himself up triumphantly.

"Very good," he said with satisfaction. "*Very* good." Then to the judge, the words coming sharp and fast, "I claim, your honor, that the so-called Henry Jenkins has no legal status as a witness in court. There is clearly no value in understanding the nature of an oath if a violation of the oath can bring no punishment in its wake. The statements of a man who can perjure himself freely have no worth. I demand they be stricken from the record!"

Turnbull was at the judge's bench in two strides.

"I had anticipated that, your honor," he said quickly. "From the very nature of the case, however, it is clear that my client can be very definitely restricted in his movements—spells, pentagrams, talismans, amulets, Exclusion Circles and what-not. I have here—which I am prepared to deliver to the bailiff of the court—a list of the various methods of confining an astral entity to a restricted area for periods ranging from a few moments to all eternity. Moreover, I have also signed a bond for five thousand dollars, prior to the beginning of the trial, which I stand ready to forfeit should my client be confined and make his escape, if found guilty of any misfeasance as a witness."

Gimbel's face, which had looked startled for a second, slowly cleared. He nodded. "The court is satisfied with the statement of the counsel for the plaintiff," he declared. "There seems no doubt that the plaintiff can be penalized for any misstatements, and the motion of the defense is denied."

Wilson looked choleric, but shrugged. "All right," he said. "That will be all."

"You may step down, Mr. Jenkins," Gimbel directed, and watched in fascination as the blood-dripping column rose and floated over the floor, along the corridor, out the door.

Turnbull approached the judge's bench again. He said, "I would like to place in evidence these notes, the diary of the late Zebulon Harley. It was presented to my client by Harley himself last fall. I call particular attention to the entry for April sixth, nineteen seventeen, in which he mentions the entrance of the United States into the First World War, and records the results of a series of eleven pinochle games played with a personage identified as 'Old Hank.' With the court's permission, I will read the entry for that day, and also various other entries for the next four years. Please note the references to someone known variously as 'Jenkins,' 'Hank Jenkins,' and—in one extremely significant passage— 'Old Invisible.' "

Wilson stewed silently during the slow reading of Harley's diary. There was anger on his face, but he paid close attention, and when the reading was over he leaped to his feet.

"I would like to know," he asked, "if the counsel for the plaintiff is in possession of any diaries *after* nineteen twenty?"

Turnbull shook his head. "Harley apparently never kept a diary, except during the four years represented in this."

"Then I demand that the court refuse to admit this diary as evidence on two counts," Wilson said. He raised two fingers to tick off the points. "In the first place, the evidence presented is frivolous. The few vague and unsatisfactory references to Jenkins nowhere specifically describe him as what he is—ghost, astral entity or what you will. Second, the evidence, even were the first point overlooked, concerns only the years up to nineteen twenty-one. The case concerns itself only with the supposed occupation of Harley Hall by the so-called Jenkins in the last twenty years—*since* 'twenty-one. Clearly, the evidence is therefore irrelevant."

Gimbel looked at Turnbull, who smiled calmly.

"The reference to 'Old Invisible' is far from vague," he said. "It is a definite indication of the astral character of my client. Furthermore, evidence as to the friendship of my client with the late Mr. Zebulon Harley before nineteen twenty-one is entirely relevant, as such a friendship, once established, would naturally be presumed to have continued indefinitely. Unless of course, the defense is able to present evidence to the contrary."

Judge Gimbel said, "The diary is admitted as evidence."

Turnbull said, "I rest my case."

There was a buzz of conversation in the courtroom while the judge looked over the diary, and then handed it to the clerk to be marked and entered.

Gimbel said, "The defense may open its case."

Wilson rose. To the clerk he said, "Russell Joseph Harley."

But young Harley was recalcitrant. "Nix," he said, on his feet, pointing at the witness chair. "That thing's got blood all over it! You don't expect me to sit down in that large puddle of blood, do you?"

Judge Gimbel leaned over to look at the chair. The drip-drop trickle of blood from the apparition who'd been testifying had left its mark. Muddy brown all down the front of the chair. Gimbel found himself wondering how the ghost managed to replenish its supply of the fluid, but gave it up.

"I see your point," he said. "Well, it's getting a bit late anyhow. The clerk will take away the present witness chair and replace it. In the interim, I declare the court recessed till tomorrow morning at ten o'clock."

III

Russell Harley noticed how the elevator boy's back registered repulsion and disapproval, and scowled. He was not a popular guest in the hotel, he knew well. Where he made his mistake, though, was in thinking that the noxious bundle of herbs about his neck was the cause of it. His odious personality had a lot to do with the chilly attitude of the management and his fellow guests.

He made his way to the bar, ignoring the heads that turned in surprise to follow the reeking comet-tail of his passage. He entered the red-leather-and-chromium drinking room, and stared about for Lawyer Wilson.

And blinked in surprise when he saw him. Wilson wasn't alone. In the booth with him was a tall, dark figure, with his back to Harley. The back alone was plenty for recognition. Nicholls!

Wilson had seen him. "Hello, Harley," he said, all smiles and affability in the presence of the man with the money. "Come on and sit down. Mr. Nicholls dropped in on me a little while ago, so I brought him over."

"Hello," Harley said glumly, and Nicholls nodded. The muscles of his cheeks pulsed, and he seemed under a strain, strangely uncomfortable in Harley's presence. Still there was a twinkle in the look he gave young Harley, and his voice was friendly enough—though supercilious—as he said:

"Hello, Harley. How is the trial going?"

"Ask him," said Harley, pointing a thumb at Wilson as he slid his knees under the booth's table and sat down. "He's the lawyer. He's supposed to know these things."

"Doesn't he?"

Harley shrugged and craned his neck for the waitress. "Oh, I guess so. . . . Rye and water!" He watched the girl appreciatively as she nodded and went off to the bar, then turned his attention back to Nicholls. "The trouble is," he said, "Wilson may think he knows, but I think he's all wet."

Wilson frowned. "Do you imply—" he began, but Nicholls put up a hand.

"Let's not bicker," said Nicholls. "Suppose you answer my question. I have a stake in this, and I want to know. How's the trial going?"

Wilson put on his most open-faced expression. "Frankly," he said, "not too well. I'm afraid the judge is on the other side. If you'd listened to me and stalled till another judge came along—"

"I had no time to stall," said Nicholls. "I have to be elsewhere within a few days. Even now, I should be on my way. Do you think we might lose the case?"

Harley laughed sharply. As Wilson glared at him he took his drink from the waitress' tray and swallowed it. The smile remained on his face as he listened to Wilson say smoothly:

"There is a good deal of danger, yes."

"Hum." Nicholls looked interestedly at his fingernails. "Perhaps I chose the wrong lawyer."

"Sure you did." Harley waved at the waitress, ordered another drink. "You want to know what else I think? I think you picked the wrong client, spelled s-t-o-o-g-e. I'm getting sick of this. This damn thing around my neck smells bad. How do I know it's any good, anyway? Far as I can see, it just smells bad, and that's all."

"It works," Nicholls said succinctly. "I wouldn't advise you to go without it. The late Hank Jenkins is not a very strong ghost—a strong one would tear you apart and chew up your herbs for dessert—but without the protection of what you wear about your neck, you would become a very uncomfortable human as soon as Jenkins heard you'd stopped wearing it."

He put down the glass of red wine he'd been inhaling without drinking, looked intently at Wilson. "I've put up the money in this," he said. "I had hoped you'd be able to handle the legal end. I see I'll have to do more. Now listen intently, because I have no intention of repeating this. There's an angle to this case that's got right by your blunted legal acumen. Jenkins claims to be an astral entity, which he undoubtedly is. Now, instead of trying to prove him a ghost, and legally dead, and therefore unfit to testify, which you have been doing, suppose you do this. . . ."

He went on to speak rapidly and to the point.

And when he left them a bit later, and Wilson took Harley up to his room and poured him into bed, the lawyer felt happy for the first time in days.

Russell Joseph Harley, a little hung over and a lot nervous, was called to the stand as first witness in his own behalf.

Wilson said, "Your name?"

"Russell Joseph Harley."

"You are the nephew of the late Zebulon Harley, who bequeathed the residence known as Harley Hall to you?"

"Yes."

Wilson turned to the bench. "I offer this copy of the late Mr. Zebulon Harley's will in evidence. All his possessions are left to his nephew and only living kin, the defendant."

Turnbull spoke from his desk. "The plaintiff in no way disputes the defendant's equity in Harley Hall."

Wilson continued, "You passed part of your childhood in Harley Hall, did you not, and visited it as a grown man on occasion?"

"Yes."

"At any time, has anything in the shape of a ghost, specter or astral entity manifested itself to you in Harley Hall?"

"No. I'd remember it."

"Did your late uncle ever mention any such manifestation to you?"

"Him? No."

"That's all."

Turnbull came up for the cross-examination.

"When, Mr. Harley, did you last see your uncle before his death?"

"It was in nineteen thirty-eight. In September, some time—around the tenth or eleventh of the month."

"How long a time did you spend with him?"

Harley flushed unaccountably. "Ah—just one day," he said.

"When before that did you see him?"

"Well, not since I was quite young. My parents moved to Pennsylvania in nineteen twenty."

"And since then—except for that one-day visit in nineteen thirty-eight —has any communication passed between your uncle and yourself?"

"No, I guess not. He was a rather queer duck—solitary. A little bit balmy, I think."

"Well, you're a loving nephew. But in view of what you've just said, does it sound surprising that your uncle never told you of Mr. Jenkins? He never had much chance to, did he?"

"He had a chance in nineteen thirty-eight, but he didn't," Harley said defiantly.

Turnbull shrugged. "I'm finished," he said.

Gimbel began to look bored. He had anticipated something more in the way of fireworks. He said, "Has the defense any further witnesses?"

Wilson smiled grimly. "Yes, your honor," he said. This was his big moment, and he smiled again as he said gently, "I would like to call Mr. Henry Jenkins to the stand."

In the amazed silence that followed, Judge Gimbel leaned forward. "You mean you wish to call the plaintiff as a witness for the defense?"

Serenely, "Yes, your honor."

Gimbel grimaced. "Call Henry Jenkins," he said wearily to the clerk, and sank back in his chair.

Turnbull was looking alarmed. He bit his lip, trying to decide whether to object to this astonishing procedure, but finally shrugged as the clerk bawled out the ghost's name.

Turnbull sped down the corridor, out the door. His voice was heard in the anteroom, then he returned more slowly. Behind him came the trickle of blood drops: *Pat. HISS. Pat. HISS—*

"One moment," said Gimbel, coming to life again. "I have no objection to your testifying, Mr. Jenkins, but the State should not be subjected to the needless expense of reupholstering its witness chair every time you do. Bailiff, find some sort of a rug or something to throw over the chair before Mr. Jenkins is sworn in."

A tarpaulin was hurriedly procured and adjusted to the chair; Jenkins materialized long enough to be sworn in, then sat.

"Tell me, Mr. Jenkins," he said, "just how many 'astral entities'—I believe that is what you call yourself—are there?"

"I have no way of knowing. Many billions."

"As many, in other words, as there have been human beings to die by violence?"

Turnbull rose to his feet in sudden agitation, but the ghost neatly evaded the trap. "I don't know. I only know there are billions."

The lawyer's cat-who-ate-canary smile remained undimmed. "And all these billions are constantly about us, everywhere, only remaining invisible. Is that it?"

"Oh, no. Very few remain on Earth. Of those, still fewer have anything to do with humans. Most humans are quite boring to us."

"Well, how many would you say are on Earth? A hundred thousand?"

"Even more, maybe. But that's a good guess."

Turnbull interrupted suddenly. "I would like to know the significance of these questions. I object to this whole line of questioning as being totally irrevelant."

Wilson was a study in legal dignity. He retorted, "I am trying to elicit some facts of major value, your honor. This may change the entire character of the case. I ask your patience for a moment or two."

"Counsel for the defense may continue," Gimbel said curtly.

Wilson showed his canines in a grin. He continued to the blood-dripping before him. "Now, the contention of your counsel is that the late Mr. Harley allowed an 'astral entity' to occupy his home for twenty years or more, with his full knowledge and consent. That strikes me as being entirely improbable, but shall we for the moment assume it to be the case?"

"Certainly! It's the truth."

"Then tell me, Mr. Jenkins, have you fingers?"

"Have I—what?"

"You heard me!" Wilson snapped. "Have you fingers, flesh-and-blood fingers, capable of making an imprint?"

"Why, no. I—"

Wilson rushed on. "Or have you a photograph of yourself—or specimens of your handwriting—or any sort of material identification? Have you any of these?"

The voice was definitely querulous. "What do you mean?"

Wilson's voice became harsh, menacing. "I mean, can you prove that *you* are the astral entity alleged to have occupied Zebulon Harley's home. Was it you—or was it another of the featureless, faceless, intangible unknowns—one of the hundreds of thousands of them that, by your own admission, are all over the face of the earth, rambling where they choose, not halted by any locks or bars? Can you prove that *you* are anyone in particular?"

"Your honor!" Turnbull's voice was almost a shriek as he found his feet at last. "My client's identity was never in question!"

"It is now!" roared Wilson. "The opposing counsel has presented a personage whom he styles 'Henry Jenkins.' Who is this Jenkins? What is he? Is he even an individual—or a corporate aggregation of these mysterious 'astral entities' which we are to believe are everywhere, but which we never see? If he is an individual, is he *the* individual? And how can we know that, even if he says he is? Let him produce evidence—photographs, a birth certificate, fingerprints. Let him bring in identifying witnesses who have known both ghosts, and are prepared to swear that these ghosts are the same ghost. Failing this, there is no case! Your honor, I demand the court declare an immediate judgment in favor of the defendant!"

Judge Gimbel stared at Turnbull. "Have you anything to say?" he asked. "The argument of the defense would seem to have every merit with it. Unless you can produce some sort of evidence as to the identity of your client, I have no alternative but to find for the defense."

For a moment there was a silent tableau. Wilson triumphant, Turnbull furiously frustrated.

How could you identify a ghost?

And then came the quietly amused voice from the witness chair.

"This thing has gone far enough," it said above the sizzle and splatter of its own leaking blood. "I believe I can present proof that will satisfy the court."

Wilson's face fell with express-elevator speed. Turnbull held his breath, afraid to hope.

Judge Gimbel said, "You are under oath. Proceed."

There was no other sound in the courtroom as the voice said, "Mr. Harley, here, spoke of a visit to his uncle in nineteen thirty-eight. I can vouch for that. They spent a night and a day together. They weren't alone. I was there."

No one was watching Russell Harley, or they might have seen the sudden sick pallor that passed over his face.

The voice, relentless, went on. "Perhaps I shouldn't have eavesdropped as I did, but old Zeb never had any secrets from me anyhow. I listened to what they talked about. Young Harley was working for a bank in Philadelphia at the time. His first big job. He needed money, and needed it bad. There was a shortage in his department. A woman named Sally—"

"Hold on!" Wilson yelled. "This has nothing to do with your identification of yourself. Keep to the point!"

But Turnbull had begun to comprehend. He was shouting, too, almost too excited to be coherent. "Your honor, my client must be allowed to speak. If he shows knowledge of an intimate conversation between the late Mr. Harley and the defendant, it would be certain proof that he enjoyed the late Mr. Harley's confidence, and thus, Q.E.D., that he is no other than the astral entity who occupied Harley Hall for so long!"

Gimbel nodded sharply. "Let me remind counsel for the defense that this is his own witness. Mr. Jenkins, continue."

The voice began again, "As I was saying, the woman's name—"

"Shut up, damn you!" Harley yelled. He sprang upright, turned beseechingly toward the judge. "He's twisting it! Make him stop! Sure, I knew my uncle had a ghost. He's it, all right, curse his black soul! He can have the house if he wants it—I'll clear out of the whole damned state!"

He broke off into babbling and turned about wildly. Only the intervention of a marshal kept him from hurtling out of the courtroom.

Banging of the gavel and hard work by the court clerk and his staff restored order in the courtroom. When the room had returned almost to normalcy, Judge Gimbel, perspiring and annoyed, said, "As far as I am concerned, identification of the witness is complete. Has the defense any further evidence to present?"

Wilson shrugged morosely. "No, your honor."

"Counsel for the plaintiff?"

"Nothing, your honor. I rest my case."

Gimbel plowed a hand through his sparse hair and blinked. "In that case," he said, "I find for the plaintiff. An order is entered hereby that the defendant, Russell Joseph Harley, shall remove from the premises of Harley Hall all spells, pentagrams, talismans and other means of exorcism employed; that he shall cease and desist from making any attempts, of whatever nature, to evict the tenant in the future; and that Henry Jenkins, the plaintiff, shall be permitted to full use and occupancy of the premises designated as Harley Hall for the full term of his natural—ah—existence."

The gavel banged. "The case is closed."

"Don't take it so hard," said a mild voice behind Russell Harley. He whirled surlily. Nicholls was coming up the street after him from the courthouse, Wilson in tow.

Nicholls said, "You lost the case, but you've still got your life. Let me buy you a drink. In here, perhaps."

He herded them into a cocktail lounge, sat them down before they had a chance to object. He glanced at his expensive wrist watch. "I have a few minutes," he said. "Then I really must be off. It's urgent."

He hailed a barman, ordered for all. Then he looked at young Harley and smiled broadly as he dropped a bill on the counter to pay for the drinks.

"Harley," he said, "I have a motto that you would do well to remember at times like these. I'll make you a present of it, if you like."

"What is it?"

" 'The worst is yet to come.' "

Harley snarled and swallowed his drink without replying. Wilson said, "What gets me is, why didn't they come to us before the trial with that stuff about this charmingly illicit client you wished on me? We'd have had to settle out of court."

Nicholls shrugged. "They had their reasons," he said. "After all, one case of exorcism, more or less, doesn't matter. But lawsuits set precedents. You're a lawyer, of sorts, Wilson; do you see what I mean?"

"Precedents?" Wilson looked at him slackjawed for a moment; then his eyes widened.

"I see you understand me." Nicholls nodded. "From now on in this state—and by virtue of the full-faith-and-credence clause of the Constitution, in *every* state of the country—a ghost has a legal right to haunt a house!"

"Good Lord!" said Wilson. He began to laugh, not loud, but from the bottom of his chest.

Harley stared at Nicholls. "Once and for all," he whispered, "tell me —what's your angle on all this?"

Nicholls smiled again.

"Think about it a while," he said lightly. "You'll begin to understand." He sniffed his wine once more, then sat the glass down gently— And vanished.

"Smee" is a muted little tale of a haunted house that manages to chill me more effectively than a lot of more melodramatic stories. ALFRED M. BURRAGE, *born in Middlesex in 1889, was a British journalist, poet, and short-story writer whose work is little known in America. This is our loss, as the few fantasies of his I've read are all first-rate.*

Smee

by A. M. Burrage

"No," said Jackson, with a deprecatory smile, "I'm sorry. I don't want to upset your game. I shan't be doing that because you'll have plenty without me. But I'm not playing any games of hide-and-seek."

It was Christmas Eve, and we were a party of fourteen with just the proper leavening of youth. We had dined well; it was the season for childish games; and we were all in the mood for playing them—all, that is, except Jackson. When somebody suggested hide-and-seek there was rapturous and almost unanimous approval. His was the one dissentient voice.

It was not like Jackson to spoil sport or refuse to do as others wanted. Somebody asked him if he were feeling seedy.

"No," he answered, "I feel perfectly fit, thanks. But," he added with a smile which softened without retracting the flat refusal, "I'm not playing hide-and-seek."

One of us asked him why not. He hesitated for some seconds before replying.

"I sometimes go and stay at a house where a girl was killed through playing hide-and-seek in the dark. She didn't know the house very well. There was a servants' staircase with a door to it. When she was pursued she opened the door and jumped into what she must have thought was one of the bedrooms—and she broke her neck at the bottom of the stairs."

We all looked concerned, and Mrs. Fernley said:

"How awful! And you were there when it happened?"

Jackson shook his head very gravely.

"No," he said, "but I was there when something else happened. Something worse."

"I shouldn't have thought anything could be worse."

"This was," said Jackson, and shuddered visibly. "Or so it seemed to me."

I think he wanted to tell the story and was angling for encouragement. A few requests, which may have seemed to him to lack urgency, he affected to ignore and went off at a tangent.

"I wonder if any of you have played a game called 'Smee'? It's a great improvement on the ordinary game of hide-and-seek. The name derives from the ungrammatical colloquialism, 'It's me.' You might care to play if you're going to play a game of that sort. Let me tell you the rules.

"Every player is presented with a sheet of paper. All the sheets are blank except one, on which is written 'Smee.' Nobody knows who is 'Smee' except 'Smee' himself—or herself, as the case may be. The lights are then turned out and 'Smee' slips from the room and goes off to hide, and after an interval the other players go off in search, without knowing whom they are actually in search of. One player meeting another challenges with the word 'Smee,' and the other player, if not the one concerned, answers 'Smee.'

"The real 'Smee' makes no answer when challenged, and the second player remains quietly by him. Presently they will be discovered by a third player who, having challenged and received no answer, will link up with the first two. This goes on until all the players have formed a chain, and the last to join is marked down for a forfeit. It's a good noisy, romping game, and in a big house it often takes a long time to complete the chain. You might care to try it; and I'll pay my forfeit and smoke one of Tim's excellent cigars here by the fire, until you get tired of it."

I remarked that it sounded a good game and asked Jackson if he had played it himself.

"Yes," he answered; "I played it in the house I was telling you about."

"And *she* was there? The girl who broke—"

"No, no," Mrs. Fernley interrupted. "He told us he wasn't there when it happened."

Jackson considered.

"I don't know if she were there or not. I'm afraid she was. I know that there were thirteen of us and there ought only to have been twelve. And I'll swear that I didn't know her name, or I think I should have gone clean off my head when I heard that whisper in the dark. No, you don't catch me playing that game, or any other like it, any more. It spoilt my nerve quite a while, and I can't afford to take long holidays. Besides, it saves a lot of trouble and inconvenience to own up at once to being a coward."

Tim Vouce, the best of hosts, smiled around at us, and in that smile there was a meaning which is sometimes vulgarly expressed by the slow closing of an eye.

"There's a story coming," he announced.

"There's certainly a story of sorts," said Jackson, "but whether it's coming or not—"

He paused and shrugged his shoulders.

"Well, you're going to pay a forfeit instead of playing?"

"Please. But have a heart and let me down lightly. It's not just a sheer cussedness on my part."

"Payment in advance," said Tim, "ensures honesty and promotes good feeling. You are therefore sentenced to tell the story here and now."

And here follows Jackson's story, unrevised by me and passed on without comment to a wider public:

Some of you, I know, have run across the Sangstons. Christopher Sangston and his wife, I mean. They're distant connections of mine—at least, Violet Sangston is. About eight years ago they bought a house between the North and South Downs on the Surrey and Sussex border, and five years ago they invited me to come and spend Christmas with them.

It was a fairly old house—I couldn't say exactly of what period—and it certainly deserved the epithet "rambling." It wasn't a particularly big house, but the original architect, whoever he may have been, had not concerned himself with economising in space, and at first you could get lost in it quite easily.

Well, I went down for that Christmas, assured by Violet's letter that I knew most of my fellow-guests and that the two or three who might be strangers to me were all "lambs." Unfortunately, I'm one of the world's workers, and I couldn't get away until Christmas Eve, although the other members of the party had assembled on the preceding day. Even then I had to cut it rather fine to be there for dinner on my first night. They were all dressing when I arrived and I had to go straight to my room and waste no time. I may even have kept dinner waiting for a bit, for I was last down, and it was announced within a minute of my entering the drawing-room. There was just time to say "hullo" to everybody

I knew, to be briefly introduced to the two or three I didn't know, and then I had to give my arm to Mrs. Gorman.

I mention this as the reason why I didn't catch the name of a tall, dark, handsome girl I hadn't met before. Everything was rather hurried and I am always bad at catching people's names. She looked cold and clever and rather forbidding, the sort of girl who gives the impression of knowing all about men and the more she knows of them the less she likes them. I felt that I wasn't going to hit it off with this particular "lamb" of Violet's, but she looked interesting all the same, and I wondered who she was. I didn't ask, because I was pretty sure of hearing somebody address her by name before very long.

Unluckily, though, I was a long way off her at table, and as Mrs. Gorman was at the top of her form that night I soon forgot to worry about who she might be. Mrs. Gorman is one of the most amusing women I know, an outrageous but quite innocent flirt, with a very sprightly wit which isn't always unkind. She can think half a dozen moves ahead in conversation just as an expert can in a game of chess. We were soon sparring, or, rather, I was "covering" against the ropes, and I quite forgot to ask her in an undertone the name of the cold, proud beauty. The lady on the other side of me was a stranger, or had been until a few minutes since, and I didn't think of seeking information in that quarter.

There was a round dozen of us, including the Sangstons themselves, and we were all young or trying to be. The Sangstons themselves were the oldest members of the party, and their son Reggie, in his last year at Marlborough, must have been the youngest. When there was talk of playing games after dinner it was he who suggested "Smee." He told us how to play it just as I've described it to you.

His father chipped in as soon as we all understood what was going to be required of us.

"If there are any games of that sort going on in the house," he said, "for goodness sake be careful of the back stairs on the first floor landing. There's a door to them and I've often meant to take it down. In the dark anybody who doesn't know the house very well might think they were walking into a room. A girl actually did break her neck on those stairs about ten years ago when the Ainsties lived here."

I asked how it happened.

"Oh," said Sangston, "there was a party here one Christmas time and they were playing hide-and-seek as you propose doing. This girl was one of the hiders. She heard somebody coming, ran along the passage to get away, and opened the door of what she thought was a bedroom, evidently with the intention of hiding behind it while her pursuer went past. Unfortunately it was the door leading to the back stairs, and that staircase is at straight and almost as steep as the shaft of a pit. She was dead when they picked her up."

We all promised for our own sakes to be careful. Mrs. Gorman said that she was sure nothing could happen to her, since she was insured by three different newspapers, and her next-of-kin was a brother whose consistent ill-luck was a byword in the family. You see, none of us had known the unfortunate girl, and as the tragedy was ten years old there was no need to pull long faces about it.

Well, we started the game almost immediately after dinner. The men allowed themselves only five minutes before joining the ladies, and then young Reggie Sangston went round and assured himself that the lights were out all over the house except in the servants' quarters and in the drawing-room where we were assembled. We then got busy with twelve sheets of paper which he twisted into pellets and shook up between his hands before passing them round. Eleven of them were blank, and "Smee" was written on the twelfth. The person drawing the latter was the one who had to hide. I looked and saw that mine was a blank. A moment later out went the electric lights, and in the darkness I heard somebody get up and creep to the door.

After a minute or so somebody gave a signal and we made a rush for the door. I for one hadn't the least idea which of the party was "Smee." For five or ten minutes we were all rushing up and down passages and in and out rooms challenging one another and answering, *"Smee?— Smee!"*

After a bit the alarums and excursions died down, and I guessed that "Smee" was found. Eventually I found a chain of people all sitting still and holding their breath on some narrow stairs leading up to a row of attics. I hastily joined it, having challenged and been answered with silence, and presently two more stragglers arrived, each racing the other to avoid being last. Sangston was one of them, indeed it was he who was marked down for a forfeit, and after a little while he remarked in an undertone, "I think we're all here now, aren't we?"

He struck a match, looked up the shaft of the staircase, and began to count. It wasn't hard, although we just about filled the staircase, for we were sitting each a step or two one above the next, and all our heads were visible.

". . . nine, ten, eleven, twelve—*thirteen*," he concluded, and then laughed. "Dash it all, that's one too many!"

The match had burnt out and he struck another and began to count. He got as far as twelve, and then uttered an exclamation.

"There *are* thirteen people here!" he exclaimed. "I haven't counted myself yet."

"Oh, nonsense!" I laughed. "You probably began with yourself, and now want to count yourself twice."

Out came his son's electric torch, giving a brighter and steadier light and we all began to count. Of course we numbered twelve. Sangston laughed.

"Well," he said, "I could have sworn I counted thirteen twice."

From halfway up the stairs came Violet Sangston's voice with a little nervous trill in it.

"I thought there was somebody sitting two steps above me. Have you moved up, Captain Ransome?"

Ransome said that he hadn't. He also said that he thought there was somebody sitting between Violet and himself. Just for a moment there was an uncomfortable Something in the air, a little cold ripple which touched us all. For that little moment it seemed to all of us, I think, that something odd and unpleasant had happened and was liable to happen again. Then we laughed at ourselves and at one another and were comfortable once more. There *were* only twelve of us, and there *could* only have been twelve of us, and there was no argument about it. Still laughing we trooped back to the drawing-room to begin again.

This time I was "Smee," and Violet Sangston ran me to earth while I was still looking for a hiding-place. That round didn't last long, and we were a chain of twelve within two or three minutes. Afterwards there was a short interval. Violet wanted a wrap fetched for her, and her husband went up to get it from her room. He was no sooner gone than Reggie pulled me by the sleeve. I saw that he was looking pale and sick.

"Quick!" he whispered, "while father's out of the way. Take me into the smoke-room and give me a brandy or a whisky or something. You know the sort of dose a fellow ought to have."

Outside the room I asked him what was the matter, but he didn't answer at first, and I thought it better to dose him first and question him afterwards. So I mixed him a pretty dark-complexioned brandy and soda which he drank at a gulp and then began to puff as if he had been running.

"I've had rather a turn," he said to me with a sheepish grin.

"What's the matter?"

"I don't know. You were 'Smee' just now, weren't you? Well, of course I didn't know who 'Smee' was, and while mother and the others ran into the west wing and found you, I turned east. There's a deep clothes cupboard in my bedroom—I'd marked it down as a good place to hide when it was my turn, and I had an idea that 'Smee' might be there. I opened the door in the dark, felt round, and touched somebody's hand. 'Smee!' I whispered, and not getting any answer I thought I had found 'Smee.'

"Well, I don't know how it was, but an odd creepy feeling came over me. I can't describe it, but I felt that something was wrong. So I turned on my electric torch and there was nobody there. Now I swear I touched a hand, and I was filling up the doorway of the cupboard at the time, so nobody could get out past me." He puffed again. "What do you make of it?" he asked.

"You imagined that you touched a hand," I answered, naturally enough.

He uttered a short laugh.

"Of course I knew you were going to say that," he said. "I must have imagined it, mustn't I?" He paused and swallowed. "I mean, it couldn't have been anything else *but* imagination, could it?"

I assured him that it couldn't, meaning what I said, and he accepted this, but rather with the philosophy of one who knows he is right but doesn't expect to be believed. We returned together to the drawing-room where, by that time, they were all waiting for us and ready to start again.

It may have been my imagination—although I'm almost sure it wasn't —but it seemed to me that all enthusiasm for the game had suddenly melted like a white frost in strong sunlight. If anybody had suggested another game I'm sure we should all have been grateful and abandoned "Smee." Only nobody did. Nobody seemed to like to. I for one, and I can speak for some of the others, too, was oppressed with the feeling that there was something wrong. I couldn't have said what I thought was wrong, indeed I didn't think about it at all, but somehow all the sparkle had gone out of the fun, and hovering over my mind like a shadow was the warning of some sixth sense which told me that there was an influence in the house which was neither sane, sound nor healthy. Why did I feel like that? Because Sangston had counted thirteen of us instead of twelve, and his son had thought he had touched somebody in an empty cupboard. No, there was more in it than just that. One would have laughed at such things in the ordinary way, and it was just that feeling of something being wrong which stopped me from laughing.

Well, we started again, and when we went in pursuit of the unknown "Smee," we were as noisy as ever, but it seemed to me that most of us were acting. Frankly, for no reason other than the one I've given you, we'd stopped enjoying the game. I had an instinct to hunt with the main pack, but after a few minutes, during which no "Smee" had been found, my instinct to play winning games and be first if possible, set me searching on my own account. And on the first floor of the west wing, following the wall which was actually the shell of the house, I blundered against a pair of human knees.

I put out my hand and touched a soft, heavy curtain. Then I knew where I was. There were tall, deeply-recessed windows with seats along the landing, and curtains over the recesses to the ground. Somebody was sitting in a corner of this window-seat behind the curtain. Aha, I had caught "Smee"! So I drew the curtain aside, stepped in, and touched the bare arm of a woman.

It was a dark night outside, and, moreover, the window was not only curtained but a blind hung down to where the bottom panes joined up with the frame. Between the curtain and the window it was as dark as the plague of Egypt. I could not have seen my hand held six inches before my face, much less the woman sitting in the corner.

"Smee?" I whispered.

I had no answer. "Smee" when challenged does not answer. So I sat down beside her, first in the field, to await the others. Then, having settled myself I leaned over to her and whispered:

"Who is it? What's your name, 'Smee'?"

And out of the darkness beside me the whisper came back: "Brenda Ford."

I didn't know the name, but because I didn't know it I guessed at once who she was. The tall, pale, dark girl was the only person in the house I didn't know by name. Ergo my companion was the tall, pale, dark girl. It seemed rather intriguing to be there with her, shut in between a heavy curtain and a window, and I rather wondered whether she was enjoying the game we were all playing. Somehow she hadn't seemed to me to be one of the romping sort. I muttered one or two commonplace questions to her and had no answer.

"Smee" is a game of silence. "Smee" and the person or persons who have found "Smee" are supposed to keep quiet to make it hard for the others. But there was nobody else about, and it occurred to me that she was playing the game a little too much to the letter. I spoke again and got no answer, and then I began to be annoyed. She was of that cold, "superior" type which affects to despise men; she didn't like me; and she was sheltering behind the rules of a game for children to be discourteous. Well, if she didn't like sitting there with me, I certainly didn't want to be sitting there with her! I half turned from her and began to hope that we should both be discovered without much more delay.

Having discovered that I didn't like being there alone with her, it was queer how soon I found myself hating it, and that for a reason very different from the one which had at first whetted my annoyance. The girl I had met for the first time before dinner, and seen diagonally across the table, had a sort of cold charm about her which had attracted while it had half angered me. For the girl who was with me, imprisoned in the opaque darkness between the curtain and the window, I felt no attraction at all. It was so very much the reverse that I should have wondered at myself if, after the first shock of the discovery that she had suddenly become repellent to me, I had no room in my mind for anything besides the consciousness that her close presence was an increasing horror to me.

It came upon me just as quickly as I've uttered the words. My flesh suddenly shrank from her as you see a strip of gelatine shrink and wither before the heat of a fire. That feeling of something being wrong had come back to me, but multiplied to an extent which turned foreboding into actual terror. I firmly believe that I should have got up and run if I had not felt that at my first movement she would have divined my intention and compelled me to stay, by some means of which I could not bear to think. The memory of having touched her bare arm made me wince and draw in my lips. I prayed that somebody else would come along soon.

My prayer was answered. Light footfalls sounded on the landing. Somebody on the other side of the curtain brushed against my knees. The curtain was drawn aside and a woman's hand fumbling in the darkness, presently rested on my shoulder. "Smee?" whispered a voice which I instantly recognised as Mrs. Gorman's.

Of course she received no answer. She came and settled down beside me with a rustle, and I can't describe the sense of relief she brought me.

"It's Tony, isn't it?" she whispered.

"Yes," I whispered back.

"You're not 'Smee' are you."

"No, she's on my other side."

She reached a hand across me, and I heard one of her nails scratch the surface of a woman's silk gown.

"Hullo, 'Smee'! How are you? *Who* are you? Oh, is it against the rules to talk? Never mind, Tony, we'll break the rules. Do you know, Tony, this game is beginning to irk me a little. I hope they're not going to run it to death by playing it all the evening. I'd like to play some game where we can all be together in the same room with a nice bright fire."

"Same here," I agreed fervently.

"Can't you suggest something when we go down? There's something rather uncanny in this particular amusement. I can't quite shed the delusion that there's somebody in this game who oughtn't to be in at all."

That was just how I had been feeling, but I didn't say so. But for my part the worst of my qualms were now gone; the arrival of Mrs. Gorman had dissipated them. We sat on talking, wondering from time to time when the rest of the party would arrive.

I don't know how long elapsed before we heard a clatter of feet on the landing and young Reggie's voice shouting, "Hullo! Hullo, there! Anybody there?"

"Yes."

"Mrs. Gorman with you?"

"Yes," I answered.

"Well, you're a nice pair! You're both forfeited. We've all been waiting for you for hours."

"Why, you haven't found 'Smee' yet," I objected.

"*You* haven't, you mean. I happen to have been 'Smee' myself."

"But 'Smee's' here with us," I cried.

"Yes," agreed Mrs. Gorman.

The curtain was stripped aside and in a moment we were blinking into the eye of Reggie's electric torch. I looked at Mrs. Gorman and then on my other side. Between me and the wall was an empty space on the window seat. I stood up at once and wished I hadn't, for I found myself sick and dizzy.

"There *was* somebody there," I maintained, "because I touched her."

"So did I," said Mrs. Gorman in a voice which had lost its steadiness. "And I don't see how she could have got up and gone without our knowing it."

Reggie uttered a queer, shaken laugh. He, too, had had an unpleasant experience that evening.

"Somebody's been playing the goat," he remarked. "Coming down?"

We were not very popular when we arrived in the drawing-room. Reggie rather tactlessly gave it out that he had found us sitting on a window-seat behind a curtain. I taxed the tall, dark girl with having pretended to be "Smee" and afterwards slipping away. She denied it. After which we settled down and played other games. "Smee" was done with for the evening, and I for one was glad of it.

Some long while later, during an interval, Sangston told me, if I wanted a drink, to go into the smoke-room and help myself. I went, and he presently followed me. I could see that he was rather peeved with me, and the reason came out during the following minute or two. It seemed that, in his opinion, if I must sit out and flirt with Mrs. Gorman —in circumstances which would have been considered highly compromising in his young days—I needn't do it during a round game and keep everybody else waiting for us.

"But there was somebody else there," I protested, "somebody pretending to be 'Smee.' I believe it was that tall, dark girl, Miss Ford, although she denied it. She even whispered her name to me."

Sangston stared at me and nearly dropped his glass.

"Miss *Who?*" he shouted.

"Brenda Ford—she told me her name was."

Sangston put down his glass and laid a hand on my shoulder.

"Look here, old man," he said, "I don't mind a joke, but don't let it go too far. We don't want all the women in the house getting hysterical. Brenda Ford is the name of the girl who broke her neck on the stairs playing hide-and-seek here ten years ago."

W. S. GILBERT, *the great English satirist, was born in 1836 and lived to write a huge number of "Bab Ballads," humorous verse from which he drew the plots of several of his comic operettas that he wrote with Arthur Sullivan. The fantastic occurs often in Gilbert (four times in the operettas alone); originally I planned to use the first-night version of the ghost scene of G&S'* Ruddigore, *but found that it suffers out of context. Here is one of the less familiar "Bab Ballads" written for* Fun *magazine. In it, two supernatural critters vie ferociously for top honors in a scareathon, in which one wonders who is the bigger dummy.*

The Ghost, the Gallant, the Gael, and the Goblin
by W. S. Gilbert

O'er unreclaimed suburban clay
　　Some years ago were hobblin',
An elderly ghost of easy ways,
　　And an influential goblin.
The ghost was a sombre spectral shape,
　　A fine old five-act fogy,
The goblin imp, a lithe young ape,
　　A fine low-comedy bogy.

And as they exercised their joints,
　　Promoting quick digestion,
They talked on several curious points,
　　And raised this pregnant question:
"Which of us two is Number One—
　　The ghostie, or the goblin?"
And o'er the point they raised in fun
　　They fairly fell a-squabblin'.

They'd barely speak, and each, in fine,
　　Grew more and more reflective,
Each thought his own particular line
　　By far the more effective.
At length they settled some one should

By each of them be haunted,
And so arranged that either could
    Exert his prowess vaunted.

"The Quaint against the Statuesque"—
    By competition lawful—
The goblin backed the Quaint Grotesque,
    The ghost the Grandly Awful.
"Now," said the goblin, "here's my plan—
    In attitude commanding,
I see a stalwart Englishman
    By yonder tailor's standing.

"The very fittest man on earth
    My influence to try on—
Of gentle, p'raps of noble birth,
    And dauntless as a lion!
Now wrap yourself within your shroud—
    Remain in easy hearing—
Observe—you'll hear him scream aloud
    When I begin appearing!"

The imp with yell unearthly—wild—
    Threw off his dark enclosure:
His dauntless victim looked and smiled
    With singular composure.
For hours he tried to daunt the youth,
    For days, indeed, but vainly—
The stripling smiled!—to tell the truth,
    The stripling smiled insanely.

For weeks the goblin weird and wild,
    That noble stripling haunted;
For weeks the stripling stood and smiled
    Unmoved and all undaunted.
The sombre ghost exclaimed, "Your plan
    Has failed you, goblin, plainly:
Now watch yon hardy Hieland man,
    So stalwart and ungainly.

"These are the men who chase the roe,
    Whose footsteps never falter,
Who bring with them where'er they go,
    A smack of old SIR WALTER.
Of such as he, the men sublime
    Who lead their troops victorious,
Whose deeds go down to after-time,
    Enshrined in annals glorious!

"Of such as he the bard has said
    'Hech thrawfu' raltie rawkie!
Wi' thecht ta' croonie clapperhead
    And fash' wi' unco pawkie!'
He'll faint away when I appear
    Upon his native heather;
Or p'raps he'll only scream with fear,
    Or p'raps the two together."

The spectre showed himself, alone,
    To do his ghostly battling,
With curdling groan and dismal moan
    And lots of chains a-rattling!
But no—the chiel's stout Gaelic stuff
    Withstood all ghostly harrying.
His fingers closed upon the snuff
    Which upwards he was carrying.

For days that ghost declined to stir,
    A foggy, shapeless giant—
For weeks that splendid officer
    Stared back again defiant!
Just as the Englishman returned
    The goblin's vulgar staring,
Just so the Scotchman boldly spurned
    The ghost's unmannered scaring.

For several years the ghostly twain
    These Britons bold have haunted,
But all their efforts are in vain—
    Their victims stand undaunted.

Unto this day the imp and ghost
   (Whose powers the imp derided)
Stand each at his allotted post—
   The bet is undecided.

BERNHARDT J. HURWOOD *is a Manhattan novelist, short-story writer and essayist who specializes in many areas, including the supernatural. He has edited and/or written many collections of short anecdotes about ghosts, some of them retold from other cultures' folklore. "The Corpse at the Inn" is one such tale, originating with an oriental tale by Pu Sung Ling. It shows an interesting variation in the role of the spectre; Western ghosts may have many guises and purposes, but Chinese phantoms often are really bodies inhabited by demons, a particularly nasty specimen of which appears below. Hurwood's stories are almost always quite brief, thus I have included three other terse accounts of unusually unnerving apparitions . . . and these three, according to the author, are not fictional, but may have "really happened." I am skeptical of that—but true or not, they are all unusually horrendous.*

A Quartet of Strange Things
by Bernhardt J. Hurwood

I: THE CORPSE AT THE INN
From the Liao Chai of Pu Sung Ling

In a remote village located in the Yang Shin district there was once an old man who, with the aid of his son, kept a roadside inn. One evening as the gathering shadows grew long and black, four weary travellers arrived and asked the landlord for a night's lodging. To their dismay the old man refused their request, explaining that all the rooms were filled. But as it had become quite dark while they talked, and there was nowhere else for them to go, the men implored the innkeeper to make room for them anywhere he could. Seeing that the four were genuinely distressed, the old man offered to put them up in a small outbuilding situated near the women's quarters. The strangers were greatly relieved and followed their host who led the way carrying a small oil lamp in one hand.

Now it happened that the innkeeper's daughter-in-law had died that day, and her corpse was laid out in the very room to which he led his unsuspecting guests. She was dressed in ceremonial paper robes and lying on a makeshift wooden bier in deep shadow at the far end of the chamber. Near the door were four simple cots and a plain wooden table upon which he placed the flickering, smoky oil lamp. Then taking his leave, he withdrew as quickly as he could without arousing suspicion and returned to the inn. The four lodgers were so exhausted that they did not notice the corpse with which they were forced to share quarters. Flinging themselves upon their couches, three of the men soon were sound asleep. The fourth, however, felt a strange premonition and lay staring at the eerie shadows cast by the sputtering lamp.

He had finally begun to doze off when suddenly he heard a creaking noise accompanied by the rustling of paper. Daring not to move anything but his eyes, he glanced sideways in the direction of the ominous sounds. By now he had become accustomed to the murky darkness, and saw at once what was happening. Fingers of ice seemed to grip his heart as he realized there was a corpse in the room. Worse yet, the dead body of the girl was rising stiffly from the bier, the dim light revealing the ghastly pallor of her lifeless face. Paralyzed with terror, the poor man beheld the animated corpse standing upright. In the next moment the dreadful creature began gliding unmistakably toward the three who slept.

As she reached the first man she bent silently over him and exhaled in his face. She rose up and repeated her action over the second and the third sleepers. The fourth man, by now half dead with fright, pulled the cover over his face, held his breath and listened for what seemed a veritable eternity. A chill came over him as she approached his bed and bent down as she had over the others. But then, hearing her footsteps recede, he stealthily peeked out from beneath his coverlet and saw her ascend the bier and stretch out, corpselike, as before.

For a few moments the man lay still. Then, ever so cautiously he stretched out one foot and kicked the nearest of his companions. But he shuddered, for it was like touching a dead man. By now the unhappy fellow had no thought but of flight. Moving as softly as he could, he reached for his clothing so that he could make a dash for the door. But no sooner had he reached under the bed than once more he heard that awful creaking and rustling. Instinctively he buried his head beneath the cover again and held his breath as he had done before. After what seemed to be an eternity the corpse came to him a second time and bent down to breathe its foul breath upon his face. Finally it retreated to the far end of the chamber to resume its place upon the bier.

Now, wasting not an instant, the traveller seized his clothes and dashed to the door as fast as he could. But he was not alone. The dead girl, too, leaped to her feet and followed him into the night. Outdoors, the man plunged wildly into the darkness, shrieking at the top of his lungs. But there was no one to hear him but his ghastly pursuer, who was close upon his heels. Raising his voice as he passed the inn door was to no avail. His screams went unheeded. So he kept running toward the main road which led to the city.

With the corpse keeping up its pace, the fleeing man looked about desperately for a place to hide. Suddenly he noticed a small roadside monastery, and rushing up to the gate, he pounded with all his might. But alas, the priests inside knew not what to make of this unexpected tumult and would not open the door. By now the corpse was only yards away. In desperation, the man ran towards a huge willow tree that stood nearby. And just in time, for the dead girl reached the tree at the precise moment her quarry managed to dodge to one side. It now became a deadly game. The corpse, her eyes glowing fiercely, like live coals, tried to seize her victim with demoniac ferocity. But each time she moved to the left he would rush to the right, and so it went until both were panting hoarsely at the brink of exhaustion. Then both the corpse and her intended victim stood motionless, staring at each other— he in mortal terror, she with the cold rage of an unnatural monster.

Suddenly the corpse lunged forward with outstretched arms to seize its victim once and for all. The man, believing that his end had finally come, fell backward, senseless to the ground. The corpse crashed into the tree with the force of a charging tiger.

By now the priests, who had been hearing the shrieks and moans, rushed out to find the cause of the disturbance. They found the unconscious stranger lying on the ground beside the tree so they carried him into the monastery. By daybreak they succeeded in bringing him to his senses, at which time he told them in detail of his horrible ordeal in the dark. When the sun was shining brightly they went out to investigate the tree and there found the corpse of the girl, hanging limply to the trunk.

The local magistrate was summoned at once, and upon arriving, he ordered that the body be removed. But this was impossible at first, for her long fingernails were imbedded too deeply in the tree. Finally she was detached and word of the night's dreadful events were sent to the inn where, by now, the three other travellers had been found dead. The innkeeper had the body of his daughter-in-law brought back, and the traveller who lived requested that he be given a certificate attesting to the truth of his tale. The magistrate complied with the man's wishes and he was accordingly sent home.

II: THE VAMPIRE OF CROGLIN GRANGE

A number of years ago two brothers and a sister rented a very old house in England called Croglin Grange. The place had no upper floor, so that all the bedrooms were at ground level. They were very fond of it and especially enjoyed the surroundings, which were peaceful and extremely charming. A belt of graceful trees separated the property from an old churchyard, and on moonlit nights the entire area presented a view of unsurpassed beauty.

One summer night, shortly after she had gone to bed, the sister, whose name was Flora, noticed what appeared to be two lights flickering in and out of the trees bordering the churchyard. Watching with mild curiosity, she gradually became aware of something dark coming towards her window. A chill of uncontrollable horror overcame her as the shapeless dark mass came closer. She wanted to get up and run from the room, but by now she was so terrified that she became paralyzed with fear.

Suddenly the hideous thing appeared at the window! Never in her life had she seen anything so ugly, so ghastly. The face was brown and shrivelled like that of a mummy, but it had fierce, blazing eyes that glared like coals from Hell itself. As she cowered in her bed the thing began scratching at the window . . . *scratch, scratch, scratch.* Thank God the window is locked, she thought, but then, to her horror, she realised that it was picking at the leading of the mullioned window. The crash of the glass falling to the floor seemed to break the spell and she leaped from the bed and ran to the door, just as a withered brown hand reached in and turned the lock.

She was so busy fumbling with the doorknob that she wasn't aware of the speed with which the monstrous horror scuttled across the room and threw itself at her. Seizing her long hair with its bony fingers, it dragged her back to the bed, forced her down, then bent over and bit her ferociously in the throat. At that instant her voice came back and she screamed with every ounce of strength that she had, while punching and kicking her hideous assailant with all her might.

Seconds later her brothers rushed into her room, and as one of them ran for a poker, the other gave chase to the creature as it ran like the wind across the lawn, over the low stone wall, and into the churchyard.

As terrible as her experience was, she refused to believe that it was anything supernatural, insisting that it had to be an attack by an escaped mental patient or prisoner. But there was no news of any such thing, and besides, how could she explain the hideous appearance of the thing? After a brief stay in hospital whilst her wound healed, and a short stay abroad, she finally returned to Croglin Grange, assuring her brothers that the chances of any such thing happening again were virtually nil. Nevertheless, thereafter they kept loaded pistols in their rooms, and tried to make her do the same, but she refused on the grounds that she could not stand guns.

After an uneventful winter the woman was awakened from a sound sleep late one March night by the familiar sound of scratching at the window. Seizing the torch she kept by her bed, she switched it on and illuminated the window. There fully bathed by the beam of light was the same ghastly brown shrivelled face with the glaring eyes, and the bony hands. A single bloodcurdling scream brought her brothers on the double, both with pistols in hand. The thing backed off and began retreating across the lawn with the two men hard on its heels. One fired a shot and hit it in the leg, but it kept running and after scrambling back over the churchyard wall, disappeared into a vault showing signs of decay and neglect.

The next day the brothers gathered a number of their neighbours together, and after revealing what had happened the night before, led them to the vault and opened it. The sight that met their eyes was shocking, and unlike anything they had ever seen. Except for one, all the coffins were broken open, and the bones of their occupants scattered on the floor. Upon opening the lid of the single coffin that was intact, they found the brown, shrivelled, hideous figure that had broken into Croglin Grange. In one leg was a fresh bullet hole. After overcoming their initial shock, they removed the dreadful body, drenched it with petrol, and burned it to cinders. Although they never knew its origin, they were never bothered by the vampire again.

III: THE OLD MAN IN YELLOW

There is hardly anything more unnerving than being followed by a hideous stranger on a lonely road at night. When the stranger proves to be *nonhuman* . . . but that is getting ahead of the story. . . .

It happened a few years ago to a young man named Elwyn Thomas, who happened to be visiting friends in a small village in South Wales. It was a warm June night and darkness was just beginning to fall when he left his friends to return to the country inn where he was staying. Judging by past experience, he reckoned on reaching it by about nine o'clock. It was exactly eight-thirty when he said good-night.

He was completely alone in the gathering dusk, and the only sounds were the occasional cries of night birds and the crunch of his own footsteps on the gravel road. Being neither superstitious nor afraid of anything he walked briskly along, glancing now and then towards the banks of an old canal off to one side of the road.

After about ten minutes he began experiencing a peculiar, creepy sensation, as if he were being watched. On an impulse, he stopped, turned around and gasped involuntarily. There, no more than a yard behind him, suspended in mid-air at eye-level, was the most hideous face he had ever seen. The putty-coloured skin was drawn tightly over the features, except for the forehead, which was lined with deep wrinkles. Thin, seemingly bloodless lips formed a crooked grin over a half-open, toothless mouth. The cheeks were hollow and corpse-like, and the eyes were wild, luminous, and piercing. Wrapped around the ghastly object were two pieces of old yellow calico, one under the jaw and tied on top of the head, the other over the forehead and tied behind.

Unable to help himself, Thomas turned and began running as fast as he could. After having covered about a hundred yards, he stopped to catch his breath and turned around again. To his horror the face was still there—as if he hadn't moved an inch. On an impulse he dropped down, grabbed a handful of gravel and hurled it at the face, then turned again and ran.

When he finally reached the inn he stopped at the path leading off the road and looked back again. The head was still behind him. Cautiously he backed up in the direction of the inn and was surprised to observe that this time the head remained above the road, grinning somewhat contemptuously. Taking courage he decided to go back, confront the apparition, and question it. But as he approached, the head began receding, its glowing eyes fixed almost malevolently on his own. Now he felt as though he had to follow. Down the road he went slowly, like a sleepwalker, until the head disappeared over a stone wall surrounding a little graveyard not far from the inn. Suddenly he felt everything begin to spin; then he lost consciousness.

When he came to again, it was late at night. He had lain at the foot of the churchyard wall for more than two hours. Groping through the darkness until he found his way back to the inn, it was with great relief that he finally retired to bed and to a restless night filled with bad dreams.

When he told the innkeeper about his experience the next day he learned that he had not been having hallucinations. An eccentric old recluse fitting the exact description of the apparition had once lived in a cottage whose ruins were quite near to the place where the face had disappeared. No one could remember exactly how long the old man had been dead, but they knew it had been many years since he had been last seen alive.

IV: THE GLOWING MAGGOT OF DOOM

Perhaps the most loathsome and terrifying apparition ever seen was a maggoty creature that was said to have haunted a little Yorkshire churchyard years ago.

The first man to see it was Mr. Mullins, the postman. It was a bright, moonlit night and he was passing the graveyard on his way home. What caught his attention was a large blob of luminous ooze issuing from the fresh grave of a recently dead villager named Peters. Wriggling like a giant, ugly glow-worm it grew bigger as it issued from the ground. Horrified, yet fascinated, Mullins followed the "thing" which now looked exactly like a giant maggot, but he had to summon all his courage, for when he saw its eyes he was forced to avert his own. They seemed to exude pure evil, and somehow appeared strangely human. The ghastly monster slithered along the ground with a caterpillar's wriggle, leaving a gleaming trail of disgusting slime in its wake. To Mullins' amazement, the maggot wriggled in and out between the tombstones, left the graveyard, and disappeared from sight when it reached the threshold of the vicar's house nearby.

The following day Mullins told his wife and his best friend about his chilling experience, and that night the three of them went to the churchyard to see if they could discover what the hideous apparition might be. Just as it had the night before, the dreadful worm oozed from Peters' grave, made its way to the vicar's house, and again disappeared at the threshold. The next day, however, the Mullinses and their friend received a severe shock. The vicar and his entire family had suddenly been taken ill, and were dead by sunset. The doctor who examined them attributed their deaths to ptomaine poisoning.

More determined than ever to get to the bottom of this horrible apparition's origin, Mullins, his wife, and their friend ventured once again to the village churchyard after dark that night. Again the hideous glowing maggot wriggled out of the grave and slithered between the tombstones, leaving the now familiar trail of slime in its path. This time they followed it to the house of the village blacksmith, into which it vanished. There was no need for it to visit him a second time, for he became ill in the morning and died before sunset, like the vicar and his family, of ptomaine poisoning.

Thoroughly alarmed, but more baffled than ever, Mullins and his companions determined to keep watch again that same night. Nothing happened. Somewhat relieved, they nevertheless decided to continue their nightly vigil at the graveyard for at least one more week. Ten nights after it had first appeared, it emerged from its customary place again only to head directly to the Mullins' house! They were horror-stricken, but powerless. That night they spent in sleepless, terrified anticipation. In the morning tragedy struck and their five-year-old son died an hour after being taken ill.

That night their hearts filled with grief and hatred, Mullins and his wife, aided by their friend, went back to the village churchyard. This time they had a plan. Equipped with a hooded lantern and spades, they dug up the grave of the late Mr. Peters.

When they finally struck the coffin, Mullins and his friend pried off the lid while Mrs. Mullins held the lantern. There, on the dead man's face was an expression of such unspeakable malevolence that they slammed the lid down and staggered back involuntarily. But after composing themselves, they put a rope around the corpse and dragged it from the grave. After resting for a few moments, they took the body to a deserted field nearby, saturated it with kerosene, and burned it to cinders. Then, returning to the cemetery, they filled in the grave and covered up all traces of their deed.

For several nights after this they went back, but the monstrous maggot of death was never seen again. Mullins later learned that the dead man had been on bad terms with both the vicar and the blacksmith. But he himself had never had any trouble with Peters. For what reason, then, did the glowing harbinger of evil visit his house? He never learned, but he thanked Providence that he never saw it again.

One of the most unusual themes of ghostly literature is that of the dead soul who receives permission to return to life, usually upon fulfilling certain divinely imposed conditions. Few such tales exist in folk literature, but the plot is quite popular in Hollywood, the most recent major version of it being Heaven Can Wait. *Perhaps two decades ago, my friend and collaborator* PARKE GODWIN *wrote a charming, funny-sad variation on the theme, in which Isolde of Irish legendry finds a way to live again. For some strange reason, Parke stuck the manuscript in a drawer and forgot about it till the 1970s, when he showed it to me while we were collaborating on* The Masters of Solitude. *He considered "The Lady of Finnigan's Hearth" an embarrassing example of a kind of writing he no longer chose to do, and was all for chucking the story into the wastebasket. But I read it, fell in love with it, and urged Parke to try it out on* FANTASTIC STORIES *magazine. Editor Ted White also was wildly enthusiastic and bought it immediately. Several months later, this wonderful, lilting love story won one of the top places in the British Fantasy Awards of 1978. The Moral:* Never trust an author on the subject of his own writing!

The Lady of Finnigan's Hearth
by Parke Godwin

Isolde, if you remember her story, was the girl queen of Cornwall in the days of King Arthur, and the sweetheart of a bad-luck knight named Tristram.

Though time and legend left their sugary crust, neither these nor any lute-twanging minstrel ever did her justice. She was a joyous, bouncing Irish hellion who died at nineteen, a bundle of brogue and bad manners, all heart and no head; a thoroughly medieval urchin whose first utterance in Glory was that she had been abducted from the world against her will and demanded immediate return. Her claim was not considered.

Isolde was not happy in Heaven. She felt that she just didn't fit in. Some—the women mostly—whispered of her not uneventful past. Others held she was a nice enough little thing if you liked them unpolished. Troubadours protested they would never have put hand to string in her behalf if they had known what she was really like. The immortal Wagner said flatly and to her face she was not worthy of the magnificent opera he had written about her. To most of the romantics she was an artistic embarrassment.

Well, it went this way most of the time. In the beginning, of course, there had been Tristram for company, but that was short-lived. Isolde came to realize that chivalry, while it might beautify a short life (the shorter the better), did not wear well in terms of the eternal. They bored each other until, mutually relieved, they finally went their separate ways.

But Paradise hung heavily upon Isolde, and her harp—an Irish model brought from home—lay discarded and mute. She passed her centuries longing for the good green world below. Such a short life; so little lived, so little known. She wanted to go back. At last when the yearning was too strong to keep silent, she planted herself before the Recording Angel and let him know her mind.

"Hear me, Angel: I said it the day I was brought here—against my will and before my time—and I say it again. I want to go *home!*"

"A very peculiar desire," the Angel acknowledged with some disappointment. "I should think you would have had time to let our place grow on you. Very peculiar." He shook his head. "But not impossible; that is, if you can pass the test. Before you can go back you must tell me what is the secret of life."

"And if I know it, I can go back? I can live again?"

The Angel's eyes were old and kind and sad. "You must know it to live at all, child. Where makes no difference."

Isolde pondered this a moment. "Well now, and where might be a good place to look?"

"I don't want to discourage you, child, but if you didn't find it down there, you probably won't find it here. However—" he had said it so often, "look where the heart is."

Isolde went away and thought for a long time, but it seemed hopeless. In her thoughtless lifetime she had never learned the secret of anything. She was doomed to Paradise, as it were, and it galled her more and more as the centuries passed. The virtuous criticized her for what she had been and the snobbish deplored her for what she was. Isolde walked Heaven alone and found no answer to the question. It was as remote from her as Hell itself.

"Well"—she decided firmly, picking up her harp—"why not?"

The Recording Angel paused in his eternal occupation and gazed up at the familiar figure. "Yes, girl?"

"I've searched my heart, Angel, and I've looked Heaven high and low and across for the secret. 'Tis not in either place."

"You must know it, nevertheless," the Angel said. "Everyone wants to go back at first. We afford the chance, but we afford it only to those grown wise enough to use a life properly. They are very few and most of them would rather leave well enough alone."

"I never lived to learn what well enough was. An end to this." Isolde raised her hand impatiently. "Open the gates and point me out the south stairway."

The Angel read her intention. "I admire your spirit, girl, but not your reasoning. They can't tell you anything constructive down *there*. I doubt if they'd even want to."

Isolde was not to be swayed. "The gates, Sir!"

"Well, if you're determined—" He opened the portals of Paradise, and she skipped through, turning to wave to him. "I'm glad you're taking the harp with you. You do play well and they never get a chance to hear a really good one."

She found the new place better suited to her. The climate was agreeable, the people generally friendly if irresponsible, and there was always something going on. Her coming caused some social stir; she was soon entrenched in the very best circle, a small but powerful clique of Salem women, stoutly traditional and privileged beyond belief.

But Hell, fun as it was, taught her no more than Heaven. Whatever the secret was, she must go *home* to find it, to the world she had left. But how? Her friends were allowed one night on Earth at All Saints' Eve, but she was only a novice. It would be ages before they would trust her with a broom for all of her natural talent. Need sharpened her craft to a fine edge. She evolved her plan and put it to work.

Isolde's closest friend was Prissy O'Gowra, a brilliant Irish witch with the most potent broomstick in the trade. Lately, Prissy's carefree spirit was vexed with a bittersweet sadness—her sudden and hopeless love for the American Secretary of State. He was to appear at an international conference in Paris. When the Prince gave her permission to go there, Prissy was ecstatic. Magic and sabbats were not for her. Their charms were flat beside what loomed in Paris. When begged for the broom, she threw it joyously to the grateful Isolde and whirled away on the west wind, trailing a snatch of *chanson*.

And so, on All Saints' Eve, Isolde flew with her friends to Gallows Hill outside Salem. The night was made for revels—raw, cold, and wet with the naked trees bending to the wind against a moonless sky. The Prince himself put in an appearance; there was a quadrille to Isolde's harp accompaniment, and as for spells, their form had never been better. The Washington Senators got another year in the cellar and four gluepots waltzed their way to the Kentucky Derby and a four-way photo finish. It was a glorious night in the finest tradition. When dawn came on dragging a thick fog behind, they sped homeward on the east wind, conscious of a social success.

But Isolde was missing.

It was sorrowfully reported that she had lost control in the fog over the Eastern Seaboard and was presumed to have crashed. Too late they insisted Isolde was too inexperienced for the flight. Now she was marooned on a world grown callous to the ancient art of witchcraft, but she had the awful O'Gowra broom in her hands and was free to roam till All Saints' next.

For days there was no laughter in Hell. Isolde had been the gayest and dearest of all the brilliant society of the Vivacious Fallen. Now she was gone and with her went some of the sparkle of damnation.

Well now, wasn't it a simple thing to let them think her lost? When she was rid of them, Isolde veered her broom a point or two to starboard and swooped down on the unsuspecting Earth, landing in a small wood. It was early morning still, and the fog coiled in erratic patterns over the ground, seeking refuge in the low places before the sun could drive it away. Isolde listened: not a soul about nor the sound of one, but through the trees the windows of a drab white house stared bleakly at her, just visible above the fog.

"Didn't I always have the luck?" she congratulated herself. " 'Tis the castle of some lord, no doubt, and I'm fair in time for breakfast."

It was her first thought to hop the broomstick and *whoosh* up to the house, but it was a grand morning for a walk. She shouldered the broom and in fifteen earthly minutes Isolde found herself in the overgrown front yard of the bald-windowed house.

"What manner of hovel is this?" she wondered. "The paint all peeling and not so much as a candle for light or a fire for warmth. It looked better from afar. An ogre lives here, no doubt—but I'll ask just for surety."

She went up to the mud-splashed door and put her hand on the knob.

> "Castle, castle, now will you tell:
> Who within your walls doth dwell?"

As one might suppose, there was no answer.

"I'll burn you for kindling, creaking scoundrel!" Isolde hissed, this time in the fairy tongue. "Now open your gawp and tell me who lives here!"

The house groaned, for it had been silent a long time. "Marty Finnigan lives here," it said mournfully. "Alone."

"Sure then, Marty Finnigan keeps a sorry house."

The house sighed deep in its timbers. "No one cares for me," it said with a tremor of self-pity.

"Oh now—and why's that?"

"It's really quite *simple*," said the house peevishly. "Because no one cares for Marty Finnigan."

"Pile o' knotholes, keep your tongue in your head!"

"Well," the house groaned sulkily, "either knock or go away." It settled once more in a manner designed to signify the interview was ended.

Isolde rapped on the door with her broom handle.

Silence.

Rap! Rap! Rap! "Halloooo! *Marty Finnigan!*"

Isolde heard muffled sounds from the second floor. Someone was up. She knocked again. "Up with your gate, Sir Finnigan, for 'tis a gentlewoman waits on your stoop in the cold and wet—"

A window rumbled up. The next instant, Isolde was drenched from hair to heels with cold water: "All right, you gah-damned kids, Halloween's over. Now *blow!*" A touseled head jutted through the window, and Marty Finnigan stared coldly down at the dampened little queen. "Oh . . . I'm sorry, lady. I thought it was those trick-or-treat punks again."

It was Isolde's hot-tempered impulse to singe him roundly with a fireball, but—*noblesse oblige,* and *noblesse* is all the easier when a man's face is no pain to a woman's eye. She gave him a graceful curtsey and asked, "Did I rouse you from slumber, Sir Finnigan?"

Marty rubbed his weekend growth of beard. "Did she wake me up, she says. No," he growled, "I was just lying there with my eyes closed. What's your problem?"

"Problem?"

"What do you want?"

"Just a morsel of bread and a place by your fire."

"A mors—" The Finnigan features contorted in disbelief. "Get lost."

"—So I can wring out the wet welcome you gave me."

"Well," Marty considered it, "I guess that's fair enough." His head disappeared, and she heard him descending the stairs. The door opened. In flannel pajamas and a ratty blue bathrobe, Marty motioned her into his house.

And Isolde moved in. She stood in the middle of the living room and tried on Marty Finnigan's house for size. It was dirty, dark, and cold—lonely most of all, with no touch of a woman's hand about it. The logs lay in the fireplace unlit and festooned with trash. The dust of the floor swirled up angrily in protest against the fresh air from the open door. In one corner, a battered coffee table displayed a week's run of coffee cups, a wrinkled necktie, two undershirts, and a pile of bills surmounted by a stale cracker, buttered and forgotten some days since.

"Cushnoo!" Isolde clucked. "What a hog-sty!"

"So excuse it." Marty shrugged. "It's the maid's day off."

He had been watching her with growing curiosity. She was small—a hair over five feet, no more—and mercurial in her movements. Her hair, impossibly red, was upswept on her head and held precariously in place with two quaint gold stays. He decided quickly that her face was made for laughter, not for looks. Her figure, if she had any, was well hidden beneath what appeared to be Methuselah's nightshirt, bunched in at the waist with the hem trailing behind like the undecided posterior of a hook-and-ladder engine.

Now Marty was many months a grass widower. Since his wife had left, a motley procession of women had left their perfumed trace about his house, but none of them were in the same league with this one for the new and different. Being essentially religious, he concluded that she had been visited upon him as some kind of penance.

"Make yourself comfortable," he mumbled, turning toward the kitchen. He shuffled sleepily out of the room. Her voice seemed to float musically through the separating wall—

"Shall I light your hearth for you? 'Tis dretful cold."

"No," he grumbled. "The flue's messed up. You couldn't burn gasoline in that thing." He filled the coffee pot with water, chuckling in spite of himself. "Well . . . she *looks* like what I'd get for Halloween, broomstick and all."

The time of year and the thought of the queer old broom summed themselves almost unconsciously in his mind. It *was* Halloween, or the day after. Marty grinned: "Oh, come *on*, Finnigan." But the wry smile softened. *Kind of a nice little thing,* he thought. *I wonder where she's from. . . .*

Isolde strolled to the fireplace, skirts switching behind her, crooning softly—

> "Oh Maeldun, son of Ailill
> Came from Aran in Thomond . . ."

She knelt beside the logs, stretched out her hand, then withdrew it, beckoning. "Come, fire: so please you, a little of your best for Marty Finnigan."

And the fire blazed up on Finnigan's hearth.

If Marty Finnigan had any true genius, it was in the brewing of coffee. Sitting by the fire, they went through two pots with toast and marmalade. Isolde missed her harp; she would have played gladly for her breakfast, but she had dropped it in her wild plunge to Earth. She stirred the fire, humming to herself, and studied the master of Finnigan's Hall. He was taller by a head and a half than her Trist had been, and leaner. His face was still young but life had happened to it. The eyes were shadowed and the frank mouth lined and drawn too taut for its fullness. The thick brown hair was fading here and there to early gray.

He'd look younger did he smile once a fortnight.

She liked the way his nose wrinkled up when he lit a cigarette. Suddenly she leaned toward him, fixing him with gray eyes: "Marty Finnigan, 'tis a handsome buck you are. Why is it no woman graces your house?"

There was a strange, far-away quality to her voice. It was inside his head, a song remembered from childhood, calling him down the years to where life could still grow green around the heart. *Stay a little,* he wanted to say. . . .

But Marty had been barren soil for the seed of impulse for a long time. He threw his cigarette into the fire. "You *are* an oddball. And you're still soggy from that bath I gave you. Wait, I'll get something you can change into so we can dry out that shroud or whatever it is of yours."

Isolde giggled. "Thank you."

"What's so funny?"

"I just bethought me," she said, "how nice your mouth would be if you let it smile a little now and then."

"You," he said with conviction, "are the *damndest*—"

"Aye," she nodded, taking a piece of toast in three huge bites. As he climbed the stairs, her voice floated after him: "But 'twas not my fault. A tedious long tale it is, and so I'll save it for a winter's night."

Marty returned presently with a faded yellow duster, flapping it vigorously to shake out the wrinkles of long storage. "Here. You're about six sizes smaller than my wife was, but it'll do."

She shrank away from it. "Your . . . wife?"

"What's the matter? She doesn't need it anymore." He dropped it in her lap but she only stared at it.

"You said nought of a wife, Marty."

"Well . . ." Marty made quite an operation out of lighting a cigarette. "She isn't here anymore. We're divorced. Her name is Alice," he concluded irrelevantly.

His glance met hers and was held. "Her name was Alice," Marty heard himself saying, "and all the things I wanted, she didn't. Not even this house. Wants me to move out so we can sell it. Maybe it's a good idea." He looked around the room with new awareness. "God, this place is cruddy."

Fortune brought me here, she thought, and here I'll stay. Plain it is that he needs a woman, and here's as good a place as any to learn what I must learn. If I work my spells right, they won't find me till All Saints' next, and what might I not do for myself *and* this sorry Marty Finnigan before then?

Isolde stood up before the fire, seeming taller than she was. She had once been a queen and the stamp never left her. And as she spoke, the flames leaped in time to the queer movements of her fingers. "Marty, have you never heard that a cricket on the hearth brings marvellous good fortune?"

"In this house," said Marty, "a cricket would die of TB."

"Then I'll be your cricket."

"What—?"

"Let me stay by your hearth and sweep your house with my broom till All Saints' next."

Marty was perplexed. "You know, the dangerous thing about you is you're so believable."

"And, Finnigan," she whispered with mock gravity, "you've grown much too wise to believe in what you see?"

He nodded. "When I found out about Santa Claus." He was vaguely disappointed in her. Only a week before, a dazzling young girl had brightened his threshold for a golden minute till Marty found she had come to sell him a pamphlet on the imminent demise of sinful Mankind.

This one, alas, was compounded of the same unstable elements. He threw the door open and pointed to the Great Beyond. "Good-bye, and take your broom with you." He handed it to her. " 'Sweep my house' . . . You couldn't sweep tennis balls with this thing."

"*Oooooh!*" Isolde was breathless at the sacrilege. "*That* be too much. Soulless imp, know that on just such a broom, Prissy O'Gowra flew the length and breadth of Eire till it carried her *whoosh!* straight into the cottage of the man who became her husband, it did. Not to *mention,* of course, her many and glorious services regarding the heathen English. Well, it's like crystal you don't know a good broom or a bargain when they be thrust in your *snout,* Sir Finnigan!"

He propelled her toward the door. "Yeah. Sure. Good-bye."

"*Unhand me, ogre!*"

He unhanded her out to the front stoop. "Get lost. Break a leg." *Slam!*

Yet her voice through the heavy door was as clear as though she were beside him: "*Just one leg, Marty?*"

"Fine."

He was on his back with a terrible pain in his left leg. The instrument of disaster lay beside him. He had tripped over that damned broom.

"Broken," Isolde crooned over him. "Fair brast below the knee, but it's a clean break and will mend soon."

"How did you—*yikes, quit pawin' at it*—how did you get in here?"

"Oh," she said airily, "I forgot my broom. But how *fortunate* you are I happened back, for here's yourself with your pin broken and like to be days in the mending by the look of it, with no one but me to get your supper—"

He saw the awful defeat of it. "Oh, no. No . . . no . . ."

"—To mend your socks and tend the fire, and take my old broom to the dreadful dust that's on your hearth and heart, Marty Finnigan. Till next All Saints' Eve!"

Isolde stood in the middle of the living room, making little swishing movements with the broom and humming to herself. For the time, at least, she was mistress of Marty's house. Of Heaven, this would suffice her. As for Hell, she had brought fair measure. The sun was well up, and it promised to be a roaring good day.

> "In Laighin fair, I met a lad.
> Who soon came courting me . . ."

She knelt by the hearth. "Prissy!" she whispered. "*Hoo,* Priss, can you hear me?"

The logs crackled furiously for a moment. She listened.

"Oh, I'm grand, Prissy. Thanks for the asking." Isolde took a ball of flame from the fire. Her dexterous fingers kneaded a fiery shamrock as she listened to the small talk of a friend. "Well, if anyone asks, you've not heard one word of me. Promise, now. What? Oh, your old broom's safe with me, and, Priss, it still works soo*peri*orly!"

Marty always said it was just magic the way she took that house and made it shine. She took care of him and so well that he put on five pounds before he was out of bed. Now and then he admitted to himself that there *was* something unworldly about her—but then she would bounce into the room and announce with convincing authority that she had just made the grandest stew this side of Hell, and could he spare a drop of the whiskey his dear uncle had sent him—just to bring out the flavor of the meat, of course?

Unworldly? In all his drab, disenchanted days, Marty had never known anything or anyone whose reality was so completely undeniable. She was as real as the luck that came with her; as real as the twenty-pound turkey which she swore on the soul of St. Bridget just traipsed into the kitchen and dropped stone dead—plucked and dressed—on Thanksgiving Day in the morning; as real as the well-paid job that materialized in a formerly uninterested office; as real as the first paycheck which Isolde set in a place of honor on the kitchen table, toasting it with a royal flourish of her teacup: "Increase, little bag of gold." Then with a wink at Marty: "And good health to the master of Finnigan's Hall."

Marty warmed to the tea, the excellent dinner, the cozy sound of logs crackling lustily on the hearth. "And praise them angels as brung it, my grandmother used to say."

She took his hands across the teacups, and her eyes held something not so heavy as sorrow nor light as laughter. "It's no angel I am, Marty." Then erect and determined: "*As* Mistress Marcianetti will discover, does she not keep her dog from howling and snapping at me when I come near."

"That's Poobah," said Marty. "He's six years older than God. Funny: you're the only one he does that to."

Nevertheless Isolde promised herself that she would inflict the venerable Poobah with fleas enough to make him a Job among canines.

"Mrs. Marcianetti has two interests in life," Marty continued. "Poobah and my welfare. I keep hoping she'll run out of home-canned tomatoes, but she never does. She brings them over about once a week, looks around, shakes her head and leaves."

"Aye, and now you have a housekeeper, and the dear old thing's got a fair crick in her neck from spying out her casement at me."

"Spying?"

"Aye, Marty: wondering who I am, and what I be to you."

He read her trailed meaning. "Well, I've been thinking about that," he started shyly. "I know this is foolish, but—" He stopped; the old fear of being hurt melted his purpose. "What I meant to say was, it's been nice having you here."

She rose and came round the table to him. "No, Marty, say what you started to say. Life's far too short to be afraid of it!"

Marty took refuge in the complicated business of lighting a cigarette. "I don't know. You just walked into this house and sort of put it on like a glove. It lives, it really lives because you're in it. When you leave—"

"When I leave—?"

"If you left, I think the life would go out of it. I think it would fall apart."

"Well, now"—her long fingers assured themselves needlessly that her hair was in place—"what a heartwarming concern for your house. And what of yourself?"

Marty blew out a great quantity of smoke. "I guess I go with the house."

Isolde knelt and took his hands. "Listen, Marty. If I knew 'twould all end this night, I'd still say those things you lack the heart to say to me: I love you. You've won me, and your hearth is mine. That's what I'd say, I would."

"Yes." He smiled, and the fear sloughed from him when he looked at her. "And a little more. Marry me and stay here always."

"I will," she whispered, her head in his lap. "I can make you happy, Finnigan."

"I know you can"—he laughed—"and when I'm too old for anything else, you can make me respectable."

"Oh, Marty, what a gallant offer. . . ."

Suddenly, she twisted away from him. Surprised, Marty saw the shadow of a frown cross her face, erasing the happiness and leaving something alien in its place. Her head was inclined sharply as if she had caught some sound beyond his hearing: a footstep lighter than thought, or perhaps a voice on the damp December wind. He started to speak but she stopped him with two fingers across his lips.

"Not a sound, Marty. There now; your supper's gone stone cold whilst you gape at me."

Isolde stood up. Resolutely, she reached for the old broom that was rarely out of her sight. "Eat, Marty. I'll not be gone a minute."

"Well, hurry back. If we're getting married, there's buckets of stuff we have to talk about."

"True," she murmured. Straight-backed and firm, she turned away from him.

Out of Marty's sight, her resolution faltered, and she shrank back from the sliding doors that closed off the living room. Beyond the doors, she heard a faint rustle of movement. Isolde clutched at her broom, quailed and retreated a step, the fear a hod of hot bricks on her heart. She took one hesitant step toward the kitchen. Then her head went up; she turned a scornful eye on the panel doors.

You need not fear the like of him, and you a queen, the proudest Leinster could spawn. Hold tight the broom. Head up. Now, in you go—

At her touch, the doors slid apart. Isolde took one sweeping step, then halted. The fear dissolved in her throat, welled up and poured out in a peal of relieved, irreverent laughter. She fell back against the doors, the helpless victim of her own mirth.

"Oh, God, no!" she gasped, " 'Tis himself . . ."

Tall, tragic, and darkly resplendent in the false ermine and sagging black tights of a stock company Hamlet, her visitor helped himself once more to the Finnigan whiskey, threw back his cape and made a sweeping obeisance before his audience of one. "To Her Majestie, Queen of the Faerie Glen," he declaimed in his best third-balcony register, adding a hint of mockery, "greetings from the Joyous Damned."

"Oh my, oh my." She was still giggling. "Expect the worst and get the best. Give ye good evening, Mr. Booth."

The gaunt young man favored her with a brilliant smile. "The same: John Wilkes Booth, your servant. I am come as herald from our court; *nay*"—Booth put up his hand in protest of her single word—"let not the fear of intrusion mar our meeting. We shall be secret kept, for the time's out of joint, and we are slipped between two broken ticks. That uninspired lout presently absorbing his supper in the scullery will hear no more of us than the wind that brought me."

"Blather, Booth. Spit it out. My supper's cooling while you hold me here."

"The price"—Booth smiled—"of materialization. One reacquires old appetites—as witness that rather artless embrace of a moment ago."

"Oooooh!" Isolde's complexion darkened a shade. "You be no gentleman, John, or the Prince either, and you can tell him that for me."

"Oh, you wrong us, Isolde. For myself, I wanted you home for our annual festival of the Bard. We do Hamlet again, echoing last year's triumph." Booth gathered the ermine to his ebonied breast, pausing for full effect. "The Prince has again chosen me to interpret the Dane. Wanton nymph, he is a lover and a critic of the arts, a gentleman and sportsman. When tidings reached him that you were gone and, through your broom, immune to recall for the nonce, he *smiled* in gracious defeat. Aloud he wished you well and ruled that no unpleasantness attend your holiday."

"Then why are you—?"

"*But*—when he heard that—that *Finnigan* declare his most unpoetic desire, he sent me on the first east wind." Booth smote his temples. "And I in the middle of a rehearsal."

"Sent you to tell me *what*, John? Can you not deliver yourself without suffering so? Tell me what?"

"Say rather to beg, Isolde. Come home now, for come you must, and it will hurt less now than later." Booth moved toward her. "Surrender your broom."

"I'll not!" she snapped, falling back. "Away with you. I'll not return before my time." She swung the broom high, wielding it like a sword. "One step more, John, and I'll sweep eternity clear of you."

Booth halted. "Listen to us, you fool, we know what life is. Madness; blind madness. What was your own time here but misery and heartbreak? What else will you find here now?"

"Life!" She hurled it at him. "Life, you wretched wreck of a soul. Life and its secret, for I left too soon to know what it was. But I'll find it, Booth. You mark me: I'll find it."

"You stole it. You can't steal life, Isolde."

"Then I'll borrow."

"And at what interest?" Booth asked. "You know the Prince never takes a loss. Come home before it is too late."

"Too late?" Isolde lowered the broom. "Tell me, John, why is't I've not been called till now? Why all a-sudden?"

The pale Booth opened his mouth to speak, then stopped. "It is late. I must go. My rehearsal . . ." He swirled the ermine around him with pathetic bravado.

"No!" Isolde demanded. "Tell me why I'm sent for *now*."

"No more . . ." The image of Booth began to blur, each line of the fine, sharp figure dissolving into an amorphous haze until only the magnificent voice remained. "Come home . . . Faerie Queen . . ."

"Back on the wind, Booth," Isolde sobbed, angry and afraid. "Tell it to the Prince, and them Above, if you can: I live! I am! For life's not borrowed, not stolen, but taken free and shaped at will—"

"*Illusion* . . ." came the faint whisper.

"No, 'tis real," she sobbed. "The knowing and the loving of it. Hear me, Booth—"

"*Heartbreak,*" said the wind.

The unoiled clock on the mantle roused itself and began to grind away the minutes. Her attention drawn by the sound, Isolde looked at the hands. Even as she watched, they seemed to move faster and faster. But she had found something. *The knowing and the loving of it:* that was something to remember.

To know and to love. That must be the secret.

"Hey, good-lookin'," Marty enticed from the kitchen, "come on! I've poured the wine."

Was that the secret? Was it?

"Hey, come on!"

"*Illusion* . . ." murmured the rain, but she did not hear it.

"Aye, Marty," she answered, "I'm coming."

Well, wasn't she a bride of two days and mistress of her own house, and that house to be put straight this Monday morning?

Marty had gone to work. Isolde stood in the middle of the living room and raised her voice: "Wake, House of Finnigan! A word with you."

The house stirred and came alive. The furniture dented and flexed itself as if supporting a body, the curtains rustled, the furnace groaned. Floors and stairs creaked with the memory of a million footsteps, and out of all these came the voice: "What do you want?"

"Obedience," Isolde snapped, "for I am your mistress now, and you'll bend to my wish and the power of my broom. Hold your roof high and gallant, as if you cost twice the gold he paid, and let no one say that Marty Finnigan's a poor man."

"I hear you," sighed the house, "but it won't work."

"And why not?"

"Because it's not real," said the house. "I need love, not spells. There is no love in you and nothing real."

"He knows I love him."

"Words," said the house. "But the belfry told the wind that the candles broke and the Book burned on the altar where you married him."

"And so I can burn you," she threatened, "if your warped temper runs against my wish. *Mind,* you'll do as I say!"

The furnace rattled violently. "I will do as you say," and the voice began to fade, "but it will only seem . . . not be . . . ."

"Enough, then," Isolde commanded. "House—be clean."

There was a rush of a great vacuum that swept every particle of dust from the floor, a flapping and rustling as the curtains and rugs shook out their lint, the swish of a hundred invisible brushes and dust rags rubbing and slapping the dust from woodwork, books, and cranny corners. In the kitchen, last night's dishes washed and dried themselves, sailing gracefully from the sink to the cupboard—and the immaculate house was quiet again.

So the happiness began for Marty Finnigan, and the world was green again. He fell asleep at night with the slight form of her curved like a kitten in his arms and woke in the morning to the joy of her nearness. Drawn by the amazement of his love he would lie on his elbow watching her asleep. Most of the time, she lay still as sleep itself but now and then she was restless and tossed fitfully, whispering aloud in some dream. Sometimes she spoke his name or a word in Irish; sometimes strange words that were like far music at the end of night, like the sound of the day itself breaking in their room.

He loved her and the love made him grow, and if everything about her seemed touched with magic, he reasoned it to this love. She had her moods, though, and when they came over her, she wanted to wander alone in the woods and meadows beyond the house. So it was on a Saturday in March that she rose out of sorts from bed and knew the blackness was on her. Without even bothering to take her broom, she kissed him good-bye almost solemnly and went out with a basket to gather herbs for salads and spells.

With herself gone, it was a slow morning for Marty. He drank coffee and read the papers, and toyed with the idea of beginning his flower bed, but gave it up before it became serious. Sprawled comfortably on the sofa, he became only gradually aware of the sound of a car turning into their lane.

His brow furrowed in a puzzled frown. He wasn't expecting company, and no one just dropped in on a Saturday morning. The frown deepened to irritation: a salesman—blood brother in Marty's eye to the Japanese beetle, the termite, and the housefly. He decided to make short, polite work of it.

The woman on the doorstep was tall and coldly beautiful. "Hello, Martin. I see you still resist shaving on weekends."

"Alice, what—"

They stared at each other for a moment.

"Well," she asked finally, "you do have some manners, don't you? Ask me inside."

Marty followed her into the living room where she stood alertly in the center of the floor, head turned slightly to one side. In this attitude, she reminded Marty of a beagle sniffing out a rabbit.

"Sit down, Alice. How about some coffee?"

She made a little grimace of distaste. "Darling, it's much too early for coffee. Coffee's for evening and regrets, but I will take a martini."

"Sorry, no gin in the house," he said. "We're both whiskey folks here."

Alice laughed drily. "You never did have any taste, Martin. By the way, where's the *new* Mrs. Finnigan? I hear she's quite young."

"Isolde's nineteen," said Marty. "She's out for a while, but she'll be back soon."

"Isolde?" Alice took a cigarette from her purse and put a lighter to it. "Makes you think of a fat soprano. But nineteen! My God, Martin, what do you talk about . . . when you talk?"

"So what's wrong with nineteen? Am I an antique?"

"Too old for *that,* anyway."

It burned Marty that she could still get to him. He thrust himself off the sofa. "All right, knock it off, Alice. What do you want?"

"And what has she *done* to this room?" Alice ignored him. "With my furniture, too." She was ill at ease in the room. It had a new brightness and charm she could never give it despite her driven search for the Room that was Her. "And that's what I came about," she concluded. "Darling, I *am* in a pinch for money, and since the furniture is mine— now that you're doing so well—I want to sell it."

She pronounced it as if the matter was settled and done; it was her way, the way she'd been from the beginning. Marty felt himself beginning to heat. "Why didn't you do this before, when it didn't matter if there was a rug on the floor or even a floor? Why now?"

"Now just a minute, Darling—"

"And dammit, don't call me 'darling.' You're the only woman in the world who could make 'darling' sound like a common noun."

"For that matter, Darling, the house itself is half mine, legally. I let you stay here because I *was* a little sorry for you. I mean, you're so helpless, Martin. It didn't matter then, but the broker says the value's gone up with the new throughway finished, and I do need the cash." Her expression softened. "I know it's been tough for you, Martin, but it's been no bed of roses for me, either. I work hard, too, and no matter how it turned out for us, give a girl credit, hmm?"

"Oh, I give you credit, Alice," Marty said quietly. Suddenly, he wanted Isolde very much. Now, when he needed her.

Go make yourself some coffee, the thought told him, and Marty acted without thinking about it. Somehow it seemed a very good idea at the moment. He left Alice so abruptly, she was startled.

"Where are you going, Martin?"

"To make coffee."

"Oh, for God's sake!" She stubbed out her cigarette with a vicious jab and threw her eyes impatiently around the room. A slight sound made her turn.

The sliding doors that led to the kitchen were drawing slowly together.

"Martin? Why did you close the doors?"

There was no answer, nor could she hear him moving in the kitchen. A deep silence had settled over the entire house, and as if a cloud had slid over the sun, the room was growing darker and somehow chilly.

A storm, she thought. *I'd better finish this up and leave.* She remembered an appointment for the early afternoon and looked at the clock on the mantle: ten thirty-three. . . .

As she looked, the clock stopped ticking.

"What . . . ?" Alice stepped to the mantle to look at it, and her eye fell on a queer old broom, the handle worn black with use and the head no more than a bundle of birch switches. She picked it up. "Shades of Halloween," she snickered, "how quaint can you be?"

"Put it down!"

Alice froze; it was as though the very sound were a pair of hands laid on her will to move. The hands loosened, and she turned. A slight red-haired girl stood behind her with cold gray eyes belying the voice that was softened now to a gentle admonishment.

"Never touch my broom," Isolde took it from her. " 'Tis the luck of Finnigan's Hearth."

Alice felt a tiny chill run like a frightened mouse down her spine. "Oh . . . hello, I didn't hear you come in. You must be Isolde."

"Aye."

"Martin and I have been having a talk." Alice attempted a patronizing grace that fell flat. "I—want to make some arrangement about the furniture and the house. But excuse me, I didn't introduce myself. I'm—"

"I know," said Isolde. "The late Mistress Finnigan."

Alice managed something like a laugh. It was a weak sound.

"Do seat yourself," Isolde invited, "and tell me your pleasure in refreshment."

Alice composed herself and prepared to do battle. She arranged her hands delicately in her lap and crossed her exquisite legs, reassured since Martin's new wife was neither beautiful nor sophisticated. It was true: Martin *must* have gotten her out of some unguarded cradle. "Well, Martin said you didn't have martini makings."

"Oh dear," Isolde laughed. "That be just like a man: not able to find a thing in his own house." She busied herself a moment at the sideboard: "For 'tis here in my hand."

She offered Alice the martini, complete to the olive. Alice blinked. There was nothing on the sideboard but a decanter of whiskey. She tasted the drink and found it superb—but with a something in its tang she couldn't place. "Perfect! Thanks so much. Whatever do you add to get this taste?"

"Herbs," said Isolde.

Those cold eyes on her; gray, but darker than before . . . like smoke. With some irritation, Alice found she was becoming increasingly nervous under that gaze. She attempted to avert it. "I think your clock has stopped."

"Aye," said Isolde, without looking at the clock, "it has."

Alice glanced at her watch. "About—well, that's queer. My watch has stopped, too."

"So it has." Isolde's smile was ice. "Time out of joint, Mistress Alice." She took the decanter from the sideboard and sat down facing Alice. "And Marty be asleep in the kitchen, but just for a bit." Her left hand carved a curious shape in the air and held a glass.

Alice gasped. "What on *earth*—!"

"When the clock rouses," Isolde purred, "so will he. Till then, we'll pass a womanly word or two."

She opened the decanter and poured. The glass was a tall one, but the liquor swelled steadily toward the brim, and Alice's jaw dropped proportionately lower as she watched it rise. "Surely, you're not going to *drink* that."

"Oh, yes." Isolde sipped at the whiskey, nodded her pleased approval, and casually drank it down. " 'Tis not pure, but only 86 proof."

Alice was shaken beyond manners. "You little fool, that's whiskey! You'll kill yourself."

She tried to rise, but her will and legs had turned to water.

"Drink up, Mistress Alice." The voice was music, but the eyes were black. Alice raised her glass; the round brim held her gaze as it spun, developing in concentric circles, drawing her in . . .

"Now," Isolde began calmly, "as to the selling of the house . . ."

. . . There was black Limbo, then Alice felt herself grasped by huge hands, and she was dragged up, up over interminable stone steps by two half-naked brutes. The rays from occasional torches glanced off the crude gold ornaments on their arms and gleamed again in their fierce blue eyes. There was no sound in her ears but the wild beating of her own heart as they passed up over hundreds of steps, ending at the entrance of a great hall. At the far end of the hall, raised on a dais, a familiar figure beckoned them forward. Alice was pushed forward to the foot of the dais.

"Kneel," a voice commanded her. "Kneel to Isolde of the blood of Leinster, daughter of a hundred unblemished kings of Eire."

"Please," Alice croaked, "please, God, this isn't real. It's insane." She raised her head to the slight, erect figure on the throne, but flinched again from the searching eyes. "You . . . what have you done to me?"

"Before I judge you," said Isolde, "one small truth out of a lying life to warm my soul upon. For what reason did you bring the pain of yourself to Marty Finnigan? And taking his heart, unworthy as you are, for what reason did you desert him?"

The truth welled out of the bottom of Alice's being. She had no power to silence it, having never known it, and it passed from her heart to her lips like a stranger.

"I was afraid," said the truth in her voice. "I had nothing to give, but I found that Martin needed giving. There was nothing inside. . . ."

". . . And what a shame it is," Isolde crooned, refilling her glass, "that you come now to talk of selling Finnigan's Hearth that we love so much and our friends, too. But here! I've forgot my graces. Do let me fill your glass like a good hostess." She leaned toward Alice, stretching out her open hand. The long fingers closed in a beckoning motion. Alice's glass was full.

Alice rubbed her eyes, shivering with unaccountable cold. She had been sitting and talking, sipping at a delicious drink and listening to a melodious voice that spoke of furniture and trifles. And yet, she seemed to have wandered out of time in a nightmare, forgotten already but leaving its chill on her mind. "What did you say? I'm afraid I . . . it's very strange. . . ."

"Drink up, Alice."

. . . And Alice groveled on the stone floor while Isolde's long finger lifted and pointed at her. "It was harm enough to take him, even more to leave. Yea, but to come *now* like a cloud in the middle of his brightest day." She leaned back, musing a moment. At a sign of her hand, a giant shadow loomed beside Alice, ready with the sword. With cold pleasure, Isolde commanded: "Give me her head."

"Don't!" Alice shrieked, cowering away from the shadow. "Please, *don't—*"

The sword came down.

". . . So will you wake now, and leave this house," Isolde whispered over the sleeping woman. "You will leave us in peace, and only in dreams will you remember the fear of me, nought but the fear—"

There was a sudden *whirr* of clockwork. The sound jarred Isolde, and she spun around. Unbidden by her, the mantle clock was ticking.

"Name of a black day," she breathed, "who is it?"

Alice woke with a violent start. She stared stupidly at her drink as if looking for a reality she might have misplaced. Between her fingers, the glass and drink dissolved to a fine smoke. Then she saw Isolde—and she remembered. She was too frightened to move, but she could scream. She was still screaming when the panel doors banged open and Marty burst into the room.

"What happened?" he looked dazedly at both women. "I must have passed out. I woke up on the floor and—"

Alice bolted out of the chair and cowered against him, her face white and contorted with fear. "Martin, she tried to kill me . . . it was in a dream . . . a man with a sword . . . there was a glass in my hand and it just disappeared . . ."

Isolde backed toward the fireplace in confusion and fright. Something had broken her spell, and now she was caught with her world falling about her head. The fear became a swelling black anger, hammering harder and faster at her temples.

"I don't know what she is," Alice moaned against Marty's shoulder, "but, Martin, she's not *human!*" She clung to him like a child sobbing out of a nightmare to the safety of a grown-up, and Marty, with the answering instinct, put his arms around her.

The last stroke of the hammer fell. Isolde gasped with a pain that bent her almost double. Only her will remained: "Take your hands from her, Marty, or I'll burn the wench in your arms!"

Marty looked up at her. For a long second, there was only the loud ticking of the clock and Alice's ragged sobbing. Then Marty pushed Alice toward the door. "Get out, Alice," he said. "Don't come back."

"Come away with me, Martin. Please, for your own sake."

But he was already closing the door on her. "No, not with you. This is something between Isolde and me, and you're a stranger, Alice. You always were. Good-bye."

He shut the door and leaned his head against it, eyes shut. From the driveway came the sound of the car started, jerked nervously into gear, and roaring down the lane.

"Marty?"

He didn't answer.

"Marty, will you turn away from me now?"

"Turn away? Turn away from what? You aren't real, are you?"

His voice was quiet and toneless with the knowing. "I know it now. I guess—always—some part of me knew, but I needed someone. Strange—sometimes when I loved you—it was like you weren't there, and I was alone. Not always, no; only a few times when I needed you so much I reached for *something,* I don't know what. Some part of me knew. I guess that's why I never asked how you came."

"From Heaven and Hell," Isolde sighed, "and all the winds between." She was tired, tired as she had not been in fifteen hundred years. "I was searching for life, and 'twas here by your fire I found it. And if I be not your first love, Marty—well you be not mine, either. But that was a long time ago, nor was it half the glory of this."

For the first time, there was something in his expression that escaped her. "Are you afraid, Marty?"

"No," Marty said quietly, "not afraid." He took a step toward the panel doors.

"Then why do you turn away?"

"Don't you know?" He wheeled on her, and Isolde began to understand the thing behind his eyes and in his voice. It was hurt. "Can't you see what you've done? Alice gave nothing, but she promised nothing. She was what she was. You promised everything when you had nothing to give that was *real*."

"And have you lacked since I came?" she asked, with the strange, sick weariness growing in her. "Have I not won your house for you, once and always?"

"Sure, and for what?" The hurt was a hard brightness in the words. "For the years we'll spend in it?"

"The years? No, we haven't got years. . . ."

"For the growing old together—when you'll never grow old, never grow up? For the children we won't have?"

She sank into a chair. "I only had a little time . . . and my broom."

"And you knew that. You knew that, and yet you couldn't know how I'd feel when you—"

"I wanted *life*, Marty!"

"Life!" he screamed at her, lunging at the broom. "With *that!*"

Her hand shut in a fist. *"Don't touch it!"*

She could have cut out her tongue before the wish was half uttered. Marty froze, paralyzed with the sudden agony. It faded slowly, leaving him white and spent.

"Thanks," he said weakly. "That was a quick death."

"God and yourself forgive me, Marty. 'Twas the last hurt I'll ever do you."

"Yes. It's killed. . . ." Marty smiled sadly at her. "Oh, my poor, scared Isolde, I couldn't have hurt you. I couldn't, but you wouldn't take the chance."

He walked out of the living room. Isolde heard his footsteps on the stairs, then in the bedroom above, and the sound of closets and drawers being opened, not in haste but with deliberateness. She rose from the chair and wandered about the living room, unable to think of what might happen. Suddenly she dropped to her knees, a little ball of misery in the middle of the floor.

"Oh, wretched!" she cursed herself, beating futile repentance into the carpet with her fists. "Worthless, white-livered slut! Be you damned twice over for the hurt in his eyes, for the love you took from him, for the life of him you stole, and yourself not fit to kiss his dead, mud-tracking boots."

After a few minutes, Marty came downstairs again, dressed to go out, carrying a small suitcase.

"Where do you go, Marty?"

"Away," he said. "I'll send someone after the rest of my things."

She bowed her head. "And not come back?"

He shook his head. "I don't want to look at this house again. Alice can sell it if she wants, I don't care. But you can work that broom till it wears out; I won't be back."

"No fear, Marty. I said 'twas the last hurt." When she looked at him, the old pride was there but it was gentled. "You've a queen's word for it."

He put his hand on the doorknob, pulled it open. "I guess I just can't take losing again. Good-bye, honey."

"Fare-you-well, Marty. The best of my heart go with you."

The door closed behind him.

Isolde fell forward, burying her face in her arms. "Heaven and Hell, Heaven and Hell, let me die once more."

"How unutterably tragic," said the petulant, cultivated voice behind her. "I really should have brought Booth along. He fairly wallows in this sort of thing."

Isolde raised her head slowly to the well-tailored man in the easy chair, pursing his lips over a tumbler of whiskey. Bitterly and without surprise she said, "Well, now's my day complete."

The Prince sipped at his whiskey, knitting fine brows. "Wonderful stuff! The woman was mad to pass this up for that drowned-olive affair. No—as a matter of fact, I hadn't intended to come myself, only to send again to ask you to come home." He gave her a charming shrug and smile. "But none of your crowd was available. Nero is throwing a party for some American Senator and Booth is still playing Hamlet. Oh! The conceit of that actor! Do you know where he kills the king in the last act? Well, as true as I'm here, whenever the mood strikes him, that unbelievable ham shoots the king with a pistol and gallops off up center bellowing *Sic Semper Tyrannis*. Still, he's in demand. The women, mostly. As for Prissy, her latest passion is Zen, and she doesn't even care about her broom, though *you've* certainly made free with it." He chuckled with reminiscent delight. "That execution effect was superb. That's why I broke your spell. I wanted to see how well you could manage *a capella*, and, my dear—you fizzled."

Isolde stared at her hands. "What's it matter now? Marty's gone. 'Tis over."

"You can't say you weren't warned. You had every chance."

"Aye, I did." She rose heavily, picked up the broom, and held it out to the Prince. " 'Tis over, let's be gone."

He waved it away. "Not for all the world. No, the moment I saw you, I knew the game was changed. There are more interesting considerations now."

Isolde was firm. "Take it. I want no more of this." Another wave of sickness rolled over her. "I said you've won. Must you rack me as well?"

"That's what I meant," said the Prince, "though I must decline the credit. You see, Faerie Queen, you're with child—what a quaint phrase!" He toasted her with his glass. "Congratulations."

"With child . . ." She dropped the broom and sank to her knees, stunned by the wonder of it. "With child! Oh saints, saints, saints, Marty, I have your child!"

"Precisely," the Prince interjected, "and you can hardly blame me for *that*. Nevertheless, you can see why I won't recall you before your time. I will even extend your visit if need be. There'll be the child."

"Marty's child!" she flared. "It belongs to him."

"Of course, Isolde, but you belong to me." An eloquent shrug of his shoulders. "Though it is an unusual case. First of its kind, actually. The possibilities are infinite. For example—how would you like to be mother of a President?" He leaned back, speculating with pleasure. "I'll make him a man of universal insight and intellectual power, a natural leader of men and irresistible to women; yet humble, possessing the common touch. A man of the people. The world will be ready for another Kennedy."

"You'll not have the power of one finger over my son!"

"Oh, stop it!" he snapped. "You're as bad as Booth. He warned you that I never operate at a loss." The Prince picked up her broom. "This is your only hold on the world, and yet its greatest power was only your own lunatic thirst for life. Well, you got everything you wanted. Now, by the same easy method, you want to sweep it all away, and still you don't understand. Not my power but your lack of it will stop you. Yet, with my way, you could have him back."

Isolde was very still for a time, seeming to accept what he said. Finally: "Aye, you do win it all . . . all. You know you can hold me here and that I won't live without Marty. But make me the small promise that Marty and his own will never lack."

The Prince was all graciousness. "They will never lack."

"And my son be happy all the days of his life?"

"Fabulously."

She gave him a cold smile. "Thanks for that."

The Prince nodded benignly. "My pleasure entirely. It's all in the family. So, it's done—now for the last." He held out the broom to her. "Take this and wish your husband back."

She hesitated. "But will he love me?"

"He will want you—not quite the same, but good enough for the time you have left."

"No—not quite the same."

He held out the broom. "But still . . ."

She took the broom. "But still."

"Now, Isolde: wish."

And Isolde wished. "Broom," she commanded, "from the world and the memory of Marty Finnigan, *sweep me out forever.*"

The Prince gasped. "Wait!"

"And that done," she raised the broom with both hands, broke it over her knee, and hurled the pieces into the fireplace, "be quit of me!" the two ends flashed into unearthly flame and disintegrated. Isolde sucked in one last breath of sweet air and held it, waiting—

A low moan ran through the foundations of the house. The curtains tore loose from every window, the paint and wallpaper peeled, the dust of months swirled in a brown cloud and settled over the furniture and the floor. All that the broom had done for her was undone, for the house had said it would only seem, and the seeming was ended.

But Isolde still stood there—corporeal, uneclipsed. She opened her eyes to the fuming anger of the Prince.

"You treacherous slut. You puling, sentimental, self-sacrificing *cow!*"

Dumbly she waited to be consumed, not hearing or caring. Marty was free of her, and what was done was done.

"Fool!" the Prince screamed at her, his voice almost a ludicrous falsetto with rage. "No one since that primal wench in Eden could have been so stupid. To writhe through the agony of this blind hog wallow of a world, not once but *twice.* To feel limbs wither and love die—*twice.* To know the death of every dream and its disillusionment—*twice.* And for what grubby little reason? Why do you think that men have clung through all time to the need for Heaven and Hell? Not for punishment, not for reward. They are refuge, both of them, from trying to find a meaning for life; the pointless end to the grisly joke. And it *is* a joke. The immense cosmic joke that you, you second-rate Guinevere, will never understand in a thousand lifetimes. Because in Heaven are all rewards for virtue except the earthly hunger for reward, and if Hell is empty after all, at least it holds no pain. Why shouldn't they be sought after and prayed for by the brave and cowardly alike, the saints and the greedy, the men who knew they walked alone and the petty bargainers who mortgaged their souls to have them loved for five minutes; why shouldn't they be refuge—these two endings that you've tossed out like an old pair of shoes? Neither gives a meaning, but both make an end to *this!*"

Something was dawning on Isolde, something so immense she dared grasp only the littlest piece of it. "Well, take me if you will. Why do you rage so?" She grinned at him. "You've lost your power over me, haven't you, Prince?"

"I wouldn't say that." But he made no move toward her.

"Yes"—the thing grew in her—"that's it: the meaning. The Secret. That's why you sent Booth when I was about to give of myself to Marty. Afraid you were that I'd learn the secret and be quit of you." She laughed in his face. "Come, try and take me. Here's my hand, Prince. Try!"

The Prince backed away from the contact. "Now, don't be hasty. Keep away from me. Don't touch me, you grimy little *human!*"

She pursued him around the room, hooting with laughter. "I've won! I'm alive, and if I lay hand or foot to you, by the Grail I'll leave a lump for every inch. *There!*"

"*Yi!*"

"And there! And there! Now, out of my house, for 'tis mine at last! Oh, Marty, Marty." She sank down on the sofa, weeping and laughing with her joy. "I'm alive. I don't know how, but I'm alive."

"Well," said the Prince nastily, keeping a safe distance from her, "at least I don't have the bother of you any more. The broom finishes that."

" 'Twas the giving," she said to herself. "The giving."

"Perhaps," the Prince conceded shortly. "I never have understood that sort of thing."

"The giving . . . such a little thing."

The Prince snorted his contempt from the doorway. "Even if I were a man, I'd call you a fool."

"Aye, Prince," she answered, and she was no longer a girl. "But if you were a fool, you'd be a man."

He inclined his head with an old-fashioned courtesy. "Well, Faerie

Queen, your world and welcome to it. Oh, don't get up. I'll let myself out."

The house was drab and dirty as the day she had come to it, unchanged in any way except that Marty was gone. But she was alive, and it was her house, and she knew what to do with it now.

His house in my hands, she thought, and his son beneath my heart. Well now! A new broom and a bucket, a brush and paint, and new curtains to be made and the kitchen to be cleaned and the lawn mowed and his garden started and . . . and what sit you here for, Mistress Finnigan, when there's your toil waiting. Just you wait, Marty, and *then* say I can give you nothing that's real . . . and, oh saints, saints, saints, I'm about to be *sick* again!

She swept and she scrubbed. She chipped and painted. She measured and she sewed. She mowed and raked until, little by little, under blistered hands that now wove no magic but her love, Finnigan's Hearth began to shine once more. She was sick in the mornings with depressing regularity but weathered it with choking curses and went about her work. The spring wind was a bouquet of moselle in her nostrils, and ancient Poobah no longer growled when she passed.

But the days went by and she found what it was to be lonely.

One afternoon, as she was rooting weeds out of the new flower bed, she heard someone call her name. Looking up, she saw a tall, white-haired man standing near the front steps. He seemed familiar but the name escaped her.

"Well, top of the morning, Mrs. Finnigan."

"And the rest of the day for yourself," she responded cordially. "What be you? An insurance peddler?"

"Good heavens, no," he laughed gently. "There's nothing sure in this world. No, I was in the area and I just thought I'd look in. I wondered if you'd found what you were looking for?"

Isolde knew him now. She curtsied in deep respect. "Sure, I forgot the face and the name. Give you good day, Angel. And how be the Blessed?"

"Tolerably well," he nodded. "You too, by your blossoming aspect. Did you find your Secret?"

Isolde wiped the perspiration from her face, leaving it streaked with brown earth. "Not all, but as much as my poor thick skull can hold."

"That's all anyone can do. Tell me, then: what is it?"

"To keep from hurt the heart of Marty Finnigan, to love him with my own, and to give to him all the days of my life."

"Well, now—" The Angel stepped back, regarding her with his kind, sad eyes. "As nicely as I've ever heard it put. Different hearts, different words, but it dresses out about the same."

"Aye, but I learned too late. He's forgot me."

"Yes, I know," said the Angel. "Your finest hour, as that Englishman said. Well, as a woman, you're going to learn that men are very forgetful anyway. It's all a question of what they forget." He indicated the flower bed. "What have you planted?"

"Roses," she said with some enthusiasm. "Marty said when the spring came . . ." the sentence trailed off. "They'll grace the look of the house," she finished, hearing the loneliness in her own voice.

"They will," the Angel said. "I wish you could send me one. But then I never sent you a wedding gift, did I? That just shows you: forgetful, every one of us. Well, let me think. What would be appropriate?" He considered the problem. "How about a new harp?"

And play it to an empty house, she thought.

"Yes," the Angel nodded, pleased with his choice. "A harp. A forgotten art, these days, but you always did have a talent for it." He took her hands in his. "Good-bye for the time, Isolde. We'll meet again, of course."

" 'Twill be my pleasure, Angel."

"Yes—well—next time, *do* plan to stay." He waved to her and disappeared around the corner of the house. Isolde went back to her digging.

A few minutes later a car turned into the lane. It was a police cruiser, manned by two bored officers and bearing a battered passenger in the rear seat. The policemen helped their charge from the car with the care one accords to a cracked Ming vase.

Isolde's heart came up into her throat. She clutched at her trowel as if it were the O'Gowra broom.

The officer gave her a weary, patient nod. "This your husband, Ma'am?"

"Oh, for sure," she swallowed. "Whatever's happened to him?"

Marty's left eye was swollen shut in a small mound of royal purple. The other was bloodshot. He was unshaven, unwashed, and the remains of his suit were only memorials to an epic struggle.

"Who did this?" Isolde snapped. "Who *dast* do this to Martin Finnigan?"

The officer gave Marty a look of professional compassion. "Couldn't

tell you all of 'em. Had complaints on him all week. Drunk and disor-
derly, damage to property, assault, four fights in three days—"

"Oh, dear God! Four?"

"Yes, Ma'am. He must've lost them all. Had him down at the station
for two days, drying him out. He wouldn't tell us where he lived." He
swung away toward the car. Marty sagged down onto the front stoop,
as bleakly silent as Stonehenge. The second policeman regarded him.

"You know, lady," he said, "I think your husband's one of those
people who just can't drink."

The first officer returned with something under his arm. He proffered
it to Marty, puzzled. "This yours, Mr. Finnigan?"

Marty's one good eye appraised the object, an ancient harp. "Hell,
no," he concluded gloomily. "What would I do with it?"

The policeman handed it to Isolde. Her arms and fingers remembered
its curve. "Well, it ain't ours, either, so you take it. All right, Ma'am, I
guess that's all. Keep him home for a while."

"My thanks, Sir."

The police car rumbled out of the lane, leaving them alone in their
world. Isolde took a deep, tired breath. There were so many things to
tell him . . . about the house and the missing of himself for days . . .
about the lonely expanse of bed at night . . . about the child.

But no: a little at a time. I'll not tell him; I'll show him, a little at a
time that what we have is real.

"Well, Marty?"

"Well, what?" he muttered. "Don't think I wanted to come back
here. They made me come back."

Isolde fought against the anger, but it rose in her throat. "And—and
so you'll be walking off again."

"Yes." Marty's voice was hoarse with fatigue. "But I wouldn't mind
an aspirin or two, if we have any."

"'We,' Finnigan? 'We' have nothing. *I* might have a draught to soothe
your head." *There's nothing but to fight him. A little of him must be
fought and beaten so all of him can win.* "But when you walk down
that road, Finnigan, what pill will you take against the next woman that
comes your way and loves you, but, pity her soul, isn't good enough,
isn't real enough, isn't perfect enough for you?"

"Don't hand me that, damn it!" Marty lunged up at her. "You know
what you are. You're a lie, an illusion," he seethed, "standing there telling me *I* don't have any guts. Telling a real person—"

"*Real!*" She jabbed a finger into his chest. "I am the realest, strongest clout of woman 'twill ever be your good fortune to look on, and, I might add, getting realer by the moment, as time and the sight of your eyes will unfold to your feeble understanding. See!" Isolde spread her hands before his face. "Those be blisters. That be callous. And do you puzzle where I got them? From work. From cleaning and painting the house that's mine now, because I stayed to care for it, whilst you walked away. And this sweat"—she was almost crying now—"is from loving your own dream enough to plant your bloody roses!"

His face cracked in the beginnings of a sardonic grin. "Looks like you used your nose to dig with."

"Does it indeed?" The nose in point was thrust as close as possible to him. "A minute at a glass will tell you you've not exactly the look of a rose yourself, Sir Finnigan. And was I blindfold with only this poor nose to tell me what I was next to, my first thought would not be any kind of flower. God, what a sorry sight you are, and yourself unwashed as a Cornish cowherd. *Crawling* home after days—"

"I did not *crawl* home," Marty bawled. "I am not staying."

"Then crawl away!"

"Don't tell me what to do in my own yard."

"*My* yard!" Isolde dropped the trowel, jabbed her fist into his stomach and kicked him in the shin. Marty doubled for a second in surprise, then grabbed at her, tucked her under one arm and spanked her until they swayed and fell onto the grass. She twisted on her back and looked up at him. Marty was very pale, but laughing. "Ah-h, hell. You're right, where else is there?"

"Marty," she said with the anger gone out of her, "will you go? Or do you come home to stay?"

"To stay." He seemed to consider it. "I think I came home to die. Honey, *please,* do we have any aspirin?"

She couldn't bear it any longer. Her arms were around him and she was sobbing. "Stay . . . stay. Please stay."

"Sure," he soothed her. "I have to. The world isn't ready for you yet, baby."

"Oh, Marty, that be finished and dead, I swear."

"Now listen," he said painfully as if each word weighed a ton, "that part is over. Let's never, never even think about it. Because people—oh, God, my head—because people like Alice . . . and other people . . . well, they're just not very broadminded."

"It's done and done." She drew him up gently. "And nothing left of it but ourselves. Our house stands tall and gallant, Finnigan. Welcome home."

Isolde led him inside and stretched him out with great care on the sofa, his head sandwiched between an icebag and the pillow. She knelt beside him and drew soft chords from the harp.

Marty stirred. "Lovely," he murmured, and then he was asleep. Isolde played softly. Now and then, when he moved, she would replace the icebag gently, as if it were a crown.

The authorship of this terrible little anecdote is uncertain, but has been ascribed to Guy de Maupassant, *a Frenchman who, born in 1854, became a leading novelist in the same naturalistic school that spawned Emile Zola. He wrote some three hundred tales as well as novels, many of them supernatural and usually tinged with tragedy.*

The Phantom Hag
by Guy de Maupassant (?)

The other evening in an old castle the conversation turned upon apparitions, each one of the party telling a story. As the accounts grew more horrible the young ladies drew closer together.

"Have you ever had an adventure with a ghost?" said they to me. "Do you not know a story to make us shiver? Come, tell us something."

"I am quite willing to do so," I replied. "I will tell you of an incident that happened to myself."

Toward the close of the autumn of 1858 I visited one of my friends, subprefect of a little city in the center of France. Albert was an old companion of my youth, and I had been present at his wedding. His charming wife was full of goodness and grace. My friend wished to show me his happy home, and to introduce me to his two pretty little daughters. I was feted and taken great care of. Three days after my arrival I knew the entire city, curiosities, old castles, ruins, etc. Every day about four o'clock Albert would order the phaeton, and we would take a long ride, returning home in the evening. One evening my friend said to me:

"Tomorrow we will go further than usual. I want to take you to the Black Rocks. They are curious old Druidical stones, on a wild and desolate plain. They will interest you. My wife has not seen them yet, so we will take her."

The following day we drove out at the usual hour. Albert's wife sat by his side. I occupied the back seat alone. The weather was gray and somber that afternoon, and the journey was not very pleasant. When we arrived at the Black Rocks the sun was setting. We got out of the phaeton, and Albert took care of the horses.

We walked some little distance through the fields before reaching the giant remains of the old Druid religion. Albert's wife wished to climb to the summit of the altar, and I assisted her. I can still see her graceful figure as she stood draped in a red shawl, her veil floating around her.

"How beautiful it is! But does it not make you feel a little melancholy?" said she, extending her hand toward the dark horizon, which was lighted a little by the last rays of the sun.

The afternoon wind blew violently, and sighed through the stunted trees that grew around the stone cromlechs; not a dwelling nor a human being was in sight. We hastened to get down, and silently retraced our steps to the carriage.

"We must hurry," said Albert; "the sky is threatening, and we shall have scarcely time to reach home before night."

We carefully wrapped the robes around his wife. She tied the veil around her face, and the horses started into a rapid trot. It was growing dark; the scenery around us was bare and desolate; clumps of fir trees here and there and furze bushes formed the only vegetation. We began to feel the cold, for the wind blew with fury; the only sound we heard was the steady trot of the horses and the sharp clear tinkle of their bells.

Suddenly I felt the heavy grasp of a hand upon my shoulder. I turned my head quickly. A horrible apparition presented itself before my eyes. In the empty place at my side sat a hideous woman. I tried to cry out; the phantom placed her fingers upon her lips to impose silence upon me. I could not utter a sound. The woman was clothed in white linen; her head was cowled; her face was overspread with a corpse-like pallor, and in place of eyes were ghastly black cavities.

I sat motionless, overcome by terror.

The ghost suddenly stood up and leaned over the young wife. She encircled her with her arms, and lowered her hideous head as if to kiss her forehead.

"What a wind!" cried Madame Albert, turning precipitately toward me. "My veil is torn."

As she turned I felt the same infernal pressure on my shoulder, and the place occupied by the phantom was empty. I looked out to the right and left—the road was deserted, not an object in sight.

"What a dreadful gale!" said Madame Albert. "Did you feel it? I cannot explain the terror that seized me; my veil was torn by the wind as if by an invisible hand; I am trembling still."

"Never mind," said Albert, smiling; "wrap yourself up, my dear; we will soon be warming ourselves by a good fire at home. I am starving."

A cold perspiration covered my forehead; a shiver ran through me; my tongue clove to the roof of my mouth, and I could not articulate a sound; a sharp pain in my shoulder was the only sensible evidence that

I was not the victim of an hallucination. Putting my hand upon my aching shoulder, I felt a rent in the cloak that was wrapped around me. I looked at it; five perfectly distinct holes—visible traces of the grip of the horrible phantom. I thought for a moment that I should die or that my reason should leave me; it was, I think, the most dreadful moment of my life.

Finally I became more calm; this nameless agony had lasted for some minutes; I do not think it is possible for a human being to suffer more than I did during that time. As soon as I had recovered my senses, I thought at first I would tell my friends all that had passed, but hesitated, and finally did not, fearing that my story would frighten Madame Albert, and feeling sure my friend would not believe me. The lights of the little city revived me, and gradually the oppression of terror that overwhelmed me became lighter.

So soon as we reached home, Madame Albert untied her veil; it was literally in shreds. I hoped to find my clothes whole and prove to myself that it was all imagination. But no, the cloth was torn in five places, just where the fingers had seized my shoulder. There was no mark, however, upon my flesh, only a dull pain.

I returned to Paris the next day, where I endeavored to forget the strange adventure; or at least when I thought of it, I would force myself to think it an hallucination.

The day after my return I received a letter from my friend Albert. It was edged with black. I opened it with a vague fear.

His wife had died the day of my return.

Ghosts often like to associate with religious orders, it seems, and here in the former capital of Sicily, a gruesome though pitiful phantom intrudes itself insidiously into the daily routine of the impressionable narrator when he visits the catacombs of the Capuchins, a branch of the Franciscan order of monks distinguished by the pointed hoods or capuches *they wear.* EUGÈNE MONTFORT, *born in 1877 in Paris, wrote novels and short stories, many of which are set in the sunny Mediterranean clime.*

The Ghost of the Capuchins
by Eugène Montfort

Adapted from the French by
Faith Lancereau
and Marvin Kaye

Toward the end of the last century, I settled for the winter in Palermo, that magnificent city whose rough, majestic architecture is softened by breezes from the Tyrrhenian Sea. My apartment was in an area called Quattro Canti, a place in the very center of town where the houses are richly ornamented and offset by statuary of antique nobility. Four Corners—for that is the meaning of the street's name—is busy morning and night with streams of natives whose features blend the *hauteur* of the proud Castilian and the more voluptuous characteristics of the Arab.

I stayed at the home of a Spanish gentleman named Herrera, whose ancestors came from Sicily. There amid the sculptured marble palaces of the Via Maqueda I dwelled, in a second-floor apartment with windows commanding all the comings and goings of Quattro Canti.

Herrera, my host, was discreet. Though my rooms were part of his home, he never showed himself to me unless I wished him to. Other than the day when he took me up to the apartment, I don't suppose I spoke with him more than twice in as many weeks.

That first day, he unlocked the door, swung it wide and allowed me to discover for myself the merits or shortcomings of the place. No word passed his lips as I investigated the simple quarters. A heavy oak table with sculptured feet distinguished one corner, and a gilded wooden Madonna rested on the bureau. An old painting of a young dark girl in

religious habit completed the décor; otherwise the place was unremark-
able, but tidy and immaculately clean.

"Who is she?" I asked, indicating the portrait of the pretty girl. She
had large, dark, bewildered eyes, and when I stepped closer and examined the canvas and the frame, I guessed it must have been painted
at least as far back as the time of Louis XIV. The painting was at the
foot of the bed, next to an armchair which I decided would be a fine
place to sit and read in. "Who is she?" I asked once more.

Herrera shrugged. "I know no more than you."

I agreed to take the rooms, and settled in that very afternoon. Days
passed, and I led a quiet existence in Palermo. My afternoons and evenings were spent in strolls in charming gardens, walks to the market or
to the port, and many visits to the Palatine Chapel, so renowned for its
beauty. I made few friends, but those I met would usually be at the
shipping mall at close of day, and there would I join them.

Thus I became thoroughly familiar with all the sights of that remarkable city . . . all except one.

On the outskirts of Palermo is a Capuchin monastery and burial catacombs famous throughout the town for vaults filled with the skeletons
of long times past. Everyone I spoke with recommended the place to
me, and my friends asserted more than once that I must not leave
Palermo before viewing the great Capuchin city of death.

Yet I stayed away from it for a long time. I do not care for things of
a macabre cast; the appurtenances of the grave fill me with loathing and
shatter my sleep.

But every week that elapsed made it harder for me to admit to my
friends that, as yet, I had not gone to the monastery. I avoided the subject as much as possible, but there came a time when the very word
"monk" ensured an unquiet evening abed, and at length I felt compelled to get it over with, so obsessive had the subject become. What
matter, I thought, whether I subsequently woke up in a sweat? The
mere thought of the place had already rendered some of my nights un-
bearable.

One morning when the weather was mild and I felt more rested and
calm than circumstances lately had permitted, I set off for the monastery. As I neared the boundary of the outer white wall that shut off the
Capuchins from the rest of the world, I thought I could detect on the
faces of the people of the neighborhood a sort of sardonic satisfaction,

as if to say, "Another going in, but he'll look different when he comes out."

By the time I was at the entryway, I felt like turning around and quietly returning to Signor Herrera's. But the distance was far, and I knew if I did not go in today, it would be harder to avoid tomorrow, so I passed the archway and spoke to the clerk.

He exchanged a few polite words, then, without further converse or preparation, opened the gate and ushered me downstairs to the burial vaults.

I was completely taken aback by the vastness of the dreadful vista. A long hallway stacked from floor to ceiling with bodies. Skeletons covered in black, gloved hands crossed at the waist, gaping sockets that once contained flesh stared sightlessly downward. At their feet, rows of glassed-in coffins held more recent human remains, while high up near the ceiling a long ledge held still more skinless piles of bones.

Everywhere, clothed skeletons leaned forward, discussing me, as it were, with silent laughter, but their joke was plain enough, though never uttered.

The monk escorted me through great galleries of the dead. Though I soon felt faint, he merely appeared bored. When I stopped, he stopped; when I stumbled forward, he resumed his pace.

The place stretched out so far I thought there must be no end. After a while—once the first shock grew duller—the hideous spectacle began to assume a ghoulish attraction of its own. I was simultaneously repulsed and fascinated by the rotted faces. The mystery of death possessed me, I sought its secrets in the downcast heads that studied the floor in a stupor, grinning with broken teeth and jaws.

Here a large skeleton rested by a smaller one, the pair posing for some morbid genius of the canvas. Over there, shreds of gray hair and bits of skin still clung to a smooth white skull, its shriveled expression atrocious, as if shrieking out the unfairness of the state of death. Yet its nearest neighbor smiled gently, sadly, while high above its head, an elder statesman reflected deeply, perhaps, on how best to legislate the improved condition of the charnel house. Two bodies away, mere surprise contorted moldering facial bones.

One skeleton stood apart from the others. Instead of leaning toward the ground, its skull pointed forward as if it had raised its head expressly to catch my eye. Its left shoulder brushed familiarly against a smaller adjacent body. I moved closer and read the name of the ghoul whose empty sockets seemed to fix me in their hypnotic command.

PIETRO CATALA
April 8, 1684

So old, then. I could not bear more. I signaled to my guide that I was anxious to return to the world of the living.

But the blue sky brought little relief as I returned to my apartment. Looking out the window, I saw the smiles of the passersby and knew they were, without realizing it, rehearsing for the final death-grin they would share with the skeletons of the vault, the grim wordless jest that ridiculed all projects and prospects we yearn for in life.

That night, I asked my landlord if he had any books on Palermo that I might borrow. He rooted about in his library, gathered up several and passed them to me. I took them to my sitting room, but did not browse in them until the following morning, when, rested by a sound sleep and in good spirits, I began to pick through the pile.

A ray of sunshine lit the apartment. I could hear joyful noises in the street, and, turning my thoughts away from the Capuchin monks and their grisly charges, I anticipated strolling through the city and taking in the good air by portside, perhaps lunching on shellfish.

But as I was about to set aside Herrera's books and quit the room, a parchment-bound old tome at the bottom of the pile arrested my attention. I picked it up, somehow compelled to examine it. Yellowed by time, it bore on the cover the following lengthy title:

Collection of Rare Facts
and Strange Happenings
in Palermo
from 1650 to 1700 A.D.

I sat down in my chair beneath the old picture and turned to the first few entries, but in truth, they were not especially interesting. I closed the book, turned it on its side to study the spine, but my fingers slipped and it fell to the floor. As it did, its leaves opened of their own accord to a place far back in the volume. My eye scanned it for an instant, then, discovering the import, I picked up the tome and read the providential passage word for word.

1684—ON APRIL 8 THERE OCCURRED A DREADFUL THING, AN
EVENT THAT WAS THE SUBJECT OF CONVERSATION FOR A LONG
TIME THEREAFTER. A YOUNG MAN OF TWENTY-THREE YEARS,
ONE PIETRO CATALA, ELDEST SON OF A RENOWNED INHABITANT
OF THE CITY, BECAME ENGAGED TO BIANCA BELFIORE, ALSO OF
AN OLD AND ILLUSTRIOUS CLAN. THEY WERE TO BE PLIGHTED TO
ONE ANOTHER, ACCORDING TO THE FAMILIES' INTENTIONS, ONE
MONTH HENCE, BUT GOD'S WAYS CANNOT BE PERCEIVED BY SIN-
NING MORTALS. AT FOUR IN THE AFTERNOON ON THE EIGHTH DAY
OF APRIL, AS THE COUPLE STROLLED ALONG THE MONREALE
ROAD ADMIRING THE BEAUTY OF THE SPRING SEASON, A VIOLENT
STORM ERUPTED. THE LOVERS TOOK REFUGE BENEATH A TREE,
BUT PROVIDENCE HURLED DOWN A GREAT LIGHTNING BOLT AND
PIETRO WAS STRUCK. HE DIED INSTANTLY, AND BIANCA, OVER-
COME BY GRIEF, FAINTED. THE BEAUTIFUL, SAD YOUNG GIRL
NEVER MARRIED ANOTHER, BUT JOINED A NEARBY CONVENT,
TAKING THE VEIL ON THE VERY DAY SHE WOULD HAVE WED
PIETRO.

As I read, I thought I saw once more the Capuchin skeleton whose
head was erect, whose name was attached to the clothing: Pietro Catala.

The air in my room, so fresh a moment earlier, now seemed to choke
me. I leaped up, grabbed my hat and left the room, slamming the door,
ran downstairs and into the street. Solitude suddenly unsettled me, I
had to be surrounded by the crowd walking along the Quattro Canti.

It was no accident, something whispered to me, that I'd especially
noted the remains of the lad whom lightning struck so long ago. The coincidence held some dreadful significance, I was afraid, though what it
might be I was powerless to discern.

I found my friends at the cafe and eagerly told them the occurrences
of the past day and morning, but they totally missed the point, treated
the affair lightly. They had neither solace nor wisdom to shed or share,
and I quickly quitted the place. Their gaiety, their idle talk was
superficial, vain; it no longer appealed to me. Behind their vacuous
laughter I heard a darker humor.

It was twilight, nearly dark. To get to the center of the city, I took a
small deserted road and walked along it distractedly, sorry I'd chosen
such a lifeless thoroughfare.

In front of me, someone walked slowly, quietly. The absence of any footfall began to worry at my nerves, and when I thought to pass him by, the most mundane of details caught my eye, and I shuddered. His clothing was too large, it looked like the black dress of a Capuchin. I tried to convince myself it was a mistake, that my overexcited brain saw resemblances that were not there. Again I considered walking faster to overtake the creature and look at his face. But I did not. Instead, I stopped in the middle of the roadway, stock-still.

What if I saw nothing there but bone, hollow cavities where eyes once were?

I waited till the silent pedestrian was far ahead of me, still treading along the road in silence, then I ducked down a side path and found another route to the well-lit and busy Maqueda Road.

I could not return yet to the empty rooms of the Quattro Canti. Instead I sought the calculated repartée of the theatre, purchasing a seat where a popular comedy was playing. But I found nothing within to smile about; on the contrary, the so-called playwright's wit seemed stupid and forced and withal so irritating that I left before the final act.

At last, late in the evening, I returned home.

I sensed nothing peculiar upon entering my room. The window was wide open and the usual street sounds wafted up to my ears. It was impossible to sleep when the windows remained open, so I closed the shutters, curtains and blinds in order to muffle the outside noise. I undressed by candlelight and as I did, noted how my room appeared enormous. I had never before heeded how the taper flickered and dimmed and created so many shadowy corners. An urge arose in me to check every cranny, to peer at each nook, even to look under my bed. For a long time, I refrained, thinking how ridiculous I was being, but in the end, I could not help but make a detailed inspection of every corner, the narrowest recesses, places not even large enough for small animals to hide.

At last, finally reassured I was the only person there, I double-checkèd the lock, then fell into the armchair, wondering why my minute scrutiny failed to calm me down, but rather increased my agitation.

I'd felt ill at ease that morning, but now the sensation was infinitely worse, hardly tolerable. An unknown, invisible presence seemed to stifle the entire room, and even the eyes of the portrait flickered in the candle flame as if lit with awareness that I was also there.

Next to the door stood a great mirror. I tried to avert my gaze from it, lest it reflect something more than the room appeared to hold. Yet time and again, it pulled me back, though I dared not look even as I dared not avoid it. The air was too warm, yet too cold; I sweated and shivered with sudden chill. Something ominous seemed to impend. My heart pounded; my breath rasped unevenly in my chest. I thought I might be growing delirious.

At last, hoping that sleep might banish all terror, I lay down on my bed, hastily throwing the bedclothes aside. I stretched out and breathed deeply, willing myself to become calm. It did not help. I began to toss and turn, but could not sleep. I blamed my insomnia on the unsnuffed candle. I usually slumber in darkness, but that night the idea of no light in the room was too hideous to bear. So I finally pulled the sheet over my face to keep the light out of my eyes.

Rest came after a long, long time.

In the middle of the night, I awoke, suddenly more nervous than I'd ever been. The sheet was still over my head. I saw nothing other than the muted glow of the candle through the cloth.

But I heard a strange sound, a kind of rubbing on the floor as if something was being dragged about the room. Not walking; more of a sliding, scuffing noise.

I didn't dare remove the sheet. I listened, teeth on edge, tight to keep them from chattering. The sliding was too deliberate and too heavy to be a small animal that might have gnawed through the woodwork into the chamber. Yet no human would walk like that, the scraping sound was dreadful to hear.

And then the noise stopped, and a silence even more terrible ensued. It was undoubtedly very late. Nothing could be heard from the street below, and now nothing disturbed the absolute stillness of my room.

I was in a cold sweat, dared not move, but with every second that I heard nothing, I grew more frightened, afraid of what might be hovering just above me in the gloom. My ignorance was an added torment, and at length I resolved I must see what was going on, no matter what it might cost me.

I lifted the sheet and gazed anxiously around the room. There by the armchair where earlier I sat knelt a black-robed figure, its back to me, its body entirely covered in the enveloping rough garb of the Capuchins.

As I gazed in horror and dread, the thing raised its arms in supplication to the old portrait of the woman. As it did, the sleeves fell back to its shoulders, and where arms should have been, I saw nothing but the outstretched bones and splayed fingers of a skeleton.

The picture itself was ringed with pale fire, and the eyes of the long-dead woman depicted in its frame seemed to turn downward to regard the foul creature below with a mixture of pity and fondness.

When I awoke, it was daylight. The room was empty, though still dark. I leaped from bed and pushed back the shutters, letting in the blessed light of morning.

The door was locked from inside, just as I'd left it.

I crossed over to the picture, telling myself such coincidences cannot occur; pictures like this are sold in every gallery or antique shop. The features were not in the least unusual, and the eyes certainly were not cast downward, nor did they seem to smile.

But when I wiped the frame clean with a damp towel, I saw centered in the middle of its bottom edge the name, Bianca Belfiore.

I returned to the Capuchin catacombs that day. The monk who admitted me looked surprised. Visitors rarely return for a second tour.

He followed me as I strode along the avenues of death, this time neither looking right nor left till I came, at last, to the remains of Pietro Catala.

I asked the monk whether he ever moved any of the skeletons. He shook his head, puzzled, and assured me he never, never, never touched them.

Yet the head of Catala now faced the ground. The eyes did not seek mine, nor did he lean any longer against the neighboring skeleton.

I gave the monk a coin and fled.

I left Palermo that morning, telling Signor Herrera I'd received a telegram calling me away immediately. He looked skeptical, knowing very well my mail passed through his hands first.

I did not wish to go to my room, so I asked him to pack my trunk and send all to the address I supplied.

Just before I left, I asked him whether he ever heard anything peculiar at night, but he shook his head.

"It is curious, though," he told me, looking as if he wanted me to say more, but knowing no gentleman pried into another's affairs. "Your room has an excellent view, and I have priced it reasonably enough. Yet I never seem to keep tenants in it for very long. . . ."

EDWARD D. HOCH *is a charming writer, incredibly prolific, yet uncompromisingly excellent. Born in 1930 in Rochester, New York, he still resides there with his wife, Pat, and contributes literally hundreds of detectival and espionage stories to* Ellery Queen's Mystery Magazine. *It is not commonly known that Ed wrote some memorable fantasy tales at the beginning of his career.* "Who Rides with Santa Anna?" *is one of the subtlest; the identity of the mysterious rider is easy to deduce, but unless one is up on dates, it is easy to miss the real riddle that the author proposes. . . .*

Who Rides with Santa Anna?
by Edward D. Hoch

Antonio Lopez de Santa Anna stood pensively on a hardened hill of sand, looking north toward a little cluster of smoldering cottonwoods that had once sheltered the walls of the Alamo Mission. For nearly two weeks, his overwhelming forces had battered at the small band of Texans and Americans. For nearly two weeks every attack had been thrown back—until now the plain between the Mexican camp and the little mission was strewn with the trappings of unsettled battle.

"Once more," Santa Anna breathed to the officer at his side. "Once more we must try it."

"But five hundred of our men have died already, President."

"What is five hundred when seven times that number still ride with us? Prepare for another attack."

And he stood there, alone, searching the horizon with his glass, swinging it from time to time back toward the shell-scarred walls of the Alamo Mission, searching for any sign of movement. Presently the officer, Juan, returned to his side.

"Yes, Juan?"

"I have passed the orders, President."

"Very good."

"But a single rider has come in from the south. . . ."

"A rider?" Santa Anna wheeled around, turning his glass toward the camp. "A messenger from Mexico City, perhaps?"

"No, President." Juan shook his head. "He is an old man—though he rides well. He wishes to speak with you."

"Very well. Bring him to me. But be ready to ride."

And presently, a little old man came slowly up the path to the place where Santa Anna stood. A short man, with a face that still seemed to retain some of the shrewdness of youth, combined now with some uncertain wisdom of age.

"Good day, great Santa Anna," the old man spoke. "How does the battle progress?" His words were an odd sort of Spanish, tempered with an accent that might have been French.

"Who are you, old man?" Santa Anna asked. "And whatever brings you to this settlement of San Antonio, before the mission of the Alamo?"

"Word reached me of your difficulties, great general. I only thought to offer my assistance."

Santa Anna smiled, revealing a crooked row of yellow teeth. "Your fighting days are over, old man. The battle today is for the younger."

But the old man stretched out a hand in protest. "I am but sixty-seven years of age, and can still ride a horse with the best of your men."

"What is one more man to me?" Santa Anna asked.

"But I can win you the battle," the little man insisted.

"You are a soldier?"

"I fought in Europe in my younger days. Many great battles!"

Santa Anna nodded. "Some day the history books will remember this as a great battle, also."

The old man took the glass from his hands and peered through it toward the cluster of cottonwoods. "That is the Alamo Mission?"

"Correct," Santa Anna replied. "My objective since February twenty-third. Only now it is more a fort than a mission."

"How many men do they have?"

"Less than two hundred, I'm sure. And with them are men like Travis, Bowie, and Crockett. If I could wipe them off the map at a single stroke, there would be no more trouble with this idea of Texas independence."

The old man dropped the glass from his eye. "I will get it for you. Draw me a map in the sand to show me the layout of the mission. Quickly."

"Well," Santa Anna began, "here are the walls . . ." He sketched quickly with his sword, somehow catching the eagerness of the old man at his side. ". . . and here is an old convent, with a courtyard. And a small hospital, and a chapel. . . ."

"I see. . . . Very well. How many men do you have?"

"Thirty-five hundred. But it's those walls—those confounded walls!"

"You have tried to scale them?"

"We have tried everything. For two weeks . . ."

"But you have cannon."

"A few. More than the defenders, certainly."

"But you have been firing into the mission rather than at the walls! That was your trouble!"

"And what would you suggest?" Santa Anna queried.

"Direct all your cannons at a single point," he said. "Breach the wall and pour your overwhelming forces through the hole."

Santa Anna listened, his eyes glued to the gems as the old man's hands manipulated the snuff. "Will you ride with me?"

"But a moment ago, you thought me too old."

"Never fear. Will you ride with me?"

"How far, Santa Anna?"

"Across all of Texas."

The old man's eyes glistened. "I will ride further. I will ride with you into Washington itself, where ten years from this date you will be emperor of all the continent."

"Then we ride! Jose," he shouted, "prepare the cannon for firing. . . ."

And the air was filled with smoke and fire and screaming, roaring death, and soon the walls of the Alamo Mission trembled and shivered.

"We ride," Santa Anna shouted. "Jose, order a full attack. The horsemen and then the foot soldiers."

"This is the last attack?"

"The last attack, Jose! The wall is breached. . . ."

And at his side, the old man wheeled his white horse high into the air. "Pass the word, Santa Anna. Not a defender must remain alive. We must wipe them out, to bring all of Texas to its knees. . . ."

And Santa Anna passed the word. . . . And then they were thundering across the plain, past the deserted dirt roads, past the crumbling cottonwoods, toward the breach in the Alamo wall. . . .

"I feel victory in my bones," Santa Anna shouted to the man at his side. "This is my day."

The old man produced a dainty jeweled snuffbox, encrusted with a glittering single letter N. Santa Anna wondered where he had gotten it. Then the old man spurred his great horse forward. "Victory, as long as we ride together. This time, I will make no mistake. This time, there will be no Waterloo."

BARBARA GALLOW *is an actress, writer and announcer for a popular New England radio station. Currently at work on a major fantasy novel, she has a gift for quietly incisive character observation that makes* Jane *both sardonic and touching. Original in its setting and loosely based on a true story,* Jane *is one of the gentler tales in this collection, but its muted ironies make it truly haunting.* . . .

Jane
by Barbara Gallow

If you ask me, the only interesting thing about WBZR-FM is our location. The music is formula album rock, but we're housed in a Victorian Gothic nightmare that's right out of a Charles Addams cartoon. It's a twenty-room, chocolate-brown shingle, former Great Estate (or so the local historical society keeps reminding us whenever we suggest knocking down a few hallowed walls to enlarge our studios) with domed turrets, wrought-iron widow's walks, enough black-oak woodwork to fill a dozen funeral parlors and a front-hall fireplace with some copper relief work that looks like the mouth of Hell. There are also a pair of hand-painted and stained-glass windows (depicting Great Ancestors) that are corny, but pretty. When the light is right, they cast rainbows on the paneled hallway.

It's a pretty strange place to locate a radio station, but then our owners are pretty strange themselves—a couple of zonked-out former hippies who went straight, hit it rich in the communications business and decided that a decaying (and consequently low-rent) mansion was a "far out" place for their latest venture, WBZR-FM, Stereo Album Rock. Or, in announcer hype, "Bi-*zarrre* Radio!" I'm told the owners came up with the call letters because they thought this house was so bizarre. Actually, it's our *music* that's bizarre. Not to mention our listeners.

My last gig was evening deejay with a Beautiful Music station in Brookline, Mass. When the beautiful music put me to sleep and I snored through a newscast, a weather report and two commercials, the program director suggested that I might not be ideally suited to their format; so I came to WBZR—weekends, eight-to-four, weekdays, whenever someone is sick, hung over or too stoned to go on. Actually, there isn't much difference between working for a BM station and an album rock station. Both of them play music for most of the hour and all the announcer has to do is come on a few times to give the news and weather, keep the commercials running, and remind the listeners what station they're tuned to. The main difference is that at WBZR I have to sound mellowed-out and into the music.

I like working weekends. Nobody else is around, I get to read a lot, drink a few dozen cups of coffee without anyone telling me how lousy it is for me, and play with Herman, my Labrador and the Eastern States K-9 frisbee champion. Or, rather, I *try* to play with Herman. Mostly he sacks out in front of the studio fireplace (one fireplace in every room, all different, none working) and chews his frisbee. I tried some light practice tosses, but quit that when he nearly went through one of the stained-glass windows on the second-floor landing. I'd hate like Hell to smash the only decent-looking thing in this building.

The one thing I *don't* do is listen to the music. Most of the other announcers sit in the booth with their headphones on, gettin' down; personally, I'd rather listen to a trash-masher than an entire album of New Wave rock. So I usually turn the studio monitors down, put my feet up on the console and stare out the window, watching the neighborhood winos take naps in the street. Sometimes I bring in my portable TV and watch ballgames or old movies. I was suffering through about my fifteenth viewing of *Demetrius and the Gladiators* when I met Jane.

Victor Mature was just being set up for the kill by the evil Messalina when Herman barked and nearly sent me through the ceiling. Normally, Herman's lethargy can only be shaken by the words "food," "frisbee" or "French poodles," but now he was growling in the direction of the outer hall, hackles up.

I couldn't remember if I had locked the front door or not. Technically, we're supposed to leave it open so any of our admiring listeners can stop by and make themselves at home (which they usually do by staring at the giant copper fireplace and the stained glass and breathing, "Oh wow, far out. Hey, you givin' away any tee shirts this week?"), but when I'm alone I prefer it locked. Once I left it open and the PM announcer walked in to find a wino passed out in the entryway.

I flipped off *Demetrius* and gave Herman an encouraging nudge.

"Go see who's out there, boy."

Herman, for all his ninety pounds of frisbee-conditioned muscle, is essentially a coward and he seemed a lot more content to stand in the doorway barking than to go into the hall. At last he ventured out and got about as far as the middle of the steps (I figured. Since I'm also essentially a coward I wasn't about to leave the studio to find out) when his barking faded into a sort of whimpering, and then nothing. Next thing, he was walking complacently back into the studio with a giant Milk-Bone in his mouth.

I stopped staring at him when I heard the scratching sound of a diamond stylus across paper and realized that I was now treating my audience to dead air. I snapped off the turntable pot and flipped up the announcer mike, "Now that was the latest chart-buster by (quick check of the label) 'Blondie,' my friends. Randy King here with you all afternoon at *double*-you, *beee, zeee, aarrr!* It is cold outside—just forty-three mean ones—and Uncle Jack in the weather center says keep your eyes peeled for some white stuff! But right now I have a little music to warm you up—Fleetwood Mac." It wasn't at all the right disc to follow "Blondie," but it was the first one I picked up, and I nearly dropped it when I saw the girl.

She was standing in the studio doorway watching me, smiling a little. At first glance, I guessed her to be about twenty; she was bundled up in a long, fur-trimmed coat and most of her hair (blonde and curly-looking) was hidden under a wide-brimmed hat with a feather. Her cheeks were rosy from the cold and she had big, round blue eyes.

And all I could think to say was, "I guess the door wasn't locked, huh?"

She smiled. "I guess it wasn't," she said in a soft, high voice, almost like a little girl's.

And my next question, equally brilliant, was, "Do you carry Milk-Bones around with you?"

She looked a little hurt. "There was a box of them sitting on the desk downstairs. I hope you don't mind. Your dog and I are friends—now."

Considering that most visitors to our station would be more likely to give Herman a swig of Colt 44 than a dog biscuit, I couldn't very well mind. And I like blondes.

I hoped the girl was an announcer (and particularly a Randy King) groupie, even though she looked too classy, but she was looking in mild distaste from me in my Schroeder sweatshirt and old jeans to the studio itself, taking in the albums stacked in the built-in bookcases, the posters of rock stars taped haphazardly on the walls, the empty soda bottles and plastic cupholders lined up along the fireplace mantle, the cigarette ashes ground into the cream shag rug.

"Is it always this . . . untidy?" she asked.

"Uh, it gets kind of messy on weekends," I apologized. "No cleaning crew till Tuesday."

"I love this house," she said abruptly, still in that sweet, little girl's voice. "I hate to see"—she gestured vaguely—"bad things happen to it."

I had the feeling that by "bad things" she meant WBZR in general, not just the bottles and ashes. Then she smiled at me, showing a set of matched dimples on each cheek.

"What must you think of me? Barging in here uninvited, taking dog biscuits and then criticizing your housekeeping? I haven't even said any of the polite things a visitor *ought* to say. You must think I'm very pushy and more than a little rude."

"No, I don't think you're rude at all," I said hastily. "I think you're just being honest. (Where do I dig up these wonderful snippets of repartee?) But, go ahead and say a few polite lies about me and the station anyway."

At this she laughed. "To be, as you say, honest, I don't know very much about the sort of music you play, but it doesn't seem very *tuneful*."

I couldn't have agreed more.

"But I know who you are. You're Randy King. I think you have a very pleasant voice."

So maybe she was a King groupie after all!

"You know me, but I don't know you," I said, trying to sound pleasant. "What's your name?"

"Jane. Plain Jane."

Jane, maybe, but definitely not plain. When she smiled she showed a perfect set of small white teeth and her blue eyes were sparkly and a little mischievous. Add to that, her nose turned up on the end and her hair *was* curly, although I couldn't tell the length because she still wore her hat. Also, as she neared me I could see she was a little older than I had first thought, despite the little kid voice—but I've nothing against women over twenty-five.

I had the strange feeling that I'd seen her before and then I thought back to her remark about loving this house.

"This isn't your first visit to the station, is it?"

"No, not nearly!" she laughed lightly. "Although I don't appear here as often as I used to. I make the others uncomfortable."

I could see why. They aren't used to seeing straight, sober visitors around here.

"You see, this is my house," she continued, very softly.

"Your house?" I asked stupidly.

"I was born and raised here," Jane said, a little sadly. "And I thought I would never leave."

"Then why *did* you?" The question just sort of slipped out. Jane gave me a strange, brief look, as though deciding how to proceed. "If it had been up to me this would still be my house and not a radio station. But of course it wasn't up to me." She flashed another of her quick smiles. "Not that I didn't try."

I smiled back, trying to picture little Jane (she wasn't very tall) fighting lawyers and corporate hotshots and maybe her parents, for all I knew, to keep from being evicted from her home. Although her family probably had a condominium in the suburbs right now.

I turned up the studio monitor for a second, to check the progress of the record and the sound of Fleetwood filled the room. Jane shook her head.

"To think, here you are sending music over the airwaves for everyone to hear and Mama once yelled at me for whistling out the window."

I laughed at that; I like anyone with a good sense of the ridiculous. Jane continued to check out the studio, as if she still couldn't believe that her old house had come to *this*.

"This was my bedroom."

"*Here?*" No wonder she was bugged about the mess.

"I had a pink room. I would have preferred brown, but Mama said pink was the proper color for girls, so . . ." She spread her hands helplessly. Her mother sounded like a candidate for the Long Live Queen Victoria Society. "My bed was on that wall, facing the fireplace. How I loved a fire on days like these! And I had a bureau and vanity over there and pictures on the walls, too, but not like *those*." Jane wrinkled her nose at the posters.

"What about the other rooms?" I didn't care all that much, but I wanted to keep her talking. When she reminisced about this old place her eyes looked even bluer and her cheeks flushed and this is corny as all Hell but I felt like a twelve-year-old with a crush.

"That big room with all the desks used to be my parents' bedroom, and the little room next to this (she meant the production studio) belonged to my brother Edward, and after . . ." she paused abruptly and made a dismissing gesture with her hand. "Well, what's past is past, I believe the saying goes," she said in a brisk voice. I think she got herself kind of shook up thinking about the good old days, because she suddenly seemed kind of flustered, as if she'd said something she shouldn't.

My experience with women is such that I can spot that "time for an exit" look a mile away, so I flipped over the Fleetwood disc (completely ignoring the fact that I was supposed to do a break; the audience prefers its music uninterrupted anyway) and plunged right in.

"I get off in an hour."

"Excuse me?"

Jane was definitely not a King groupie or she'd have picked up the cue. "I get off work in an hour, if you'd like to go out for a drink or something . . ." and I never saw such a look of total disbelief in my life.

"You want me to *go* somewhere with you?" she asked, just to rub in the absurdity of it, I figured. "But I *can't!*"

That gave me a little hope. Maybe she had a boyfriend who'd kill her (or me) if he caught her fooling around with another man. She's just the sort of woman who brings out the macho protector spirit.

"I'm not making a play or anything," I lied. "I'd just like to see you again."

"You would? Really?" Jane seemed genuinely pleased. "I'd like that. Truly." She had a conspirator's gleam in her eye that was cute as hell. "I could come here again and visit. But not weekdays; it's too . . . crowded then."

Nothing could have suited me better. "Next week then?" I asked, trying not to pant. "Same time, same station—excuse the pun."

She nodded eagerly. "But I have to go now," she half-whispered, sort of drifting back towards the door.

I offered to walk her downstairs, but she laughed and said it wasn't necessary. Then she was gone and Herman and I sat looking at each other glumly. Some of the life had left the room.

Two days later, I got a call at six-thirty in the morning. The mid-morning deejay was "bummed out, you know," and wouldn't be in. So I prepared to face the full-time weekday staffers of WBZR.

After being at work about an hour, the "Have a good day" and "Hey, I hear you man," level of conversation sent me running to the coffee machine in desperate need of a fix. I hoped the pantry would be deserted, but I was out of luck: Karen Sykes, the business manager, was there ahead of me. Since some form of chitchat is obligatory at these brief meetings of the weekday and weekend staffs, I told Karen about my visit from Jane.

She gave me one long look over the top of her oversized executive eyeglasses. "I don't believe it," she said definitively.

"Why would I lie?" I said, resisting the urge to answer with the trendy, "Be-*lieve* it!" "What a sweet lady she is," I couldn't help adding, but I doubt if Karen heard me because she was busy bawling into the reception hall, "Sheila, you'll *never* believe it! *Jane* is back!"

That got a reaction. Four people jammed into the little pantry and stared at me. I felt like I was in a miniature Star Chamber.

"Wow, Jane's really back? That's far out!"

"I thought we'd scared her away for good!"

That got me. "Why the hell would you want to scare away a sweet girl like Jane? After all, this *is* her house!"

"*Was,* man. *Was* her house," said the production chief, known lovingly as Freaky Freddy. "We don't want her around here *now.*"

"You actually saw her and talked to her?" Karen asked.

"That's what I said, isn't it?" I'd about had it with these clowns.

Freaky Freddy was impressed. "Oh wow, that is far out, man. Really saw her in person. Wow. Most people only *hear* her," he tittered a little. "She likes to keep a low profile, you know?"

With these jokers around, who could blame her?

Karen was shaking her head like a doctor on a tough case. "So she's back again," she muttered.

"Yeah, and she's coming to visit me again *next* Sunday," I said with I think justifiable bravado.

This was too much for Freddy. "Oh wow, man, he's got a date with *Jane!*" And he headed for the safety of his production studio.

The others cleared out too, except for Karen. "I really can't believe this," she said.

I was getting pretty tired of that refrain. What was the big deal anyway? I couldn't help comparing Karen mentally with Jane. Or contrasting, I should say. I'm not really a chauvinist, but there was just something so much more—I can't help it—*feminine* about Jane. Almost an old-fashioned gentility. And I couldn't wait for Sunday to come, I can tell you.

For the first time in ages I dressed up to go to work. Oh not a suit and tie, but a real sharp cable-knit sweater and corduroy pants. I even gave Herman a clean frisbee to chew on.

Jane came in wearing the same coat and hat, even though it wasn't nearly as cold out. Her cheeks were just as rosy, her hair just as blonde and her eyes as blue and sparkly as I'd remembered them. She appeared in the studio doorway with a shy little smile on her face that showed all her dimples.

I was all set today, though. I had a double album on the turntable and I'd already promised my listeners that they were gonna be treated, yes indeed, to one solid hour of music, music, music. And I left the TV set at home.

And with all that I still couldn't come up with a decent opening line. "I was so afraid you weren't gonna come, today," I said.

"Oh, but I promised and I always keep my word," Jane said in that enchanting light, sweet voice. Then she giggled. "Although I must say I never used to be in the habit of making assignations with men."

Mostly we talked about ourselves, our families, schools and all that stuff that sounded so trivial coming from me and so sweet coming from her. I tried to talk politics and films and all that trendy nonsense, but Jane either didn't know or didn't care much about them. So I ended up telling her what I hadn't told anyone in a long time: that I truly intended one day to write the great American novel.

"I do *so* admire writers!" she said. "I know you'll write a good book. You're more sensitive than most." Here she paused. "That's why I'm here, you see." She turned her head away, suddenly uncomfortable.

That shy admission had more effect on me than the sexiest come-on. I think I'd have jumped off the roof at that moment if she had asked me.

"Jane, I haven't been able to get you off my mind all week. Are you sure you couldn't go out with me just once?" I wheedled.

"No!" she flared suddenly. "How can you even think it?" I just about fell off my chair. She amended quickly. "You know so little about me, Randy. Less than you think."

The thought hit me like a bolt and even as I was asking the question she was saying, "I have a husband."

Well. And well again. What did I expect? Beautiful women get snapped up pretty quickly.

"I'm sorry," she said sadly. "I ought to have told you, but I never dreamed . . ." She twisted her hands. "He isn't with me now, you see, but . . . but he wants me to join him. I haven't made up my mind." She seemed to be talking more to herself than to me.

"Stay with me!" I burst out. I've never made a declaration to a woman before.

Jane looked at me with a strange, faraway look in her eyes. "How I would like to stay *here*," she said. "But the others don't want me."

"Well who cares about the others!" I said, in near exasperation. "*I* want you. And I think you want me."

"What good company you would be!" she said passionately.

"Herman's good company, too," I added; Herman was beginning to sniff the air suspiciously. I think he can smell "involvement" and he hates to be excluded.

"Yes, it's been so long since I had a dog," she whispered quickly. She stood in front of me, smiling down from those blue eyes and very slowly reached out her hand to me.

I felt almost hypnotized, lost in her terrific eyes, and I raised my hand to hers.

My hand had nearly closed on her fingertips, when she drew her hand away quickly, almost angrily.

"What am I thinking of!" she said. "I must go."

The whole scene was moving too fast for my feeble brain to comprehend. I could have sworn she'd just offered herself to me. I hated to think she was just another tease. I guess she knew what I was thinking, because she looked at me beseechingly.

"I like you so very much, Randy. You're the first man since Andrew —my husband—that I have ever wanted to spend my . . . all of my time with. But I cannot. You aren't mine to have."

Before I could think of a rejoinder for this unlikely speech she had practically flown out the door, leaving the studio cold and still. And all I could think of was that I still didn't know her last name.

"Bradford was the family name," Karen told me on Thursday, when I went in to collect my paycheck. "I don't know what her husband's name would have been."

"*Would* have been? You talk like he's dead."

Karen laughed in a particularly superior way as she stamped her signature on my check. "Well, I should certainly think he *is*," she said. "After all, he'd be about a hundred and twenty today!"

A hundred and twenty. "And Jane," I asked tonelessly. "How old is Jane?"

Karen shrugged. "Oh I don't know how old she'd be now, but I heard she was pretty young when she died. Only in her late twenties." She thrust my paycheck at me. "Have a nice day."

I've been doing a lot of walking lately. Around this crummy neighborhood where WBZR, where the old Bradford estate, is located. And around the crummy neighborhood where I live. A hundred years ago my block didn't exist. And this neighborhood was the best in the city; of all the fine houses, the Bradford mansion was the finest. Is still. The hand-carved woodwork is as solid now as it was then. The fireplaces, of copper and rose marble and curly maple, still flame to life when the sun hits them. And the beautiful stained-glass windows send rainbows running along the walls, just like the crystal prisms in my grandmother's chandelier used to do. All of these things have been so carefully preserved by the lady of the house. The lady with whom I could gladly spend all *my* days.

"Jane? Jane, I know you're here. Come in; please come in."

It's only Saturday morning, but there's no reason to wait for Sunday afternoon now. I think I feel the way a groom must the night before a wedding.

Herman barks in greeting, and Jane is standing in the doorway, her feather hat in her hands. Her curly blonde hair falls halfway down her back and I can't wait to run my fingers through it.

"I was afraid you wouldn't come back after last week," I tell her. "But it's okay, now."

"Yes," she says, in her little girl's voice. "Now you know."

"Now I know," I say with a grin.

Jane smiles sadly. "So now you know why I must leave."

I stare at her. "What?"

She nods. "I've been so very foolish."

"What do you mean, leave? This is your *home*."

"Not any more," she says gazing around wistfully. "My time has passed. This house belongs to the living." She says the last word very pointedly and fixes me with a blue-eyed gaze.

I get out of my chair and go to her. "This house belongs to *you* . . . and to me." I reach out for her.

She steps backward and shakes her head. "You mustn't touch me, don't you see?"

"Yes I *do* see and . . . and I *want* you. I want to be with you forever. That's all I care about." She starts to speak, but I don't let her. "Look, Jane, I've always loved you a little. Even before I really met you; I know that now."

"Yes, I know," she says. "That's why I let you see me. But that was a mistake." Her voice drops to a whisper. "I am very fond of you, Randy."

"Then take my hand."

"I can't do that—not to you and not to me." She adds lightly, "After all, I could not bear to have you tire of me and my house after fifty years or so."

"Jane—"

"I'm going to join Andrew now, as I should have done years ago"—she is drifting away from my outstretched hand—"and you must stay where *you* belong."

She disappears into the hall and I follow, Herman at my heels.

The hall is empty.

But Jane is still there, with the sunlight shining on her curly yellow hair, red cheeks and sparkling blue eyes, gazing at me from the hand-painted, stained-glass window at the top of the second-floor landing.

And I hear, a whisper inside my head, "Take care of my house for me, Randy."

To most readers, WASHINGTON IRVING, *born in New York in 1783, is merely the author of* "Rip Van Winkle" *and* "The Legend of Sleepy Hollow," *but though those tales have justly become folk classics, the rest of Irving's work is worthy of a revival of interest, richly endowed as it is with fascinating travel notes of a bygone England that Irving's* Sketch Book *makes one long to revisit—as well as several excellent early American examples of fantasy literature. One such is the following Grand Guignol-esque nightmare, also known as* "The Tale of the German Student."

The Tale of the German Student
by Washington Irving

On a stormy night, in the tempestuous times of the French Revolution, a young German was returning to his lodgings, at a late hour, across the old part of Paris. The lightning gleamed, and the loud claps of thunder rattled through the lofty narrow streets—but I should first tell you something about this young German.

Gottfried Wolfgang was a young man of good family. He had studied for some time at Gottingen, but being of a visionary and enthusiastic character, he had wandered into those wild and speculative doctrines which have so often bewildered German students. His secluded life, his intense application, and the singular nature of his studies, had an effect on both mind and body. His health was impaired; his imagination diseased. He had been indulging in fanciful speculations on spiritual essences, until, like Swedenborg, he had an ideal world of his own around him. He took up a notion, I do not know from what cause, that there was an evil influence hanging over him; an evil genius or spirit seeking to ensnare him and insure his perdition. Such an idea working on his melancholy temperament produced the most gloomy effects. He became haggard and desponding. His friends discovered the mental malady preying upon him, and determined that the best cure was a change of scene; he was sent, therefore, to finish his studies amidst the splendors and gayeties of Paris.

Wolfgang arrived in Paris at the breaking out of the Revolution. The popular delirium at first caught his enthusiastic mind, and he was captivated by the political and philosophical theories of the day, but the scenes of blood which followed shocked his sensitive nature, disgusted him with society and the world, and made him more than ever a recluse.

He shut himself up in a solitary apartment in the Pays Latin, the quarter of students. There, in a gloomy street not far from the monastic walls of the Sorbonne, he pursued his favorite speculations. Sometimes he spent hours in the great libraries of Paris, those catacombs of departed authors, rummaging among their hoards of dusty and obsolete works in quest of food for his unhealthy appetite. He was, in a manner, a literary ghoul, feeding in the charnel-house of decayed literature.

Wolfgang, though solitary and recluse, was of an ardent temperament, but for a time it operated merely upon his imagination. He was too shy and ignorant of the world to make any advances to the fair, but he was a passionate admirer of female beauty, and in his lonely chamber would often lose himself in reveries on forms and faces which he had seen, and his fancy would deck out images of loveliness far surpassing the reality.

While his mind was in this excited and sublimated state, a dream produced an extraordinary effect upon him. It was of a female face of transcendent beauty. So strong was the impression made, that he dreamed of it again and again. It haunted his thoughts by day, his slumbers by night; in fine, he became passionately enamored of his shadow of a dream. This lasted so long that it became one of those fixed ideas which haunt the minds of melancholy men, and are at times mistaken for madness.

Such was Gottfried Wolfgang, and such his situation at the time I mentioned. He was returning home late one stormy night, through some of the old and gloomy streets of the Marais, the ancient part of Paris. The loud claps of thunder rattled among the high houses of the narrow streets. He came to the Place de la Greve, the square where public executions are performed. The lightning quivered about the pinnacles of the ancient Hotel de Ville, and shed flickering gleams over the open space in front. As Wolfgang was crossing the square, he shrank back with horror at finding himself close by the guillotine. It was the height of the Reign of Terror (when this dreadful instrument of death stood ever ready, and its scaffold was continually running with the blood of the virtuous and the brave. It had that very day been actively employed in the work of carnage, and there it stood in grim array, amidst a silent and sleeping city, waiting for fresh victims.

Wolfgang's heart sickened within him, and he was turning shuddering from the horrible engine, when he beheld a shadowy form, cowering as it were at the foot of the steps which led up to the scaffold. A succession of vivid flashes of lightning revealed it more distinctly. It was a female figure, dressed in black. She was seated on one of the lower steps of the scaffold, leaning forward, her face hid in her lap; and her long disheveled tresses hanging to the ground, streaming with the rain which fell in torrents. Wolfgang paused. There was something awful in this solitary monument of woe. The female had the appearance of being above the common order. He knew the times to be full of vicissitude, and that many a fair head, which had been pillowed on down, now wandered houseless. Perhaps this was some poor mourner whom the dreadful ax had rendered desolate, and who sat here heartbroken on the strand of existence, from which all that was dear to her had been launched into eternity.

He approached, and addressed her in the accents of sympathy. She raised her head and gazed wildly at him. What was his astonishment at beholding, by the bright glare of the lightning, the very face which had haunted him in his dreams. It was pale and disconsolate, but ravishingly beautiful.

Trembling with violent and conflicting emotions, Wolfgang again accosted her. He spoke something of her being exposed at such an hour of the night, and to the fury of such a storm, and offered to conduct her to her friends. She pointed to the guillotine with a gesture of dreadful signification.

"I have no friend on earth," said she.

"But you have a home," said Wolfgang.

"Yes—in the grave!"

The heart of the student melted at the words.

"If a stranger dare make an offer," said he, "without danger of being misunderstood, I would offer my humble dwelling as a shelter; myself as a devoted friend. I am friendless myself in Paris, and a stranger in the land; but if my life could be of service, it is at your disposal, and should be sacrificed before harm or indignity should come to you."

There was an honest earnestness in the young man's manner that had its effect. His foreign accent, too, was in his favor; it showed him not to be a hackneyed inhabitant of Paris. Indeed, there is an eloquence in true enthusiasm that is not to be doubted. The homeless stranger confided herself implicitly to the protection of the student.

He supported her faltering steps across the Pont Neuf, and by the place where the statue of Henry the Fourth had been overthrown by the populace. The storm had abated, and the thunder rumbled at a distance. All Paris was quiet; that great volcano of human passion slumbered for a while, to gather fresh strength for the next day's eruption. The student conducted his charge through the ancient streets of the Pays Latin, and by the dusky walls of the Sorbonne, to the great dingy hotel which he inhabited. The old portress who admitted them stared with surprise at the unusual sight of the melancholy Wolfgang with a female companion.

On entering his apartment, the student, for the first time, blushed at the scantiness and indifference of his dwelling. He had but one chamber —an old-fashioned salon—heavily carved, and fantastically furnished with the remains· of former magnificence, for it was of those hotels in the quarter of the Luxembourg Palace which had once belonged to nobility. It was lumbered with books and papers, and all the usual apparatus of a student, and his bed stood in a recess at one end.

When lights were brought, and Wolfgang had a better opportunity of contemplating the stranger, he was more than ever intoxicated by her beauty. Her face was pale, but of a dazzling fairness, set off by a profusion of raven hair that hung clustering about it. Her eyes were large and brilliant, with a singular expression approaching almost to wildness. As far as her black dress permitted her shape to be seen, it was of perfect symmetry. Her whole appearance was highly striking, though she was dressed in the simplest style. The only thing approaching to an ornament which she wore, was a broad black band round her neck, clasped by diamonds.

The perplexity now commenced with the student how to dispose of the helpless being thus thrown upon his protection. He thought of abandoning his chamber to her, and seeking shelter for himself elsewhere. Still he was so fascinated by her charms, there seemed to be such a spell upon his thoughts and senses, that he could not tear himself from her presence. Her manner, too, was singular and unaccountable. She spoke no more of the guillotine. Her grief had abated. The attentions of the student had first won her confidence, and then, apparently, her heart. She was evidently an enthusiast like himself, and enthusiasts soon understand each other.

In the infatuation of the moment, Wolfgang avowed his passion for her. He told her the story of his mysterious dream, and how she had possessed his heart before he had even seen her. She was strangely affected by his recital, and acknowledged to have felt an impulse toward him equally unaccountable. It was the time for wild theory and wild actions. Old prejudices and superstitions were done away; everything was under the sway of the "Goddess of Reason." Among other rubbish of the old times, the forms and ceremonies of marriage began to be considered superfluous bonds for honorable minds. Social compacts were the vogue. Wolfgang was too much of a theorist not to be tainted by the liberal doctrines of the day.

"Why should we separate?" said he. "Our hearts are united; in the eye of reason and honor we are as one. What need is there of sordid forms to bind high souls together?"

The stranger listened with emotion; she had evidently received illumination at the same school.

"You have no home nor family," continued he; "let me be everything to you, or rather let us be everything to one another. If form is necessary, form shall be observed—there is my hand. I pledge myself to you forever."

"Forever?" said the stranger, solemnly.

"Forever!" repeated Wolfgang.

The stranger clasped the hand extended to her. "Then I am yours," murmured she, and sank upon his bosom.

The next morning the student left his bride sleeping, and sallied forth at an early hour to seek more spacious apartments, suitable to the change in his situation. When he returned, he found the stranger lying with her head hanging over the bed, and one arm thrown over it. He spoke to her, but received no reply. He advanced to awaken her from her uneasy posture. On taking her hand, it was cold—there was no pulsation—her face was pallid and ghastly—in a word, she was a corpse.

Horrified and frantic, he alarmed the house. A scene of confusion ensued. The police were summoned.

As the officer of police entered the room, he started back on beholding the corpse.

"Great heaven!" cried he; "how did this woman come here?"

"Do you know anything about her?" said Wolfgang eagerly.

"Do I?" exclaimed the police officer; "she was guillotined yesterday."

He stepped forward, undid the black collar round the neck of the corpse, and the head rolled on the floor!

The student burst into a frenzy. "The fiend! The fiend has gained possession of me!" shrieked he; "I am lost forever."

They tried to soothe him, but in vain. He was possessed with the frightful belief that an evil spirit had reanimated the dead body to ensnare him. He went distracted, and died in a madhouse.

When the great supernatural periodical, Weird Tales, *went out of business, an enormous void opened in American fantasy publishing. But in the 1960s, Robert A. (Doc) Lowndes made a brave effort to recapture the* Weird Tales *spirit with his short-lived* Magazine of Horror. *"Doorslammer" is one of the more evanescent tales to derive from an early issue of MOH, but it has a way of sticking with one when more garish stories have faded from memory.* DONALD A. WOLLHEIM *heads up the science fiction paperback house, DAW Books, and is especially distinguished for having edited what is presumed to be the very first science fiction anthology in U.S. publishing history,* The Pocket Book of Science Fiction *(1943).*

Doorslammer
by Donald A. Wollheim

From somewhere down the darkened hall a door slammed.

I looked up from my papers, looked at Mr. Wilkins questioningly. It was ten-thirty at night and I had supposed we were alone in the office, probably alone in the whole gigantic office building.

"The cleaning woman come back?" I queried. She had been in an hour ago, dusting and mopping and emptying the waste baskets. It was a disturbance and a distraction. We wanted to get the books straightened out and we needed peace and quiet to do it.

Wilkins shook his head. "It was nothing. Let's get on with this."

I frowned, annoyed, went back to my ledgers. I finished four more pages, saw that the work was finished on this book. It wasn't going to be such a long job at that. I'd figured on being at the office until maybe one in the morning. I leaned back, looked up.

Wilkins looked up just then, caught my eye, smiled a bit. I saw he'd probably realized just how close we were to being through.

"I'm done with this one," I said. "Going to stretch my legs a bit." He watched me, said nothing. I got up, walked over to the water cooler at the door, took a drink, looked out into the dark corridor leading towards the editorial offices. I couldn't see what door had slammed. They were all shut, all the little cubbyholes at the far end, the ones with the view of the river from twenty stories up, the best offices reserved for the sensitive souls in Editorial—with the big brains and the lowest salaries.

I walked down the hall towards that end. It was dark and deserted, and there were no lights behind the chilled glass windows of the doors.

It's eerie in an office building after hours, darned eerie. I came back. Wilkins had finished his ledger, was leaning back, lighting a cigarette.

"Nobody there," I said. "But somebody slammed a door before. I heard it. And there's no drafts."

He nodded soberly. "I know. I heard it too. Often hear it late at night like this. It's nobody. Only Alice."

"Alice?" I asked. "Thought you said we were alone. Is Alice the cleaning woman's name?"

He shook his head. "No, not Mrs. Flaherty. Just Alice . . . You remember."

I sat down. "Who're you kidding? I don't remember any Alice."

Wilkins looked at me, took his cigarette out of his mouth. "Oh, that's right. You never knew her. You came after her time. Well . . . it's Alice, anyway. Alice Kingsley, I think was her name. Alice C. Kingsley. Mrs."

"So?" I said. "So this Alice is working here tonight. Why doesn't she come in and say hello? One of those stuck-up editors?"

"Alice isn't working here tonight," said Wilkins mildly. "She hasn't been working here for a couple of years. Not here. Not nowhere."

"So who are you talking about?" I asked, beginning to get a little piqued. "First you say Alice, then no—so what Alice is here now?"

"I don't know," he said. "I really don't know for sure. We just think it's Alice. I mean the Kingsley girl. She was a knockout too. A real looker."

For a moment he looked dreamy, as if thinking of some girl he'd maybe had an infatuation for. I could have knocked him on the head. "What are you handing me? Make sense, man. You're a hell of an accountant, sitting there like a goof dreaming of some girl."

He wasn't offended. "Yeah, I guess so. But Alice got us all that way. She was . . . well, you just couldn't look at her without thinking of blue skies and green fields, of Spring mornings and college campuses. She didn't belong in a city office. She was . . . well, she looked like a kid fresh from some rah-rah field."

"Uh huh," I said. "Does your wife know about the way you feel about this chick?"

"Ahh," he shook his head, "you won't believe it, but she wouldn't mind. Alice was that way. She was out of this world—I mean the big-city world. The women didn't seem to object to her. Somehow she just didn't seem to compete. She was in love, you see, and offered no rivalry. She was also nuts."

"Boy, what a picture you're building up. Sweet innocence, a knock-out, lovely, but nuts. Come down to Earth, man." I sat down myself, glanced out at the dark corridor back over my shoulder.

He went on again, this time paying no attention to me, just talking.

"Alice was hired as an assistant editor to the short story department. She was fresh from college, somewhere in the Midwest, and she never lost that look. You don't find it often. She had the blackest hair and the fairest skin, and the brightest, shiniest eyes you ever saw.

"She was like a kid in many ways. Never seemed to have any mind for other folks. She was a door slammer. I remember a big fight she had the first week she was here. Slammed the door going out of Miss Burn-side's office and boy, did that queen bee get sore. You know what a touchy old bat the boss' secretary is. You should have heard her give Alice the mouth. And Alice didn't answer back. Just looked at her like a child of twelve would look, sort of wide-eyed and wondering what kind of curious animal this was. Afterwards, Alice only remarked that Miss Burnside must be crazy.

"Fact is, we got to thinking that it wasn't Burnsy that was cracked. Alice just never learned some things. She'd step on people's toes and expect them to pardon her like they'd forgive a pretty brat. It took a while for us to learn. She never stopped slamming doors. Got so we all knew when she was around.

"You should have seen the fellows try to date up Alice. Not one of them got to first base. She just seemed so darned innocent and starry that nothing impressed her. Later, we found out why. She was married, you see. Still loved her husband. He was some fellow she'd met in col-lege, married there.

"We envied him until we found out that one day he'd run off, just skipped out, vanished. That was the day Alice graduated. She came home with her diploma, in that college town to the boarding house they were living in, and he'd gone. Left no notice, just went. Quit.

"Alice went home to her folks—I think they're Des Moines people—threw a wingding, was laid up, left town, came to New York, got a job. Here. She was brilliant, but there was always something . . .

"It's hard to explain to a fellow who never saw her. You'd be amazed at what she could get away with. None of her bosses—the men that is—could get mad at her. She did her work too well for that, yet she never seemed to be present in spirit. I think they were afraid she'd quit if they pressed her too hard to learn some manners. Having her around was a pleasure—just to see that Springlike air. You don't find it around the city, you just don't.

"But there was something else, though. I remember once going down in the elevator with her, and with Joe Simpkins, her boss, the short story editor, you know. She never said goodnight to us, just brushed past and walked off down the street, her brow a little puzzled as if wondering herself what she was doing here away from the green fields. Joe and I walked a block watching her, and then Joe turned to me and said, 'You know, I keep saying to myself that Alice is as nutty as fruit cake. I keep thinking it every once in a while. It sort of bothers me.'

"I knew what he meant, too. Exactly what he meant. Anyway, Alice was with the firm about six months and everybody loved her and everybody knew when you heard a door slam, it was just Alice going somewhere.

"Miss Burnside never forgave her. They had another fight one afternoon and Burnsy gave it to her good. Told her she should wake up and stop acting like a spoiled brat. Burnsy said something else, too. Said she could understand how her husband would walk out on her."

Wilkins stopped, frowned to himself in thought, lit another cigarette. "Alice took it from her without really listening, her usual trick. But the next day it seemed to bother her, because she actually took to closing doors gently. It amazed us all.

"And then one morning, about eleven, the door slammed—violently. Alice was off again, we thought, but we didn't know the whole of it.

"Joe Simpkins told us at lunchtime. He said Alice was very upset. It seems she'd read a manuscript that morning, some short story in the mail unsolicited pile. Something about a guy that fell in love only to find a mirage. Typical college young-love sort of yarn. We saw afterwards who wrote it. Some fellow in California. Last name was Kingsley.

"Alice didn't do much work that afternoon. Just seemed to forget every now and then and sort of visit. She'd drop in on the other readers, sort of stand around vacantly, just sort of dreamy, then breeze out, slamming the door behind her. We were getting real sore after an afternoon of that and Joe swore if she didn't stop it, he'd have to do something. Maybe get rid of her, fire her. Good as she was, he couldn't have people being disrupted.

"He didn't have to fire her though. The door of her own office slammed around four o'clock. When it was half past five and the other girls were leaving, someone looked in and her office was empty and the window open.

"Yeah, it was in the papers. There was quite a funeral, too. She had quite a mob of young fellows there. Nobody ever suspected them, but I think they couldn't help themselves. She was a sort of dream, a dream of sun and fleecy white clouds such as you somehow don't get with city girls. I didn't go myself. They kept the coffin closed.

"Anyway, that was two years ago. Alice made an impression on people that lasted. Nobody that knew her can ever quite get over her. And maybe things feel the same way. We got door trouble in this office, late at night or on quiet afternoons. Nobody pays any attention to it any more."

I looked at him, thinking to myself that he was really going in the deep end. You wouldn't believe he could be such a matter-of-fact, adding and subtracting machine accountant. There was something in his eyes, something perplexed, lit up and yet maybe a little pained.

"Well, enough of this. Let's get this work cleaned up. I want to get home tonight." Wilkins shoved another ledger at me, opened up the other remaining one, and we bent over our tasks again.

Somewhere down the hall a door slammed. I looked up, caught Wilkins' eye. He shrugged.

"It's nothing. Just Alice."

When M. G. Lewis wrote the famous Gothic horror novel, The Monk, *the literary hacks of the day were swift to leap on the bandwagon and grind out innumerable imitations. Here is one of the better examples, a c. 1798 ghostly scene in a crypt which, like the Lewis original, dares to suggest the apostles of Church may be less than holy. The theme may be viewed as part of the logical process of spiritual redefinition that began long before the Renaissance and is raging in today's world.*

The Monk of Horror
or The Conclave of Corpses

Anonymous

Some three hundred years since, when the convent of Kreutzberg was in its glory, one of the monks who dwelt therein, wishing to ascertain something of the hereafter of those whose bodies lay all undecayed in the cemetery, visited it alone in the dead of night for the purpose of prosecuting his inquiries on that fearful subject. As he opened the trap-door of the vault a light burst from below; but deeming it to be only the lamp of the sacristan, the monk drew back and awaited his departure concealed behind the high altar. The sacristan emerged not, however, from the opening; and the monk, tired of waiting, approached, and finally descended the rugged steps which led into the dreary depths. No sooner had he set foot on the lower-most stair, than the well-known scene underwent a complete transformation in his eyes. He had long been accustomed to visit the vault, and whenever the sacristan went thither, he was almost sure to be with him. He therefore knew every part of it as well as he did the interior of his own narrow cell, and the arrangement of its contents was perfectly familiar to his eyes. What, then, was his horror to perceive that this arrangement, which even but that morning had come under his observation as usual, was altogether altered, and a new and wonderful one substituted in its stead.

A dim lurid light pervaded the desolate abode of darkness, and it just sufficed to give to his view a sight of the most singular description.

On each side of him the dead but imperishable bodies of the long-buried brothers of the convent sat erect in their lidless coffins, their cold, starry eyes glaring at him with lifeless rigidity, their withered fingers locked together on their breasts, their stiffened limbs motionless and still. It was a sight to petrify the stoutest heart; and the monk's quailed before it, though he was a philosopher, and a sceptic to boot. At the upper end of the vault, at a rude table formed of a decayed coffin, or something which once served the same purpose, sat three monks. They were the oldest corpses in the charnel-house, for the inquisitive brother knew their faces well; and the cadaverous hue of their cheeks seemed still more cadaverous in the dim light shed upon them, while their hollow eyes gave forth what looked to him like flashes of flame. A large book lay open before one of them, and the others bent over the rotten table as if in intense pain, or in deep and fixed attention. No word was said; no sound was heard; the vault was as silent as the grave, its awful tenants still as statues.

Fain would the curious monk have receded from this horrible place; fain would he have retraced his steps and sought again his cell, fain would he have shut his eyes to the fearful scene; but he could not stir from the spot, he felt rooted there; and though he once succeeded in turning his eyes to the entrance of the vault, to his infinite surprise and dismay he could not discover where it lay, nor perceive any possible means of exit. He stood thus for some time. At length the aged monk at the table beckoned him to advance. With slow tottering steps he made his way to the group, and at length stood in front of the table, while the other monks raised their heads and glanced at him with fixed, lifeless looks that froze the current of his blood. He knew not what to do; his senses were fast forsaking him; Heaven seemed to have deserted him for his incredulity. In this moment of doubt and fear he bethought him of a prayer, and as he proceeded he felt himself becoming possessed of a confidence he had before unknown. He looked on the book before him. It was a large volume, bound in black, and clasped with bands of gold, with fastenings of the same metal. It was inscribed at the top of each page.

"*Liber Obedientiae.*"

He could read no further. He then looked, first in the eyes of him before whom it lay open, and then in those of his fellows. He finally glanced around the vault on the corpses who filled every visible coffin in its dark and spacious womb. Speech came to him, and resolution to use it. He addressed himself to the awful beings in whose presence he stood, in the words of one having authority with them.

"*Pax vobis,*" 'twas thus he spake—"Peace be to ye."

"*Hic nulla pax,*" replied an aged monk, in a hollow, tremulous tone, bearing his breast the while—"Here is no peace."

He pointed to his bosom as he spoke, and the monk, casting his eye upon it, beheld his heart within surrounded by living fire, which seemed to feed on it but not consume it. He turned away in affright, but ceased not to prosecute his inquiries.

"*Pax vobis, in nomine Domini,*" he spake again—"Peace be to ye, in the name of the Lord."

"*Hic non pax,*" the hollow and heartrending tones of the ancient monk who sat at the right of the table were heard to answer.

On glancing at the bared bosom of this hapless being also the same sight was exhibited—the heart surrounded by a devouring flame, but still remaining fresh and unconsumed under its operation. Once more the monk turned away and addressed the aged man in the centre.

"*Pax vobis, in nomine Domini,*" he proceeded.

At these words the being to whom they were addressed raised his head, put forward his hand, and closing the book with a loud clap, said—

"Speak on. It is yours to ask, and mine to answer."

The monk felt reassured, and his courage rose with the occasion.

"Who are ye?" he inquired; "who may ye be?"

"We know not!" was the answer, "alas! we know not!"

"We know not, we know not!" echoed in melancholy tones the denizens of the vault.

"What do ye here?" pursued the querist.

"We await the last day, the day of the last judgement! Alas for us! woe! woe!"

"Woe! woe!" resounded on all sides.

The monk was appalled, but still he proceeded.

"What did ye to deserve such doom as this? What may your crime be that deserves such dole and sorrow?"

As he asked the question the earth shook under him, and a crowd of skeletons uprose from a range of graves which yawned suddenly at his feet.

"These are our victims," answered the old monk. "They suffered at our hands. We suffer now, while they are at peace; and we shall suffer."

"For how long?" asked the monk.

"For ever and ever!" was the answer.

"For ever and ever, for ever and ever!" died along the vault.

"May God have mercy on us!" was all the monk could exclaim.

The skeletons vanished, the graves closing over them. The aged men disappeared from his view, the bodies fell back in their coffins, the light fied, and the den of death was once more enveloped in its usual darkness.

On the monk's revival he found himself lying at the foot of the altar. The grey dawn of a spring morning was visible, and he was fain to retire to his cell as secretly as he could, for fear he should be discovered.

From thenceforth he eschewed vain philosophy, says the legend, and, devoting his time to the pursuit of true knowledge, and the extension of the power, greatness, and glory of the Church, died in the odour of sanctity, and was buried in that holy vault, where his body is still visible.

Here is a lovely, offbeat tale by an unknown author: of a traveling salesman whose experience with trains is not dissimilar to old Vanderdecken's problem with his ship, The Flying Dutchman. Ghost stories can be charming!

The Parlor-Car Ghost
Anonymous

All draped with blue denim—the seaside cottage of my friend, Sara Pyne. She asked me to go there with her when she opened it to have it set in order for the summer. She confessed that she felt a trifle nervous at the idea of entering it alone. And I am always ready for an excursion. So much blue denim rather surprised me, because blue is not complimentary to Sara's complexion—she always wears some shade of red, by preference. She perceived my wonder; she is very nearsighted, and therefore sees everything by some sort of sixth sense.

"You do not like my portieres and curtains and table-covers," said she. "Neither do I. But I did it to accommodate. And now he rests well in his grave, I hope."

"Whose grave, for pity's sake?"

"Mr. J. Billington Price's."

"And who is he? He doesn't sound interesting."

"Then I will tell you about him," said Sara, taking a seat directly in front of one of those curtains. "Last autumn I was leaving this place for New York, traveling on the fast express train known as the Flying Yankee. Of course, I thought of the Flying Dutchman and Wagner's musical setting of the uncanny legend, and how different things are in these days of steam, etc. Then I looked out of the window at the landscape, the horizon that seemed to wheel in a great curve as the train sped on. Every now and then I had an impression at the 'tail of the eye' that a man was sitting in a chair three or four numbers in front of me on the opposite side of the car. Each time that I saw this shape I looked at the chair and ascertained that it was unoccupied. But it was an odd trick of vision. I raised my lorgnette, and the chair showed emptier than before. There was nobody in it, certainly. But the more I knew that it was vacant the more plainly I saw the man. Always with the corner of my eye. It made me nervous. When passengers entered the car I dreaded lest they might take that seat. What would happen if they should? A bag was put in the chair—that made me uncomfortable. The bag was re-

moved at the next station. Then a baby was placed in the seat. It began
to laugh as though someone had gently tickled it. There was something
odd about that chair—thirteen was its number. When I looked away
from it the impression was strong upon me that some person sitting
there was watching me.

"Really, it would not do to humor such fancies. So I touched the
electric button, asked the porter to bring me a table, and taking from
my bag a pack of cards, proceeded to divert myself with a game of patience. I was puzzling where to put a seven of spades. 'Where can it go?'
I murmured to myself. A voice behind me prompted: 'Play the four of
diamonds on the five, and you can do it.' I started. The only occupants
of the car, besides me, were a bridal couple, a mother with three little
children, and a typical preacher of one of the straitest sects. Who had
spoken? 'Play up the four, madam,' repeated this voice.

"I looked fearfully over my shoulder. At first I saw a bluish cloud,
like cigar smoke, but inodorous. Then the vision cleared, and I saw a
young man whom I knew by a subtle intuition to be the occupant, seen
and not seen, of chair number thirteen. Evidently he was a traveling
salesman—and a ghost. Of course, a drummer's ghost sounds ridiculous
—they're so extremely alive! Or else you would expect a dead drummer
to be particularly dead and not 'walk.' This was a most commonplace-
looking ghost, cordial, pushing, businesslike. At the same time, his face
had an expression of utter despair and horror which made him still
more preposterous. Of course it is not nice to let a stranger speak to
one, even on so impersonal a topic as a four of diamonds. But a ghost—
there can't be any rule of etiquette about talking with a ghost! My dear,
it was dreadful! That forward creature showed me how to play all the
cards, and then begged me to lay them out again, in order that he might
give me some clever points. I was too much amazed and disturbed to
speak. I could only place the cards at his suggestion. This I did so as
not to appear to be listening to the empty air, and be supposed to be a
crazy woman. Presently the ghost spoke again, and told me his story.

" 'Madam,' he said, 'I have been riding back and forth on this car
ever since February 22, 189—. Seven months and eleven days. All this
time I have not exchanged a word with anyone. For a drummer, that is
pretty hard, you may believe! You know the story of the Flying Dutchman? Well, that is very nearly my case. A curse is upon me and will not
be removed until some kind soul——. But I'm getting ahead of my text.
That day there were four of us, traveling for different houses. One of
the boys was in wool, one in baking powder, one in boots and shoes,

and myself in cotton goods. We met on the road, took seats together and fell into talking shop.

" 'Those fellows told big lies about their sales, Washington's Birthday though it was. The baking powder man raised the amount of the bills of goods which he had sold better than a whole can of his stuff could have done. I admitted the straight truth, that I had not yet been able to make a sale. And then I swore—not in a light-minded, chipper style of verbal trimmings, but a great, round, heaven-defying oath—that I would sell a case of blue denims on that trip if it took me forever. We became dry with talk, and when the train stopped at Rivermouth, we went out to have some beer. It is good there, you know—pardon me, I forgot that I was speaking to a lady. Well, we had to run to get aboard. I missed my footing, fell under the wheels, and the next thing that I knew they were holding an inquest over my remains; while I, disemboweled, was sitting on a corner of the undertaker's table, wondering which of the coroner's jury was likely to want a case of blue denims.

" 'Then I remembered my wicked oath, and understood that I was a soul doomed to wander until I could succeed in selling that bill of goods. I spoke once or twice, offering the denims under value, but nobody noticed me. Verdict: accidental death; negligence of deceased; railroad corporation not to blame; deceased got out for beer at his own risk. The other drummers took charge of the remains, and wrote a beautiful letter to my relatives about my social qualities and my impressive conversation. I wish it had been less impressive that time! I might have lied about my sales, or I might have said that I hoped for better luck. But after that oath there was nothing for it. Back and forth, back and forth, on this road, in chair number thirteen, to all eternity. Nobody suspects my presence. They sit on my knees—I'm playing in luck when it is a nice baby as it was this afternoon! They pile wraps, bags, even railway literature on me. They play cards under my nose—and what duffers some of them are! You, madam, are the first person who has perceived me; and therefore I ventured to speak to you, meaning no offense. I can see that you are sorry for me. Now, if you recall the story of the Flying Dutchman, he was saved by the charity of a good woman. In fact, Senta married him. Now I'm not asking anything of that size. I see that you wear a wedding ring, and no doubt you make some man's happiness. I wasn't a marrying man myself, and, naturally, am not a marrying ghost. And that has nothing to do with the matter anyway. But if you could—I don't suppose you would have any use for them—but if you were disposed to do a turn of good, solid, Christian charity—I should be everlastingly grateful, and you may have that case of denims at $72.50. And that quality is quoted today at $80. Does it go, madam?'

"The speech of the poor ghost was not very eloquent, but his eyes had an intense, eager glare, which was terrible. Something—pity, fear, I do not know what—compelled me. I decided to do without that white and gold evening cloak. Instead, I gave $72.50 to the ghost and took from him a receipt for the sum, signed J. Billington Price. Then he smiled contentedly, thanked me with emotion, and returned to chair number thirteen. Several times on the journey, although I did not perceive him again, I felt dazed. When the train arrived at New York, and I, with the other passengers, dismounted, it seemed to me that a strong hand passed under my elbow, steadying me down the steps. As I walked the length of the station my bag—not heavy at any time—appeared to become weightless. I believe that the parlor-car ghost walked beside me, carrying the bag, whose handle still remained in my other hand. Indeed, once or twice I thought I felt the touch of cold fingers against mine. Since then I have no reason to suppose that the poor ghost is not at rest. I hope he is.

"But I never expected nor wished for the blue denims. The next day, however, a dray belonging to a great wholesale house backed up to our door and delivered a case of denims, with a receipted bill for the same. What was I to do? I could not go about selling blue denims; I could not give them away without exciting comment. So I furnished the cottage with them—and you know the effect on my complexion. Pity me, dear! And credit me, frivolous woman as I am, with having saved a soul at the expense of my own vanity. My story is told. What do you think about it?"

"The Red Room" is a remarkable study of terror created by the power of suggestion, but to say any more would be to tip off the final revelation. H. G. WELLS *wrote a generous quantity of weird and speculative tales, as well as those justly famous, oft-dramatized and/or filmed classics of science fiction,* The Time Machine, The War of the Worlds, The Invisible Man, The Food of the Gods *and* The Island of Doctor Moreau. *Born in 1866, Wells was the central dramatic figure of the exciting film,* Time After Time . . . *and still seems far ahead of most of his literary successors.*

The Red Room
by H. G. Wells

"I can assure you," said I, "that it will take a very tangible ghost to frighten me." And I stood up before the fire with my glass in my hand.

"It is your own choosing," said the man with the withered arm, and glanced at me askance.

"Eight-and-twenty years," said I, "I have lived, and never a ghost have I seen as yet."

The old woman sat staring hard into the fire, her pale eyes wide open. "Ay," she broke in; "and eight-and-twenty years you have lived and never seen the likes of this house, I reckon. There's a many things to see, when one's still but eight-and-twenty." She swayed her head slowly from side to side. "A many things to see and sorrow for."

I half suspected the old people were trying to enhance the spiritual terrors of their house by their droning insistence. I put down my empty glass on the table and looked about the room, and caught a glimpse of myself, abbreviated and broadened to an impossible sturdiness, in the queer old mirror at the end of the room. "Well," I said, "if I see anything tonight, I shall be so much the wiser. For I come to the business with an open mind."

"It's your own choosing," said the man with the withered arm once more.

I heard the sound of a stick and a shambling step on the flags in the passage outside, and the door creaked on its hinges as a second old man entered, more bent, more wrinkled, more aged even than the first. He supported himself by a single crutch, his eyes were covered by a shade, and his lower lip, half-averted, hung pale and pink from his decaying yellow teeth. He made straight for an arm-chair on the opposite side of the table, sat down clumsily, and began to cough. The man with the withered arm gave this new-comer a short glance of positive dislike; the old woman took no notice of his arrival, but remained with her eyes fixed steadily on the fire.

"I said—it's your own choosing," said the man with the withered arm, when the coughing had ceased for a while.

"It's my own choosing," I answered.

The man with the shade became aware of my presence for the first time, and threw his head back for a moment and sideways, to see me. I caught a momentary glimpse of his eyes, small and bright and inflamed. Then he began to cough and splutter again.

"Why don't you drink?" said the man with the withered arm, pushing the beer towards him. The man with the shade poured out a glassful with a shaky arm that splashed half as much again on the deal table. A monstrous shadow of him crouched upon the wall and mocked his action as he poured and drank. I must confess I had scarce expected these grotesque custodians. There is to my mind something inhuman in senility, something crouching and atavistic; the human qualities seem to drop from old people insensibly day by day. The three of them made me feel uncomfortable, with their gaunt silences, their bent carriage, their evident unfriendliness to me and to one another.

"If," said I, "you will show me to this haunted room of yours, I will make myself comfortable there."

The old man with the cough jerked his head back so suddenly that it startled me, and shot another glance of his red eyes at me from under the shade; but no one answered me. I waited a minute, glancing from one to the other.

"If," I said a little louder, "if you will show me to this haunted room of yours, I will relieve you from the task of entertaining me."

"There's a candle on the slab outside the door," said the man with the withered arm, looking at my feet as he addressed me. "But if you go to the red room to-night—"

("This night of all nights!" said the old woman.)

"You go alone."

"Very well," I answered. "And which way do I go?"

"You go along the passage for a bit," said he, "until you come to a door, and through that is a spiral staircase, and half-way up that is a landing and another door covered with baize. Go through that and down the long corridor to the end, and the red room is on your left up the steps."

"Have I got that right?" I said, and repeated his directions. He corrected me in one particular.

"And are you really going?" said the man with the shade, looking at me again for the third time, with that queer, unnatural tilting of the face.

("This night of all nights!" said the old woman.)

"It is what I came for," I said, and moved towards the door. As I did so, the old man with the shade rose and staggered round the table, so as to be closer to the others and to the fire. At the door I turned and looked at them, and saw they were all close together, dark against the firelight, staring at me over their shoulders, with an intent expression on their ancient faces.

"Good-night," I said, setting the door open.

"It's your own choosing," said the man with the withered arm.

I left the door wide open until the candle was well alight, and then I shut them in and walked down the chilly, echoing passage.

I must confess that the oddness of these three old pensioners in whose charge her ladyship had left the castle, and the deep-toned, old fashioned furniture of the housekeeper's room in which they foregathered, affected me in spite of my efforts to keep myself at a matter-of-fact phase. They seemed to belong to another age, an older age, an age when things spiritual were different from this of ours, less certain; an age when omens and witches were credible, and ghosts beyond denying. Their very existence was spectral; the cut of their clothing, fashions born in dead brains. The ornaments and conveniences of the room about them were ghostly—the thoughts of vanished men, which still haunted rather than participated in the world of to-day. But with an effort I sent such thoughts to the right-about. The long, draughty subterranean passage was chilly and dusty, and my candle flared and made the shadows cower and quiver. The echoes rang up and down the spiral staircase, and a shadow came sweeping up after me, and one fled before me into the darkness overhead. I came to the landing and stopped there for a moment, listening to a rustling that I fancied I heard; then, satisfied of the absolute silence, I pushed open the baize-covered door and stood in the corridor.

The effect was scarcely what I expected, for the moonlight, coming in by the great window on the grand staircase, picked out everything in vivid black shadow or silvery illumination. Everything was in its place: the house might have been deserted on the yesterday instead of eighteen months ago. There were candles in the sockets of the sconces, and whatever dust had gathered on the carpets or upon the polished flooring was distributed so evenly as to be invisible in the moonlight. I was about to advance, and stopped abruptly. A bronze group stood upon the landing, hidden from me by the corner of the wall, but its shadow fell with marvellous distinctness upon the white panelling, and gave me the impression of someone crouching to waylay me. I stood rigid for half a minute perhaps. Then, with my hand in the pocket that held my revolver, I advanced, only to discover a Ganymede and Eagle glistening in the moonlight. That incident for a time restored my nerve, and a porcelain Chinaman on a buhl table, whose head rocked silently as I passed him, scarcely startled me.

The door to the red room and the steps up to it were in a shadowy corner. I moved my candle from side to side, in order to see clearly the nature of the recess in which I stood before opening the door. Here it was, thought I, that my predecessor was found, and the memory of that story gave me a sudden twinge of apprehension. I glanced over my shoulder at the Ganymede in the moonlight, and opened the door of the red room rather hastily, with my face half turned to the pallid silence of the landing.

I entered, closed the door behind me at once, turned the key I found in the lock within, and stood with the candle held aloft, surveying the scene of my vigil, the great red room of Lorraine Castle, in which the young duke had died. Or, rather, in which he had begun his dying, for he had opened the door and fallen headlong down the steps I had just ascended. That had been the end of his vigil, of his gallant attempt to conquer the ghostly tradition of the place; and never, I thought, had apoplexy better served the ends of superstition. And there were other and older stories that clung to the room, back to the half-credible beginning of it all, the tale of a timid wife and the tragic end that came to her husband's jest of frightening her. And looking around that large shadowy room, with its shadowy window bays, its recesses and alcoves, one could well understand the legends that had sprouted in its black corners, its germinating darkness. My candle was a little tongue of flame in its vastness, that failed to pierce the opposite end of the room, and left an ocean of mystery and suggestion beyond its island of light.

I resolved to make a systematic examination of the place at once, and dispel the fanciful suggestions of its obscurity before they obtained a hold upon me. After satisfying myself of the fastening of the door, I began to walk about the room, peering round each article of furniture, tucking up the valances of the bed, and opening its curtains wide. I pulled up the blinds and examined the fastenings of the several windows before closing the shutters, leant forward and looked up the blackness of the wide chimney, and tapped the dark oak panelling for any secret opening. There were two big mirrors in the room, each with a pair of sconces bearing candles, and on the mantelshelf, too, were more candles in china candlesticks. All these I lit one after the other. The fire was laid,—an unexpected consideration from the old housekeeper,—and I lit it, to keep down any disposition to shiver, and when it was burning well, I stood round with my back to it and regarded the room again. I had pulled up a chintz-covered arm-chair and a table, to form a kind of barricade before me, and on this lay my revolver ready to hand. My precise examination had done me good, but I still found the remoter darkness of the place, and its perfect stillness, too stimulating for the imagination. The echoing of the stir and crackling of the fire was no sort of comfort to me. The shadow in the alcove, at the end in particular, had that undefinable quality of a presence, that odd suggestion of a lurking living thing, that comes so easily in silence and solitude. At last, to reassure myself, I walked with a candle into it, and satisfied myself that there was nothing tangible there. I stood that candle upon the floor of the alcove, and left it in that position.

By this time I was in a state of considerable nervous tension, although to my reason there was no adequate cause for the condition. My mind, however, was perfectly clear. I postulated quite unreservedly that nothing supernatural could happen, and to pass the time I began to string some rhymes together, Ingoldsby fashion, of the original legend of the place. A few I spoke aloud, but the echoes were not pleasant. For the same reason I also abandoned, after a time, a conversation with myself upon the impossibility of ghosts and haunting. My mind reverted to the three old and distorted people downstairs, and I tried to keep it upon that topic. The sombre reds and blacks of the room troubled me; even with seven candles the place was merely dim. The one in the alcove flared in a draught, and the fire-flickering kept the shadows and penumbra perpetually shifting and stirring. Casting about for a remedy, I recalled the candles I had seen in the passage, and, with a slight effort, walked out into the moonlight, carrying a candle and leaving the door open, and presently returned with as many as ten. These I put in various knick-knacks of china with which the room was sparsely adorned, lit and placed where the shadows had lain deepest, some on the floor, some in the window recesses, until at last my seventeen candles were so arranged that not an inch of the room but had the direct light of at least one of them. It occurred to me that when the ghost came, I could warn him not to trip over them. The room was now quite brightly illuminated. There was something very cheery and reassuring in these little streaming flames, and snuffing them gave me an occupation, and afforded a reassuring sense of the passage of time.

Even with that, however, the brooding expectation of the vigil weighed heavily upon me. It was after midnight that the candle in the alcove suddenly went out, and the black shadow sprang back to its place. I did not see the candle go out; I simply turned and saw that the darkness was there, as one might start and see the unexpected presence of a stranger. "By Jove!" said I aloud; "that draught's a strong one!" and, taking the matches from the table, I walked across the room in a leisurely manner to relight the corner again. My first match would not strike, and as I succeeded with the second, something seemed to blink on the wall before me. I turned my head involuntarily, and saw that the two candles on the little table by the fireplace were extinguished. I rose at once to my feet.

"Odd!" I said. "Did I do that myself in a flash of absent-mindedness?"

I walked back, relit one, and as I did so, I saw the candle in the right sconce of one of the mirrors wink and go right out, and almost immediately its companion followed it. There was no mistake about it. The flame vanished, as if the wicks had been suddenly nipped between a finger and a thumb, leaving the wick neither glowing nor smoking, but black. While I stood gaping, the candle at the foot of the bed went out, and the shadows seemed to take another step towards me.

"This won't do!" said I, and first one and then another candle on the mantelshelf followed.

"What's up?" I cried, with a queer high note getting into my voice somehow. At that the candle on the wardrobe went out, and the one I had relit in the alcove followed.

"Steady on!" I said. "These candles are wanted," speaking with a half-hysterical facetiousness, and scratching away at a match the while for the mantel candlesticks. My hands trembled so much that twice I missed the rough paper of the matchbox. As the mantel emerged from darkness again, two candles in the remoter end of the window were eclipsed. But with the same match I also relit the larger mirror candles, and those on the floor near the doorway, so that for the moment I seemed to gain on the extinctions. But then in a volley there vanished four lights at once in different corners of the room, and I struck another match in quivering haste, and stood hesitating whither to take it.

As I stood undecided, an invisible hand seemed to sweep out the two candles on the table. With a cry of terror, I dashed at the alcove, then into the corner, and then into the window, relighting three, as two more vanished by the fireplace; then, perceiving a better way, I dropped the matches on the iron-bound deed-box in the corner, and caught up the bedroom candlestick. With this I avoided the delay of striking matches; but for all that the steady process of extinction went on, and the shadows I feared and fought against returned, and crept in upon me, first a step gained on this side of me and then on that. It was like a ragged storm-cloud sweeping out the stars. Now and then one returned for a minute, and was lost again. I was now almost frantic with the horror of coming darkness, and my self-possession deserted me. I leaped panting and dishevelled from candle to candle, in a vain struggle against that remorseless advance.

I bruised myself on the thigh against the table, I sent a chair headlong, I stumbled and fell and whisked the cloth from the table in my fall. My candle rolled away from me, and I snatched another as I rose. Abruptly this was blown out, as I swung it off the table, by the wind of my sudden movement, and immediately the two remaining candles followed. But there was light still in the room, a red light that staved off the shadows from me. The fire! Of course, I could thrust my candle between the bars and relight it!

I turned to where the flames were dancing between the glowing coals, and splashing red reflections upon the furniture, made two steps towards the grate, and incontinently the flames dwindled and vanished, the glow vanished, the reflections rushed together and vanished, and as I thrust the candle between the bars, darkness closed upon me like the shutting of an eye, wrapped about me in a stifling embrace, sealed my vision, and crushed the last vestiges of reason from my brain. The candle fell from my hand. I flung out my arms in a vain effort to thrust that ponderous blackness away from me, and, lifting up my voice, screamed with all my might—once, twice, thrice. Then I think I must have staggered to my feet. I know I thought suddenly of the moonlit corridor, and, with my head bowed and my arms over my face, made a run for the door.

But I had forgotten the exact position of the door, and struck myself heavily against the corner of the bed. I staggered back, turned, and was either struck or struck myself against some other bulky furniture. I have a vague memory of battering myself thus, to and fro in the darkness, of a cramped struggle, and of my own wild crying as I darted to and fro, of a heavy blow at last upon my forehead, a horrible sensation of falling that lasted an age, of my last frantic effort to keep my footing, and then I remember no more.

I opened my eyes in daylight. My head was roughly bandaged, and the man with the withered arm was watching my face. I looked about me, trying to remember what had happened, and for a space I could not recollect. I turned to the corner, and saw the old woman, no longer abstracted, pouring out some drops of medicine from a little blue phial into a glass. "Where am I?" I asked. "I seem to remember you, and yet I cannot remember who you are."

They told me then, and I heard of the haunted Red Room as one who hears a tale. "We found you at dawn," said he, "and there was blood on your forehead and lips."

It was very slowly I recovered my memory of my experience. "You believe now," said the old man, "that the room is haunted?" He spoke no longer as one who greets an intruder, but as one who grieves for a broken friend.

"Yes," said I; "the room is haunted."

"And you have seen it. And we, who have lived here all our lives, have never set eyes upon it. Because we have never dared. . . . Tell us, is it truly the old earl who—"

"No," said I; "it is not."

"I told you so," said the old lady, with the glass in her hand. "It is his poor young countess who was frightened—"

"It is not," I said. "There is neither ghost of earl nor ghost of countess in that room, there is no ghost there at all; but worse, far worse—"

"Well?" they said.

"The worst of all the things that haunt poor mortal man," said I; "and that is, in all its nakedness—*Fear!* Fear that will not have light nor sound, that will not bear with reason, that deafens and darkens and overwhelms. It followed me through the corridor, it fought against me in the room—"

I stopped abruptly. There was an interval of silence. My hand went up to my bandages.

Then the man with the shade sighed and spoke. "That is it," said he. "I knew that was it. A Power of Darkness. To put such a curse upon a woman! It lurks there always. You can feel it even in the daytime, even of a bright summer's day, in the hangings, in the curtains, keeping behind you however you face about. In the dusk it creeps along the corridor and follows you, so that you dare not turn. There is Fear in that room of hers—black Fear, and there will be—so long as this house of sin endures."

A Gathering of Ghosts
by Craig Shaw Gardner

(1)

"Life is short, death inevitable, and, as the wise men say, it is best to do what one can with your poor, short life. However, should one manage a rich, short life, or even a short life on a moderate income, the 'best' the wise men speak of can be of a better quality altogether."

from *The Teachings of Ebenezum*
Volume 2

It was all luck, I guess you could say. Bad luck. Not that there had been any real catastrophes. Just a string of small misfortunes; beginning, I guess, with that misunderstanding in the tiny kingdom of Melifox, where the ruler had refused to pay us simply because a technicality in a spell had caused most of his wealth to vanish.

I looked to my master, the great wizard Ebenezum, as he descended the hill before me. Even on the steep path we took now, his tread was sure, his dark wizard's robes, tastefully inlaid with silver thread, flowing proud behind him. No matter what hardships we faced on our journey from the Western Kingdoms, no matter how great my master's affliction, Ebenezum would not bow.

It occurred to me, then, that our string of luck really began with my master's sneezing fits. It was the great wizard's battle with a particularly powerful demon from the seventh Netherhell that did it. In the end, of course, my master managed to send the demon back to the foul place from which it came. But my master did not escape the battle unscathed, for he discovered shortly thereafter that, should he even be in the presence of magic, he would begin to sneeze violently.

Now, a malady of this nature might have defeated many a lesser wizard. But not Ebenezum. He still managed to ply his trade, using his wits rather than spells to solve his clients' problems. It became apparent, however, that the mage's malady would not go away of its own accord, and, due to the nature of the affliction, Ebenezum could not cure it through the use of magic. We therefore took to the road, searching for some wizard great enough to cure my master's ills, though we might have to travel to far Vushta, city of a thousand forbidden delights, before we found one as great as that.

And Vushta began to seem more of a possibility with every passing day. What with being chased out of one kingdom and not being particularly welcome in the next two, we hadn't had a chance to meet many wizards at all. Then there'd been the mercenaries King Urfoo of Melifox had sent to kill us, and the seven straight days of rain, and the incident with the giant swamp rats. I didn't even want to think of those.

But still my master walked on, proud and tall, to far, forbidden Vushta. And I would follow him there, and anywhere. Even with his affliction, Ebenezum was the greatest wizard I had ever seen!

I touched my walking stick to my forehead in a silent salute to the man before me. It was then that I lost my footing and slid down the hill, colliding with my master.

Our fall ended in a cluster of bushes at the valley bottom. Not looking at me, the wizard stood with a groan that was like the rumble of an approaching storm. He turned, much too slowly, to face me. I watched the eyes beneath bushy brows and awaited the inevitable.

"Wuntvor," the mage said, his voice like an earthquake splitting a mountainside. "If you can't watch where you put your—"

My master stopped midsentence, and stared over my head. I started to stammer an apology, but the wizard waved me to silence.

"What do you hear, 'prentice?" he asked.

I listened, but heard nothing. I told him so.

"Exactly," he replied. "Nothing at all. 'Tis the midst of summer, deep in the wood, yet I do not see a single bird nor hear an insect. Though I must admit, the absence of the latter does not upset me overmuch." The mage scratched at a pink welt beneath his long, white beard. We had had a great deal of experience, ever since the seven days of rain, with clouds of mosquitoes and biting gnats.

"Methinks, Wunt, something is amiss."

I listened for a moment more. My master was right. The forest was silent, the only sounds the breathing of the wizard and myself. I had never heard quiet like this except perhaps on the coldest days of winter. A chill went up my back, surprising in the summer's heat.

My master dusted off his robes. "We seem to have landed near a clearing." He nodded down what remained of the hill. "Perhaps we shall find some habitation, even someone who can explain the nature of this place. Until then, we will bask in the absence of mosquitoes." He scratched his neck absently as he started down the hill. "Always look at the bright side, Wunt."

I hurriedly gathered up the foodstuffs, books, and magical paraphernalia that had fallen from my pack and followed my master's wizardly strides. He, as usual, carried nothing, preferring, as he often said, to keep his hands free for quick conjuring, his mind free for quick thought. I scrambled after him over the uneven ground, avoiding what underbrush there was. But the brush thinned rapidly as we walked, and we found ourselves facing a large clearing of bare earth, broken only by a ring of seven large boulders in its center.

"Now we've even lost the grasses," Ebenezum rumbled. "Come, Wunt, we'll find the cause of this." He took great strides across the bare ground, clouds of dust rising with every step. I followed close behind, doing my best not to cough.

When we reached the first boulder, something jumped.

"Boo!" the something said. I dropped my pack, but Ebenezum simply stood there and watched the apparition.

"Indeed," he said after a moment.

"Boo! Boo! Boo! Boo!" the creature confronting us shrieked. On closer inspection, I could see that it was definitely human, with long gray hair covering the face and brown rags concealing the body. The person raised frail hands and rushed us on unsteady legs.

Neither of us moved. Our attacker stopped, out of breath. "Not going to work, is it?" she wheezed at last. It was an old woman; her speaking voice was cracked and high.

Ebenezum stroked his moustache. "Is what not going to work?"

"Can't scare you away, huh?" She parted the long hair that covered her face and peered at the sky. "Probably too late for you to get away, anyhow. Might as well sit down and wait." She looked around for a likely rock and sat.

"Indeed," Ebenezum repeated. "Wait for what?"

"You don't know?" The woman's eyes widened in wonder. "Sir, you are in the dreaded Valley of Vrunge!"

"Indeed," Ebenezum said when it became apparent the woman planned to say no more.

"Now don't tell me you've never heard of it. What, do you come from the ignorant Western Kingdoms?" The woman laughed derisively. "Everyone knows of the Valley of Vrunge and the dread curse that falls upon it once every one hundred and thirty-seven years. Not that this place is all that friendly at any time—" She spat on the parched earth. "—but there is one night, every one hundred thirty-seven years, when all hell breaks loose. One night when no one then in the valley will get out alive!"

I didn't like the direction the woman's speech was taking. I swallowed hard and cleared my throat. "Ma'am, would you mind telling us just when that night is?"

"Haven't I made it clear?" The crone laughed again. "This is the cursed night of the Valley of Vrunge. It begins when the sun passes yonder hills." She pointed behind me.

I followed her arm and looked at the sun, already touching the tops of the western hills, then turned to Ebenezum. He stared above me, lost in thought. As I mentioned, our luck seemed to be running true to its course.

"If we are all due to die," Ebenezum said at last, "what are you doing here?"

The old woman looked away from us. "I have my reasons, which I'm sure would be of little interest to anyone but me. Let us just say that once this land was green and fair, and it was ruled over by a princess as lovely as the land itself. But a dark time came upon the earth, and the sky rained toads, and the princess became afraid. But her suitor, the handsome—"

"You're quite right," Ebenezum interrupted. "No one would be interested in that at all. You've decided to die because the sky rained toads?"

The woman sighed and watched the sun disappear behind the hilltop. "Not exactly. I've worn this old body out; I'm due to die. I just thought I'd see old Maggie out in style."

"Maggie?" Ebenezum scratched his insect bite thoughtfully. "That wouldn't be short for Magredel?" He peered into her ancient face.

"Oh, I haven't used that name in years. Not since I got away from those dull Western Kingdoms. Used to practice witchery thereabouts for a time, that's probably where you heard of me. Didn't specialize much, though. More of a general practitioner."

"Maggie?" Ebenezum repeated. "As in Old Aunt Maggie?"

Maggie squinted her eyes in turn. "Say, do I know you from someplace?"

There was an explosion directly behind me. All three of us spun to see a tall, pale apparition atop the tallest of the seven stones.

"Greetings, lady and gentlemen!" the apparition cried with a swirl of its white robe. "And welcome to curse night!"

"Greetings to you, too, Death," Maggie replied. "I hope tonight will be up to your usual standards?"

Death laughed, a high, echoey sound that came near to scaring the life from me. When I mentioned it later to Ebenezum, he said no doubt that was the desired reaction.

The apparition atop the stone disappeared.

"That was our introduction," Maggie remarked. "Soon the fun begins."

I was appalled. "F-fun?" I stammered. "How do you know what happens next?"

"Simple." The crone flashed a toothless smile. "I've been through this night once before."

(2)

"Your average ghost is a much more complex and interesting individual than is generally imagined. Just because someone is dragging chains or has one's head perpetually in flames does not necessarily make them of a lesser class. Some ghosts, especially those with heads still attached and mouths to speak through, are actually quite good conversationalists, with otherworldly stories by the score. In addition, ghosts generally subscribe to the happy custom of disappearing completely at dawn, a habit many living associates and relations might do well to cultivate."

from *The Teachings of Ebenezum*
Volume 6 (Appendix B)

Death had vanished, and the silence was again complete. My master cleared his throat.

"Ebenezum!" the old woman cried. "Of course! I'd recognize that nervous cough anywhere. Poor little Ebby, always coughing or scratching or tugging or doing something. He never could sit still." She winked in my direction. "You know, in the whole first year he studied under me, he didn't get one spell straight? You should have seen the things that showed up in our kitchen!" She laughed.

My master cast a worried glance at the rock where Death had stood. "Please, Aunt Maggie. I don't think this is the proper time to discuss—"

"Oh, keep your cap on!" The woman clapped Ebenezum on the shoulder. "We have a little time. It always takes them a while to get organized. When you only have a performance once every one hundred thirty-seven years, you tend to get a bit rusty."

"But what's going to happen?" I asked. I noticed my hand hurt from my tight grip on the walking stick.

"Ghosts, ghosts and more ghosts." The old woman spat on the ground. "Death is fond of games. He plays a game with every living thing, one in which he's always the victor. Some games he likes more than others, and those great conflicts he brings here, to play over and over again in his arena in the Valley of Vrunge!"

"The spirits just play games?" I asked. That didn't sound so bad.

"All of life is a game, remember. Death brings along the best of all his games, ranging from a nation at war to two people in love."

She jumped and screamed.

"Tickle, tickle, tickle," said a high voice from nowhere.

"Poltergeists! Boo! Boo! Boo! Away from here!" Maggie waved her hands about wildly. "More and more ghosts will appear throughout the night. And Death will try to snare you in his games. Beware, he always wins!" She screamed and jumped again.

"Boo, boo, boo?" the voice from nowhere asked. "That's passé, lady. These days, long, sensitive moans are much more the thing in ghostly circles."

"So it begins. I'm sorry, Ebby, you had to stumble into this!" She ran and screamed as "tickle, tickle, tickle!" chased her around the circle of boulders.

Ebenezum sneezed once and blew his nose on a silver-inlaid sleeve. "Just a minor spirit. Hardly bothers me at all."

I realized then that this was the first time Ebenezum's malady had affected him since we entered the cursed valley. Perhaps the severity of our situation was effecting a cure. Ebenezum had not sneezed once in the presence of Death!

My master shook his head when I explained my theory. "Why should I sneeze? Death is the most natural thing in the world." He pulled at his beard. "And I fear that, should we fail to devise a plan of action, Death will become all too familiar to both of us."

It was then that the beast leapt at me. All I could see was the huge mouth, giant, sharp teeth, slavering tongue. I leapt aside and felt claws of ice graze my shoulder. I rolled over with a groan and looked at my master. He stood at the ready, feet spread, sleeves back, hands in conjuring position. But the clearing was quiet again.

Ebenezum blew his nose. "The apparitions will try to divide us."

A great wind sprang up. My master had to shout to be heard. "Stay close! If we're separated—"

The wizard sneezed as three ghosts on a sled grabbed him and whisked him high in the air. Ghosts, sled and sneezing Ebenezum disappeared around the stones.

Night had fallen completely, and I was alone.

But then there was a crowd around me, sitting on long rows of seats, one atop another, as if they were built on a hillside. The crowd roared, and I saw they were watching a group of uniformed men on a green lawn, a few of whom were running but most of whom were standing still.

A man carrying a big silver box walked up the steps toward me. "Hot dogs!" he cried. "Hot dogs!"

He wasn't real, I told myself. This whole place was beyond my understanding. I stepped aside to let him pass. He stopped next to me anyway.

"Hot dog, mister?"

It was only with a mental effort that I kept from shivering. I looked down at the stout oak staff I used for a walking stick. My grip was firm. If the apparition tried anything, I'd swing at him. And then again, from what I'd heard of ghosts, I might swing through him as well.

With some trepidation, I asked, "What's a hot dog?"

"Like I thought," the spirit nodded sagely, "you're an outsider. So this is your first ball game? Well, you picked a good one, buddy."

I looked out over the field below us. "Ball game," I repeated, struggling to comprehend.

"Yeah," the apparition replied. "*The* ball game. People had counted the Red Sox out, but they came around. Now Torrez will blow the Yankees away! Seventy-eight is going to be our year. It *has* to be."

I looked closely at the spirit, hoping that some gesture or facial mannerism would help me to understand his ravings. All I saw was the haunted look, deep in his eyes.

"Has to be?" I asked.

"Well, yeah." The ghost paused. "I mean, the Sox have to win. Otherwise—" He shuddered. "Do you have any idea what it would be like to have to sell hot dogs throughout eternity?"

He didn't wait for an answer but walked up the stairs beyond me. I turned down to the "ball game" on the field below. I felt a sudden, near overwhelming urge to be drawn into that game and find out just what could move the hot dog spirit to such a frenzy. I'd watch the shifting patterns of men on the bright green lawn, and sooner or later some great secret would be revealed, a joyous revelation that would make my whole existence take on new meaning!

Something in the back of my head told me to turn away. I remembered Aunt Maggie's warning about Death and games.

The ball game disappeared. In its place stood Death.

"There you are," the creature said in his sonorous voice. "I've been looking all over for you. These curse evenings can be so long and boring, sometimes I like to indulge in games to help pass the time. Tell me, do you know how to play 'Red Light, Green Light'?"

Death stood much closer than he had before. I stared at the thin layer of pale skin pulled tight over his skull, and at the shadows where there should have been eyes. Yet his smile was ingratiating; you wanted to believe in what he told you. I decided he would make a good seller of used pack animals on market day.

"Well?" Death prompted.

"No!" I stammered. "I—I don't know the rules!"

"Oh, is that all?" Death reached out to touch my arm. "I'll explain everything. I'm very good with rules."

"No! I have to find my master!" I pulled away from the creature's hand and ran blindly.

Suddenly a pit yawned before me. A pit filled with sharpened spikes, and the roaring creature, all mouth and teeth and claws. I tried to stop, to step backward, but I was over the edge, falling, falling.

Someone barked a command behind me; my master's voice. I found myself on solid ground, standing by Ebenezum. All the ghosts were gone.

Ebenezum sneezed repeatedly, rocking with the force emitted by his nose.

"Temporary exorcism spell," he gasped at last. "Best I can manage."

I did a short jig on the parched earth while my master caught his breath. Ebenezum had freed himself from the sledding spirits! Hope once again rose within my breast.

I asked him how he had accomplished his escape.

The wizard shrugged. "I sneezed my way free. The ghosts were ready for sorcery, a battle of wits, anything but extreme nasal activity. They simply evaporated before the onslaught of my nose."

"That's wonderful!" I cried. "We'll be free of this cursed valley in no time!"

Ebenezum shook his head. "Death does not make the same mistake twice. The next set of apparitions will be ready for my malady."

Aunt Maggie appeared around one of the seven great boulders. She staggered over to Ebenezum's feet and collapsed.

She groaned, then turned and looked at my master. "It's gone! The poltergeist is gone!"

The wizard nodded solemnly. "Exorcism spell."

Maggie sighed in relief. "It kept taunting me, begging me to tickle it back. You can't give in to those things. It would have all been over." She looked at Ebenezum. "Exorcism? That means you followed your calling and graduated into wizardry! I did hesitate to ask you. In the early days, you were very determined, but your aptitude was sometimes less than—"

Ebenezum cleared his throat. " 'Tis only a temporary spell. Death's power is greater than common magic, and the ghosts will push through presently. We must come up with a more permanent solution."

Maggie laughed. "I pulled through this cursed night once, with the aid of magic. Maybe we can do so again. And gain my kingdom back in the bargain!" She slapped my master's shoulder. "So one of my students made good? Let's see you do your stuff. Nothing fancy; a bird out of thin air, water into wine, something to tickle an old woman's fancy."

Ebenezum fixed her with a wizardly stare. "We are in peril for our lives. I need to concentrate." He stalked off and disappeared into the circle of stone.

Maggie shook her head and smiled. "A great wizardly manner. He must be raking in the business." She sighed. "Wish I could work magic the way I used to. After a while, the body wears out. Can toss off a little spell now and again, when I'm feeling spry. But the big ones are beyond my reach."

I hesitated to tell her that, due to my master's affliction, just about all the spells that could save us from our present predicament were beyond his reach as well. Best not to upset her; I was upset enough for both of us.

"But let me tell you my story, and you'll understand why I'm here," she began. "You've already learned of the fair kingdom and the beautiful princess. And then, of course, there were the raining toads. And did I tell you about the princess's handsome suitor, Unwin, killed on their wedding day? No? Well, that's a good place to—"

Maggie jumped and screamed.

"Tickle, tickle, tickle," the disembodied voice chortled. The exorcism spell was over.

A cool breeze blew in my ear. "Hey, big boy," a woman whispered. "What's a fellow like you doing without a date on a night like this?"

I turned to gaze on the most beautiful apparition I had ever seen. I was speechless. She was slender and pale, with long, silver hair. And she wore no clothing at all, ghostly or otherwise. At certain angles, you could see right through her, but at other angles she was more than my eyes could bear.

"Oh, the silent type," she said, and took my hand, her fingers intertwining with mine. Her touch was ice and sent thrills up my arm and across my shoulders. She leaned close, and her breath was the breeze of Autumn. Her lips parted, close to mine. I wanted to kiss those lips more than I wanted life itself.

"I know a little game we can play," the full, cool lips said. "It's called Spin-the-Bottle."

Yes, yes, whatever it was, yes! All those girls I'd known in the Western Kingdoms, women I'd longed for on our travels overland, they were nothing to me now.

But my beloved was pulled away from me and sent spinning through the air, her ectoplasm flying in every direction.

"I can still toss off a spell or two." Maggie smiled. "Got to watch out for Succubi. Not good for your health."

"Crone!" Death was before us. "What would you know of love? Your body has been old and withered for a hundred years. An empty shell which can no longer be filled. Or, can it?"

Death waved his hand and a young man materialized at his side.

"Unwin?" The old woman's voice was little more than a whisper. "Is that you, Unwin?"

"Magredel!" the young man cried. "What's happened to you?"

"It's not me, Unwin. It's you. You've been away. I haven't seen you in so long!"

The old woman was crying.

"Consider, woman," Death said. "Come with me and you will be together always."

But Maggie turned on him, anger replacing sorrow. "No! You've stolen my kingdom for centuries! I'll be with Unwin soon enough! I must free what was tricked from me!"

"Such harsh words." Death examined his skeletal hand. "I have need of this place. My ghosts need their exercise." He looked at me, and I shivered where I stood. "Come, Wuntvor; let's leave these lovers alone while they talk things over. I'll give you the guided tour."

Without thinking, I found myself following him. Death smiled. "Simon says put your hands in the air."

It took all my willpower to keep my hands at my sides.

"We'll find one yet." Death's hands were full of small rectangles, which he fanned out before him. "How about a little 'Go Fish'?"

I found myself staring at the rectangles. I looked the other way.

"My kingdom," Death said.

There were apparitions everywhere. Armies fighting; women laughing, people in costumes familiar and unfamiliar, crawling across the ground, climbing the trees, flying through the air in strange machines.

"Amazing," I said despite myself.

Death nodded. "The paperwork alone is staggering. Yet we pull it off, every one hundred thirty-seven years. It's a shame our audience has to be so small. The Vrunge Curse is my masterpiece. Here are all the great moments of humanity, past, present, future, played out over and over again, from men at war to men at play, games of chance to games of love. A pity. Perhaps I should advertise."

Death coughed gently. "Tell me, Wuntvor. Who is the greatest magician in all the Western Kingdoms?"

Was he trying to trick me? I'd stay firm to my beliefs. "Why, Ebenezum, of course."

"Right!" Death cried as a gong sounded somewhere nearby. "Wuntvor, you've just won an additional five years on your life!"

We were surrounded by bright light. The ghosts all sat in a large amphitheatre now, whistling and cheering. The succubus I had almost kissed stood a little bit to one side, next to a large board that read "5." She was wearing some sort of spangled costume that managed to look more revealing than her nudity had before.

"Okay!" Death smiled broadly. "Now, Wunt, for ten additional years! Tell us, who is the ruler of Melifox?"

The crowd whistled and stamped their feet. Urgent music came from somewhere. The succubus smiled her magnificent smile.

"Uh—King Urfoo the Brave!" I blurted.

"Right, for ten more years!"

The crowd went wild. The spangled beauty flipped a couple of cards over the board to one that read "15."

"All right! All right!" Death raised his hands for silence. "Now it's time for the question we've all been waiting for. Double or nothing!"

The crowd cheered.

"Now, Wuntvor, are you ready to double your life span?"

"Yes! Yes!" the crowd chanted. I nodded my head. Why not? This was easy.

"All right! The big question, Wuntvor, to double your life span or erase it altogether! Who was the famous chamberlain of the Eastern Kingdoms, three centuries ago, who used to mutter to himself, "One of these days, one of these days . . .""

"What?" I asked. How could I know something like that?

"Quick, Wuntvor! The Quiz Lady has set the clock. You have fifteen seconds to answer, or pay the penalty, on 'Forfeit Your Life!' "

What? What could I do? I didn't know anything about the Eastern Kingdoms. The dramatic music was back, louder than ever. The crowd was roaring. I couldn't think. Why hadn't I listened to Maggie and kept away from these games?

"Ten!" the crowd chanted. "Nine! Eight! Seven! Six! Five!"

"Gangway! Gangway! Boo! Boo! Boo!" The entire crowd turned to look at Aunt Maggie, riding atop Ebenezum's shoulders as the wizard rushed into our midst. And Maggie was holding Ebenezum's nose!

"Batwom Ignatius, Wuntvor!" my master cried. "Batwom Ignatius!"

"Batwom Ignatius?" I replied.

"Is right!" Death exclaimed. "You've doubled your life! Barring illness or accident, of course."

The crowd started to go wild, but Maggie chanted a few guttural syllables and Ebenezum waved his hands. The crowd noise receded.

Ebenezum sneezed once, loudly, as Aunt Maggie climbed down from his back. I asked him how he knew about Ignatius.

"Had to learn it for my wizard finals," he replied. "It's amazing the useless knowledge they make you pack into your skull."

"Such a pitiful spell," Death remarked. "Why did you do it? They'll all be back in a moment."

"I wanted to talk to you alone," the wizard replied.

"Your affliction will come back, too, when they return. Is that what you're afraid of? Come with me, Ebenezum, and you need never sneeze again."

"Perhaps I will." Ebenezum tugged at his sleeves. "I have heard, Death, that you are fond of games. Will you play one with me?"

Death sneered. "You toy with me, wizard. No one toys with Death! Quick, what will it be? Parchesi? Contract Bridge? Fifty-two pickup?"

The wizard pulled on his beard for a moment, then intoned, "Arm wrestling."

Death shrugged. "If you insist." He snapped his fingers and a table and chairs materialized between them.

"Now the terms." Ebenezum looked Death in the eye socket. "If I win, the three of us go free, and Maggie regains her kingdom. If I lose, I am yours."

Death smiled. "For someone of your eminence, anything. After you." He indicated a chair.

Ebenezum sat. I thought that the ghostly crowd noises were somewhat closer. Ebenezum would have to hurry, or his nose might betray him.

Death smoothed his snow-white robe and sat opposite my master. His smile, if anything, was broader than before.

"Shall we begin, dear wizard?"

Ebenezum put his elbow to the table. Death did the same. Their hands clasped.

The ghostly crowd was definitely closer. I could see pale flickerings across the clearing.

"Now!" Death said, and Ebenezum tensed his whole body. There was no movement beyond the constant quiver where the two hands met.

And then the ghosts were back upon us, swirling in on top of us, all talking and screaming and laughing at once. "I'm hit!" "You're out!" "Got you!" "Hot dogs!" "Tickle, tickle, tickle!"

"Dishonest Death!" Maggie screamed. "This was to be an even contest, without your ghostly consorts!"

Death laughed. Maggie said something else that I didn't quite catch. And Ebenezum sneezed.

And what a sneeze. Ghosts went flying. Death pulled back in alarm and was caught in the gale, along with his table and chair.

It was silent all around. I saw the first light of dawn in the east.

"Will they be back?" I asked, my voice little more than a whisper.

The sun peeked over the hill, and Ebenezum's chair evaporated beneath him. He sat on the ground rather suddenly.

"Alas, Wuntvor," the wizard said. "I fear they haven't the ghost of a chance." Then he blew his nose.

(3)

"On occasion, a wizard may find himself taking a job that has no monetary rewards. For a good wizard, these jobs will be few and far between, but they happen to us all. They are a wizard's duty, and they do have their benefits, such as letting them be known, loudly and in great detail, anyplace you travel through the kingdom just before the tax collector is due."

from *The Teachings of Ebenezum*
Volume 16

Ebenezum and Maggie sat on one of the great stones so recently toppled by the wizard's sneezing attack, while I surveyed in wonder the devastation a single great sneeze could bring to this already bleak land.

"How?" was my only question.

"Ebby never could keep a secret from me." Maggie cackled. "But his aversion to sorcery presented something of a problem if we were to survive the night."

My master pulled at his beard. "I freed you from Unwin, remember."

"All I had to do was choose to talk to you rather than him. Unwin always was impossibly jealous. Flew off in an ectoplasmic snit. Which made you sneeze about five times."

Ebenezum tried to say something, but Maggie kept right on talking. "That's when I had the idea. If he always sneezed around the supernatural, what if he really sneezed! We couldn't take away his problem, so the two of us worked up a little spell that would increase Ebby's nasal power a hundredfold!"

"Indeed," Ebenezum said, rubbing his nose, which was sore from blowing.

"And now we're safe. And the kingdom is free. Or is it?" Maggie spat on the ground. "Death is such a trickster. I was so afraid of him when Unwin died, I gave in and let him give me five lifetimes for what he termed 'occasional use of my kingdom.' What he didn't tell me was that nothing could live in the kingdom between the times he used it." She looked around her. "Has he kept his word? If only there was a sign."

She slapped Ebenezum's shoulder. "But you still haven't heard my story."

Ebenezum looked out over the hills. "Alas, teacher, we have a long way to travel. Shoulder your pack, Wunt. We'd best move before the sun gets too high."

"You'll sit here and listen!" Maggie commanded. "Ebby never did have any manners. From the beginning. Once there was a beautiful kingdom and a fair princess. But all was not well, for one day came the dreaded rain of—"

"Ow!" I yelled. Something had bitten my arm.

Ebenezum jumped up. "Biting gnats! They're all over us!"

Maggie threw her hands up to the heavens. "My kingdom is saved!"

"Drop us a note when 'tis a little better developed!" the wizard called over his shoulder. "We'll visit then!" And we were once again traveling, somewhat more rapidly than before, with frequent slapping of arms and legs, in the general direction of Vushta.

Born in Kent, England, in 1869, ALGERNON BLACKWOOD is one of the most famous fantasy writers in all English literature. His precise, sometimes journalistic style is coupled with themes of striking originality. "The Woman's Ghost Story" is unusually gentle for him, but its humanistic tone is quietly passionate.

The Woman's Ghost Story
by Algernon Blackwood

"Yes," she said, from her seat in the dark corner, "I'll tell you an experience if you care to listen. And, what's more, I'll tell it briefly, without trimmings—I mean without unessentials. That's a thing story-tellers never do, you know," she laughed. "They drag in all the unessentials and leave their listeners to disentangle; but I'll give you just the essentials, and you can make of it what you please. But on one condition: that at the end you ask no questions, because I can't explain it and have no wish to."

We agreed. We were all serious. After listening to a dozen prolix stories from people who merely wished to "talk" but had nothing to tell, we wanted "essentials."

"In those days," she began, feeling from the quality of our silence that we were with her, "in those days I was interested in psychic things, and had arranged to sit up alone in a haunted house in the middle of London. It was a cheap and dingy lodging-house in a mean street, unfurnished. I had already made a preliminary examination in daylight that afternoon, and the keys from the caretaker, who lived next door, were in my pocket. The story was a good one—satisfied me, at any rate, that it was worth investigating; and I won't weary you with details as to the woman's murder and all the tiresome elaboration as to *why* the place was *alive*. Enough that it was.

"I was a good deal bored, therefore, to see a man, whom I took to be the talkative old caretaker, waiting for me on the steps when I went in at 11 P.M., for I had sufficiently explained that I wished to be there alone for the night.

" 'I wished to show you *the* room,' he mumbled, and of course I couldn't exactly refuse, having tipped him for the temporary loan of a chair and table.

" 'Come in, then, and let's be quick,' I said.

"We went in, he shuffling after me through the unlighted hall up to the first floor where the murder had taken place, and I prepared myself to hear his inevitable account before turning him out with the half-crown his persistence had earned. After lighting the gas I sat down in the arm-chair he had provided—a faded, brown plush arm-chair—and turned for the first time to face him and get through with the performance as quickly as possible. And it was in that instant I got my first shock. The man was *not* the caretaker. It was not the old fool, Carey, I had interviewed earlier in the day and made my plans with. My heart gave a horrid jump.

" 'Now who are *you,* pray?' I said. 'You're not Carey, the man I arranged with this afternoon. Who are you?'

"I felt uncomfortable, as you may imagine. I was a 'psychical researcher,' and a young woman of new tendencies, and proud of my liberty, but I did not care to find myself in an empty house with a stranger. Something of my confidence left me. Confidence with women, you know, is all humbug after a certain point. Or perhaps you don't know, for most of you are men. But anyhow my pluck ebbed in a quick rush, and I felt afraid.

" 'Who are you?' I repeated quickly and nervously. The fellow was well dressed, youngish and good-looking, but with a face of great sadness. I myself was barely thirty. I am giving you essentials, or I would not mention it. Out of quite ordinary things comes this story. I think that's why it has value.

" 'No,' he said; 'I'm the man who was frightened to death.'

"His voice and his words ran through me like a knife, and I felt ready to drop. In my pocket was the book I had brought to make notes in. I felt the pencil sticking in the socket. I felt, too, the extra warm things I had put on to sit up in, as no bed or sofa was available—a hundred things dashed through my mind, foolishly and without sequence or meaning, as the way is when one is really frightened. Unessentials leaped up and puzzled me, and I thought of what the papers might say if it came out, and what my 'smart' brother-in-law would think, and whether it would be told that I had cigarettes in my pocket, and was a free-thinker.

" 'The man who was frightened to death!' I repeated aghast.

" 'That's me,' he said stupidly.

"I stared at him just as you would have done—any one of you men now listening to me—and felt my life ebbing and flowing like a sort of hot fluid. You needn't laugh! That's how I felt. Small things, you know, touch the mind with great earnestness when terror is there—*real terror*. But I might have been at a middle-class tea party, for all the ideas I had: they were so ordinary!

" 'But I thought you were the caretaker I tipped this afternoon to let me sleep here!' I gasped. 'Did—did Carey send you to meet me?'

" 'No,' he replied in a voice that touched my boots somehow. 'I am the man who was frightened to death. And what is more, I am frightened *now!*'

" 'So am I!' I managed to utter, speaking instinctively. 'I'm simply terrified.'

" 'Yes,' he replied in that same odd voice that seemed to sound within me. 'But you are still in the flesh, and I—*am not!*'

"I felt the need for vigorous self-assertion. I stood up in that empty, unfurnished room, digging the nails into my palms and clenching my teeth. I was determined to assert my individuality and my courage as a new woman and a free soul.

" 'You mean to say you are not in the flesh!' I gasped. 'What in the world are you talking about?'

"The silence of the night swallowed up my voice. For the first time I realised that darkness was over the city; that dust lay upon the stairs; that the floor above was untenanted and the floor below empty. I was alone in an unoccupied and haunted house, unprotected, and a woman. I chilled. I heard the wind round the house, and knew the stars were hidden. My thoughts rushed to policemen and omnibuses, and everything that was useful and comforting. I suddenly realised what a fool I was to come to such a house alone. I was icily afraid. I thought the end of my life had come. I was an utter fool to go in for psychical research when I had not the necessary nerve.

" 'Good God!' I gasped. 'If you're not Carey, the man I arranged with, who are you?'

"I was really stiff with terror. The man moved slowly towards me across the empty room. I held out my arm to stop him, getting up out of my chair at the same moment, and he came to a halt just opposite to me, a smile on his worn, sad face.

" 'I told you who I am,' he repeated quietly with a sigh, looking at me with the saddest eyes I have ever seen, 'and I am frightened *still.*'

"By this time I was convinced that I was entertaining either a rogue or a madman, and I cursed my stupidity in bringing the man in without having seen his face. My mind was quickly made up, and I knew what to do. Ghosts and psychic phenomena flew to the winds. If I angered the creature my life might pay the price. I must humour him till I got to the door, and then race for the street. I stood bolt upright and faced him. We were about of a height, and I was a strong, athletic woman who played hockey in winter and climbed Alps in summer. My hand itched for a stick, but I had none.

" 'Now, of course, I remember,' I said with a sort of stiff smile that was very hard to force. 'Now I remember your case and the wonderful way you behaved. . . .'

"The man stared at me stupidly, turning his head to watch me as I backed more and more quickly to the door. But when his face broke into a smile I could control myself no longer. I reached the door in a run, and shot out on to the landing. Like a fool, I turned the wrong way, and stumbled over the stairs leading to the next storey. But it was too late to change. The man was after me, I was sure, though no sound of footsteps came; I dashed up the next flight, tearing my skirt and banging my ribs in the darkness, and rushed headlong into the first room I came to. Luckily the door stood ajar, and, still more fortunate, there was a key in the lock. In a second I had slammed the door, flung my whole weight against it, and turned the key.

"I was safe, but my heart was beating like a drum. A second later it seemed to stop altogether, for I saw that there was someone else in the room besides myself. A man's figure stood between me and the window, where the street lamps gave just enough light to outline his shape against the glass. I'm a plucky woman, you know, for even then I didn't give up hope, but I may tell you that I have never felt so vilely frightened in all my born days. I had locked myself in with him!

"The man leaned against the window, watching me where I lay in a collapsed heap upon the floor. So there were two men in the house with me, I reflected. Perhaps the other rooms were occupied too! What could it all mean? But, as I stared something changed in the room, or in me—hard to say which—and I realised my mistake, so that my fear, which had so far been physical, at once altered its character and became *psychical*. I became afraid in my soul instead of in my heart, and I knew immediately who this man was.

" 'How in the world did you get up here?' I stammered to him across the empty room, amazement momentarily stemming my fear.

" 'Now, let me tell you,' he began, in that odd far-away voice of his that went down my spine like a knife. 'I'm in different space, for one thing, and you'd find me in any room you went into; for according to your way of measuring, I'm *all over the house*. Space is a bodily condition, but I am out of the body, and am not affected by space. It's my condition that keeps me here. I want something to change my condition for me, for then I could get away. What I want is sympathy. Or, really, more than sympathy; I want affection—I want *love!*'

"While he was speaking I gathered myself slowly upon my feet. I wanted to scream and cry and laugh all at once, but I only succeeded in sighing, for my emotion was exhausted and a numbness was coming over me. I felt for the matches in my pocket and made a movement towards the gas-jet.

" 'I should be much happier if you didn't light the gas,' he said at once, 'for the vibrations of your light hurt me a good deal. You need not be afraid that I shall injure you. I can't touch your body to begin with, for there's a great gulf fixed, you know; and really this half-light suits me best. Now, let me continue what I was trying to say before. You know, so many people have come to this house to see me, and most of them have seen me, and one and all have been terrified. If only, oh! if only someone would be *not* terrified, but kind and loving to me! Then, you see, I might be able to change my condition and get away.'

"His voice was so sad that I felt tears start somewhere at the back of my eyes; but fear kept all else in check, and I stood shaking and cold as I listened to him.

" 'Who are you then? Of course Carey didn't send you, I know now,' I managed to utter. My thoughts scattered dreadfully and I could think of nothing to say. I was afraid of a stroke.

" 'I know nothing about Carey, or who he is,' continued the man quietly, 'and the name my body had I have forgotten, thank God; but I am the man who was frightened to death in this house ten years ago, and I have been frightened ever since, and am frightened still; for the succession of cruel and curious people who come to this house to see the ghost, and thus keep alive its atmosphere of terror, only helps to render my condition worse. If only someone would be kind to me— *laugh,* speak gently and rationally with me, cry if they like, pity, comfort, soothe me—anything but come here in curiosity and tremble as you are now doing in that corner. Now, madam, won't you take pity on me?' His voice rose to a dreadful cry. "Won't you step out into the middle of the room and try to love me a little?'

"A horrible laughter came gurgling up in my throat as I heard him, but the sense of pity was stronger than the laughter, and I found myself actually leaving the support of the wall and approaching the centre of the floor.

" 'By God!' he cried, at once straightening up against the window, 'you have done a kind act. That's the first attempt at sympathy that has been shown me since I died, and I feel better already. In life, you know, I was a misanthrope. Everything went wrong with me, and I came to hate my fellow men so much that I couldn't bear to see them even. Of course, like begets like, and this hate was returned. Finally I suffered from horrible delusions, and my room became haunted with demons that laughed and grimaced, and one night I ran into a whole cluster of them near the bed—and the fright stopped my heart and killed me. It's hate and remorse, as much as terror, that clogs me so thickly and keeps me here. If only someone could feel pity, and sympathy, and perhaps a little love for me, I could get away and be happy. When you came this afternoon to see over the house I watched you, and a little hope came to me for the first time. I saw you had courage, originality, resource— *love*. If only I could touch your heart, without frightening you, I knew I could perhaps tap that love you have stored up in your being there, and thus borrow the wings for my escape!'

"Now I must confess my heart began to ache a little, as fear left me and the man's words sank their sad meaning into me. Still, the whole affair was so incredible, and so touched with unholy quality, and the story of a woman's murder I had come to investigate had so obviously nothing to do with this thing, that I felt myself in a kind of wild dream that seemed likely to stop at any moment and leave me somewhere in bed after a nightmare.

"Moreover, his words possessed me to such an extent that I found it impossible to reflect upon anything else at all, or to consider adequately any ways and means of action or escape.

"I moved a little nearer to him in the gloom, horribly frightened, of course, but with the beginnings of a strange determination in my heart.

" 'You women,' he continued, his voice plainly thrilling at my approach, 'you wonderful women, to whom life often brings no opportunity of spending your great love, oh, if you only could know how many of *us* simply yearn for it! It would save our souls, if you but knew. Few might find the chance that you now have, but if you only spent your love freely, without definite object, just letting it flow openly for all who need, you would reach hundreds and thousands of souls like me, and *release us!* Oh, madam, I ask you again to feel with me, to be kind and gentle—and if you can to love me a little.'

"My heart did leap within me and this time the tears did come, for I could not restrain them. I laughed too, for the way he called me 'madam' sounded so odd, here in this empty room at midnight in a London street, but my laughter stopped dead and merged in a flood of weeping when I saw how my change of feeling had affected him. He had left his place by the window and was kneeling on the floor at my feet, his hands stretched out towards me, and the first signs of a kind of glory about his head.

" 'Put your arms round me and kiss me, for the love of God!' he cried. 'Kiss me, oh, kiss me, and I shall be freed! You have done so much already—now do this!'

"I stuck there, hesitating, shaking, my determination on the verge of action, yet not quite able to compass it. But the terror had almost gone.

" 'Forget that I'm a man and you're a woman,' he continued in the most beseeching voice I ever heard. 'Forget that I'm a ghost, and come out boldly and press me to you with a great kiss, and let your love flow into me. Forget yourself just for one minute and do a brave thing! Oh, love me, *love me*, LOVE ME! and I shall be free!'

"The words, or the deep force they somehow released in the centre of my being, stirred me profoundly, and an emotion infinitely greater than fear surged up over me and carried me with it across the edge of action. Without hesitation I took two steps forward towards him where he knelt, and held out my arms. Pity and love were in my heart at that moment, genuine pity, I swear, and genuine love. I forgot myself and my little tremblings in a great desire to help another soul.

" 'I love you! poor, aching, unhappy thing! I love you,' I cried through hot tears, 'and I am not the least bit afraid in the world.'

"The man uttered a curious sound, like laughter, yet not laughter, and turned his face up to me. The light from the street below fell on it, but there was another light, too, shining all round it that seemed to come from the eyes and skin. He rose to his feet and met me, and in that second I folded him to my breast and kissed him full on the lips again and again."

All our pipes had gone out, and not even a skirt rustled in that dark studio as the story-teller paused a moment to steady her voice, and put a hand softly up to her eyes before going on again.

"Now, what can I say, and how can I describe to you, all you sceptical men sitting there with pipes in your mouths, the amazing sensation I experienced of holding an intangible, impalpable thing so closely to my heart that it touched my body with equal pressure all the way down, and then melted away somewhere into my very being? For it was like seizing a rush of cool wind and feeling a touch of burning fire the moment it had struck its swift blow and passed on. A series of shocks ran all over and all through me; a momentary ecstasy of flaming sweetness and wonder thrilled down into me; my heart gave another great leap—and then I was alone.

"The room was empty. I turned on the gas and struck a match to prove it. All fear had left me, and something was singing round me in the air and in my heart like the joy of a spring morning in youth. Not all the devils or shadows or hauntings in the world could then have caused me a single tremor.

"I unlocked the door and went all over the dark house, even into kitchen and cellar and up among the ghostly attics. But the house was empty. Something had left it. I lingered a short hour, analysing, thinking, wondering—you can guess what and how, perhaps, but I won't detail, for I promised only essentials, remember—and then went out to sleep the remainder of the night in my own flat, locking the door behind me upon a house no longer haunted.

"But my uncle, Sir Henry, the owner of the house, required an account of my adventure, and of course I was in duty bound to give him some kind of a true story. Before I could begin, however, he held up his hand to stop me.

" 'First,' he said, 'I wish to tell you a little deception I ventured to practise on you. So many people have been to that house and seen the ghost that I came to think the story acted on their imaginations, and I wished to make a better test. So I invented for their benefit another story, with the idea that if you did see anything I could be sure it was not due merely to an excited imagination.'

" 'Then what you told me about a woman having been murdered, and all that, was not the true story of the haunting?'

" 'It was not. The true story is that a cousin of mine went mad in that house, and killed himself in a fit of morbid terror following upon years of miserable hypochondriasis. It is his figure that investigators see.'

" 'That explains, then,' I gasped . . .

" 'Explains what?'

"I thought of that poor struggling soul, longing all these years for escape, and determined to keep my story for the present to myself.

" 'Explains, I mean, why I did not see the ghost of the murdered woman,' I concluded.

" 'Precisely,' said Sir Henry, 'and why, if you had seen anything, it would have had value, inasmuch as it could not have been caused by the imagination working upon a story you already knew.' "

One of the most dangerous kinds of ghost is the handsome or beautiful spirit who lures a member of the opposite sex to his or her destruction. One might argue whether such creatures really are incubi and succubi or just ordinary ghosts with a grudge against the opposite sex. Whatever their origin . . . they are especially insidious; but then those who seek comeliness above all other attributes ought to be wary of the results, no matter what plane the object of their affection dwells on. . . .

The Phantom Woman

Anonymous

He took an all-possessing, burning fancy to her from the first. She was neither young nor pretty, so far as he could see—but she was wrapped round with mystery. That was the key of it all; she was noticeable in spite of herself. Her face at the window, sunset after sunset; her eyes, gazing out mournfully through the dusty panes, hypnotized the lawyer. He saw her through the twilight night after night, and he grew at length to wait through the days in a feverish waiting for dusk, and that one look at an unknown woman.

She was always at the same window on the ground floor, sitting doing nothing. She looked beyond, so the infatuated solicitor fancied, at him. Once he even thought that he detected the ghost of a friendly smile on her lips. Their eyes always met with a mute desire to make acquaintance. This romance went on for a couple of months.

Gilbert Dent assured himself that nothing in this life can possibly remain stationary, and he cudgeled his brain for a respectable manner of introducing himself to his idol.

He had hardly arrived at this point when he received a shock. There came an evening when she was not at the window.

Next morning he walked down Wood Lane on his way to the office. He always went by train, but he felt a strong disinclination to go through another day without a sight of her. His heart began to beat like a schoolgirl's as he drew near the house. If she should be at the window. He was almost disposed to take his courage in his hand and call on her, and—yes, even—tell her in a quick burst that she had mysteriously become all the world to him. He could see nothing ridiculous in this course; the possibility of her being married, or having family ties of any sort, had simply never occurred to him.

However, she was not at the window; what was more, there was a sinister silence, a sort of breathlessness about the whole place.

It was a very hot morning in late August. He looked a long time, but no face came, and no movement stirred the house.

He went his way, walking like a man who has been heavily knocked on the brow and sees stars still. That afternoon he left the office early, and in less than an hour stood at the gate again. The window was blank. He pushed the gate back—it hung on one hinge—and walked up the drive to the door. There were five steps—five steps leading up to it. At the foot he wheeled aside sharply to the window; he had a sick dread of looking through the small panes—why he could not have told.

When at last he found courage to look he saw that there was a small round table set just under the window—a work table to all appearance; one of those things with lots of little compartments all round and a lid in the middle which shut over a well-like cavity for holding pieces of needlework. He remembered that his mother had one—thirty years before.

Round the edge of the table was gripped a small, delicate hand. Gilbert Dent's eyes ran from this bloodless hand and slim wrist to a shoulder under a coarse stuff bodice—to a rather wasted throat, which was bare and flung back.

So this was the end—before the beginning. He saw her. She was dead; twisted on the floor with a ghastly face turned up toward the ceiling, and stiff fingers caught in desperation round the work table.

He stumbled away along the path and into the lane.

For a long time he could not realize the horror of this thing. The influence of the decayed house hung over him—nothing seemed real. It was quite dark when he moved away from the gate, and went in the direction of the nearest police station. That she was dead—this woman whose very name he did not know, although she influenced him so powerfully—he was certain; one look at the face would have told anyone that. That she was murdered he more than suspected. He had seen no blood about; there had been no mark on the long, bare throat, and yet the word rushed in his ears, "Murder."

Later on he went back with a police officer.

They broke into the house and entered the room. It was in utter darkness, of course, by now. Dent, his fingers trembling, struck a match. It flared round the walls and lighted them for a moment before he let it fall on the dusty floor.

The policeman began to light his lantern and turned it stolidly on the window. He had no reason for delay; he was eager to get to the bottom of the business. His professional zeal was whetted; this promised to be a mystery with a spice in it.

He turned the light full on the window; he gave a strange, choked cry, half of rage, half of apprehension. Then he went up to Gilbert Dent, who stood in the middle of the room with his hands before his eyes, and took his shoulder and shook it none too gently.

"There ain't nobody," he said.

Dent looked wildly at the window—the recess was empty except for the work table. The woman was gone.

They searched the house; they minutely inspected the garden. Everything was normal; everything told the same mournful tale—of desertion, of death, of long empty years. But they found no woman, nor trace of one.

"This house," said the policeman, looking suspiciously into the lawyer's face, "has been empty for longer than I can remember. Nobody'll live in it. They do say something about foul play a good many years ago. I don't know about that. All I do know is that the landlord can't get it off his hands."

It was doubtful if Gilbert Dent heard one word of what the man was saying. He was too stunned to do anything but creep home—when he was allowed to go—and let himself stealthily into his own house with a latch key; he was afraid even of himself. He did not go to bed that night.

As for the mystery of the woman, the matter was allowed to drop; it ended—officially. There was a shrug and a grin at the police station. The impression there was that the lawyer had been drinking—that the dead woman in the empty room was a gruesome freak of his tipsy brain.

*   *   *

A week or so later Dent called on his brother, Ned—the one near relation he had. Ned was a doctor; perhaps he was a shade more matter-of-fact than Gilbert; at all events, when the latter told his story of the house and the woman, he attributed the affair solely to liver.

"You are overworked"—the elder brother looked at the younger's yellow face. "An experience of this nature is by no means uncommon. Haven't you heard of people having their pet 'spooks'?"

"But this was a real woman," he declared. "I—I, well, I was in love with her. I had made up my mind to marry her—if I could."

Ned gave him a keen, swift glance.

"We'll go to Brighton tomorrow," he said, with quiet decision. "As for your work, everything must be put aside. You've run completely down. You ought to have been taken in hand before."

They went to Brighton, and it really seemed as if Ned was right, and that the woman at the window had been merely a nervous creation. It seemed so, that is, for nearly three weeks, and then the climax came.

It was in the twilight—she had always been part of it—that Gilbert Dent saw her again; the woman that he had found lying dead.

They were walking, the two brothers, along the cliffs.

The wind was blowing in their faces, the sea was booming beneath the cliff. Ned had just said it was about time they turned back to the hotel and had some dinner, when Gilbert with a cry leapt forward to the very edge of the flat grass path on which they were strolling. The movement was so sudden that his brother barely caught him in time. They struggled and swayed on the very edge of the cliff for a second; Gilbert, possessed by some sudden frenzy, seemed resolved to go over, but the other at last dragged him backward, and they rolled together on the close, thick turf.

At this point Gilbert opened his eyes and tried to get on his feet.

"Better?" asked his brother, cheerfully, holding out a helping hand. "Strange! The sea has that effect on some people. Didn't think that you were one of them."

"What effect?"

"Vertigo, my dear fellow."

"Ned," said the other solemnly, "I saw her. It is not worth your while to try to account for anything. I have been inclined to think that you were right—that she, the woman at the window, was a fancy, that I had fallen in love with a creation of my own brain; but I saw her again tonight. You must have seen her yourself—she was within a couple of feet of you. Why did you not try and save her? It was nothing short of murder to let her go over like that. I did my best."

"You certainly did—to kill us both," said Ned, grimly.

Gilbert gave him a wild look.

After luncheon Ned persuaded him to rest—watched him fall asleep, and then went out.

In the porch of the hotel he was met by a waiter on his return who told him that Gilbert had left about a quarter of an hour after he had himself gone out.

Directly he heard this he feared the worst; having, as is usual in such cases, a very hazy idea of what the worst might be. Of course he must follow without a moment's delay; but a reference to the timetable told him that there was not another train for an hour, and that was slow.

It was already getting dusk when he arrived there. He felt certain that Gilbert would go there. He got to the end of the lane and walked up it slowly, examining every house. There would be no difficulty in recognizing the one he wanted; Gilbert had described it in detail more than once.

He stood outside the loosely hanging gate at last, and stared through the darkness at the shabby stucco front and rank garden.

He went down a flight of steps to the back door, and finding it unfastened, stepped into a stone passage. It was one of the problems of the place that he should have avoided the main entrance door with a half-admitted dread, and that, only half admitting still, he was afraid to mount the long flight of stone stairs leading from the servants' quarters. However, he pulled himself together and went up to the room.

It was quite dark inside. He heard something scuttle across the floor; he felt the grit and dust of years under his feet. He struck a match—just as Gilbert had done—and looked first at the recess in which the window was built. The match flared round the room for a moment and gave him a flash picture of his surroundings. He saw the stripes of gaudy paper moving almost imperceptibly, like tentacles of some sea monster, from the wall; he saw a creature—it looked like a rat—scurry across the floor from the window to the great mantelpiece of hard white marble.

If he had seen nothing more than this.

He saw in detail all that the first match had flashed at him. He saw his brother lying on the floor; a ghastly coincidence, his hand was caught round the edge of the work table as hers had been. The other hand was clenched across his breast; there was a look of great agony on his face.

A dead face, of course. This was the end of the affair. He was lying dead by the window where the woman had sat every night at dusk and smiled at him.

The second match went out; the brother of the dead man struck a third. He looked again and closely. Then he staggered to his feet and gave a cry. It rang through the empty rooms and echoed without wearying down the long, stone passages in the basement.

Gilbert's head was thrown back; his chin peaked to the ceiling. On his throat were livid marks. The doctor saw them distinctly; he saw the grip of small fingers; the distinct impression of a woman's little hand.

*   *   *

The curious thing about the whole story—the most curious thing, perhaps—is that no other eye ever saw those murderous marks. So there was no scandal, no chase after the murderer, no undiscovered crime. They faded; when the doctor saw his brother again in the full light and in the presence of others his throat was clear. And the post-mortem proved that death was due to natural causes.

So the matter stands, and will.

But where the house and its overgrown garden stood runs a new road with neat red and white villas.

Whatever secret it knew—if any—it kept discreetly.

Ned Dent is morbid enough to go down the smart new road in the twilight sometimes and wonder.

An anonymous rendition of a folk tale that seems to recur in any country with lots of ice and the need for negotiating the same on skates . . . a good example of the missioned spirit whose duty it is to protect.

The Spectre Bride

Anonymous

The winter nights up at Sault Ste. Marie are as white and luminous as the Milky Way. The silence that rests upon the solitude appears to be white also. Nature has included sound in her arrestment. Save the still white frost, all things are obliterated. The stars are there, but they seem to belong to heaven and not to earth. They are at an immeasurable height, and so black is the night that the opaque ether rolls between them and the observer in great liquid billows.

In such a place it is difficult to believe that the world is peopled to any great extent. One fancies that Cain has just killed Abel, and that there is need for the greatest economy in the matter of human life.

The night Ralph Hagadorn started out for Echo Bay he felt as if he were the only man in the world, so complete was the solitude through which he was passing. He was going over to attend the wedding of his best friend, and was, in fact, to act as the groomsman. Business had delayed him, and he was compelled to make his journey at night. But he hadn't gone far before he began to feel the exhilaration of the skater. His skates were keen, his legs fit for a longer journey than the one he had undertaken, and the tang of the frost was to him what a spur is to a spirited horse.

He cut through the air as a sharp stone cleaves the water. He could feel the tumult of the air as he cleft it. As he went on he began to have fancies. It seemed to him that he was enormously tall—a great Viking of the Northland, hastening over icy fiords to his love. That reminded him that he had a love—though, indeed, that thought was always present with him as a background for other thoughts. To be sure, he had not told her she was his love, because he had only seen her a few times and the opportunity had not presented itself. She lived at Echo Bay, too, and was to be the maid of honor to his friend's bride—which was another reason why he skated on almost as swiftly as the wind, and why, now and then, he let out a shout of exhilaration.

The one drawback in the matter was that Marie Beaujeu's father had money, and that Marie lived in a fine house and wore otter skin about her throat and little satin-lined mink boots on her feet when she went sledding, and that the jacket in which she kept a bit of her dead mother's hair had a black pearl in it as big as a pea. These things made it difficult—nay, impossible—for Ralph Hagadorn to say anything more than "I love you." But that much he meant to have the satisfaction of saying, no matter what came of it.

With this determination growing upon him he swept along the ice which gleamed under the starlight. Indeed, Venus made a glowing path toward the west and seemed to reassure him. He was sorry he could not skim down that avenue of light from the love star, but he was forced to turn his back upon it and face toward the northeast.

It came to him with a shock that he was not alone. His eyelashes were a good deal frosted and his eyeballs blurred with the cold, and at first he thought it an illusion. But he rubbed his eyes hard and at length made sure that not very far in front of him was a long white skater in fluttering garments who sped over the snows fast as ever werewolf went. He called aloud, but there was no answer, and then he gave chase, setting his teeth hard and putting a tension on his firm young muscles. But however fast he might go the white skater went faster. After a time he became convinced, as he chanced to glance for a second at the North Star, that the white skater was leading him out of his direct path. For a moment he hesitated, wondering if he should not keep to his road, but the strange companion seemed to draw him on irresistibly, and so he followed.

Of course it came to him more than once that this might be no earthly guide. Up in those latitudes men see strange things when the hoar frost is on the earth. Hagadorn's father, who lived up there with the Lake Superior Indians and worked in the copper mines, had once welcomed a woman at his hut on a bitter night who was gone by morning, and who left wolf tracks in the snow—yes, it was so, and John Fontanelle, the half-breed, could tell you about it any day—if he were alive. (Alack, the snow where the wolf tracks were is melted now!)

Well, Hagadorn followed the white skater all the night, and when the ice flushed red at dawn and arrows of lovely light shot up into the cold heavens, she was gone, and Hagadorn was at his destination. Then, as he took off his skates while the sun climbed arrogantly up to his place above all other things, Hagadorn chanced to glance lakeward, and he saw there was a great wind-rift in the ice and that the waves showed blue as sapphires beside the gleaming ice. Had he swept along his intended path, watching the stars to guide him, his glance turned upward, all his body at magnificent momentum, he must certainly have gone into that cold grave. The white skater had been his guardian angel!

Much impressed, he went up to his friend's house, expecting to find there the pleasant wedding furore. But someone met him quietly at the door, and his friend came downstairs to greet him with a solemn demeanor.

"Is this your wedding face?" cried Hagadorn. "Why, really, if this is the way you are affected, the sooner I take warning the better."

"There's no wedding today," said his friend.

"No wedding? Why, you're not——"

"Marie Beaujeu died last night——"

"Marie——"

"Died last night. She had been skating in the afternoon, and she came home chilled and wandering in her mind, as if the frost had got in it somehow. She got worse and worse and talked all the time of you."

"Of me?"

"We wondered what it all meant. We didn't know you were lovers."

"I didn't know it myself; more's the pity."

"She said you were on the ice. She said you didn't know about the big breaking up, and she cried to us that the wind was off shore. Then she cried that you could come in by the old French Creek if you only knew——"

"I came in that way," interrupted Hagadorn.

"How did you come to do that? It's out of your way."

So Hagadorn told him how it came to pass.

And that day they watched beside the maiden, who had tapers at her head and feet, and over in the little church the bride who might have been at her wedding said prayers for her friend. Then they buried her in her bridesmaid's white, and Hagadorn was there before the altar with her, as he intended from the first. At midnight the day of the burial her friends were married in the gloom of the cold church, and they walked together through the snow to lay their bridal wreaths on her grave.

Three nights later Hagadorn started back again to his home. They wanted him to go by sunlight, but he had his way and went when Venus made her bright path on the ice. He hoped for the companionship of the white skater. But he did not have it. His only companion was the wind. The only voice he heard was the baying of a wolf on the north shore. The world was as white as if it had just been created and the sun had not yet colored nor man defiled it.

Can there be ghosts of things to come? Among fantasists, the following story by the author of "The Lady or the Tiger?" is nearly as popular as that remarkable puzzle tale. FRANK R. STOCKTON, *born in 1834 in Philadelphia, worked on several magazines and newspapers and produced a large number of novels and short stories, many too sugary for today's taste. But often one finds gems in his collected works, and the story of the semibarbaric princess and her doomed lover who must open one of two doors is recognized as a classic of English letters. (Equally maddening is its less familiar sequel, "The Discourager of Hesitancy," which only compounds the riddle with a second insoluble anecdote.) Here is another fine Stockton tale.*

The Philosophy of
Relative Existences

by Frank R. Stockton

In a certain summer, not long gone, my friend Bentley and I found ourselves in a little hamlet which overlooked a placid valley, through which a river gently moved, winding its way through green stretches until it turned the end of a line of low hills and was lost to view. Beyond this river, far away, but visible from the door of the cottage where we dwelt, there lay a city. Through the mists which floated over the valley we could see the outlines of steeples and tall roofs; and buildings of a character which indicated thrift and business stretched themselves down to the opposite edge of the river. The more distant parts of the city, evidently a small one, lost themselves in the hazy summer atmosphere.

Bentley was young, fair-haired, and a poet; I was a philosopher, or trying to be one. We were good friends, and had come down into this peaceful region to work together. Although we had fled from the bustle and distractions of the town, the appearance in this rural region of a city, which, so far as we could observe, exerted no influence on the quiet character of the valley in which it lay, aroused our interest. No craft plied up and down the river; there were no bridges from shore to shore; there were none of those scattered and half-squalid habitations which generally are found on the outskirts of a city; there came to us no distant sound of bells; and not the smallest wreath of smoke rose from any of the buildings.

In answer to our inquiries our landlord told us that the city over the river had been built by one man, who was a visionary, and who had a great deal more money than common sense. "It is not as big a town as you would think, sirs," he said, "because the general mistiness of things in this valley makes them look larger than they are. Those hills, for instance, when you get to them are not as high as they look to be from here. But the town is big enough, and a good deal too big; for it ruined its builder and owner, who when he came to die had not money enough left to put up a decent tombstone at the head of his grave. He had a queer idea that he would like to have his town all finished before anybody lived in it, and so he kept on working and spending money year after year and year after year until the city was done and he had not a cent left. During all the time that the place was building hundreds of people came to him to buy houses or to hire them, but he would not listen to anything of the kind. No one must live in his town until it was all done. Even his workmen were obliged to go away at night to lodge. It is a town, sirs, I am told, in which nobody has slept for even a night. There are streets there, and places of business, and churches, and public halls, and everything that a town full of inhabitants could need; but it is all empty and deserted, and has been so as far back as I can remember, and I came to this region when I was a little boy."

"And is there no one to guard the place?" we asked; "no one to protect it from wandering vagrants who might choose to take possession of the buildings?"

"There are not many vagrants in this part of the country," he said; "and if there were, they would not go over to that city. It is haunted."

"By what?" we asked.

"Well, sirs, I scarcely can tell you; queer beings that are not flesh and blood, and that is all I know about it. A good many people living hereabouts have visited that place once in their lives, but I know of no one who has gone there a second time."

"And travellers," I said; "are they not excited by curiosity to explore that strange uninhabited city?"

"Oh, yes," our host replied; "almost all visitors to the valley go over to that queer city—generally in small parties, for it is not a place in which one wishes to walk about alone. Sometimes they see things, and sometimes they don't. But I never knew any man or woman to show a fancy for living there, although it is a very good town."

This was said at suppertime, and, as it was the period of full moon, Bentley and I decided that we would visit the haunted city that evening. Our host endeavored to dissuade us, saying that no one ever went over there at night; but as we were not to be deterred, he told us where we would find his small boat tied to a stake on the river-bank. We soon crossed the river, and landed at a broad, but low, stone pier, at the land end of which a line of tall grasses waved in the gentle night wind as if they were sentinels warning us from entering the silent city. We pushed through these, and walked up a street fairly wide, and so well paved that we noticed none of the weeds and other growths which generally denote desertion or little use. By the bright light of the moon we could see that the architecture was simple, and of a character highly gratifying to the eye. All the buildings were of stone and of good size. We were greatly excited and interested, and proposed to continue our walks until the moon should set, and to return on the following morning—"to live here, perhaps," said Bentley. "What could be so romantic and yet so real? What could conduce better to the marriage of verse and philosophy?" But as he said this we saw around the corner of a cross-street some forms as of people hurrying away.

"The spectres," said my companion, laying his hand on my arm.

"Vagrants, more likely," I answered, "who have taken advantage of the superstition of the region to appropriate this comfort and beauty to themselves."

"If that be so," said Bentley, "we must have a care for our lives."

We proceeded cautiously, and soon saw other forms fleeing before us and disappearing, as we supposed, around corners and into houses. And now suddenly finding ourselves upon the edge of a wide, open public square, we saw in the dim light—for a tall steeple obscured the moon— the forms of vehicles, horses, and men moving here and there. But before, in our astonishment, we could say a word one to the other, the moon moved past the steeple, and in its bright light we could see none of the signs of life and traffic which had just astonished us.

Timidly, with hearts beating fast, but with not one thought of turning back, nor any fear of vagrants,—for we were now sure that what we had seen was not flesh and blood, and therefore harmless,—we crossed the open space and entered a street down which the moon shone clearly. Here and there we saw dim figures, which quickly disappeared; but, approaching a low stone balcony in front of one of the houses, we were surprised to see, sitting thereon and leaning over a book which lay open upon the top of the carved parapet, the figure of a woman who did not appear to notice us.

"That is a real person," whispered Bentley, "and she does not see us."

"No," I replied; "it is like the others. Let us go near it."

We drew near to the balcony and stood before it. At this the figure raised its head and looked at us. It was beautiful, it was young; but its substance seemed to be of an ethereal quality which we had never seen or known of. With its full, soft eyes fixed upon us, it spoke:—

"Why are you here?" it asked. "I have said to myself that the next time I saw any of you I would ask you why you come to trouble us. Cannot you live content in your own realms and spheres, knowing, as you must know, how timid we are, and how you frighten us and make us unhappy? In all this city there is, I believe, not one of us except myself who does not flee and hide from you whenever you cruelly come here. Even I would do that, had not I declared to myself that I would see you and speak to you, and endeavor to prevail upon you to leave us in peace."

The clear, frank tones of the speaker gave me courage. "We are two men," I answered, "strangers in this region, and living for the time in the beautiful country on the other side of the river. Having heard of this quiet city, we have come to see it for ourselves. We had supposed it to be uninhabited, but now that we find that this is not the case, we would assure you from our hearts that we do not wish to disturb or annoy any one who lives here. We simply came as honest travellers to view the city."

The figure now seated herself again, and as her countenance was nearer to us, we could see that it was filled with pensive thought. For a moment she looked at us without speaking. "Men!" she said. "And so I have been right. For a long time I have believed that the beings who sometimes come here, filling us with dread and awe, are men."

"And you," I exclaimed—"who are you, and who are these forms that we have seen, these strange inhabitants of this city?"

She gently smiled as she answered: "We are the ghosts of the future. We are the people who are to live in this city generations hence. But all of us do not know that, principally because we do not think about it and study about it enough to know it. And it is generally believed that the men and women who sometimes come here are ghosts who haunt the place."

"And that is why you are terrified and flee from us?" I exclaimed. "You think we are ghosts from another world?"

"Yes," she replied; "that is what is thought, and what I used to think."

"And you," I asked, "are spirits of human beings yet to be?"

"Yes," she answered; "but not for a long time. Generations of men, I know not how many, must pass away before we are men and women."

"Heavens!" exclaimed Bentley, clasping his hands and raising his eyes to the sky, "I shall be a spirit before you are a woman."

"Perhaps," she said again, with a sweet smile upon her face, "you may live to be very, very old."

But Bentley shook his head. This did not console him. For some minutes I stood in contemplation, gazing upon the stone pavement beneath my feet. "And this," I ejaculated, "is a city inhabited by the ghosts of the future, who believe men and women to be phantoms and spectres?"

She bowed her head.

"But how is it," I asked, "that you discovered that you are spirits and we mortal men?"

"There are so few of us who think of such things," she answered, "so few who study, ponder, and reflect. I am fond of study, and I love philosophy; and from the reading of many books I have learned much. From the book which I have here I have learned most; and from its teachings I have gradually come to the belief, which you tell me is the true one, that we are spirits and you men."

"And what book is that?" I asked.

"It is *The Philosophy of Relative Existences,* by Rupert Vance."

"Ye gods!" I exclaimed, springing upon the balcony, "that is my book, and I am Rupert Vance." I stepped toward the volume to seize it, but she raised her hand.

"You cannot touch it," she said. "It is the ghost of a book. And did you write it?"

"Write it? No," I said; "I am writing it. It is not yet finished."

"But here it is," she said, turning over the last pages. "As a spirit book it is finished. It is very successful; it is held in high estimation by intelligent thinkers; it is a standard work."

I stood trembling with emotion. "High estimation!" I said. "A standard work!"

"Oh, yes," she replied with animation; "and it well deserves its great success, especially in its conclusion. I have read it twice."

"But let me see these concluding pages," I exclaimed. "Let me look upon what I am to write."

She smiled, and shook her head, and closed the book. "I would like to do that," she said, "but if you are really a man you must not know what you are going to do."

"Oh, tell me, tell me," cried Bentley from below, "do you know a book called *Stellar Studies,* by Arthur Bentley? It is a book of poems."

The figure gazed at him. "No," it said presently; "I never heard of it."

I stood trembling. Had the youthful figure before me been flesh and blood, had the book been a real one, I would have torn it from her.

"O wise and lovely being!" I exclaimed, falling on my knees before her, "be also benign and generous. Let me but see the last page of my book. If I have been of benefit to your world; more than all, if I have been of benefit to you, let me see, I implore you—let me see how it is that I have done it."

She rose with the book in her hand. "You have only to wait until you have done it," she said, "and then you will know all that you could see here." I started to my feet, and stood alone upon the balcony.

"I am sorry," said Bentley, as we walked toward the pier where we had left our boat, "that we talked only to that ghost girl, and that the other spirits were all afraid of us. Persons whose souls are choked up with philosophy are not apt to care much for poetry; and even if my book is to be widely known, it is easy to see that she may not have heard of it."

I walked triumphant. The moon, almost touching the horizon, beamed like red gold. "My dear friend," said I, "I have always told you that you should put more philosophy into your poetry. That would make it live."

"And I have always told you," said he, "that you should not put so much poetry into your philosophy. It misleads people."

"It didn't mislead that ghost girl," said I.

"How do you know?" said Bentley. "Perhaps she is wrong, and the other inhabitants of the city are right, and we may be the ghosts after all. Such things, you know, are only relative. Anyway," he continued, after a little pause, "I wish I knew that those ghosts were now reading the poem which I am going to begin tomorrow."

This short ambiguity is intense and upsetting in its implications, and it is by a writer who claims to have seen the black-hooded figures mentioned herein. Z. Z. JEROMM is the pen name of an actor who claims considerable personal concourse with the world of the spectral.

21 *Main Street No.*
by Z. Z. Jeromm

It is my belief and the belief of my family as well as those who have lived here before me that there are sites—call them châteaus, call them estates, or apartments, or houses, or what you will—that are designated to be forever occupied by ghosts. I do not know why this should be so. I know only that it is. There are some who will dispute this—on both planes, I imagine. They are wrong. Let me cite the facts in my own case.

People have lived here, in this same general locale, maybe even in this very room, where I am now sitting alone at my desk in these dark and lonely hours that pass between dusk and daylight—my wife and children being long asleep in their beds—for some hundreds of years. The portraits that hang, dusty and neglected on the peeling walls in the west wing, are testimony enough to this, and I say dusty and neglected, for that wing is one we rarely visit; it holding such unhappy memories for us.

There is nothing—at least, nothing I know of—that should attract us to this place; rather the reverse, I should say. The weather is rarely pleasant—unenthusiastic rain by day and truculent fog by night; the contour of the land hereabouts is flat and uninteresting; the vegetation on it, boringly ordinary, and of culture—well, the less said, the better. There are no opera houses, no symphony halls, no theatres, no dance companies that visit. There is one tiny museum filled with the most trivial of artifacts and hung with paintings that have been daubed by brushes dipped in the most awful of garish tints and held by hands boasting of the least of small talents. Oh yes, there is one very old movie house with its original seats still intact and which still proudly shows films on its original screen. I have heard—for I have never graced it with my presence—that they distribute to their coarse audiences printed sheets containing the dialogue to these films rather than use and perhaps wear out their sound equipment, but this may be an exaggeration.

I mention all the above merely to illustrate the singular lack of clear motive in most people in even those choices which affect them deeply. What has attracted my ancestors to this place I don't know; any more than I know why I, myself, am here.

It is not a happy place; this house we live in, not a happy home. It has seen more than its share of tears and madness; of murders and suicides; of hauntings and exorcisms; this last a rather futile gesture designed, I should imagine, to satisfy church personnel who must keep up their pride, real estate agents who must keep up the values of those properties they handle, and all those misguided do-gooders who earn their livings toiling in the wastelands of the mass media and who must, needless to say, keep up their circulation.

Certainly, those much publicized exorcisms didn't help us.

Nor any of the others.

For the creatures are here still, now as then; coming and going day and night as they please, in their black hooded capes that fall in heavy folds to the floor, shrouding their evil in shadow; huddling in their damnable semicircles; cackling in high-pitched voices; using for their own ends the energies from the bodies of those poor, still-alive—God help them—souls. There is no defense against them; nothing to stop them in their hysterical glee from reaching into the minds of the inhabitants of this house, twisting and turning them till those minds fill with paranoid fears and suspicions and they turn on each other. I, like you, was taught that good triumphs over evil, that love is stronger than hate. Why then is it that in this house brother has killed brother, that no animal or bird or even rodent is safe, that parents destroy their own issue and each other rather than allow the sickness they feel in their breasts to burst beyond these bounds into outrageous acts against the innocent?

But in here, too, we are—were—innocent.

It was not—is not—our fault that these creatures exist. Where do they come from? I do not know. Where do they hide during those times we do not see them? Again, I do not know.

I know only that I am lonely. I should like to be either alive or dead; not a shadow in this gray world; living in this house of fear with a wife I can no longer touch, and with children whose laughter no longer rings out and who walk sadly through these rooms like the ghosts they are; like the ghosts we are.

All of us; my ancestors and possibly yours; crowding each other, jostling monstrous memories that permit no rest.

And we cannot leave.

Who are they, these creatures that hold us? Bind us to this place? Or, are they themselves bound? Held fast in the grip of an evil even beyond theirs?

Are they controlled by others?

By you, perhaps?

Yes, you, sitting solid and self-satisfied in your armchair reading these lines. Is it your love for us—or that emotion you glorify with the name—so earth-bound, so possessive, so selfish that we must forever stay to satisfy your puny longings?

Think hard.

But for your soul's sake as for ours—be honest, be merciful.

There is a new family moving in here tomorrow.

I am afraid for them.

Shakespearean actors, like most theatre people, are superstitious; a whole subclassification of taboo might be written about the production of plays by The Bard. Much of this lore is wonderfully evoked in the following eerie, amusing and ultimately glorious novella by FRITZ LEIBER, *son of a once-renowned actor of the same name. One of America's finest fantasists, Leiber here portrays the world of the touring "rep" company with rich atmosphere, and it is no surprise, since he spent two seasons himself as a Shakespearean actor in his father's company; his stage name was Francis Lathrop.*

Four Ghosts in Hamlet
by Fritz Leiber

Actors are a superstitious lot, probably because chance plays a big part in the success of a production of a company or merely an actor—and because we're still a little closer than other people to the gypsies in the way we live and think. For instance, it's bad luck to have peacock feathers on stage or say the last line of a play at rehearsals or whistle in the dressing room (the one nearest the door gets fired) or sing "God Save the Sovereign" on a railway train. (A Canadian company got wrecked that way.)

Shakespearean actors are no exceptions. They simply travel a few extra superstitions, such as the one which forbids reciting the lines of the Three Witches, or anything from *Macbeth,* for that matter, except at performances, rehearsals, and on other legitimate occasions. This might be a good rule for outsiders too—then there wouldn't be the endless flood of books with titles taken from the text of *Macbeth*—you know, *Brief Candles, Tomorrow and Tomorrow, The Sound and the Fury, A Poor Player, All Our Yesterdays,* and those are all just from one brief soliloquy.

And our company, the Governor's company, has a rule against the Ghost in *Hamlet* dropping his greenish cheesecloth veil over his helmet-framed face until the very moment he makes each of his entrances. Hamlet's dead father mustn't stand veiled in the darkness of the wings.

This last superstition commemorates something which happened not too long ago, an actual ghost story. Sometimes I think it's the greatest ghost story in the world—though certainly not from my way of telling it, which is gossipy and poor, but from the wonder blazing at its core.

It's not only a true tale of the supernatural, but also very much a story about people, for after all—and before everything else—ghosts are people.

The ghostly part of the story first showed itself in the tritest way imaginable: three of our actresses (meaning practially all the ladies in a Shakespearean company) took to having sessions with a Ouija board in the hour before curtain time and sometimes even during a performance when they had long offstage waits, and they became so wrapped up in it and conceited about it and they squeaked so excitedly at the revelations which the planchette spelled out—and three or four times almost missed entrances because of it—that if the Governor weren't such a tolerant commander-in-chief, he would have forbidden them to bring the board to the theater. I'm sure he was tempted to and might have, except that Props pointed out to him that our three ladies probably wouldn't enjoy Ouija sessions one bit in the privacy of a hotel room, that much of the fun in operating a Ouija board is in having a half-exasperated, half-intrigued floating audience, and that when all's done the basic business of all ladies is glamour, whether of personal charm or of actual witchcraft, since the word means both.

Props—that is, our property man, Billy Simpson—was fascinated by their obsession, as he is by any new thing that comes along, and might very well have broken our Shakespearean taboo by quoting the Three Witches about them, except that Props has no flair for Shakespearean speech at all, no dramatic ability whatsoever, in fact he's the one person in our company who never acts even a bit part or carries a mute spear on stage, though he has other talents which make up for this deficiency —he can throw together a papier-mache bust of Pompey in two hours, or turn out a wooden prop dagger all silvery bladed and hilt-gilded, or fix a zipper, and that's not all.

As for myself, I was very irked at the ridiculous alphabet board, since it seemed to occupy most of Monica Singleton's spare time and satisfy all her hunger for thrills. I'd been trying to promote a romance with her—a long touring season becomes deadly and cold without some sort of heart-tickle—and for a while I'd made progress. But after Ouija came along, I became a ridiculous Guildenstern mooning after an unattainable unseeing Ophelia—which were the parts I and she actually played in *Hamlet*.

I cursed the idiot board with its childish corner-pictures of grinning suns and smirking moons and windblown spirits, and I further alienated Monica by asking her why wasn't it called a Nenein or No-No board (Ninny board!) instead of a Yes-Yes board? Was that, I inquired, because all spiritualists are forever accentuating the positive and behaving like a pack of fawning yes-men?—yes, we're here; yes, we're your uncle Harry; yes, we're happy on this plane; yes, we have a doctor among us who'll diagnose that pain in your chest; and so on.

Monica wouldn't speak to me for a week after that.

I would have been even more depressed except that Props pointed out to me that no flesh-and-blood man can compete with ghosts in a girl's affections, since ghosts being imaginary have all the charms and perfections a girl can dream of, but that all girls eventually tire of ghosts, or if their minds don't, their bodies do. This eventually did happen, thank goodness, in the case of myself and Monica, though not until we'd had a grisly, mind-wrenching experience—a night of terrors before the nights of love.

So Ouija flourished and the Governor and the rest of us put up with it one way or another, until there came that three-night stand in Wolverton, when its dismal uncanny old theater tempted our three Ouija-women to ask the board who was the ghost haunting the spooky place and the swooping planchette spelled out the name S-H-A-K-E-S-P-E-A-R-E. . . .

But I am getting ahead of my story. I haven't introduced our company except for Monica, Props, and the Governor—and I haven't identified the last of those three.

We call Gilbert Usher the Governor out of sheer respect and affection. He's about the last of the old actor-managers. He hasn't the name of Gielgud or Olivier or Evans or Richardson, but he's spent most of a lifetime keeping Shakespeare alive, spreading that magical a-religious gospel in the more remote counties and the Dominions and the United States, like Benson once did. Our other actors aren't names at all—I refuse to tell you mine!—but with the exception of myself they're good troupers, or if they don't become that the first season, they drop out. Gruelingly long seasons, much uncomfortable traveling, and small profits are our destiny.

This particular season had got to that familiar point where the plays are playing smoothly and everyone's a bit tireder than he realizes and the restlessness sets in. Robert Dennis, our juvenile, was writing a novel of theatrical life (he said) mornings at the hotel—up at seven to slave at it, our Robert claimed. Poor old Guthrie Boyd had started to drink again, and drink quite too much, after an abstemious two months which had astonished everyone.

Francis Farley Scott, our leading man, had started to drop hints that he was going to organize a Shakespearean repertory company of his own next year and he began to have conspiratorial conversations with Gertrude Grainger, our leading lady, and to draw us furtively aside one by one to make us hypothetical offers, no exact salary named. F.F. is as old as the Governor—who is our star, of course—and he has no talents at all except for self-infatuation and a somewhat grandiose yet impressive fashion of acting. He's portly like an opera tenor and quite bald and he travels an assortment of thirty toupees, ranging from red to black shot with silver, which he alternates with shameless abandon—they're for wear offstage, not on. It doesn't matter to him that the company knows all about his multicolored artificial toppings, for we're part of his world of illusion, and he's firmly convinced that the stage-struck local ladies he squires about never notice, or at any rate mind the deception. He once gave me a lecture on the subtleties of suiting the color of your hair to the lady you're trying to fascinate—her own age, hair color, and so on.

Every year F.F. plots to start a company of his own—it's a regular midseason routine with him—and every year it comes to nothing, for he's as lazy and impractical as he is vain. Yet F.F. believes he could play any part in Shakespeare or all of them at once in a pinch; perhaps the only F. F. Scott Company which would really satisfy him would be one in which he would be the only actor—a Shakespearean monologue; in fact, the one respect in which F.F. is not lazy is in his eagerness to double as many parts as possible in any single play.

F.F.'s yearly plots never bother the Governor a bit—he keeps waiting wistfully for F.F. to fix him with an hypnotic eye and in a hoarse whisper ask *him* to join the Scott company.

And I of course was hoping that now at last Monica Singleton would stop trying to be the most exquisite ingenue that ever came tripping Shakespeare's way (rehearsing her parts even in her sleep, I guessed, though I was miles from being in a position to know that for certain) and begin to take note and not just advantage of my devoted attentions.

But then old Sybil Jameson bought the Ouija board and Gertrude Grainger dragooned an unwilling Monica into placing her fingertips on the planchette along with theirs "just for a lark." Next day Gertrude announced to several of us in a hushed voice that Monica had the most amazing undeveloped mediumistic talent she'd ever encountered, and from then on the girl was a Ouija-addict. Poor tight-drawn Monica, I suppose she had to explode out of her self-imposed Shakespearean discipline somehow, and it was just too bad it had to be the board instead of me. Though come to think of it, I shouldn't have felt quite so resentful of the board, for she might have exploded with Robert Dennis, which would have been infinitely worse, though we were never quite sure of Robert's sex. For that matter I wasn't sure of Gertrude's and suffered agonies of uncertain jealousy when she captured my beloved. I was obsessed with the vision of Gertrude's bold knees pressing Monica's under the Ouija board, though with Sybil's bony ones for chaperones, fortunately.

Francis Farley Scott, who was jealous too because this new toy had taken Gertrude's mind off their annual plottings, said rather spitefully that Monica must be one of those grabby girls who have to take command of whatever they get their fingers on, whether it's a man or a planchette, but Props told me he'd bet anything that Gertrude and Sybil had "followed" Monica's first random finger movements like the skillfulest dancers guiding a partner while seeming to yield, in order to coax her into the business and make sure of their third.

Sometimes I thought that F.F. was right and sometimes Props and sometimes I thought that Monica had a genuine supernatural talent, though I don't ordinarily believe in such things, and that last really frightened me, for such a person might give up live men for ghosts forever. She was such a sensitive, subtle, wraith-cheeked girl and she could get so keyed up and when she touched the planchette her eyes got such an empty look, as if her mind had traveled down into her fingertips or out to the ends of time and space. And once the three of them gave me a character reading from the board which embarrassed me with its accuracy. The same thing happened to several other people in the company. Of course, as Props pointed out, actors can be pretty good character analysts whenever they stop being egomaniacs.

After reading characters and foretelling the future for several weeks, our Three Weird Sisters got interested in reincarnation and began asking the board and then telling us what famous or infamous people we'd been in past lives. Gertrude Grainger had been Queen Boadicea, I wasn't surprised to hear. Sybil Jameson had been Cassandra. While Monica was once mad Queen Joanna of Castile and more recently a prize hysterical patient of Janet at the Salpetriere—touches which irritated and frightened me more than they should have. Billy Simpson—Props—had been an Egyptian silversmith under Queen Hatshepsut and later a servant of Samuel Pepys; he heard this with a delighted chuckle. Guthrie Boyd had been the Emperor Claudius and Robert Dennis had been Caligula. For some reason I had been both John Wilkes Booth and Lambert Simnel, which irritated me considerably, for I saw no romance but only neurosis in assassinating an American president and dying in a burning barn, or impersonating the Earl of Warwick, pretending unsuccessfully to the British throne, being pardoned for it—of all things!—and spending the rest of my life as a scullion in the kitchen of Henry VII and his son. The fact that both Booth and Simnel had been actors of a sort—a poor sort—naturally irritated me the more. Only much later did Monica confess to me that the board had probably made those decisions because I had had such a "tragic, dangerous, defeated look"—a revelation which surprised and flattered me.

Francis Farley Scott was flattered too, to hear he'd once been Henry VIII—he fancied all those wives and he wore his golden-blond toupee after the show that night—until Gertrude and Sybil and Monica announced that the Governor was a reincarnation of no less than William Shakespeare himself. That made F.F. so jealous that he instantly sat down at the prop table, grabbed up a quill pen, and did an impromptu rendering of Shakespeare composing Hamlet's "To be or not to be" soliloquy. It was an effective performance, though with considerably more frowning and eye-rolling and trying of lines for sound than I imagine Willy S. himself used originally, and when F.F. finished, even the Governor, who'd been standing unobserved in the shadows beside Props, applauded with the latter.

Governor kidded the pants off the idea of himself as Shakespeare. He said that if Willy S. were ever reincarnated it ought to be as a world-famous dramatist who was secretly in his spare time the world's greatest scientist and philosopher and left clues to his identity in his mathematical equations—that way he'd get his own back at Bacon, or rather the Baconians.

Yet I suppose if you had to pick someone for a reincarnation of Shakespeare, Gilbert Usher wouldn't be a bad choice. Insofar as a star and director ever can be, the Governor is gentle and self-effacing—as Shakespeare himself must have been, or else there would never have arisen that ridiculous Bacon-Oxford-Marlowe-Elizabeth-take-your-pick-who-wrote-Shakespeare controversy. And the Governor has a sweet melancholy about him, though he's handsomer and, despite his years, more athletic than one imagines Shakespeare being. And he's generous to a fault, especially where old actors who've done brave fine things in the past are concerned.

This season his mistake in that last direction had been in hiring Guthrie Boyd to play some of the more difficult older leading roles, including a couple F.F. usually handles: Brutus, Othello, and, besides those, Duncan in *Macbeth,* Kent in *King Lear,* and the Ghost in *Hamlet.*

Guthrie was a bellowing hard-drinking bear of an actor, who'd been a Shakespearean star in Australia and successfully smuggled some of his reputation west—he learned to moderate his bellowing, while his emotions were always simple and sincere, though explosive—and finally even spent some years in Hollywood. But there his drinking caught up with him, probably because of the stupid film parts he got, and he failed six times over. His wife divorced him. His children cut themselves off. He married a starlet and she divorced him. He dropped out of sight.

Then after several years the Governor ran into him. He'd been rusticating in Canada with a stubborn teetotal admirer. He was only a shadow of his former self, but there was some substance to the shadow —and he wasn't drinking. The Governor decided to take a chance on him—although the company manager Harry Grossman was dead set against it—and during rehearsals and the first month or so of performances it was wonderful to see how old Guthrie Boyd came back, exactly as if Shakespeare were a restorative medicine.

It may be stuffy or sentimental of me to say so, but you know, I think Shakespeare's good for people. I don't know of an actor, except myself, whose character hasn't been strengthened and his vision widened and charity quickened by working in the plays. I've heard that before Gilbert Usher became a Shakespearean, he was a more ruthlessly ambitious and critical man, not without malice, but the plays mellowed him, as they've mellowed Props's philosophy and given him a zest for life.

Because of his contact with Shakespeare, Robert Dennis is a less strident and pettish swish (if he is one), Gertrude Grainger's outbursts of cold rage have an undercurrent of queenly make-believe, and even Francis Farley Scott's grubby little seductions are probably kinder and less insultingly illusionary.

In fact I sometimes think that what civilized serenity the British people possess, and small but real ability to smile at themselves, is chiefly due to their good luck in having had William Shakespeare born one of their company.

But I was telling how Guthrie Boyd performed very capably those first weeks, against the expectations of most of us, so that we almost quit holding our breaths—or sniffing at his. His Brutus was workmanlike, his Kent quite fine—that bluff, rough, honest part suited him well—and he regularly got admiring notices for his Ghost in *Hamlet.* I think his years of living death as a drinking alcoholic had given him an understanding of loneliness and frozen abilities and despair that he put to good use—probably unconsciously—in interpreting that small role.

He was really a most impressive figure in the part, even just visually. The Ghost's basic costume is simple enough—a big all-enveloping cloak that brushes the ground-cloth, a big dull helmet with the tiniest battery light inside its peak to throw a faint green glow on the Ghost's features, and over the helmet a veil of greenish cheesecloth that registers as mist to the audience. He wears a suit of stage armor under the cloak, but that's not important and at a pinch he can do without it, for his cloak can cover his entire body.

The Ghost doesn't switch on his helmet-light until he makes his entrance, for fear of it being glimpsed by an edge of the audience, and nowadays because of that superstition or rule I told you about, he doesn't drop the cheesecloth veil until the last second either, but when Guthrie Boyd was playing the part that rule didn't exist and I have a vivid recollection of him standing in the wings, waiting to go on, a big bearish inscrutable figure about as solid and unsupernatural as a bushy seven-foot evergreen covered by a gray tarpaulin. But then when Guthrie would switch on the tiny light and stride smoothly and silently on stage and his hollow distant tormented voice boomed out, there'd be a terrific shivery thrill, even for us backstage, as if we were listening to words that really had traveled across black windy infinite gulfs from the Afterworld or the Other Side.

At any rate Guthrie was a great Ghost, and adequate or a bit better than that in most of his other parts—for those first nondrinking weeks. He seemed very cheerful on the whole, modestly buoyed up by his comeback, though sometimes something empty and dead would stare for a moment out of his eyes—the old drinking alcoholic wondering what all this fatiguing sober nonsense was about. He was especially looking forward to our three-night stand at Wolverton, although that was still two months in the future then. The reason was that both his children—married and with families now, of course—lived and worked at Wolverton and I'm sure he set great store on proving to them in person his rehabilitation, figuring it would lead to a reconciliation and so on.

But then came his first performance as Othello. (The Governor, although the star, always played Iago—an equal role, though not the title one.) Guthrie was almost too old for Othello, of course, and besides that, his health wasn't good—the drinking years had taken their toll of his stamina and the work of rehearsals and of first nights in eight different plays after years away from the theater had exhausted him. But somehow the old volcano inside him got seething again and he gave a magnificent performance. Next morning the papers raved about him and one review rated him even better than the Governor.

That did it, unfortunately. The glory of his triumph was too much for him. The next night—*Othello* again—he was drunk as a skunk. He remembered most of his lines—though the Governor had to throw him about every sixth one out of the side of his mouth—but he weaved and wobbled, he planked a big hand on the shoulder of every other character he addressed to keep from falling over, and he even forgot to put in his false teeth the first two acts, so that his voice was mushy. To cap that, he started really to strangle Gertrude Grainger in the last scene, until that rather brawny Desdemona, unseen by the audience, gave him a knee in the gut; then, after stabbing himself, he flung the prop dagger high in the flies so that it came down with two lazy twists and piercing the ground-cloth buried its blunt point deep in the soft wood of the stage floor not three feet from Monica, who plays Iago's wife, Emilia, and so was lying dead on the stage at that point in the drama, murdered by her villainous husband—and might have been dead for real if the dagger had followed a slightly different trajectory.

Since a third performance of *Othello* was billed for the following night, the Governor had no choice but to replace Guthrie with Francis Farley Scott, who did a good job (for him) of covering up his satisfaction at getting his old role back. F.F., always a plushy and lascivious-eyed Moor, also did a good job with the part, coming in that way without even a brush-up rehearsal, so that one critic, catching the first and third shows, marveled how we could change big roles at will, thinking we'd done it solely to demonstrate our virtuosity.

Of course the Governor read the riot act to Guthrie and carried him off to a doctor, who without being prompted threw a big scare into him about his drinking and his heart, so that he just might have recovered from his lapse, except that two nights later we did *Julius Caesar* and Guthrie, instead of being satisfied with being workmanlike, decided to recoup himself with a really rousing performance. So he bellowed and groaned and bugged his eyes as I suppose he had done in his palmiest Australian days. His optimistic self-satisfaction between scenes was frightening to behold. Not too terrible a performance, truly, but the critics all panned him and one of them said, "Guthrie Boyd played Brutus —a bunch of vocal cords wrapped up in a toga."

That tied up the package and knotted it tight. Thereafter Guthrie was

medium pie-eyed from morning to night—and often more than medium.
The Governor had to yank him out of Brutus too (F.F. again replacing), but being the Governor he didn't sack him. He put him into a couple of bit parts—Montano and the Soothsayer—in *Othello* and *Caesar*
and let him keep on at the others, and he gave me and Joe Rubens and
sometimes Props the job of keeping an eye on the poor old sot and
making sure he got to the theater by the half hour and if possible not
too plastered. Often he played the Ghost or the Doge of Venice in his
street clothes under cloak or scarlet robe, but he played them. And
many were the nights Joe and I made the rounds of half the local bars
before we corraled him. The Governor sometimes refers to Joe Rubens
and me in mild derision as "the American element" in his company, but
just the same he depends on us quite a bit; and I certainly don't mind
being one of his trouble-shooters—it's a joy to serve him.

All this may seem to contradict my statement about our getting to the
point, about this time, where the plays were playing smoothly and the
monotony setting in. But it doesn't really. There's always something
going wrong in a theatrical company—anything else would be abnormal;
just as the Samoans say no party is a success until somebody's dropped
a plate or spilled a drink or tickled the wrong woman.

Besides, once Guthrie had got Othello and Brutus off his neck, he
didn't do too badly. The little parts and even Kent he could play passa-
bly whether drunk or sober. King Duncan, for instance, and the Doge in
The Merchant are easy to play drunk because the actor always has a
couple of attendants to either side of him, who can guide his steps if he
weaves and even hold him up if necessary—which can turn out to be an
effective dramatic touch, registering as the infirmity of extreme age.

And somehow Guthrie continued to give that same masterful performance as the Ghost and get occasional notices for it. In fact Sybil
Jameson insisted he was a shade better in the Ghost now that he was in-
variably drunk; which could have been true. And he still talked about
the three-night stand coming up in Wolverton, though now as often with
gloomy apprehension as with proud fatherly anticipation.

Well, the three-night stand eventually came. We arrived at Wolverton
on a nonplaying evening. To the surprise of most of us, but especially
Guthrie, his son and daughter were there at the station to welcome him
with their respective spouses and all their kids and numerous in-laws
and a great gaggle of friends. Their cries of greeting when they spotted
him were almost an organized cheer and I looked around for a brass
band to strike up.

I found out later that Sybil Jameson, who knew them, had been sending them all his favorable notices, so that they were eager as weasels to be reconciled with him and show him off as blatantly as possible.

When he saw his children's and grandchildren's faces and realized the cries were for him, old Guthrie got red in the face and beamed like the sun, and they closed in around him and carried him off in triumph for an evening of celebrations.

Next day I heard from Sybil, whom they'd carried off with him, that everything had gone beautifully. He'd drunk like a fish, but kept marvellous control, so that no one but she noticed, and the warmth of the reconciliation of Guthrie to everyone, complete strangers included, had been wonderful to behold. Guthrie's son-in-law, a pugnacious chap, had got angry when he'd heard Guthrie wasn't to play Brutus the third night, and he declared that Gilbert Usher must be jealous of his magnificent father-in-law. Everything was forgiven twenty times over. They'd even tried to put old Sybil to bed with Guthrie, figuring romantically, as people will about actors, that she must be his mistress. All this was very fine, and of course wonderful for Guthrie, and for Sybil too in a fashion, yet I suppose the unconstrained night-long bash, after two months of uninterrupted semicontrolled drunkenness, was just about the worst thing anybody could have done to the old boy's sodden body and laboring heart.

Meanwhile on that first evening I accompanied Joe Rubens and Props to the theater we were playing at Wolverton to make sure the scenery got stacked right and the costume trunks were all safely arrived and stowed. Joe is our stage manager besides doing rough or Hebraic parts like Caliban and Tubal—he was a professional boxer in his youth and got his nose smashed crooked. Once I started to take boxing lessons from him, figuring an actor should know everything, but during the third lesson I walked into a gentle right cross and, although it didn't exactly stun me, there were bells ringing faintly in my head for six hours afterwards and I lived in a world of faery and that was the end of my fistic career. Joe is actually a most versatile actor—for instance, he understudies the Governor in Macbeth, Lear, Iago, and of course Shylock —though his brutal moon-face is against him, especially when his make-up doesn't include a beard. But he dotes on being genial and in the States he often gets a job by day playing Santa Claus in big department stores during the month before Christmas.

The Monarch was a cavernous old place, very grimy backstage, but with a great warren of dirty little dressing rooms and even a property room shaped like an L stage left. Its empty shelves were thick with dust.

There hadn't been a show in the Monarch for over a year, I saw from the yellowing sheets thumbtacked to the callboard as I tore them off and replaced them with a simple black-crayoned HAMLET: TO-NIGHT AT 8:30.

Then I noticed, by the cold inadequate working lights, a couple of tiny dark shapes dropping down from the flies and gliding around in wide swift circles—out into the house too, since the curtain was up. Bats, I realized with a little start—the Monarch was really halfway through the lich gate. The bats would fit very nicely with *Macbeth*, I told myself, but not so well with *The Merchant of Venice*, while with Hamlet they should neither help nor hinder, provided they didn't descend in nightfighter squadrons; it would be nice if they stuck to the Ghost scenes.

I'm sure the Governor had decided we'd open at Wolverton with *Hamlet* so that Guthrie would have the best chance of being a hit in his children's home city.

Billy Simpson, shoving his properties table into place just in front of the dismal L of the prop room, observed cheerfully, "It's a proper haunted house. The girls'll find some rare ghosts here, I'll wager, if they work their board."

Which turned out to be far truer than he realized at the time—I think.

"Bruce!" Joe Rubens called to me. "We better buy a couple of rat traps and set them out. There's something scuttling back of the drops."

But when I entered the Monarch next night, well before the hour, by the creaky thick metal stage door, the place had been swept and tidied a bit. With the ground-cloth down and the *Hamlet* set up, it didn't look too terrible, even though the curtain was still unlowered, dimly showing the house and its curves of empty seats and the two faint green exit lights with no one but myself to look at them.

There was a little pool of light around the callboard stage right, and another glow the other side of the stage beyond the wings, and lines of light showing around the edges of the door of the second dressing room, next to the star's.

I started across the dark stage, sliding my shoes softly so as not to trip over a cable or stage-screw and brace, and right away I got the magic electric feeling I often do in an empty theater the night of a show. Only this time there was something additional, something that started a shiver crawling down my neck. It wasn't, I think, the thought of the bats which might now be swooping around me unseen, skirling their inaudibly shrill trumpet calls, or even of the rats which *might* be watching sequin-eyed from behind trunks and flats, although not an hour ago Joe had told me that the traps he'd actually procured and set last night had been empty today.

No, it was more as if all of Shakespeare's characters were invisibly there around me—all the infinite possibilities of the theater. I imagined Rosalind and Falstaff and Prospero standing arm-in-arm watching me with different smiles. And Caliban grinning down from where he silently swung in the flies. And side by side, but unsmiling and not arm-in-arm: Macbeth and Iago and Dick the Three Eyes—Richard III. And all the rest of Shakespeare's myriad-minded good-evil crew.

I passed through the wings opposite and there in the second pool of light Billy Simpson sat behind his table with the properties for *Hamlet* set out on it: the skulls, the foils, the lantern, the purses, the parchmenty letters, Ophelia's flowers, and all the rest. It was odd Props having everything ready quite so early and a bit odd too that he should be alone, for Props has the un-actorish habit of making friends with all sorts of locals, such as policemen and porters and flower women and newsboys and shopkeepers and tramps who claim they're indigent actors, and even inviting them backstage with him—a fracture of rules which the Governor allows since Props is such a sensible chap. He has a great liking for people, especially low people, Props has, and for all the humble details of life. He'd make a good writer, I'd think, except for his utter lack of dramatic flair and story-skill—a sort of prosiness that goes with his profession.

And now he was sitting at his table, his stooped shoulders almost inside the doorless entry to the empty-shelfed prop room—no point in using it for a three-night stand—and he was gazing at me quizzically. He has a big forehead—the light was on that—and a tapering chin—that was in shadow—and rather large eyes, which were betwixt the light and the dark. Sitting there like that, he seemed to me for a moment (mostly because of the outspread props, I guess) like the midnight Master of the Show in *The Rubaiyat* round whom all the rest of us move like shadow shapes.

Usually he has a quick greeting for anyone, but tonight he was silent, and that added to the illusion.

"Props," I said, "this theater's got a supernatural smell."

His expression didn't change at that, but he solemnly sniffed the air in several little whiffles adding up to one big inhalation, and as he did so he threw his head back, bringing his weakish chin into the light and shattering the illusion.

"Dust," he said after a moment. "Dust and old plush and scenery water-paint and sweat and drains and gelatin and greasepaint and powder and a breath of whisky. But the supernatural . . . no, I can't smell that. Unless . . ." And he sniffed again, but shook his head.

I chuckled at his materialism—although that touch about whisky did seem fanciful, since I hadn't been drinking and Props never does and Guthrie Boyd was nowhere in evidence. Props has a mind like a notebook for sensory details—and for the minutiae of human habits too. It was Props, for instance, who told me about the actual notebook in which John McCarthy (who would be playing Fortinbras and the Player King in a couple of hours) jots down the exact number of hours he sleeps each night and keeps totting them up, so he knows when he'll have to start sleeping extra hours to average the full nine he thinks he must get each night to keep from dying.

It was also Props who pointed out to me that F.F. is much more careless gumming his offstage toupees to his head than his theater wigs— a studied carelessness, like that in tying a bowtie, he assured me; it indicated, he said, a touch of contempt for the whole offstage world.

Props isn't *only* a detail-worm, but it's perhaps because he is one that he has sympathy for all human hopes and frailties, even the most trivial, like my selfish infatuation with Monica.

Now I said to him, "I didn't mean an actual smell, Billy. But back there just now I got the feeling anything might happen tonight."

He nodded slowly and solemnly. With anyone but Props I'd have wondered if he weren't a little drunk. Then he said, "You were on a stage. You know, the science fiction writers are missing a bet there. We've got time machines right now. Theaters. Theaters are time machines and spaceships too. They take people on trips through the future and the past and the elsewhere and the might-have-been—yes, and if it's done well enough, give them glimpses of Heaven and Hell."

I nodded back at him. Such grotesque fancies are the closest Props ever comes to escaping from prosiness.

I said, "Well, let's hope Guthrie gets aboard the spaceship before the curtain up-jets. Tonight we're depending on his children having the sense to deliver him here intact. Which from what Sybil says about them is not to be taken for granted."

Props stared at me owlishly and slowly shook his head. "Guthrie got here about ten minutes ago," he said, "and looking no drunker than usual."

"That's a relief," I told him, meaning it.

"The girls are having a Ouija session," he went on, as if he were determined to account for all of us from moment to moment. "They smelt the supernatural here, just as you did, and they're asking the board to name the culprit." Then he stooped so that he looked almost hunchbacked and he felt for something under the table.

I nodded. I'd guess the Ouija part from the lines of light showing around the door of Gertrude Grainger's dressing room.

Props straightened up and he had a pint bottle of whisky in his hand. I don't think a loaded revolver would have dumbfounded me as much. He unscrewed the top.

"There's the Governor coming in," he said tranquilly, hearing the stage door creak and evidently some footsteps my own ears missed. "That's seven of us in the theater before the hour."

He took a big slow swallow of whisky and recapped the bottle, as naturally as if it were a nightly action. I goggled at him without comment. What he was doing was simply unheard of—for Billy Simpson.

At that moment there was a sharp scream and a clatter of thin wood and something twangy and metallic falling and a scurry of footsteps. Our previous words must have cocked a trigger in me, for I was at Gertrude Grainger's dressing-room door as fast as I could sprint—no worry this time about tripping over cables or braces in the dark.

I yanked the door open and there by the bright light of the bulbs framing the mirror were Gertrude and Sybil sitting close together with the Ouija board face down on the floor in front of them along with a flimsy wire-backed chair, overturned. While pressing back into Gertrude's costumes hanging on the rack across the little room, almost as if she wanted to hide behind them liked bedclothes, was Monica pale and staring-eyed. She didn't seem to recognize me. The dark-green heavily brocaded costume Gertrude wears as the Queen in *Hamlet,* into which Monica was chiefly pressing herself, accentuated her pallor. All three of them were in their street clothes.

I went to Monica and put an arm around her and gripped her hand. It was cold as ice. She was standing rigidly.

While I was doing that, Gertrude stood up and explained in rather haughty tones what I told you earlier: about them asking the board who the ghost was haunting the Monarch tonight and the planchette spelling out S-H-A-K-E-S-P-E-A-R-E . . .

"I don't know why it startled you so, dear," she ended crossly, speaking to Monica. "It's very natural his spirit should attend performances of his plays."

I felt the slim body I clasped relax a little. That relieved me. I was selfishly pleased at having got an arm around it, even under such public and unamorous circumstances, while at the same time my silly mind was thinking that if Props had been lying to me about Guthrie Boyd having come in no more drunken than usual (this new Props who drank straight whisky in the theater could lie too, I supposed), why then we could certainly use William Shakespeare tonight, since the Ghost in *Hamlet* is the one part in all his plays Shakespeare himself is supposed to have acted on the stage.

"I don't know why myself now," Monica suddenly answered from beside me, shaking her head as if to clear it. She became aware of me at last, started to pull away, then let my arm stay around her.

The next voice that spoke was the Governor's. He was standing in the doorway, smiling faintly, with Props peering around his shoulder. Props would be as tall as the Governor if he ever straightened up, but his stoop takes almost a foot off his height.

The Governor said softly, a comic light in his eyes, "I think we should be content to bring Shakespeare's plays to life, without trying for their author. It's hard enough on the nerves just to *act* Shakespeare."

He stepped forward with one of his swift, naturally graceful movements and kneeling on one knee he picked up the fallen board and planchette. "At all events I'll take these in charge for tonight. Feeling better now, Miss Singleton?" he asked as he straightened and stepped back.

"Yes, quite all right," she answered flusteredly, disengaging my arm and pulling away from me rather too quickly.

He nodded. Gertrude Grainger was staring at him coldly, as if about to say something scathing, but she didn't. Sybil Jameson was looking at the floor. She seemed embarrassed, yet puzzled too.

I followed the Governor out of the dressing room and told him, in case Props hadn't, about Guthrie Boyd coming to the theater early. My momentary doubt of Props's honesty seemed plain silly to me now, although his taking that drink remained an astonishing riddle.

Props confirmed me about Guthrie coming in, though his manner was a touch abstracted.

The Governor nodded his thanks for the news, then twitched a nostril and frowned. I was sure he'd caught a whiff of alcohol and didn't know to which of us two to attribute it—or perhaps even to one of the ladies, or to an earlier passage of Guthrie this way.

He said to me, "Would you come into my dressing room for a bit, Bruce?"

I followed him, thinking he'd picked me for the drinker and wondering how to answer—best perhaps simply silently accept the fatherly lecture—but when he'd turned on the lights and I'd shut the door, his first question was, "You're attracted to Miss Singleton, aren't you, Bruce?"

When I nodded abruptly, swallowing my morsel of surprise, he went on softly but emphatically, "Then why don't you quit hovering and playing Galahad and really go after her? Ordinarily I must appear to frown on affairs in the company, but in this case it would be the best way I know of to break up those Ouija sessions, which are obviously harming the girl."

I managed to grin and tell him I'd be happy to obey his instructions— and do it entirely on my own initiative too.

He grinned back and started to toss the Ouija board on his couch, but instead put it and the planchette carefully down on the end of his long dressing table and put a second question to me.

"What do you think of some of this stuff they're getting over the board, Bruce?"

I said, "Well, that last one gave me a shiver, all right—I suppose because . . ." and I told him about sensing the presence of Shakespeare's characters in the dark. I finished, "But of course the whole idea is nonsense," and I grinned.

He didn't grin back.

I continued impulsively, "There was one idea they had a few weeks back that impressed me, though it didn't seem to impress you. I hope you won't think I'm trying to butter you up, Mr. Usher. I mean the idea of you being a reincarnation of William Shakespeare."

He laughed delightedly and said, "Clearly you don't yet know the difference between a player and a playwright, Bruce. Shakespeare striding about romantically with head thrown back?—and twirling a sword and shaping his body and voice to every feeling handed him? Oh no! I'll grant he might have played the Ghost—it's a part within the scope of an average writer's talents, requiring nothing more than that he stand still and sound off sepulchrally."

He paused and smiled and went on. "No, there's only one person in this company who might be Shakespeare come again, and that's Billy

Simpson. Yes, I mean Props. He's a great listener and he knows how to put himself in touch with everyone and then he's got that rat-trap mind for every hue and scent and sound of life, inside or out the mind. And he's very analytic. Oh, I know he's got no poetic talent, but surely Shakespeare wouldn't have that in *every* reincarnation. I'd think he'd need about a dozen lives in which to gather material for every one in which he gave it dramatic form. Don't you find something very poignant in the idea of a mute inglorious Shakespeare spending whole humble lifetimes collecting the necessary stuff for one great dramatic burst? Think about it some day."

I was doing that already and finding it a fascinating fantasy. It crystalized so perfectly the feeling I'd got seeing Billy Simpson behind his property table. And then Props did have a high-foreheaded poet-schoolmaster's face like that given Shakespeare in the posthumous engravings and woodcuts and portraits. Why, even their initials were the same. It made me feel strange.

Then the Governor put his third question to me.

"He's drinking tonight, isn't he? I mean Props, not Guthrie."

I didn't say anything, but my face must have answered for me—at least to such a student of expressions as the Governor—for he smiled and said, "You needn't worry. I wouldn't be angry with him. In fact, the only other time I know of that Props drank spirits by himself in the theater, I had a great deal to thank him for." His lean face grew thoughtful. "It was long before your time, in fact it was the first season I took out a company of my own. I had barely enough money to pay the printer for the three-sheets and get the first-night curtain up. After that it was touch and go for months. Then in mid-season we had a run of bad luck—a two-night heavy fog in one city, an influenza scare in another, Harvey Wilkins' Shakespearean troupe two weeks ahead of us in a third. And when in the next town we played it turned out the advance sale was very light—because my name was unknown there and the theater an unpopular one—I realized I'd have to pay off the company while there was still money enough to get them home, if not the scenery.

"That night I caught Props swigging, but I hadn't the heart to chide him for it—in fact I don't think I'd have blamed anyone, except perhaps myself, for getting drunk that night. But then during the performance the actors and even the union stagehands we travel began coming to my dressing room by ones and twos and telling me they'd be happy to work without salary for another three weeks, if I thought that might give us a chance of recouping. Well, of course I grabbed at their offers and we got a spell of brisk pleasant weather and we hit a couple of places starved for Shakespeare, and things worked out, even to paying all the back salary owed before the season was ended.

"Later on I discovered it was Props who had put them all up to doing it."

Gilbert Usher looked up at me and one of his eyes was wet and his lips were working just a little. "I couldn't have done it myself," he said, "for I wasn't a popular man with my company that first season—I'd been riding everyone much too hard and with nasty sarcasms—and I hadn't yet learned how to ask anyone for help when I really needed it. But Billy Simpson did what I couldn't, though he had to nerve himself for it with spirits. He's quick enough with his tongue in ordinary circumstances, as you know, particularly when he's being the friendly listener, but apparently when something very special is required of him, he must drink himself to the proper pitch. I'm wondering . . ."

His voice trailed off and then he straightened up before his mirror and started to unknot his tie and he said to me briskly, "Better get dressed now, Bruce. And then look in on Guthrie, will you?"

My mind was churning some rather strange thoughts as I hurried up the iron stairs to the dressing room I shared with Robert Dennis. I got on my Guildenstern make-up and costume, finishing just as Robert arrived; as Laertes, Robert makes a late entrance and so needn't hurry to the theater on *Hamlet* nights. Also, although we don't make a point of it, he and I spend as little time together in the dressing room as we can.

Before going down I looked into Guthrie Boyd's. He wasn't there, but the lights were on and the essentials of the Ghost's costume weren't in sight—impossible to miss that big helmet!—so I assumed he'd gone down ahead of me.

It was almost the half hour. The house lights were on, the curtain down, more stage lights on too, and quite a few of us about. I noticed that Props was back in the chair behind his table and not looking particularly different from any other night—perhaps the drink had been a once-only aberration and not some symptom of a crisis in the company.

I didn't make a point of hunting for Guthrie. When he gets costumed early he generally stands back in a dark corner somewhere, wanting to be alone—perchance to sip, aye, there's the rub!—or visits with Sybil in her dressing room.

I spotted Monica sitting on a trunk by the switchboard, where backstage was brightest lit at the moment. She looked ethereal yet springlike in her blond Ophelia wig and first costume, a pale green one. Recalling my happy promise to the Governor, I bounced up beside her and asked her straight out about the Ouija business, pleased to have something to the point besides the plays to talk with her about—and really not worrying as much about her nerves as I suppose I should have.

She was in a very odd mood, both agitated and abstracted, her gaze going back and forth between distant and near and very distant. My questions didn't disturb her at all, in fact I got the feeling she welcomed them, yet she genuinely didn't seem able to tell me much about why she'd been so frightened at the last name the board had spelled. She told me that she actually did get into a sort of dream state when she worked the board and that she'd screamed before she'd quite comprehended what had shocked her so; then her mind had blacked out for a few seconds, she thought.

"One thing though, Bruce," she said. "I'm not going to work the board any more, at least when the three of us are alone like that."

"That sounds like a wise idea," I agreed, trying not to let the extreme heartiness of my agreement show through.

She stopped peering around as if for some figure to appear that wasn't in the play and didn't belong backstage, and she laid her hand on mine and said, "Thanks for coming so quickly when I went idiot and screamed."

I was about to improve this opportunity by telling her that the reason I'd come so quickly was that she was so much in my mind, but just then Joe Rubens came hurrying up with the Governor behind him in his Hamlet black to tell me that neither Guthrie Boyd nor his Ghost costume was to be found anywhere in the theater.

What's more, Joe had got the phone numbers of Guthrie's son and daughter from Sybil and rung them up. The one phone hadn't answered, while on the other a female voice—presumably a maid's—had informed him that everyone had gone to see Guthrie Boyd in *Hamlet.*

Joe was already wearing his cumbrous chain-mail armor for Marcellus—woven cord silvered—so I knew I was elected. I ran upstairs and in the space of time it took Robert Dennis to guess my mission and advise me to try the dingiest bars first and have a drink or two myself in them, I'd put on my hat, overcoat, and wristwatch and left him.

So garbed and as usual nervous about people looking at my ankles, I sallied forth to comb the nearby bars of Wolverton. I consoled myself with the thought that if I found Hamlet's father's ghost drinking his way through them, no one would ever spare a glance for my own costume.

Almost on the stroke of curtain I returned, no longer giving a damn what anyone thought about my ankles. I hadn't found Guthrie or spoken to a soul who'd seen a large male imbiber—most likely of Irish whisky—in great-cloak and antique armor, with perhaps some ghostly green light cascading down his face.

Beyond the curtain the overture was fading to its sinister close and the backstage lights were all down, but there was an angry hushed-voice dispute going on stage left, where the Ghost makes all his entrances and exits. Skipping across the dim stage in front of the blue-lit battlements of Elsinore—I still in my hat and overcoat—I found the Governor and Joe Rubens and with them John McCarthy all ready to go on as the Ghost in his Fortinbras armor with a dark cloak and some green gauze over it.

But alongside them was Francis Farley Scott in a very similar get-up —no armor, but a big enough cloak to hide his King costume and a rather more impressive helmet than John's.

They were all very dim in the midnight glow leaking back from the dimmed-down blue floods. The five of us were the only people I could see on this side of the stage.

F.F. was arguing vehemently that he must be allowed to double the Ghost with King Claudius because he knew the part better than John and because—this was the important thing—he could imitate Guthrie's voice perfectly enough to deceive his children and perhaps save their illusions about him. Sybil had looked through the curtain hole and seen them and all of their yesterday crowd, with new recruits besides, occupying all of the second, third, and fourth rows center, chattering with excitement and beaming with anticipation. Harry Grossman had confirmed this from the front of the house.

I could tell that the Governor was vastly irked at F.F. and at the same time touched by the last part of his argument. It was exactly the sort of sentimental heroic rationalization with which F.F. cloaked his insatiable yearnings for personal glory. Very likely he believed it himself.

John McCarthy was simply ready to do what the Governor asked him. He's an actor untroubled by inward urgencies—except things like keeping a record of the hours he sleeps and each penny he spends—though with a natural facility for portraying on stage emotions which he doesn't feel one iota.

The Governor shut up F.F. with a gesture and got ready to make his decision, but just then I saw that there was a sixth person on this side of the stage.

Standing in the second wings beyond our group was a dark figure like a tarpaulined Christmas tree topped by a big helmet of unmistakable general shape despite its veiling. I grabbed the Governor's arm and pointed at it silently. He smothered a large curse and strode up to it and rasped, "Guthrie, you old Son of a B! Can you go on?" The figure gave an affirmative grunt.

Joe Rubens grimaced at me as if to say "Show business!" and grabbed a spear from the prop table and hurried back across the stage for his entrance as Marcellus just before the curtain lifted and the first nervous, superbly atmospheric lines of the play rang out, loud at first, but then going low with unspoken apprehension.

"Who's there?"

"Nay, answer me; stand, and unfold yourself."

"Long live the king!"

"Bernardo?"

"He."

"You come most carefully upon your hour."

" 'Tis now struck twelve; get thee to bed, Francisco."

"For this relief much thanks; 'tis bitter cold and I am sick at heart."

"Have you had quiet guard?"

"Not a mouse stirring."

With a resigned shrug, John McCarthy simply sat down. F.F. did the same, though *his* gesture was clench-fisted and exasperated. For a moment it seemed to me very comic that two Ghosts in *Hamlet* should be sitting in the wings, watching a third perform. I unbuttoned my overcoat and slung it over my left arm.

The Ghost's first two appearances are entirely silent ones. He merely goes on stage, shows himself to the soldiers, and comes off again. Nevertheless there was a determined little ripple of hand-clapping from the audience—the second, third, and fourth rows center greeting their patriarchal hero, it seemed likely. Guthrie didn't fall down at any rate and he walked reasonably straight—an achievement perhaps rating applause, if anyone out there knew the degree of intoxication Guthrie was probably burdened with at this moment—a cask-bellied Old Man of the Sea on his back.

The only thing out of normal was that he had forgot to turn on the little green light in the peak of his helmet—an omission which hardly mattered, certainly not on this first appearance. I hurried up to him when he came off and told him about it in a whisper as he moved off toward a dark backstage corner. I got in reply, through the inscrutable green veil, an exhalation of whisky and three affirmative grunts: one, that he knew it; two, that the light was working; three, that he'd remember to turn it on next time.

Then the scene had ended and I darted across the stage as they changed to the room-of-state set. I wanted to get rid of my overcoat. Joe Rubens grabbed me and told me about Guthrie's green light not being on and I told him that was all taken care of.

"Where the hell was he all the time we were hunting for him?" Joe asked me.

"I don't know," I answered.

By that time the second scene was playing, with F.F., his Ghost-coverings shed, playing the King as well as he always does (it's about his best part) and Gertrude Grainger looking very regal beside him as the Queen, her namesake, while there was another flurry of applause, more scattered this time, for the Governor in his black doublet and tights beginning about his seven hundredth performance of Shakespeare's longest and meatiest role.

Monica was still sitting on the trunk by the switchboard, looking paler than ever under her make-up, it seemed to me, and I folded my overcoat and silently persuaded her to use it as a cushion. I sat beside her and she took my hand and we watched the play from the wings.

After a while I whispered to her, giving her hand a little squeeze, "Feeling better now?"

She shook her head. Then leaning toward me, her mouth close to my ear, she whispered rapidly and unevenly, as if she just had to tell someone, "Bruce, I'm frightened. There's something in the theater. I don't think that was Guthrie playing the Ghost."

I whispered back, "Sure it was. I talked with him."

"Did you see his face?" she asked.

"No, but I smelled his breath," I told her and explained to her about him forgetting to turn on the green light. I continued, "Francis and John were both ready to go on as the Ghost, though, until Guthrie turned up. Maybe you glimpsed one of them before the play started and that gave you the idea it wasn't Guthrie."

Sybil Jameson in her Player costume looked around at me warningly. I was letting my whispering get too loud.

Monica put her mouth so close that her lips for an instant brushed my ear and she mouse-whispered, "I don't mean another *person* playing the Ghost—not that exactly. Bruce, there's *something* in the theater."

"You've got to forget that Ouija nonsense," I told her sharply. "And buck up now," I added, for the curtain had just gone down on Scene Two and it was time for her to get on stage for her scene with Laertes and Polonius.

I waited until she was launched into it, speaking her lines brightly enough, and then I carefully crossed the stage behind the backdrop. I was sure there was no more than nerves and imagination to her notions, though they'd raised shivers on me, but just the same I wanted to speak to Guthrie again and see his face.

When I'd completed my slow trip (you have to move rather slowly, so the drop won't ripple or bulge), I was dumbfounded to find myself witnessing the identical backstage scene that had been going on when I'd got back from my tour of the bars. Only now there was a lot more light because the scene being played on stage was a bright one. And Props was there behind his table, watching everything like the spectator he basically is. But beyond him were Francis Farley Scott and John McCarthy in their improvised Ghost costumes again, and the Governor and Joe with them, and all of them carrying on that furious lipreader's argument, now doubly hushed.

I didn't have to wait to get close to them to know that Guthrie must have disappeared again. As I made my way toward them, watching their silent antics, my silly mind became almost hysterical with the thought that Guthrie had at last discovered that invisible hole every genuine alcoholic wishes he had, into which he could decorously disappear and drink during the times between his absolutely necessary appearances in the real world.

As I neared them, Donald Fryer (our Horatio) came from behind me, having made the trip behind the backdrop faster than I had, to tell the Governor in hushed gasps that Guthrie wasn't in any of the dressing rooms or anywhere else stage right.

Just at that moment the bright scene ended, the curtain came down, the drapes before which Ophelia and the others had been playing swung back to reveal again the battlements of Elsinore, and the lighting shifted back to the midnight blue of the first scene, so that for the moment it was hard to see at all. I heard the Governor say decisively, *"You* play the Ghost," his voice receding as he and Joe and Don hurried across the stage to be in place for their proper entrance. Seconds later there came the dull soft hiss of the main curtain opening and I heard the Governor's taut resonant voice saying, "The air bites shrewdly; it is very cold," and Don responding as Horatio with, "It is a nipping and an eager air."

By that time I could see again well enough—see Francis Farley Scott and John McCarthy moving side by side toward the back wing through which the Ghost enters. They were still arguing in whispers. The explanation was clear enough: each thought the Governor had pointed at him in the sudden darkness—or possibly in F.F.'s case was pretending he so thought. For a moment the comic side of my mind, grown a bit hysterical by now, almost collapsed me with the thought of twin Ghosts entering the stage side by side. Then once again, history still repeating itself, I saw beyond them that other bulkier figure with the unmistakable shrouded helmet. They must have seen it too for they stopped dead just before my hands touched a shoulder of each of them. I circled quickly past them and reached out my hands to put them lightly on the third figure's shoulders, intending to whisper, "Guthrie, are you okay?" It was a very stupid thing for one actor to do to another—startling him just before his entrance—but I was made thoughtless by the memory of Monica's fears and by the rather frantic riddle of where Guthrie could possibly have been hiding.

But just then Horatio gasped, "Look, my lord, it comes," and Guthrie moved out of my light grasp onto the stage without so much as turning his head—and leaving me shaking because where I'd touched the rough buckram-braced fabric of the Ghost's cloak I'd felt only a kind of insubstantiality beneath instead of Guthrie's broad shoulders.

I quickly told myself that was because Guthrie's cloak had stood out from his shoulders and his back as he had moved. I had to tell myself something like that. I turned around. John McCarthy and F.F. were standing in front of the dark prop table and by now my nerves were in such a state that their paired forms gave me another start. But I tiptoed after them into the downstage wings and watched the scene from there.

The Governor was still on his knees with his sword held hilt up like a cross doing the long speech that begins, "Angels and ministers of grace defend us!" And of course the Ghost had his cloak drawn around him so you couldn't see what was under it—and the little green light still wasn't lit in his helmet. Tonight the absence of that theatric touch made him a more frightening figure—certainly to me, who wanted so much to see Guthrie's ravaged old face and be reassured by it. Though there was still enough comedy left in the ragged edges of my thoughts that I could imagine Guthrie's pugnacious son-in-law whispering angrily to those around him that Gilbert Usher was so jealous of his great father-in-law that he wouldn't let him show his face on the stage.

Then came the transition to the following scene where the Ghost has led Hamlet off alone with him—just a five-second complete darkening of the stage while a scrim is dropped—and at last the Ghost spoke those first lines of "Mark me" and "My hour is almost come, When I to sulphurous and tormenting flames Must render up myself."

If any of us had any worries about the Ghost blowing up on his lines or slurring them drunkenly, they were taken care of now. Those lines were delivered with the greatest authority and effect. And I was almost certain that it was Guthrie's rightful voice—at least I was at first—but doing an even better job than the good one he had always done of getting the effect of distance and otherworldliness and hopeless alienation from all life on Earth. The theater became silent as death, yet at the same time I could imagine the soft pounding of a thousand hearts, thousands of shivers crawling—and I *knew* that Francis Farley Scott, whose shoulder was pressed against mine, was trembling.

Each word the Ghost spoke was like a ghost itself, mounting the air and hanging poised for an impossible extra instant before it faded towards eternity.

Those great lines came: "I am thy father's spirit; Doomed for a certain term to walk the night . . ." and just at that moment the idea came to me that Guthrie Boyd might be dead, that he might have died and be lying unnoticed somewhere between his children's home and the theater —no matter what Props had said or the rest of us had seen—and that his ghost might have come to give a last performance. And on the heels of that shivery impossibility came the thought that similar and perhaps even eerier ideas must be frightening Monica. I knew I had to go to her.

So while the Ghost's words swooped and soared in the dark—marvellous black-plumed birds—I again made that nervous cross behind the back-drop.

Everyone stage right was standing as frozen and absorbed—motionless loomings—as I'd left John and F.F. I spotted Monica at once. She'd moved forward from the switchboard and was standing, crouched a little, by the big floodlight that throws some dimmed blue on the back-drop and across the back of the stage. I went to her just as the Ghost was beginning his exit stage left, moving backward along the edge of the light from the flood, but not quite in it, and reciting more lonelily and eerily than I'd ever heard them before those memorable last lines:

"Fare thee well at once!
"The glow-worm shows the matin to be near,
"And 'gins to pale his uneffectual fire;
"Adieu, adieu! Hamlet, remember me."

One second passed, then another, and then there came two unexpected bursts of sound at the same identical instant: Monica screamed and a thunderous applause started out front, touched off by Guthrie's people, of course, but this time swiftly spreading to all the rest of the audience.

I imagine it was the biggest hand the Ghost ever got in the history of the theater. In fact, I never heard of him getting a hand before. It certainly was a most inappropriate place to clap, however much the performance deserved it. It broke the atmosphere and the thread of the scene.

Also, it drowned out Monica's scream, so that only I and a few of those behind me heard it.

At first I thought I'd made her scream, by touching her as I had Guthrie, suddenly, like an idiot, from behind. But instead of shrinking or dodging away she turned and clung to me, and kept clinging too even after I'd drawn her back and Gertrude Grainger and Sybil Jameson had closed in to comfort her and hush her gasping sobs and try to draw her away from me.

By this time the applause was through and Governor and Don and Joe were taking up the broken scene and knitting together its finish as best they could, while the floods came up little by little, changing to rosy, to indicate dawn breaking over Elsinore.

Then Monica mastered herself and told us in quick whispers what had made her scream. The Ghost, she said, had moved for a moment into the edge of the blue floodlight, and she had seen for a moment through his veil, and what she had seen had been a face like Shakespeare's. Just that and no more. Except that at the moment when she told us—later she became less certain—she was sure it was Shakespeare himself and no one else.

I discovered then that when you hear something like that you don't exclaim or get outwardly excited. Or even inwardly, exactly. It rather shuts you up. I know I felt at the same time extreme awe and a renewed irritation at the Ouija board. I was deeply moved, yet at the same time pettishly irked, as if some vast adult creature had disordered the toy world of my universe.

It seemed to hit Sybil and even Gertrude the same way. For the moment we were shy about the whole thing, and so, in her way, was Monica, and so were the few others who had overheard in part or all what Monica had said.

I knew we were going to cross the stage in a few more seconds when the curtain came down on that scene, ending the first act, and stage-lights came up. At least I knew that I was going across. Yet I wasn't looking forward to it.

When the curtain did come down—with another round of applause from out front—and we started across, Monica beside me with my arm still tight around her, there came a choked-off male cry of horror from ahead to shock and hurry us. I think about a dozen of us got stage left about the same time, including of course the Governor and the others who had been on stage.

F.F. and Props were standing inside the doorway to the empty prop room and looking down into the hidden part of the L. Even from the side, they both looked pretty sick. Then F.F. knelt down and almost went out of view, while Props hunched over him with his natural stoop.

As we craned around Props for a look—myself among the first, just beside the Governor, we saw something that told us right away that this Ghost wasn't ever going to be able to answer that curtain call they were still fitfully clapping for out front, although the house lights must be up by now for the first intermission.

Guthrie Boyd was lying on his back in his street clothes. His face looked gray, the eyes staring straight up. While swirled beside him lay the Ghost's cloak and veil and the helmet and an empty fifth of whisky.

Between the two conflicting shocks of Monica's revelation and the body in the prop room, my mind was in a useless state. And from her helpless incredulous expression I knew Monica felt the same. I tried to put things together and they wouldn't fit anywhere.

F.F. looked up at us over his shoulder. "He's not breathing," he said. "I think he's gone." Just the same he started loosing Boyd's tie and shirt and pillowing his head on the cloak. He handed the whisky bottle back to us through several hands and Joe Rubens got rid of it.

The Governor sent out front for a doctor and within two minutes Harry Grossman was bringing us one from the audience who'd left his seat number and bag at the box office. He was a small man—Guthrie would have made two of him—and a bit awestruck, I could see, though holding himself with greater professional dignity because of that, as we made way for him and then crowded in behind.

He confirmed F.F.'s diagnosis by standing up quickly after kneeling only for a few seconds where F.F. had. Then he said hurriedly to the Governor, as if the words were being surprised out of him against his professional caution, "Mr. Usher, if I hadn't heard this man giving that great performance just now, I'd think he'd been dead for an hour or more."

He spoke low and not all of us heard him, but I did and so did Monica, and there was Shock Three to go along with the other two, raising in my mind for an instant the grisly picture of Guthrie Boyd's spirit, or some other entity, willing his dead body to go through with that last performance. Once again I unsuccessfully tried to fumble together the parts of this night's mystery.

The little doctor looked around at us slowly and puzzledly. He said, "I take it he just wore the cloak over his street clothes?" He paused. Then, "He *did* play the Ghost?" he asked us.

The Governor and several others nodded, but some of us didn't at once and I think F.F. gave him a rather peculiar look, for the doctor cleared his throat and said, "I'll have to examine this man as quickly as possible in a better place and light. Is there—?" The Governor suggested the couch in his dressing room and the doctor designated Joe Rubens and John McCarthy and Francis Farley Scott to carry the body. He passed over the Governor, perhaps out of awe, but Hamlet helped just the same, his black garb most fitting.

It was odd the doctor picked the older men—I think he did it for dignity. And it was odder still that he should have picked two ghosts to help carry a third, though he couldn't have known that.

As the designated ones moved forward, the doctor said, "Please stand back, the rest of you."

It was then that the very little thing happened which made all the pieces of this night's mystery fall into place—for me, that is, and for Monica too, judging from the way her hand trembled in and then tightened around mine. We'd been given the key to what had happened. I won't tell you what it was until I've knit together the ends of this story.

The second act was delayed perhaps a minute, but after that we kept to schedule, giving a better performance than usual—I never knew the Graveyard Scene to carry so much feeling, or the bit with Yorick's skull to be so poignant.

Just before I made my own first entrance, Joe Rubens snatched off my street hat—I'd had it on all this while—and I played all of Guildenstern wearing a wrist-watch, though I don't imagine anyone noticed.

F.F. played the Ghost as an off-stage voice when he makes his final brief appearance in the Closet Scene. He used Guthrie's voice to do it, imitating him very well. It struck me afterwards as ghoulish—but right.

Well before the play ended, the doctor had decided he could say that Guthrie had died of a heart seizure, not mentioning the alcoholism. The minute the curtain came down on the last act, Harry Grossman informed Guthrie's son and daughter and brought them backstage. They were much moved, though hardly deeply smitten, seeing they'd been out of touch with the old boy for a decade. However, they quickly saw it was a Grand and Solemn Occasion and behaved accordingly, especially Guthrie's pugnacious son-in-law.

Next morning the two Wolverton papers had headlines about it and Guthrie got his biggest notices ever in the Ghost. The strangeness of the event carried the item around the world—a six-line filler, capturing the mind for a second or two, about how a once-famous actor had died immediately after giving a performance as the Ghost in *Hamlet,* though in some versions, of course, it became Hamlet's Ghost.

The funeral came on the afternoon of the third day, just before our last performance in Wolverton, and the whole company attended along with Guthrie's children's crowd and many other Wolvertonians. Old Sybil broke down and sobbed.

Yet to be a bit callous, it was a neat thing that Guthrie died where he did, for it saved us the trouble of having to send for relatives and probably take care of the funeral ourselves. And it did give old Guthrie a grand finish, with everyone outside the company thinking him a hero-martyr to the motto The Show Must Go On. And of course we knew too that in a deeper sense he'd really been that.

We shifted around in our parts and doubled some to fill the little gaps Guthrie had left in the plays, so that the Governor didn't have to hire another actor at once. For me, and I think for Monica, the rest of the season was very sweet. Gertrude and Sybil carried on with the Ouija sessions alone.

And now I must tell you about the very little thing which gave myself and Monica a satisfying solution to the mystery of what had happened that night.

You'll have realized that it involved Props. Afterwards I asked him straight out about it and he shyly told me that he really couldn't help me there. He'd had this unaccountable devilish compulsion to get drunk and his mind had blanked out entirely from well before the performance until he found himself standing with F.F. over Guthrie's body at the end of the first act. He didn't remember the Ouija scare or a word of what he'd said to me about theaters and time machines—or so he always insisted.

F.F. told us that after the Ghost's last exit he'd seen him—very vaguely in the dimness—lurch across backstage into the empty prop room and that he and Props had found Guthrie lying there at the end of the scene. I think the queer look F.F.—the old reality-fuddling rogue!—gave the doctor was to hint to him that *he* had played the Ghost, though that wasn't something I could ask him about.

But the very little thing— When they were picking up Guthrie's body and the doctor told the rest of us to stand back, Props turned as he obeyed and straightened his shoulders and looked directly at Monica and myself, or rather a little over our heads. He appeared compassionate yet smilingly serene as always and for a moment transfigured, as if he were the eternal observer of the stage of life and this little tragedy were only part of an infinitely vaster, endlessly interesting pattern.

I realized at that instant that Props could have done it, that he'd very effectively guarded the doorway to the empty prop room during our searches, that the Ghost's costume could be put on or off in seconds (though Props's shoulders wouldn't fill the cloak like Guthrie's), and that I'd never once before or during the play seen him and the Ghost at the same time. Yes, Guthrie had arrived a few minutes before me . . . and died . . . and Props, nerved to it by drink, had covered for him.

While Monica, as she told me later, knew at once that here was the great-browed face she'd glimpsed for a moment through the greenish gauze.

Clearly there had been four ghosts in *Hamlet* that night—John McCarthy, Francis Farley Scott, Guthrie Boyd, and the fourth who had really played the role. Mentally blacked out or not, knowing the lines from the many times he'd listened to *Hamlet* performed in this life, or from buried memories of times he'd taken the role in the days of Queen Elizabeth the First, Billy (or Willy) Simpson, or simply Willy S., had played the Ghost, a good trouper responding automatically to an emergency.

Here is another legend of the sea, of a tar who sails forlornly like the Flying Dutchman, though his itinerant vigil may not be forever—a thought which frightens him, poor ghost. SARALEE TERRY is the pseudonym of an obscure novelist who writes humorous verse on napkins.

The Ghost of Sailboat Fred
by Saralee Terry

From Plymouth to Cape Finistere,
Each sailor, to a man,
Will quake and shake in mortal fear
On spying "the Dutchman."

For Vanderdecken's flying boat
Presages doom at sea;
Don't hail his sail when you're afloat,
Or wrecked ye'll surely be.

But now I sing of Sailboat Fred
Who terrifies no he-man.
Tars laugh and chaff at this poor dead
Befuddled little seaman.

When Freddie breathed, he loved to fish
Upon a placid stream;
Poor lad, he had no other wish
For loafing was his dream.

One day on deck he fell asleep
And snoozed till it was morning.
A bog of fog was sair acreep
And soon, without a warning

A fearful storm began to rage
With furious commotion;
It broke the yoke of his moorage
And swept him to the ocean.

Green Freddie rode the sea so wide
Yet could not find the land;
His sail so frail bobbed on the tide
And never touched the sand.

And now his spectre seeks the beach,
As sailors laugh with glee;
His ghost the coast still tries to reach
Because he's late for tea

And every day that he's not home
Just makes his wife more mad.
Each year, the fear that she will roam
And find him scares him bad.

'Twould mean her patience was no more
And she would have his head . . .
And not a lot of help he'd score
Just from the fact he's dead!

There are several peculiar legends associated with Christmas Eve, one of which is that at midnight, animals briefly enjoy the power of human speech. "The Fisherman's Story" is another Yule legend of peasant superstition concerning fishing for gain on that holiday. ANATOLE LE BRAZ, *born in 1859 in Saint-Servais, Brittany, was a professor of philosophy who wrote a small number of books and tales dealing with the legends of his native province, among which is the strange story that follows. Its translator and adapter,* FAITH LANCEREAU, *has trimmed the original of its conversational prolixity. A native and resident of New York City, she is a psychologist specializing in chronic mental illness; she is devoted to cats and fantasy literature.*

The Fisherman's Story

Adapted by Faith Lancereau
from a tale by Anatole Le Braz

We were all gathered at the home of Jean Menguy and his family on the hilly ridge of Crec'h, overlooking the sea. Christmas was near, and we sat about the fire talking of the miracles and events of that holiest of nights.

Everyone had something to say except Cloarec, the pilot. He sat quietly sucking his pipe. Under his thick, bushy brows, his blue eyes turned inward as if he remembered things long past.

"Cloarec," I said, "you are so quiet. Surely you have some story of the season just waiting to be told."

His face, which was always brick-red—having been cooked over and over by the salty sea air—now became fiery red. With embarrassment, he stuttered, "When it comes to tales like the one I have in mind, there is little to wait for. I still do not know what really happened. But it taught me never to go fishing on Christmas Eve. . . ."

Removing the pipe from his mouth, he shook the ash on his thumb, passed the back of his hand under his nose, and sniffed. Then, in the characteristic accents of Brittany, he began his story.

I was about your age, John Junior, when this occurred. Take heed and always listen to the advice of your elders.

One Christmas Eve, I decided I would put out to sea to fish. My father tried to dissuade me from going because it was a Holy Night, but I replied, "Christmas or not, whether you will or won't come, the winds are northwest, and it is a blessed time for turbot, so I'm going."

The previous week had been impossible for putting out the nets. There was a heavy haze like you see sometimes in Ireland, and it darkened the sky for six consecutive days. I was, therefore, doubly eager to go on Christmas Eve, when the sky was lightly overcast and the north wind was well-tempered and not too cold. The ocean was calm and gray with large swells, not choppy; one might wait till mid-March to find such good conditions again for fishing.

"But," my father said, "you would do better to lose the fish than lose your soul. Do not go out tonight, son!"

"And where is there a commandment of God or of the Church forbidding me to earn a living on Christmas Eve?" I demanded. "Isn't it just as necessary to eat tomorrow as any other day?"

"A clever argument to which I have no reply," my father admitted, "yet I was always told that Christmas Eve, beginning at midnight, is a mysterious time and better left alone. However, you are an adult, and if you insist on going, I cannot stop you. But please take one bit of advice with you."

"Yes?"

"If anything strange should happen, hoist your anchor as fast as you can, raise its cross in the air, make your crew kneel and sing 'The Song of Nédélek.'* Do not forget."

I shrugged my shoulders and set out for port. With me were five crew members, all rough tars like myself, all more concerned with keeping the pot boiling in this world, than in assuring themselves a place in the next. Except for the little cabin boy, Dudored (who died twenty years ago of yellow fever in Montevideo), all are still alive. There were the brothers Pierre and René Balanec from Roc'h-vrân, Louis Rudono from Cosquer, and Gonery Mezcam of Kerampoullou.

The five joined me at the landing, their heavy boots on, their oilskin hats tied under their chins. Ten minutes later, with all sails set, we steered toward the Seven Isles.

The breeze was just right, but we were the only anglers out. All other ships were still tied to the pier. Pierre pointed at the fishermen who, with folded arms, lounged on the embankment of the old battery. "Idlers," he spat. "Probably not ten sous in any of their pockets for cel-

* A Christmas carol of Brittany.

ebrating Christmas, yet they loaf around instead of preparing for the holiday."

Rudono agreed with Balanec and worried we all would be expected to treat the shirkers once High Mass ended.

But I knew there was another reason why they did not set out to sea. Uneasily, I mentioned to my crew the discussion I'd had with my father.

"Bah!" Pierre scoffed. "An old woman's idea."

All but Dudored agreed. Working on one of the lines, our cabin boy timidly murmured something about his grandfather being lost forever just after midnight on Christmas Eve, but none of the others paid any attention.

Soon we were in the waters of the Ile aux Moines and let down our lines. But contrary to our expectations, the fish weren't biting. We thought the gentle weather would bring them to the surface, but they seemed in no hurry to leave their dark hiding places in the depths. After an hour or so with nothing to show for the time spent, Pierre suggested we move farther out to sea, and I agreed.

It started out as a good move. As soon as we hit the windward side of the islands, we brought in fish each and every time we put out the net. Our spirits rose with the abundance of our catch; it began to look as if we would empty the sea of fish, and our cabin boy, Dudored, barely had enough time to take the catch out of the nets before the next was hauled into the boat.

The more fish we caught, the more we laughed and chaffed one another. The hours slipped by unnoticed. We didn't even mark the onset of darkness. Our eyes saw nothing but the gray-green waters that lifted the ship with their long regular waves and brought turbot to our lines.

Dudored alone had thoughts of a darker nature, though I did not realize it at the time. But the approach of night bothered him, and finally he spoke to me.

"It's getting late, pilot," he said; "it'll be hard to go in with the ebb tide."

He was right. The tide and the northwest wind would work against us if we didn't hurry to catch the eddy at Seven Isles while the water was still deep enough to get over it. Sea currents are terrible and cannot be approached as if one were jumping a hurdle. So I agreed with Dudored and ordered our departure.

But the other men objected. The more fish they caught, the more they wanted. Pierre's brother, René, when he heard the suggestion originated with Dudored, scowled deeply. "What business is it of his, that unweaned calf?" he growled thickly. "Did we ask him what time it is?"

"No," I said, "but maybe we should listen, anyhow. Look at the horizon. Darkness is falling."

"Let it fall. One last pull on the net, pilot."

He was indeed angry, all of the others were, too—Louis, Pierre, Gonery. To be truthful, I also was annoyed at our cabin boy, so I did not fight them. We stayed.

Cloarec paused to relight his pipe. Bending over the fireplace, he took an ember in his hand and put it to the bowl of the tiny clay pipe. Inhaling, his cheeks become so hollow they seemed to touch the inner walls of his face.

Somewhere outside the house, a cricket began to chirp.

"I regret," he said at last, "that I, too, was so transfigured by the profit motive as to jeopardize the lives of six men, but I spare nothing now, the facts are so few, as it is.

"And now I come to the evil part of my tale."

We finally finished pulling things together on board ship. Our sails were set, and I sat down at the rudder to tack when, shooting a glance at the foresail, I saw it flutter slightly, then grow calm. That was ominous. If the wind disappeared and the waves subsided, we would be in a bad fix. Stranded, at the very least, until half-tide, and even escaping then would mean hard work on the oars. Then we'd still have to wait three or four hours in the dark before being able to set sail for port.

The laughter that claimed us earlier was suddenly gone. My five companions, sitting on the benches at their posts, some facing forward, some backward, distractedly watched the deepening darkness.

Nevertheless, I held on to the hope of reaching the formidable embankment at the right moment. We sailed toward it, and indeed were only a few hundred yards away, when René began to shout obscenities.

"What's wrong with you?" I snapped.

"A horrible mess," he replied, looking west toward the high sea. "There's nothing over there but drizzle."

Louis Rudono looked the same way, then muttered, "No doubt about it. Fog coming."

And they were right. Turning quickly, I saw a confounding fog invading the horizon, a fog weaving a soft weft between sky and water.

"Damn," Pierre muttered, "that's what muzzled the wind."

The sea curled round the sides of the boat. Foam streamed in our wake, and the oak planks shook beneath us. We were in the channel between the islands.

"Hey, cabin boy," I stood up and called, "come steer as best you can. The rest of you, to the oars!" I myself joined them.

Now note carefully how Mezcam and I took the oars on the starboard side, while the brothers Balanec were seated to port. At the prow, Louis Rudono kept a lookout for rocks. He had good eyes, and I thought if anyone could spot trouble ahead, Louis could.

Remember how we were situated: Louis at the prow; little Dudored at the helm; the other four on the oars right and left.

I gave the word and we pulled hard. The vessel responded and we fairly flew over the water. Pierre, an enormous man, groaned loud with the effort.

But no matter how fast we rowed, we could not outrun the fog. Little by little, it overtook us. In the final minutes before it did, we saw the last remnant of daylight gleam eerily on the face of the sea.

Then darkness enveloped the boat, and the fog muffled us in an enormous floating wall of mist. For a little while, we could still make out a light on the Ile aux Moines, suspended like a ghostly star in the distance, but presently, it, too, turned into a blurred halo and vanished.

"That's the last light," Louis said over his shoulder. "Boy, steer to starboard, do you hear?"

"Aye, aye," he answered from his post behind us. His high-pitched voice sounded hoarse.

Now a glacial dampness penetrated our limbs. The fog was around and in us, its strange smoky smell stinging our throats and lungs. We held to the oars, still trying to maneuver across the rapids. Every minute I asked Louis what he saw, if anything.

"Whitecaps." He dipped his hand below the bow. "The water's choppy; we're still in the channel, I think."

The acrid fog stank in our nostrils, the curtain of shadow and night imprisoned us and it became difficult even to see one another seated close by. I reached out and touched Gonery's jersey to assure myself that he hadn't left his seat and that the gigantic silhouette my eyes squinted at was really him. Even the sides of the boat were indistinct against the deeper gloom of the night.

Then from the bow of the boat, as if from far off, our lookout's voice sounded, thin and hard to hear, "We're no longer going forward, friends. We're drifting."

There was nothing we could do. We let go of the oars and sat in near-silence, broken only by the slap-slap of the waves against the sides of our ship. Destiny now was the pilot.

At least, I thought, we would drift into the high sea and be more secure while waiting for the tide to change. If we stayed in the channel waters, we might run upon the reefs. However it turned out, I was sure we would not reach port until dawn.

We glided along, shadows that seemed more like specters than mortals. Wrapped in oilskin, visors pulled down, hands in sleeves, we said nothing, no longer able to talk, to open the mouth was to swallow fog. I thought the dreadful smell must be like the waters of Hell.

Even the noise of the ocean itself eventually faded away. Total silence. We floated alone as if we had ceased to exist, six lost souls on a sea of death.

The silence was suddenly broken by the weak voice of the cabin boy. I could not hear him.

"What, Dudored?"

"I said there is a seventh person on board."

Everyone leaped to their feet.

"What kind of idiocy are you saying?" I snarled at him, furious and frightened at the same time.

Pierre sneered. "The little fool can't count higher than five!"

"Or else he's blind," taunted his brother René.

"Damn you," Dudored swore faintly, "then count yourselves."

I did. Or tried to. But the hazy figures in the fog could not be identified. There, at front, that must be Louis, yes, over there the brothers, but had Mezcam moved? I was not sure, so I counted again. Seven.

"Yes," Pierre whispered, "there is one more on board."

Each had to do it for himself, none took the others' words for it. And every man reached the same tally.

We had started out as six, but there were seven silhouettes etched against the blackness of night.

"Call the roll," Rudono implored me.

I did so, naming each according to age, Pierre first, then Gonery Mezcam. Both answered.

"Louis?"

"Here!"

"René?"

"Here."

"Dudored?"

"Here."

Louis Rudono burst out, "The one who didn't answer is over by me!" He gestured at a figure leaning on the mast, rushed forward to grab him by the collar, but lowered his fist fast when Pierre yelled, "Ass! It's me you're aiming your fist at!"

And then no one said anything further for a long time. My heart beat fast, my skin prickled with terror that longed to cry out and break the heavy silence. Deep breaths on all sides, eyes averted lest the comrade whose face one sought turned out to be the mysterious stranger who came out of the night.

I meditated nervously on the nature of the inexplicable seventh passenger. Was he human or a wraith? A ghost was dreadful to contemplate, but the weight of another body might be too much for our small vessel to bear.

And then the cabin boy spoke again.

"Pilot! The back of the boat is sinking. The inner planks are almost at sea level!"

Pierre let out a cry of pure fear, and the same thought occurred to us all. Our supernatural visitor, whatever his nature, meant to drag us into the midnight depths of the sea.

I shouted that we must throw all we could overboard in order to lighten the load.

All the fish went first.

Total havoc. Everything within reach splashed overboard, but nothing helped, the ship was not lightened.

"Only an inch before we're engulfed," the little cabin boy screamed.

I felt around frantically for anything else that could be tossed into the water, came across the anchor, hefted it high . . . then stopped.

The words of my father rushed into my mind.

"Wait!" I cried out. "Throw nothing else." Then I raised the cross of the anchor above my head and began to sing, "In a town of Galilee—"

The hymn of Nédélek.

Later the others told me they thought I'd gone crazy, but Dudored joyfully said that as soon as I started to chant, the boat rose once more.

They all joined in on the second verse, Pierre Balanec bellowing like some great church organ.

And then a call from the fog, "Ho, there! Beware of what's alongside, sail nearer to the wind!"

We never found out who spoke. It was not Louis, our lookout. But turning to the indicated side of the ship, we all saw with dread and wonder the great rocks of Triagoz. The sea had almost run us on them.

Had we been under sail with the slightest breeze, we would have been pounded mercilessly, even as we foundered. But Louis saw the lighthouse immediately after the strange warning, and we set to the oars with renewed strength. Soon the watchman greeted us, a lantern in his hand.

"Listen," he said as he tethered our line to the pier, "the midnight mass on the mainland."

And all of us crossed ourselves.

The pilot's pipe had gone out. He stared at it a moment, reflecting on the odd history he'd told us there in Jean Menguy's seaside house.

"Well, that's my tale," he said. "We returned to port by six a.m. without a single fish. My father regarded me with silent knowledge and wonder, but never asked any questions."

"And the seventh?" I asked. "When do you think he disappeared? And who, or what was he?"

Cloarec bowed his curly head and shrugged his shoulders. "I have told you all I know, or wish to know." Blinking his small blue eyes, so full of dreams beneath his bushy brows, he added, "Do not seek for more, but remember always that you must never go fishing on Christmas Eve."

Here is an example of a "historical" haunted house that once existed—so the nameless author says—about ten miles north of Atlantic City. I have the strange feeling that I read some local reference to the very place a few years ago while researching the Miss America Pageant for a series of articles . . . but like ghosts themselves, the reference remains elusive. Still, the site of this sea-haunted hostel ought to be capable of investigation.

The Old Mansion

Anonymous

Down on Long Beach, that narrow strip of sand which stretches along the New Jersey coast from Barnegat Inlet on the north to Little Egg Harbor Inlet on the south, the summer sojourner at some one of the numerous resorts, which of late years have sprung up every few miles, may, in wandering over the sand dunes just across the bay from the village of Manahawkin, stumble over some charred timbers or vestiges of crumbling chimneys, showing that once, years back, a human habitation has stood there. If the find rouses the jaded curiosity of the visitor sufficiently to impel him to question the weather-beaten old bayman who sails him on his fishing trips he will learn that these relics mark the site of one of the first summer hotels erected on the New Jersey coast.

"That's where the Old Mansion stood," he will be informed by Captain Nate or Captain Sam, or whatever particular captain it may chance to be, and if by good fortune it chances to be Captain Jim, he will hear a story that will pleasantly pass away the long wait for a sheepshead bite.

It was my good luck to have secured Captain Jim for a preceptor in the angler's art during my vacation last summer, and his stories and reminiscences of Long Beach were not the least enjoyable features of the two weeks' sojourn.

Captain Jim was not garrulous. Few of the baymen are. They are a sturdy, self-reliant, and self-controlled people, full of strong common sense, but still with that firm belief in the supernatural which seems inherent in dwellers by the sea.

"The Old Mansion," said Captain Jim, "or the Mansion of Health, for that was its full name, was built away back in 1822, so I've heard my father say. There had been a tavern close by years before that was kept by a man named Cranmer, and people used to come from Philadelphia by stage, sixty miles through the pines, to 'Hawkin, and then cross here by boat. Some would stop at Cranmer's and others went on down the beach to Homer's which was clear down at End by the Inlet. Finally some of the wealthy people concluded that they wanted better accommodations than Cranmer gave, so they formed the Great Swamp Long Beach Company, and built the Mansion of Health. I've heard that when it was built it was the biggest hotel on the coast, and was considered a wonder. It was 120 feet long, three stories high, and had a porch running all the way around it, with a balcony on top. It was certainly a big thing for those days. I've heard father tell many a time of the stage loads of gay people that used to come rattling into 'Hawkin, each stage drawn by four horses, and sometimes four or five of them a day in the summer. A good many people, too, used to come in their own carriages, and leave them over on the mainland until they were ready to go home. There were gay times at the Old Mansion then, and it made times good for the people along shore, too."

"How long did the Old Mansion flourish, Captain?" I asked.

"Well, for twenty-five or thirty years people came there summer after summer. Then they built a railroad to Cape May, and that, with the ghosts, settled the Mansion of Health."

"What do you mean by the ghosts?" I demanded.

"Well, you see," said Captain Jim, cutting off a mouthful of navy plug, "the story got around that the old house was haunted. Some people said there were queer things seen there, and strange noises were heard that nobody could account for, and pretty soon the place got a bad name and visitors were so few that it didn't pay to keep it open any more."

"But how did it get the name of being haunted, Captain Jim?" I persisted.

"Why, it was this way," continued the mariner. "Maybe you've heard of the time early in the fifties when the Powhatan was wrecked on the beach here, and every soul on board was lost. She was an emigrant ship, and there were over 400 people aboard—passengers and crew. She came ashore here during the equinoctial storm in September. There wasn't any life-saving stations in them days, and everyone was drowned. You can see the long graves now over in the 'Hawkin churchyard, where the bodies were buried after they came ashore. They put them in three long trenches that were dug from one end of the burying-ground to the other. The only people on the beach that night was the man who took care of the Old Mansion. He lived there with his family, and his son-in-law lived with him. He was the wreckmaster for this part of the coast, too. It

wasn't till the second day that the people from 'Hawkin could get over
to the beach, and by that time the bodies had all come ashore, and the
wreckmaster had them all piled up on the sand. I was a youngster, then,
and came over with my father, and, I tell you, it was the awfullest sight
I ever saw—them long rows of drowned people, all lying there with their
white, still faces turned up to the sky. Some were women, with their
dead babies clasped tight in their arms, and some were husbands and
wives, whose bodies came ashore locked together in a death embrace.
I'll never forget that sight as long as I live. Well, when the coroner
came and took charge he began to inquire whether any money or valuables had been found, but the wreckmaster declared that not a solitary
coin had been washed ashore. People thought this was rather singular,
as the emigrants were, most of them, well-to-do Germans, and were
known to have brought a good deal of money with them, but it was concluded that it had gone down with the ship. Well, the poor emigrants
were given pauper burial, and the people had begun to forget their suspicions until three or four months later there came another storm, and
the sea broke clear over the beach, just below the Old Mansion, and
washed away the sand. Next morning early two men from 'Hawkin
sailed across the bay and landed on the beach. They walked across on
the hard bottom where the sea had washed across, and, when about half
way from the bay, one of the men saw something curious close up
against the stump of an old cedar tree. He called the other man's attention to it, and they went over to the stump. What they found was a pile
of leather money-belts that would have filled a wheelbarrow. Every one
was cut open and empty. They had been buried in the sand close by the
old stump, and the sea had washed away the covering. The men didn't
go any further.

"They carried the belts to their boats and sailed back to 'Hawkin as
fast as the wind would take them. Of course, it made a big sensation,
and everybody was satisfied that the wreckmaster had robbed the bodies, if he hadn't done anything worse, but there was no way to prove it,
and so nothing was done. The wreckmaster didn't stay around here long
after that, though. The people made it too hot for him, and he and his
family went away South, where it was said he bought a big plantation
and a lot of slaves. Years afterward the story came to 'Hawkin somehow that he was killed in a barroom brawl, and that his son-in-law was
drowned by his boat upsettin' while he was out fishin'. I don't furnish
any affidavits with that part of the story, though.

"However, after that nobody lived in the Old Mansion for long at a
time. People would go there, stay a week or two, and leave—and at last

it was given up entirely to beach parties in the day time, and ghosts at night."

"But, Captain, you don't really believe the ghost part, do you?" I asked.

Captain Jim looked down the bay, expectorated gravely over the side of the boat, and answered, slowly:

"Well, I don't know as I would have believed in 'em if I hadn't seen the ghost."

"What!" I exclaimed; "you saw it? Tell me about it. I've always wanted to see a ghost, or next best thing, a man who has seen one."

"It was one August, about 1861," said the captain. "I was a young feller then, and with a half dozen more was over on the beach cutting salt hay. We didn't go home at nights, but did our own cooking in the Old Mansion kitchen, and at nights slept on piles of hay upstairs. We were a reckless lot of scamps, and reckoned that no ghosts could scare us. There was a big full moon that night, and it was as light as day. The muskeeters was pretty bad, too, and it was easier to stay awake than go to sleep. Along toward midnight me and two other fellers went out on the old balcony, and began to race around the house. We hollered and yelled, and chased each other for half an hour or so, and then we concluded we had better go to sleep, so we started for the window of the room where the rest were. This window was near one end on the ocean side, and as I came around the corner I stopped as if I had been shot, and my hair raised straight up on top of my head. Right there in front of that window stood a woman looking out over the sea, and in her arms she held a little child. I saw her as plain as I see you now. It seemed to me like an hour she stood there, but I don't suppose it was a second; then she was gone. When I could move I looked around for the other boys, and they were standing there paralyzed. They had seen the woman, too. We didn't say much, and we didn't sleep much that night, and the next night we bunked out on the beach. The rest of the crowd made all manner of fun of us, but we had had all the ghost we wanted, and I never set foot inside the old house after that."

"When did it burn down, Captain?" I asked, as Jim relapsed into silence.

"Somewhere about twenty-five years ago. A beach party had been roasting clams in the old oven, and in some way the fire got to the woodwork. It was as dry as tinder, and I hope the ghosts were all burnt up with it."

Few ghost stories occur in science-fiction; the genres tend to be exclusive by definition. But once in a while, some clever writer manages to concoct a conceit that fits both categories of fantastic literature. Such a tale is "The Haunting of Y-12," a delicious "club" story in the tradition of Lord Dunsany's wonderful "Jorkens" series. AL SARRANTONIO is an editor whose science-fiction appears in major genre periodicals regularly. He is one of a new breed of editor-writers whose taste and energy will do much to shape the best of the future output in American speculative fiction.

The Haunting of Y-12
by Al Sarrantonio

It was business time for the Genial Hauntings Club. Seated after dinner in the well-polished leather chairs of the Club's smoking room, pulled up before a glowing fire which threw dark, warm shadows across the walls and ceiling, with brim-filled brandy glasses and lit cigars or pipes, the Members called on the stranger to tell his story. This, of course, was Tradition at the GHC, for this was the one time during the year, on the Eve of Christmas (or, Dickens' Spirits' Eve, as it was whimsically called at the Club), when a new member might earn admission. Not that admission was so difficult to earn, for the nominee, sponsored by one of the present Members (in this case Porutto, a small, olive-skinned fellow of indistinct nationality with glasses and cool brown eyes, an adventurer by trade who was in the habit of tapping his pipe thoughtfully against his palm), need only tell a story. And the story need only be a true one, a story of ghosts—not a tall order for admission to an establishment known as the Genial Hauntings Club; but perhaps yes, since true stories of ghosts do not jump out of every shadow.

The Members settled themselves in—Thomas, the painter; Maye and Podwin, the writers of somewhat Mutt and Jeff-esque proportions who had cowritten many popular fictions, mostly in the science and fantasy categories; Hewetson, Butler of the Club (an exalted position, akin to Secretary); Petrone, the social scientist; Jenick, the light-bearded editor and wit; Ballestaire, the actor; and the others; even Michelle, the somewhat fiery-tempered World Traveler—and the stranger began his tale.

"Well," he said, drawing himself up in his chair and taking a last leisurely puff on his cigar, "my story begins with a computer." He was a young man of short-medium height, working his way toward stocky, with a florid moustache and tight shiny eyes behind his rimless glasses; there was an air of nervous certainty about him, as if he knew what he was about but hadn't quite discovered how to make others believe it yet.

"A haunted computer," he continued, pausing a moment for effect. And then drawing himself up once again with a sigh, he began in earnest.

These events (he said) occurred some twelve years ago, and the computer, called the Y-12, was lodged in my place of employment, what was then known as a Think Tank. There was a rush-rush project underway, and some very odd things began to happen to a man named Lonnigan.

Robert Lonnigan was in charge of our project, whose task it was to develop one of the first table-top computers; you have to remember that at one time a computer that would now rest on your thumbnail would fill an entire drawing room. Anyway, some strange things began to occur.

Lonnigan was working alone one night when the prototype of the Y-12 suddenly turned itself on and began to type out a message which read, "Robert, are you there?"

Lonnigan was a bit shocked of course, but realizing that there was such a thing as a practical joke and that whatever had happened should not have happened, he turned off the computer and went back to work. But once again Y-12 turned itself on and typed out, "Robert, are you there?" and then added, "This is father."

This shook Lonnigan. There was something eerily familiar about the words, and he had a slight feeling of déjà vu. His own father had died a few years previously, but being of the kind of mind that builds computers he was not about to admit to the possibility that his father's spirit had taken over Y-12. Still, something made his skin crawl about the whole thing.

He quickly checked through all of the input files, which only he had access to, and discovered that no one had programmed Y-12—not officially, anyway—for anything that would include the kind of phrasing the machine had evidenced. And as for practical jokes, he couldn't figure out how it could have been rigged up since he was supposed to see every program that went in and since security was so tight due to government involvement in the project; no research assistant was going to jeopardize his security clearance and career by pulling a scary—and somewhat sick—stunt on the program manager. Lonnigan was resolved, that night if possible, to find out what was going on.

He set up Y-12 for two-way conversation using the IBM keyboard and printout and queried, "Identify program: 'Robert, are you there? This is father.'"

There was no response.

He tried the same command, in as many variations as he could think of, but Y-12 remained silent. There was not even an acknowledgment of the query as a viable one, and according to Y-12 itself, no such statement had ever been made by the computer nor could be, since it did not exist in its memory banks.

Lonnigan was dumbfounded, and shut off the computer, beginning to think that maybe he was going crazy. He was bundling up to leave for the night, and had just turned off the lights in the lab, when Y-12 suddenly turned itself on again and repeated once more, "Robert, are you there? This is father. Please answer me."

A chill went up Lonnigan's spine and that feeling of déjà vu gripped him again, and he stood staring at the machine he had built, the machine he had turned off with his own hands, its amber and green lights now blinking on and off in the darkness and typing out repeatedly on its printer, "Robert, are you there? Please answer. Robert, are you there? Please answer." Lonnigan finally ended it by shutting down the computer completely and pulling the plug from the power outlet. He then left quickly, fearing that Y-12 would somehow turn itself back on despite the fact that its power source had been disconnected.

The following morning the bleary-eyed project manager assembled our entire staff and gave us a small speech, demanding that if anyone had tampered with Y-12 he should make himself known. No one stepped forward. Lonnigan pleaded with us, asking that if anyone knew anything at all about what had happened the night before, he should step forward now because he was endangering the entire project. We remained mute to a man, and I must admit we began to look at him a bit strangely.

There was talk throughout that day that perhaps Lonnigan needed a rest. A decision had actually been made to put him on at least temporary suspension when Y-12 suddenly burst into life with myself and about ten others present and began once more to type out its ghost message.

When the pandemonium died down, Lonnigan set us all to work. It was imperative, he said, that whatever was wrong with Y-12 be corrected before the government, which was funding the project, found out and all hell broke loose. One of my friends, a man named Boylston, asked, "But what if it really is haunted?" and Lonnigan, his face showing things he didn't want to show, answered, "Don't even think about it."

Every nut and bolt on the Y-12 computer was removed, turned over, and, more often than not, replaced. Every circuit was tapped, checked and rechecked, each memory bank drained and carefully reprogrammed. Nearly three days later, when we were through, Y-12 looked exactly as it had before. "Let's hope we've driven it out," Lonnigan said as we ran it through a test program. "Driven what out?" asked Boylston, and the look Lonnigan turned on him made him not ask again.

Y-12 ran through the program perfectly, and then ran through it again perfectly. There was a general sigh of relief. But then, almost as soon as it had been shut down, it blinked back into life and began to type: "Robert, are you there?"

There was complete silence in the room, and Lonnigan's face went white. Heaven knows what thoughts were running through his mind then. Whatever they were he shook his head and refused to dwell on them.

He ordered the lab sealed, ordered Y-12 pulled to pieces again. "Check every component twice, change everything that can be changed. We've got a government man coming tomorrow, dammit, so I want it finished before he gets here."

No one moved, and all eyes were on him, with the same silent statement.

Lonnigan went into a rage. "That's not my father in there, dammit! It's a bug! This is a machine. We built it, we can tear it down, we can smash it to bits and it can't talk back; there's a reason for what happened, and I want to know what it is! It's *not my father!*"

From across the room Y-12 burst into life and typed out, "Robert, please answer me."

"Get to it now!" Lonnigan screamed, and stalked from the room.

An hour before dawn the job was completed, and we all sat huddled across the room from Y-12, drinking coffee. No one spoke; all attention was fastened on the computer, or on Robert Lonnigan who sat huddled over a drafting table, a set of blueprints pinned out beneath his eyes. He was studying those prints minutely, almost obsessively, and muttering to himself under his breath. He looked drawn and haggard.

"There's something here. . . . I know it. Something . . ."

At that moment Y-12 began to clatter and blink into life. Everyone in the room, including Lonnigan, jumped.

"Robert, are you there? This is father. Can you hear me? This is father—"

"Ah!" cried Lonnigan suddenly, grabbing the schematic and waving it aloft. There was a look of triumph on his face, and deep relief. "By God, I know what it is," he said. "I should kick myself for not solving this before. Everyone come and look at this."

He spread the diagram out on the drafting table as we gathered around it. Behind us, Y-12 went on, "Can you hear me? Please answer. This is father—" and some of us glanced back nervously.

"Don't worry about the damn computer," said Lonnigan. "We've got some real work ahead of us before that government man gets here. Look at this section." He indicated a portion of the left upper corner of the sheet. "What happened was this, and it really is fantastic. We took every component out of Y-12, at least two times, right? And some were even replaced."

"A couple of times," I said.

"Right," continued Lonnigan. "But what we forgot about was the fact that some of the components of Y-12 were taken whole from other, earlier units and jerry-rigged into this one."

"So?" said my friend Boylston, who was still casting worried looks over his shoulder at the computer. "We've always done that; it's better than redesigning whole circuits that are basically the same. It just eliminates redundancy."

"Well, that's basically true. But in this case we used a component that was haunted."

Lonnigan savored the looks he got from us for a moment.

"Now before you bolt for the doors, listen to me. Do you remember where we got this component here from?" Again he indicated the upper left corner of the blueprint.

"Sure," I piped in. "From the A-6 model."

"Right. And the A-6 unit we used was one of the first ever manufactured. In fact, I'll wager it was the first off the line. And look at this," he said, pointing to a specific area; "we used almost the whole thing intact."

"No we didn't," I protested. "We went through a lot of circuitry, but we bypassed most of it."

"Ah, but not all of it; this whole section over here was part of the memory banks of the original machine."

"Yes, but we *bypassed* it," I insisted.

"Did we?" This was as an accusation from Lonnigan. "Ever since this business started, I've had the eerie feeling that I had heard some of what Y-12 was saying before. Well, it suddenly came to me.

"When I was fresh out of school I worked briefly with a man named Fleishman Bushyager—a brilliant man, but a little on the dotty side. He was elderly at the time, and pretty close to retirement age; the A-6 project, in any case, was supposed to be his last. You must remember this is a long time ago, and that I haven't thought about any of these things in years, so I may be a little fuzzy on a few points. But this is basically how the story goes.

"Part of the reason Bushyager was being herded out after the A-6 project was the fact that he began to come up with a few strange ideas; his son Robert died in an automobile accident and, like Arthur Conan Doyle, the old man became obsessed with trying to reach his son beyond the grave. He was actually working on some computer circuitry to aid him in this—a sort of computerized medium. Some of the higher-ups found out about it and since Bushyager was a big man they couldn't get rid of him outright; so they ordered him to restrict himself to A-6 work alone while they put through, behind his back, paperwork for his retirement.

"The old man was just about ready to leave by the time I got there, but one day he showed me some of the designs and one of his programs in particular. I stared and stared at this blueprint for hours and then it suddenly all wrapped up in my mind. One of the designs for the final A-6 computer actually contained, embedded in the circuitry, the design for Bushyager's medium. And though it was hidden, it could still do the old man's work for him, though in secret. He'd arranged things in such a way that his input would never show up on a readout, but the way we cannibalized the circuitry freed, as it were, the program for the first time. If you look closely, you can even see how Y-12 turned itself on. A bit eerie, but there's your ghost. The Y-12 really was haunted—in a way. And the Robert our ghost was calling for was Robert Bushyager.

"Well," said Lonnigan, "we haven't much time before that government man arrives. Let's unhook that circuitry and patch it up, and clean this place up. At least we didn't have to see any real ghosts, right?"

"Amen," we all agreed.

"This," said the stranger, sipping at his brandy and relighting his cold cigar, "nearly ends my story. The A-6 circuitry was altered and fixed, and the ghost in Y-12 appeared no more. In fact, my story would end here if not for one thing. You see, a curious thing ensued. During the cleanup before the government inspector arrived that morning, I took the printout sheets from Y-12's ghost messages. I put them into a drawer, intending to show them to my wife when I was able to tell her the story after the security lid on the Y-12 project was lifted, and promptly forgot about them. A few years later, when I was leaving my position for a new one, I came across them while cleaning out my desk; I almost tossed them in the waste basket but then remembered what they were and took a close look. And I found, as I said, a curious thing."

The stranger paused, and, with his eyes, took in his audience who, he was delighted to see, was a captive one; even the somewhat impatient Hewetson was leaning forward in his chair, his attention fixed on the stranger's next words. "And what I found," the stranger continued, "was that between the lines of type, in the blank spaces, a kind of raised lettering had appeared. And, on rubbing at this lettering lightly with a pencil, I discovered a most chilling and interesting message. I tried to get in touch with Robert Lonnigan, who was not to be found; and I tried to get in touch with old Bushyager who, it turned out, was dead—which only deepened my feeling of alarm. For there, printed between all the lines of Fleishman Bushyager's input, was a strange message."

There was a moment of silence and then, with a flourish, the stranger produced the very printout he had been speaking of, spreading it out before their eager eyes.

"I, Robert Bushyager," it read, "am here." And on the very last line, at the end of the printout, "And I, Fleishman Bushyager, with him." And under that, "Tell the other Robert his father forgives him."

"Capital!" cried Porutto, the stranger's sponsor, and there were cries of delight all around.

And, after another filling of glasses and stoking of the red-coaled fire, a vote was made, and a toast proposed and accepted, and another member of the Genial Hauntings Club welcomed.

Opera lovers know and love Offenbach's strikingly offbeat Tales of
Hoffmann, *but few are probably aware that the Hoffmann of the title is* E.
T. HOFFMANN, *the German macabre writer who, born in 1776, lived to write
many unforgettable tales of the strange and psychologically unsettling ways
of often-artistic characters. Tschaikovsky based his* Nutcracker *ballet on one
of Hoffmann's stories, and* The Cremona Violin *doubtless inspired Mme. Bla-
vatsky to write* "The Ensouled Violin". *The following ghost story is a
wholly independent prologue of Hoffmann's short story,* "Automata."

Untitled Ghost Story
by E. T. Hoffmann

A considerable time ago I was invited to a little evening gathering,
where our friend Vincent was, along with some other people. I was de-
tained by business, and did not arrive till very late. I was all the more
surprised not to hear the slightest sound as I came up to the door of the
room. Could it be that nobody had been able to come? I gently opened
the door. There sat Vincent, opposite me, with the others, around a little table; and they were all staring, stiff and motionless like so many
statues, in the profoundest silence up at the ceiling. The lights were on a
table at some distance, and nobody took any notice of me. I went
nearer, full of amazement, and saw a glittering gold ring suspended
from the ceiling, swinging back and forth in the air, and presently beginning to move in circles. One after another they said, "Wonderful!"
"Most wonderful!" "Most inexplicable!" "Curious!" and so on. I could
no longer contain myself, and cried out, "For Heaven's sake, tell me
what you are doing."

At this they all jumped up. But Vincent cried, in that shrill voice of
his: "Creeping Tom! You come slinking in like a sleepwalker, interrupting the most important and interesting experiments. Let me tell you
that a phenomenon which the incredulous have classed without a moment's hesitation as fabulous, has just been verified by this company.
We wished to see whether the pendulum swings of a suspended ring can
be controlled by the concentrated human will. I undertook to fix my
will upon it; and thought as hard as I could of circular oscillations. The
ring, which is fixed to the ceiling by a silk thread, remained motionless
for a very long time, but at last it began to swing, and it was just beginning to go in circles when you came in and interrupted us."

"But what if it were not your will," I said, "so much as the draught of air when I opened the door which set the ring in motion?"

"Materialist!" cried Vincent. Everybody laughed.

"The pendulum oscillations of rings nearly drove me crazy at one time," said Theodore. "This is absolutely certain, and anyone can convince himself of it: the oscillations of a plain gold ring, suspended by a fine thread over the palm of the hand, unquestionably take the direction which the unspoken will directs them to take. I cannot tell you how profoundly and how eerily this phenomenon affected me. I used to sit for hours at a time making the ring go swinging in the most varied directions, as I willed it; and at last I went to the length of making an oracle of it. I would say, mentally, 'If such and such a thing is going to happen, let the ring swing between my thumb and little finger; if it is not going to happen, let it swing at right angles to that direction,' and so on."

"Delightful," said Lothair. "You set up within yourself a higher spiritual principle to speak to you mystically when you conjure it up. Here we have the true 'spiritus familiaris,' the Socratic daemon. From here there is only a very short step to ghosts and supernatural stories, which might easily have their *raison d'être* in the influence of some exterior spiritual principle."

"And I mean to take just this step," said Cyprian, "by telling you, right here and now, the most terrible supernatural story I have ever heard. The peculiarity of this story is that it is vouched for by persons of credibility, and that the manner in which it has been brought to my knowledge, or recollection, has to do with the excited or (if you prefer) disorganized condition which Lothair observed me to be in a short time ago."

Cyprian stood up; and, as was his habit when his mind was occupied, and he needed a little time to arrange his words, he walked several times up and down the room. Presently he sat down, and began:—

"You may remember that some little time ago, just before the last campaign, I was paying a visit to Colonel von P—— at his country house. The colonel was a good-tempered, jovial man, and his wife quietness and simpleness personified. At the time I speak of, the son was away with the army, so that the family circle consisted, besides the colonel and his lady, of two daughters and an elderly French lady who was trying to persuade herself that she was fulfilling the duties of a governess—though the young ladies appeared to be beyond the period of being 'governed.' The elder of the two daughters was a most lively and cheerful girl, vivacious even to ungovernability; not without plenty of brains, but so constituted that she could not go five yards without cutting at least three entrechats. She sprang in the same fashion in her conversation and everything that she did, restlessly from one thing to another. I myself have seen her within the space of five minutes work at needlework, read, draw, sing, dance, or cry about her poor cousin who was killed in battle and then while the tears were still in her eyes burst into a splendid infectious burst of laughter when the Frenchwoman spilled the contents of her snuffbox over the pug. The pug began to sneeze frightfully, and the old lady cried, *'Ah, che fatalità! Ah carino! Poverino!'* (She always spoke to the dog in Italian because he was born in Padua.) Moreover, this young lady was the loveliest blonde ever seen, and for all her odd caprices, full of the utmost charm, goodness, kindliness, and attractiveness, so that whether she wanted to or not she exerted the most irresistible charm over everyone.

"Her younger sister was the greatest possible contrast to her (her name was Adelgunda). I try in vain to find words in which to express to you the extraordinary impression which this girl produced upon me when I first saw her. Picture to yourselves the most exquisite figure, and the most marvellously beautiful face; but her cheeks and lips wear a deathly pallor, and she moves gently, softly, slowly, with measured steps; and then, when you hear a low-toned word from her scarcely opened lips you feel a sort of shudder of spectral awe. Of course I soon got over this eerie feeling, and, when I managed to get her to emerge from her deep self-absorbed condition and converse, I was obliged to admit that the strangeness, the eeriness, was only external; and by no means came from within. In the little she said she displayed a delicate womanliness, a clear head, and a kindly disposition. She had not a trace of overexcitability, though her melancholy smile, and her glance, heavy as if with tears, seemed to speak of some morbid bodily condition producing a hostile influence on her mental state. It struck me as very strange that the whole family, not excepting the French lady, seemed to get into a state of anxiety as soon as anyone began to talk to this girl, and tried to interrupt the conversation, often breaking into it in a very forced manner. But the most extraordinary thing of all was that, as soon as it was eight o'clock in the evening, the young lady was reminded, first by the French lady and then by her mother, sister, and father, that it was time to go to her room, just as little children are sent to bed so that they will not overtire themselves. The French lady went with her, so that neither of them ever appeared at supper, which was at nine o'clock.

The lady of the house, probably noticing my surprise at those proceedings, threw out (by way of preventing indiscreet inquiries) a sort of sketchy statement to the effect that Adelgunda was in very poor health, that, particularly about nine in the evening, she was liable to feverish attacks, and that the doctors had ordered her to have complete rest at that time. I saw there must be more in the affair than this, though I could not imagine what it might be; and it was only today that I ascertained the terrible truth, and discovered what the events were which have wrecked the peace of that happy circle in the most frightful manner.

"Adelgunda was at one time the most blooming, vigorous, cheerful creature to be seen. Her fourteenth birthday came, and a number of her friends and companions had been invited to spend it with her. They were all sitting in a circle in the shrubbery, laughing and amusing themselves, taking little heed that the evening was getting darker and darker, for the soft July breeze was blowing refreshingly, and they were just beginning thoroughly to enjoy themselves. In the magic twilight they set about all sorts of dances, pretending to be elves and woodland sprites. Adelgunda cried, 'Listen, children! I shall go and appear to you as the White Lady whom our gardener used to tell us about so often while he was alive. But you must come to the bottom of the garden, where the old ruins are.' She wrapped her white shawl round her, and went lightly dancing down the leafy path, the girls following her, in full tide of laughter and fun. But Adelgunda had scarcely reached the old crumbling arches, when she suddenly stopped, and stood as if paralyzed in every limb. The castle clock struck nine.

"'Look, look!' cried she, in a hollow voice of the deepest terror. 'Don't you see it? the figure—close before me—stretching her hand out at me. Don't you see her?'

"The children saw nothing whatever; but terror came upon them, and they all ran away, except one, more courageous than the rest, who hastened up to Adelgunda, and was going to take her in her arms. But Adelgunda, turning pale as death, fell to the ground. At the screams of the other girl everybody came hastening from the castle, and Adelgunda was carried in. At last she recovered from her faint, and, trembling all over, told them that as soon as she reached the ruins she saw an airy form, as if shrouded in mist, stretching its hand out towards her. Of course everyone ascribed this vision to some deceptiveness of the twilight; and Adelgunda recovered from her alarm so completely that night that no further evil consequences were anticipated, and the whole affair was supposed to be at an end. However, it turned out altogether other-

wise. The next evening, when the clock struck nine, Adelgunda sprang
up, in the midst of the people about her, and cried, 'There she is! there
she is. Don't you see her—just before me?'

"Since that unlucky evening, Adelgunda declared that as soon as the
clock struck nine, the figure stood before her, remaining visible for several seconds, although no one but herself could see anything of it, or
trace by any psychic sensation the proximity of an unknown spiritual
principle. So that poor Adelgunda was thought to be out of her mind;
and, in a strange perversion of feeling, the family were ashamed of this
condition of hers. I have told you already how she was dealt with in
consequence. There was, of course, no lack of doctors, or of plans of
treatment for ridding the poor soul of the *idée fixe,* as people were
pleased to term the apparition which she said she saw. But nothing had
any effect; and she implored, with tears, to be left in peace, inasmuch as
the form which in its vague, uncertain traits had nothing terrible or
alarming about it no longer caused her any fear; although for a time
after seeing it she felt as if her inner being and all her thoughts and
ideas were turned out from her, and were hovering, bodiless, outside of
her. At last the colonel made the acquaintance of a celebrated doctor
who had the reputation of being specially clever in the treatment of the
mentally afflicted. When this doctor heard Adelgunda's story he laughed
aloud, and said nothing could be easier than to cure a condition of the
kind, which resulted solely from an overexcited imagination. The idea of
the appearing of the spectre was so intimately associated with the
striking of nine o'clock that the mind could not dissociate them. So that
all that was necessary was to effect this separation by external means.
About this there would be no difficulty, as it was only necessary to
deceive the patient as to the time, and let nine o'clock pass without her
being aware of it. If the apparition did not then appear, she would be
convinced herself that it was an illusion; and measures to give tone to
the general system would be all that would then be necessary to complete the cure.

"This unfortunate advice was taken. One night all the clocks at the
castle were put back an hour—the hollow, booming tower clock included—so that, when Adelgunda awoke in the morning, although she
did not know it, she was really an hour wrong in her time. When evening came, the family were assembled, as usual, in a cheerful corner
room; no stranger was present, and the mother constrained herself to
talk about all sorts of cheerful subjects. The colonel began (as was his
habit, when in specially good humour) to carry on an encounter of wit

with the old French lady, in which Augusta, the older of the daughters, aided and abetted him. Everybody was laughing, and more full of enjoyment than ever. The clock on the wall struck eight (although it was really nine o'clock) and Adelgunda fell back in her chair, pale as death. Her work dropped from her hands; she rose, with a face of horror, stared before her into the empty part of the room, and murmured, in a hollow voice, 'What! an hour early! Don't you see it? Don't you see it? Right before me!'

"Everyone rose up in alarm. But as none of them saw the smallest vestige of anything, the colonel cried, 'Calm yourself, Adelgunda, there is nothing there! It is a vision of your brain, only your imagination. We see nothing, nothing whatever; and if there really were a figure close to you we should see it as well as you! Calm yourself.'

" 'Oh God!' cried Adelgunda, 'they think I am out of my mind. See! it is stretching out its long arm, it is making signs to me!'

"And, as though she were acting under the influence of another, without exercise of her own will, with eyes fixed and staring, she put her hand back behind her, took up a plate which chanced to be on the table, held it out before her into vacancy, and let it go.

"The plate did not drop, but floated about among the persons present, and then settled gently on the table. Augusta and her mother fainted; and these fainting fits were succeeded by violent nervous fever. The colonel forced himself to retain his self-control, but the profound impression which this extraordinary occurrence made on him was evident in his agitated and disturbed condition.

"The French lady had fallen on her knees and prayed in silence with her face turned to the floor, and both she and Adelgunda remained free from evil consequences. The mother very soon died. Augusta survived the fever; but it would have been better had she died. She who, when I first saw her, was an embodiment of vigorous, magnificent youthful happiness, is now hopelessly insane, and that in a form which seems to me the most terrible and gruesome of all the forms of *idée fixe* ever heard of. For she thinks she is the invisible phantom which haunts Adelgunda; and therefore she avoids everyone, or, at all events, refrains from speaking, or moving if anybody is present. She scarce dares to breathe, because she firmly believes that if she betrays her presence in any way everyone will die. Doors are opened for her, and her food is set down, she slinks in and out, eats in secret, and so forth. Can a more painful condition be imagined?

"The colonel, in his pain and despair, followed the colours to the next campaign, and fell in the victorious engagement at W——. It is re-markable, most remarkable that since then Adelgunda has never seen the phantom. She nurses her sister with the utmost care, and the French lady helps her. Only this very day Sylvester told me that the uncle of these poor girls is here, taking the advice of our celebrated R——, as to the means of cure to be tried in Augusta's case. God grant that the cure may succeed, improbable as it seems."

When Cyprian finished, the friends all kept silence, looking medita-tively before them. At last Lothair said, "It is certainly a very terrible ghost story. I must admit it makes me shudder, although the incident of the hovering plate is rather trifling and childish."

"Not so fast, my dear Lothair," Ottmar interrupted. "You know my views about ghost stories, and the manner in which I swagger towards visionaries; maintaining, as I do, that often as I have thrown down my glove to the spirit world challenging it to enter the lists with me, it has never taken the trouble to punish me for my presumption and irrever-ence. But Cyprian's story suggests another consideration. Ghost stories may often be mere chimeras; but, whatever may have been at the bot-tom of Adelgunda's phantom, and the hovering plate, this much is cer-tain: that on that evening, in the family of Colonel von P—— something happened which produced in three of the persons present such a shock to the system that the result was the death of one and the insanity of an-other; if we do not ascribe at least indirectly the colonel's death to it, too. For I happen to remember that I heard from officers who were on the spot, that he suddenly dashed into the thick of the enemy's fire as if impelled by the furies. Then the incident of the plate differs so com-pletely from anything in the ordinary *mise en scène* of supernatural sto-ries. The hour when it happened is so remote from ordinary super-natural use and wont, and the event so simple that its improbability acquires probability, and thereby becomes gruesome to me. But if one were to assume that Adelgunda's imagination carried along those of her father, mother and sister—that it was only within her brain that the plate moved about—would not this vision of the imagination striking three people dead in a moment, like a shock of electricity, be the most terri-ble supernatural event imaginable?"

"Certainly," said Theodore, "and I share with you, Ottmar, your opinion that the very horror of the incident lies in its utter simplicity. I can imagine myself enduring fairly well the sudden alarm produced by some fearful apparition; but the weird actions of some invisible thing would infallibly drive me mad. The sense of the most utter, most helpless powerlessness must grind the spirit to dust. I remember that I could hardly resist the profound terror which made me afraid to sleep in my room alone, like a silly child, when I once read of an old musician who was haunted in a terrible manner for a long time (almost driving him out of his mind) by an invisible being which used to play on his piano in the night, compositions of the most extraordinary kind, with the power and the technique of the most accomplished master. He heard every note, saw the keys going up and down, but never any form of a player."

"Really," Lothair said, "the way in which this class of subject is flourishing among us is becoming unendurable, I have admitted that the incident of that accursed plate produced the profoundest impression on me. Ottmar is right; if events are to be judged by their results, this is the most terrible supernatural story conceivable. Therefore I pardon the disturbed condition which Cyprian displayed earlier in the evening, and which has passed away considerably now. But not another word on the subject of supernatural horrors."

Spectral hounds occur more than once in genre fiction: the original version of Faulkner's "The Hound" concerned a departed canine who sought revenge for its own, and its master's murders; you don't have to be a Doyle buff to be acquainted with the Hound of the Baskervilles. *Here is another nasty mutt, courtesy of* AMBROSE BIERCE *who grew from a poverty-stricken Connecticut childhood to become one of America's best-known essayists and prosodists. The essence of Bierce is savagely withering satire; he was so disenchanted with his fellows that it is little wonder he disappeared to Mexico and was never again heard from. He was born in 1842, but it is unlikely that anyone will ever know when he left this plane—probably with a disgusted sneer on his lip.*

Staley Fleming's Hallucination
by Ambrose Bierce

Of two men who were talking one was a physician.

"I sent for you, Doctor," said the other, "but I don't think you can do me any good. Maybe you can recommend a specialist in psychopathy. I fancy I'm a bit loony."

"You look all right," the physician said.

"You shall judge—I have hallucinations. I wake every night and see in my room, intently watching me, a big black Newfoundland dog with a white forefoot."

"You say you wake; are you sure about that? 'Hallucinations' are sometimes only dreams."

"Oh, I wake, all right. Sometimes I lie still a long time, looking at the dog as earnestly as the dog looks at me—I always leave the light going. When I can't endure it any longer I sit up in bed—and nothing is there!"

" 'M, 'm—what is the beast's expression?"

"It seems to me sinister. Of course I know that, except in art, an animal's face in repose has always the same expression. But this is not a real animal. Newfoundland dogs are pretty mild-looking, you know; what's the matter with this one?"

"Really, my diagnosis would have no value: I am not going to treat the dog."

The physician laughed at his own pleasantry, but narrowly watched his patient from the corner of his eye. Presently he said: "Fleming, your description of the beast fits the dog of the late Atwell Barton."

Fleming half rose from his chair, sat again and made a visible attempt at indifference. "I remember Barton," he said, "I believe he was—it was reported that—wasn't there something suspicious in his death?"

Looking squarely now into the eyes of his patient, the physician said: "Three years ago the body of your old enemy, Atwell Barton, was found in the woods near his home and yours. He had been stabbed to death. There have been no arrests; there was no clue. Some of us had 'theories.' I had one. Have you?"

"I? Why, bless your soul, what could I know about it? You remember that I left for Europe almost immediately afterward—a considerable time afterward. In the few weeks since my return you could not expect me to construct a 'theory.' In fact, I have not given the matter a thought. What about his dog?"

"It was first to find the body. It died of starvation on his grave."

We do not know the inexorable law underlying coincidences. Staley Fleming did not, or he would perhaps not have sprung to his feet as the night wind brought in through the open window the long wailing howl of a distant dog. He strode several times across the room in the steadfast gaze of the physician; then, abruptly confronting him, almost shouted: "What has all this to do with my trouble, Dr. Halderman? You forget why you were sent for."

Rising, the physician laid his hand upon his patient's arm and said, gently: "Pardon me. I cannot diagnose your disorder off-hand—tomorrow, perhaps. Please go to bed, leaving your door unlocked; I will pass the night here with your books. Can you call me without rising?"

"Yes, there is an electric bell."

"Good. If anything disturbs you push the button without sitting up. Good night."

Comfortably installed in an armchair, the man of medicine stared into the glowing coals and thought deeply and long, but apparently to little purpose, for he frequently rose and opening a door leading to the staircase, listened intently; then resumed his seat. Presently, however, he fell asleep, and when he woke it was past midnight. He stirred the failing fire, lifted a book from the table at his side and looked at the title. It was Denneker's *Meditations*. He opened it at random and began to read:

"Forasmuch as it is ordained of God that all flesh hath spirit and thereby taketh on spiritual powers, so, also, the spirit hath powers of the flesh, even when it is gone out of the flesh and liveth as a thing apart, as many a violence performed by wraith and lemure sheweth. And there be those who say that man is not single in this, but the beasts have the like evil inducement, and—"

The reading was interrupted by a shaking of the house, as by the fall of a heavy object. The reader flung down the book, rushed from the room, and mounted the stairs to Fleming's bedchamber. He tried the door, but contrary to his instructions it was locked. He set his shoulder against it with such force that it gave way. On the floor near the disordered bed, in his night clothes, lay Fleming gasping away his life.

The physician raised the dying man's head from the floor and observed a wound in the throat. "I should have thought of this," he said, believing it suicide.

When the man was dead an examination disclosed the unmistakable marks of an animal's fangs deeply sunken into the jugular vein.

But there was no animal.

Mirrors and cameras traditionally have been objects of distrust in folk tradition, probably because they are believed to have the power to entrap an essential part of the human soul. Here is an anonymous rendition of that theme; the plot is often encountered in oral ghost tales.

The Dead Woman's Photograph
Anonymous

Virgil Hoyt is a photographer's assistant up at St. Paul, and a man of a good deal of taste. He has been in search of the picturesque all over the West, and hundreds of miles to the north in Canada, and can speak three or four Indian dialects, and put a canoe through the rapids. That is to say, he is a man of an adventurous sort and no dreamer. He can fight well and shoot well and swim well enough to put up a winning race with the Indian boys, and he can sit all day in the saddle and not dream about it at night.

Wherever he goes he uses his camera.

"The world," Hoyt is in the habit of saying to those who sit with him when he smokes his pipe, "was created in six days to be photographed. Man—and especially woman—was made for the same purpose. Clouds are not made to give moisture, nor trees to cast shade. They were created for the photographer."

In short, Virgil Hoyt's view of the world is whimsical, and he doesn't like to be bothered with anything disagreeable. That is the reason that he loathes and detests going to a house of mourning to photograph a corpse. The horribly bad taste of it offends him partly, and partly he is annoyed at having to shoulder, even for a few moments, a part of someone's burden of sorrow. He doesn't like sorrow, and would willingly canoe 500 miles up the cold Canadian rivers to get rid of it. Nevertheless, as assistant photographer, it is often his duty to do this very kind of thing.

Not long ago he was sent for by a rich Jewish family at St. Paul to photograph the mother, who had just died. He was very much put out, but he went. He was taken to the front parlor, where the dead woman lay in her coffin. It was evident that there was some excitement in the household and that a discussion was going on, but Hoyt wasn't concerned, and so he paid no attention to the matter.

The daughter wanted the coffin turned on end, in order that the corpse might face the camera properly, but Hoyt said he could overcome the recumbent attitude and make it appear that the face was taken in the position it would naturally hold in life, and so they went out and left him alone with the dead.

The face was a strong and positive one, such as may often be seen among Jewish matrons. Hoyt regarded it with some admiration, thinking to himself that she was a woman who had been used to having her own way. There was a strand of hair out of place, and he pushed it back from her brow. A bud lifted its head too high from among the roses on her breast and spoiled the contour of the chin, so he broke it off. He remembered these things later very distinctly and that his hand touched her bare face two or three times.

Then he took the photographs and left the house.

He was very busy at the time and several days elapsed before he was able to develop the plates. He took them from the bath, in which they had lain with a number of others, and went to work upon them. There were three plates, he having taken that number merely as a precaution against any accident. They came up well, but as they developed he became aware of the existence of something in the photograph which had not been apparent to his eye. The mysterious always came under the head of the disagreeable with him, and was therefore to be banished, so he made only a few prints and put the things away out of sight. He hoped that something would intervene to save him from attempting an explanation.

But it is a part of the general perplexity of life that things do not intervene as they ought and when they ought, so one day his employer asked him what had become of those photographs. He tried to evade him, but it was futile, and he got out the finished photographs and showed them to him. The older man sat staring at them a long time.

"Hoyt," said he, at length, "you're a young man, and I suppose you have never seen anything like this before. But I have. Not exactly the same thing, but similar phenomena have come my way a number of times since I went into the business, and I want to tell you there are things in heaven and earth not dreamt of——"

"Oh, I know all that tommy-rot," cried Hoyt, angrily, "but when anything happens I want to know the reason why, and how it is done."

"All right," said his employer, "then you might explain why and how the sun rises."

But he humored the younger man sufficiently to examine with him the bath in which the plates were submerged and the plates themselves.

All was as it should be. But the mystery was there and could not be done away with.

Hoyt hoped against hope that the friends of the dead woman would somehow forget about the photographs, but of course the wish was unreasonable, and one day the daughter appeared and asked to see the photographs of her mother.

"Well, to tell the truth," stammered Hoyt, "those didn't come out as well as we could wish."

"But let me see them," persisted the lady. "I'd like to look at them, anyway."

"Well, now," said Hoyt, trying to be soothing, as he believed it was always best to be with women—to tell the truth, he was an ignoramus where women were concerned—"I think it would be better if you didn't see them. There are reasons why——" he ambled on like this, stupid man that he was, and of course the Jewess said she would see those pictures without any further delay.

So poor Hoyt brought them out and placed them in her hand, and then ran for the water pitcher, and had to be at the bother of bathing her forehead to keep her from fainting.

For what the lady saw was this: Over face and flowers and the head of the coffin fell a thick veil, the edges of which touched the floor in some places. It covered the features so well that not a hint of them was visible.

"There was nothing over mother's face," cried the lady at length.

"Not a thing," acquiesced Hoyt. "I know, because I had occasion to touch her face just before I took the picture. I put some of her hair back from her brow."

"What does it mean, then?" asked the lady.

"You know better than I. There is no explanation in science. Perhaps there is some in psychology."

"Well," said the lady, stammering a little and coloring, "mother was a good woman, but she always wanted her own way, and she always had it, too."

"Yes?"

"And she never would have her picture taken. She didn't admire herself. She said no one should ever see a picture of hers."

"So?" said Hoyt, meditatively. "Well, she's kept her word, hasn't she?"

The two stood looking at the pictures for a time. Then Hoyt pointed to the open blaze in the grate.

"Throw them in," he commanded. "Don't let your father see them—don't keep them yourself. They wouldn't be good things to keep."

"That's true enough," said the lady, slowly. And she threw them in the fire. Then Virgil Hoyt brought out the plates and broke them before her eyes.

And that was the end of it—except that Hoyt sometimes tells the story to those who sit beside him when his pipe is lighted.

BRAM STOKER *is the justly famous author of* Dracula, *the book which both defined and effectively ended the vampire horror novel—since no fantasist has ever written anything to surpass it on its own terms. Born in Dublin in 1847, Stoker lived a vigorous life as actor Henry Irving's personal manager and wrote a small number of mostly weird novels and tales in his spare time. His first and perhaps rarest work of fiction was* Under the Sunset, *consisting of a series of darkly poetic episodes about the land of Death where the pale ghosts of the living may be sought. "The Castle of the King" is a self-contained chapter from that work, a bleak odyssey to the shores of night. It is astounding that the haunted Irishman thought he was writing the following tone poem for children!*

The Castle of the King
by Bram Stoker

When they told the poor Poet that the One he loved best was lying sick in the shadow of danger, he was nigh distraught.

For weeks past he had been alone; she, his Wife, having gone afar to her old home to see an aged grandsire ere he died.

The Poet's heart had for some days been oppressed with a strange sorrow. He did not know the cause of it; he only knew with the deep sympathy which is the poet's gift, that the One he loved was sick. Anxiously had he awaited tidings. When the news came, the shock, although he expected a sad message, was too much for him, and he became nigh distraught.

In his sadness and anxiety he went out into the garden which long years he had cultured for Her. There, amongst the bright flowers, where the old statues stood softly white against the hedges of yew, he lay down in the long uncut summer grass, and wept with his head buried low.

He thought of all the past—of how he had won his Wife and how they loved each other; and to him it seemed a sad and cruel thing that she was afar and in danger, and he not near to comfort her or even to share her pain.

Many many thoughts came back to him, telling the story of the weary years whose gloom and solitude he had forgotten in the brightness of his lovely home.—

How in youth they twain had met and in a moment loved. How his poverty and her greatness had kept them apart. How he had struggled and toiled in the steep and rugged road to fame and fortune.

How all through the weary years he had striven with the single idea of winning such a place in the history of his time, that he should be able to come and to her say, "I love you," and to her proud relations, "I am worthy, for I too have become great."

How amid all this dreaming of a happy time which might come, he had kept silent as to his love. How he had never seen her or heard her voice, or even known her habitation, lest, knowing, he should fail in the purpose of his life.

How time—as it ever does to those who work with honesty and singleness of purpose—crowned the labours and the patience of his life.

How the world had come to know his name and reverence and love it as of one who had helped the weak and weary by his example; who had purified the thoughts of all who listened to his words; and who had swept away baseness before the grandeur and simpleness of his noble thoughts.

How success had followed in the wake of fame.

How at length even to his heart, timorous with the doubt of love, had been borne the thought that he had at last achieved the greatness which justified him in seeking the hand of her he loved.

How he had come back to his native place, and there found her still free.

How when he had dared to tell her of his love she had whispered to him that she, too, had waited all the years, for that she knew that he would come to claim her at the end.

How she had come with him as his bride into the home which he had been making for her all these years. How, there, they had lived happily; and had dared to look into the long years to come for joy and content without a bar.

How he thought that even then, when though somewhat enfeebled in strength by the ceaseless toil of years and the care of hoping, he might look to the happy time to come.

But, alas! for hope; for who knoweth what a day may bring forth? Only a little while ago his Dear One had left him hale, departing in the cause of duty; and now she lay sick and he not nigh to help her.

All the sunshine of his life seemed passing away. All the long years of waiting and the patient continuance in well-doing which had crowned

their years with love, seemed as but a passing dream, and was all in
vain—all, all in vain.

Now with the shadow hovering over his Beloved One, the cloud
seemed to be above and around them, and to hold in its dim recesses
the doom of them both.

"Why, oh why," asked the poor Poet to the viewless air, "did love
come to us? Why came peace and joy and happiness, if the darkening
wings of peril shadow the air around her, and leave me to weep alone?"

Thus he moaned, and raved, and wept; and the bitter hours went by
him in his solitude.

As he lay in the garden with his face buried in the long grass, they
came to him and told him with weeping, that tidings—sad, indeed—had
come.

As they spoke he lifted his poor head and gazed at them; and they
saw in the great, dark, tender eyes that now he was quite distraught. He
smiled at them sadly, as though not quite understanding the import of
their words. As tenderly as they could they tried to tell him that the
One he loved best was dead.

They said:—

"She has walked in the Valley of the Shadow;" but he seemed to understand them not.

They whispered,

"She has heard the Music of the Spheres," but still he comprehended
not.

Then they spoke to him sorrowfully and said:

"She now abides in the Castle of the King."

He looked at them eagerly, as if to ask:

"What castle? What king?"

They bowed their heads; and as they turned away weeping they murmured to him softly—

"The Castle of the King of Death."

He spake no word; so they turned their weeping faces to him again.
They found that he had risen and stood with a set purpose on his face.
Then he said sweetly:

"I go to find her, that where she abideth, I too may there abide."

They said to him:

"You cannot go. Beyond the Portal she is, and in the Land of
Death."

Set purpose shone in the Poet's earnest, loving eyes as he answered them for the last time:

"Where she has gone, there go I too. Through the Valley of the Shadow shall I wend my way. In these ears also shall ring the Music of the Spheres. I shall seek, and I shall find my Beloved in the Halls of the Castle of the King. I shall clasp her close—even before the dread face of the King of Death."

As they heard these words they bowed their heads again and wept, and said:

"Alas! alas!"

The poet turned and left them; and passed away. They fain would have followed; but he motioned them that they should not stir. So, alone, in his grief he went.

As he passed on he turned and waved his hand to them in farewell. Then for a while with uplifted hand he stood, and turned him slowly all around.

Suddenly his outstretched hand stopped and pointed. His friends looking with him saw, where, away beyond the Portal, the idle wilderness spread. There in the midst of desolation the mist from the marshes hung like a pall of gloom on the far off horizon.

As the Poet pointed there was a gleam of happiness—very very faint it was—in his poor sad eyes, distraught with loss, as if afar he beheld some sign or hope of the Lost One.

Swiftly and sadly the Poet fared on through the burning day.

The Rest Time came; but on he journeyed. He paused not for shade or rest. Never, even for an instant did he stop to cool his parched lips with an icy draught from the crystal springs.

The weary wayfarers resting in the cool shadows beside the fountains raised their tired heads and looked at him with sleepy eyes as he hurried. He heeded them not; but went ever onward with set purpose in his eyes, as though some gleam of hope bursting through the mists of the distant marshes urged him on.

So he fared on through all the burning day, and all the silent night. In the earliest dawn, when the promise of the still unrisen sun quickened the eastern sky into a pale light, he drew anigh the Portal. The horizon stood out blackly in the cold morning light.

There, as ever, stood the Angels who kept watch and ward, and oh, wondrous! although invisible to human eyes, they were seen of him.

As he drew nigh they gazed at him pityingly and swept their great wings out wide, as if to shelter him. He spake; and from his troubled heart the sad words came sweetly through the pale lips:

"Say, Ye who guard the Land, has my Beloved One passed hither on the journey to the Valley of the Shadow, to hear the Music of the Spheres, and to abide in the Castle of the King?"

The Angels at the Portal bowed their heads in token of assent; and they turned and looked outward from the Land to where, far off in the idle wilderness, the dank mists crept from the lifeless bosom of the marsh.

They knew well that the poor lonely Poet was in quest of his Beloved One; so they hindered him not, neither urged they him to stay. They pitied him much for that much he loved.

They parted wide, that through the Portal he might pass without let.

So, the Poet went onwards into the idle desert to look for his Beloved One in the Castle of the King.

For a time he went through gardens whose beauty was riper than the gardens of the Land. The sweetness of all things stole on the senses like the odours from the Isles of the Blest.

The subtlety of the King of Death, who rules in the Realms of Evil, is great. He has ordered that the way beyond the Portal be made full of charm. Thus those straying from the paths ordained for good see around them such beauty that in its joy the gloom and cruelty and guilt of the desert are forgotten.

But as the Poet passed onwards the beauty began to fade away.

The fair gardens looked as gardens do when the hand of care is taken off, and when the weeds in their hideous luxuriance choke, as they spring up, the choicer life of the flowers.

From cool alleys under spreading branches, and from crisp sward which touched as soft as velvet the Wanderer's aching feet, the way became a rugged stony path, full open to the burning glare. The flowers began to lose their odour, and to dwarf to stunted growth. Tall hemlocks rose on every side, infecting the air with their noisome odour.

Great fungi grew in the dark hollows where the pools of dank water lay. Tall trees, with branches like skeletons, rose—trees which had no leaves, and under whose shadow to pause were to die.

Then huge rocks barred the way. These were only passed by narrow, winding passages, overhung by the ponderous cliffs above, which ever threatened to fall and engulph the Sojourner.

Here the night began to fall; and the dim mist rising from the far-off marshes, took weird shapes of gloom. In the distant fastnesses of the mountains the wild beasts began to roar in their cavern lairs. The air became hideous with the fell sounds of the night season.

But the poor Poet heeded not ill sights or sounds of dread. Onward he went ever—unthinking of the terrors of the night. To him there was no dread of darkness—no fear of death—no consciousness of horror. He sought his Beloved One in the Castle of the King; and in that eager quest all natural terrors were forgot.

So fared he onward through the livelong night. Up the steep defiles he trod. Through the shadows of the huge rocks he passed unscathed. The wild animals came around him roaring fiercely—their great eyes flaming like fiery stars through the blackness of the night.

From the high rocks great pythons crawled and hung to seize their prey. From the crevices of the mountain steeps, and from cavernous rifts in the rocky way poisonous serpents glided and rose to strike.

But close though the noxious things came, they all refrained to attack; for they knew that the lonely Sojourner was bound for the Castle of their King.

Onward still, onward he went—unceasing—pausing not in his course—but pressing ever forward in his quest.

When daylight broke at last, the sun rose on a sorry sight. There toiling on the rocky way, the poor lonely Poet went ever onwards, unheeding of cold or hunger or pain.

His feet were bare, and his footsteps on the rock-strewn way were marked by blood. Around and behind him, and afar off keeping equal pace on the summits of the rocky ridges, came the wild beasts that looked on him as their prey, but that refrained from touching him because he sought the Castle of their King.

In the air wheeled the obscene birds who follow ever on the track of the dying and the lost. Hovered the bare-necked vultures with eager eyes, and hungry beaks. Their great wings flapped lazily in the idle air as they followed in the Wanderer's track. The vultures are a patient folk, and they await the falling of the prey.

From the cavernous recesses in the black mountain gorges crept, with silent speed, the serpents that there lurk. Came the python, with his colossal folds and endless coils, whence looked forth cunningly the small flat head. Came the boa and all his tribe, which seize their prey by force and crush it with the dread strictness of their embrace. Came the hooded snakes and all those which with their venom destroy their prey. Here, too, came those serpents most terrible of all to their quarry—

which fascinate with eyes of weird magic and by the slow gracefulness of their approach.

Here came or lay in wait, subtle snakes, which take the colour of herb, or leaf, or dead branch, or slimy pool, amongst which they lurk, and so strike their prey unsuspecting.

Great serpents there were, nimble of body, which hang from rock or branch. These griping tight to their distant hold, strike downward with the rapidity of light as they hurl their whip-like bodies from afar upon their prey.

Thus came forth all these noxious things to meet the Questing Man, and to assail him. But when they knew he was bound for the dread Castle of their King, and saw how he went onward without fear, they abstained from attack.

The deadly python and the boa towering aloft, with colossal folds, were passive, and for the nonce, became as stone. The hooded serpents drew in again their venomous fangs. The mild, deep earnest eyes of the fascinating snake became lurid with baffled spleen, as he felt his power to charm was without avail. In its deadly descent the hanging snake arrested its course, and hung a limp line from rock or branch.

Many followed the Wanderer onwards into the desert wilds, waiting and hoping for a chance to destroy.

Many other perils also were there for the poor Wanderer in the desert idleness. As he went onward the rocky way got steeper and darker. Lurid fogs and deadly chill mists arose.

Then in this path along the trackless wilderness were strange and terrible things.

Mandrakes—half plant, half man—shrieked at him with despairing cry, as, helpless for evil, they stretched out their ghastly arms in vain.

Giant thorns arose in the path; they pierced his suffering feet and tore his flesh as onward he trod. He felt the pain, but he heeded it not.

In all the long, terrible journey he had but one idea other than his eager search for his Beloved One. He thought that the children of men might learn much from the journey towards the Castle of the King, which began so fair, amidst the odorous gardens and under the cool shadow of the spreading trees. In his heart the Poet spake to the multitude of the children of men; and from his lips the words flowed like music, for he sang of the Golden Gate which the Angels call TRUTH.

"Pass not the Portal of the Sunset Land!
Pause where the Angels at their vigil stand.

> Be warned! and press not though the gates lie wide,
> But rest securely on the hither side.
> Though odorous gardens and cool ways invite,
> Beyond are darkest valleys of the night.
> Rest! Rest contented.— Pause whilst undefiled,
> Nor seek the horrors of the desert wild."

Thus treading down all obstacles with his bleeding feet, passed ever onwards, the poor distraught Poet, to seek his Beloved One in the Castle of the King.

Even as onward he went the life that is of the animals seemed to die away behind him. The jackals and the more cowardly savage animals slunk away. The lions and tigers, and bears, and wolves, and all the braver of the fierce beasts of prey which followed on his track even after the others had stopped, now began to halt in their career.

They growled low and then roared loudly with uplifted heads; the bristles of their mouths quivered with passion, and the great white teeth champed angrily together in baffled rage. They went on a little further; and stopped again roaring and growling as before. Then one by one they ceased, and the poor Poet went on alone.

In the air the vultures wheeled and screamed, pausing and halting in their flight, as did the savage beasts. These too ceased at length to follow in air the Wanderer in his onward course.

Longest of all kept up the snakes. With many a writhe and stealthy onward glide, they followed hard upon the footsteps of the Questing Man. In the blood marks of his feet upon the flinty rocks they found a joy and hope, and they followed ever.

But time came when the awful aspect of the places where the Poet passed checked even the serpents in their track—the gloomy defiles whence issue the poisonous winds that sweep with desolation even the dens of the beasts of prey—the sterile fastnesses which march upon the valleys of desolation. Here even the stealthy serpents paused in their course; and they too fell away. They glided back, smiling with deadliest rancour, to their obscene clefts.

Then came places where plants and verdure began to cease. The very weeds became more and more stunted and inane. Farther on they declined into the sterility of lifeless rock. Then the most noxious herbs that grew in ghastly shapes of gloom and terror lost even the power to harm, which outlives their living growth. Dwarfed and stunted even of evil, they were compact of the dead rock. Here even the deadly Upas tree could strike no root into the pestiferous earth.

Then came places where, in the entrance to the Valley of the Shadow, even solid things lost their substance, and melted in the dank and cold mists which swept along.

As he passed, the distraught Poet could feel not solid earth under his bleeding feet. On shadows he walked, and amid them, onward through the Valley of the Shadow to seek his Beloved One in the Castle of the King.

The Valley of the Shadow seemed of endless expanse. Circled by the teeming mist, no eye could pierce to where rose the great mountains between which the Valley lay.

Yet they stood there—Mount Despair on the one hand, and the Hill of Fear upon the other.

Hitherto the poor bewildered brain of the Poet had taken no note of all the dangers, and horrors, and pains which surrounded him—save only for the lesson which they taught. But now, lost as he was in the shrouding vapour of the Valley of the Shadow, he could not but think of the terrors of the way. He was surrounded by grisly phantoms that ever and anon arose silent in the mist, and were lost again before he could catch to the full their dread import.

Then there flashed across his soul a terrible thought—

Could it be possible that hither his Beloved One had travelled? Had there come to her the pains which shook his own form with agony? Was it indeed necessary that she should have been appalled by all these surrounding horrors?

At the thought of her, his Beloved One, suffering such pain and dread, he gave forth one bitter cry that rang through the solitude—that cleft the vapour of the Valley, and echoed in the caverns of the mountains of Despair and Fear.

The wild cry prolonged with the agony of the Poet's soul rang through the Valley, till the shadows that peopled it woke for the moment into life-in-death. They flitted dimly along, now melting away and anon springing again into life—till all the Valley of the Shadow was for once peopled with quickened ghosts.

Oh, in that hour there was agony to the poor distraught Poet's soul.

But presently there came a calm. When the rush of his first agony passed, the Poet knew that to the Dead came not the horrors of the journey that he undertook. To the Quick alone is the horror of the passage to the Castle of the King. With the thought came to him such peace that even there—in the dark Valley of the Shadow—stole soft music that sounded in the desert gloom like the Music of the Spheres.

Then the poor Poet remembered what they had told him; that his Beloved One had walked through the Valley of the Shadow, that she had known the Music of the Spheres, and that she abode in the Castle of the King. So he thought that as he was now in the Valley of the Shadow, and as he heard the Music of the Spheres, that soon he should see the Castle of the King where his Beloved One abode. Thus he went on in hope.

But alas! that very hope was a new pain that ere this he wot not of.

Hitherto he had gone on blindly, recking not of where he went or what came a-nigh him, so long as he pressed onward on his quest; but now the darkness and the peril of the way had new terrors, for he thought of how they might arrest his course. Such thoughts made the way long indeed, for the moments seemed an age with hoping. Eagerly he sought for the end to come, when, beyond the Valley of the Shadow through which he fared, he should see rising the turrets of the Castle of the King.

Despair seemed to grow upon him; and as it grew there rang out, ever louder, the Music of the Spheres.

Onward, ever onward, hurried in mad haste the poor distraught Poet. The dim shadows that peopled the mist shrank back as he passed, extending towards him warning hands with long gloomy fingers of deadly cold. In the bitter silence of the moment, they seemed to say:

"Go back! Go back!"

Louder and louder rang now the Music of the Spheres. Faster and faster in mad, feverish haste rushed the Poet, amid the shrinking Shadows of the gloomy valley. The peopling shadows as they faded away before him, seemed to wail in sorrowful warning:

"Go back! Go back!"

Still in his ears rang ever the swelling tumult of the music.

Faster and faster he rushed onward; till, at last, wearied nature gave way and he fell prone to earth, senseless, bleeding, and alone.

After a time—how long he could not even guess—he awoke from his swoon.

For awhile he could not think where he was; and his scattered senses could not help him.

All was gloom and cold and sadness. A solitude reigned around him, more deadly than aught he had ever dreamt of. No breeze was in the air; no movement of a passing cloud. No voice or stir of living thing in earth, or water, or air. No rustle of leaf or sway of branch—all was silent, dead, and deserted. Amid the eternal hills of gloom around, lay the valley devoid of aught that lived or grew.

The sweeping mists with their multitude of peopling shadows had gone by. The fearsome terrors of the desert even were not there. The Poet, as he gazed around him, in his utter loneliness, longed for the sweep of the storm or the roar of the avalanche to break the dread horror of the silent gloom.

Then the Poet knew that through the Valley of the Shadow had he come; that scared and maddened though he had been, he had heard the Music of the Spheres. He thought that now hard by the desolate Kingdom of Death he trod.

He gazed all around him, fearing lest he should see anywhere the dread Castle of the King, where his Beloved One abode; and he groaned as the fear of his heart found voice:

"Not here! oh not here, amid this awful solitude."

Then amid the silence around, upon distant hills his words echoed:

"Not here! oh not here," till with the echoing and reechoing rock, the idle wilderness was peopled with voices.

Suddenly the echo voices ceased.

From the lurid sky broke the terrible sound of the thunder peal. Along the distant skies it rolled. Far away over the endless ring of the grey horizon it swept—going and returning—pealing—swelling—dying away. It traversed the æther, muttering now in ominous sound as of threats, and anon crashing with the voice of dread command.

In its roar came a sound as of a word:

"Onward."

To his knees the Poet sank and welcomed with tears of joy the sound of the thunder. It swept away as a Power from Above the silent desolation of the wilderness. It told him that in and above the Valley of the Shadow rolled the mighty tones of Heaven's command.

Then the Poet rose to his feet, and with new heart went onwards into the wilderness.

As he went the roll of the thunder died away, and again the silence of desolation reigned alone.

So time wore on; but never came rest to the weary feet. Onwards, still onwards he went, with but one memory to cheer him—the echo of the thunder roll in his ears, as it pealed out in the Valley of Desolation:

"Onward! Onward!"

Now the road became less and less rocky, as on his way he passed. The great cliffs sank and dwindled away, and the ooze of the fens crept upward to the mountain's feet.

At length the hills and hollows of the mountain fastnesses disappeared. The Wanderer took his way amid mere trackless wastes, where was nothing but quaking marsh and slime.

On, on he wandered; stumbling blindly with weary feet on the endless road.

Over his soul crept ever closer the blackness of despair. Whilst amid the mountain gorges he had been wandering, some small cheer came from the hope that at any moment some turn in the path might show him his. journey's end. Some entry from a dark defile might expose to him, looming great in the distance—or even anigh him—the dread Castle of the King. But now with the flat desolation of the silent marsh around him, he knew that the Castle could not exist without his seeing it.

He stood for a while erect, and turned him slowly round, so that the complete circuit of the horizon was swept by his eager eyes. Alas! never a sight did he see. Nought was there but the black line of the horizon, where the sad earth lay against the level sky. All, all was compact of a silent gloom.

Still on he tottered. His breath came fast and laboured. His weary limbs quivered as they bore him feebly up. His strength—his life—was ebbing fast.

On, on, he hurried, ever on, with one idea desperately fixed in his poor distraught mind—that in the Castle of the King he should find his Beloved One.

He stumbled and fell. There was no obstacle to arrest his feet; only from his own weakness he declined.

Quickly he arose and went onward with flying feet. He dreaded that should he fall he might not be able to arise again.

Again he fell. Again he rose and went on his way desperately, with blind purpose.

So for a while went he onwards, stumbling and falling; but arising ever and pausing not on his way. His quest he followed, of his Beloved One abiding in the Castle of the King.

At last so weak he grew that when he sank he was unable to rise again.

Feebler and feebler he grew as he lay prone; and over his eager eyes came the film of death.

But even then came comfort; for he knew that his race was run, and that soon he would meet his Beloved One in the Halls of the Castle of the King.

To the wilderness his thoughts he spoke. His voice came forth with a feeble sound, like the moaning before a storm of the wind as it passes through reeds in the grey autumn:

"A little longer. Soon I shall meet her in the Halls of the King; and we shall part no more. For this it is worth to pass through the Valley of the Shadow and to listen to the Music of the Spheres with their painful hope. What boots it though the Castle be afar? Quickly speed the feet of the dead. To the fleeting spirit all distance is but a span. I fear not now to see the Castle of the King; for there, within its chiefest Hall, soon shall I meet my Beloved—to part no more.

Even as he spoke he felt that the end was nigh.

Forth from the marsh before him crept a still, spreading mist. It rose silently, higher—higher—enveloping the wilderness for far around. It took deeper and darker shades as it arose. It was as though the Spirit of Gloom were hid within, and grew mightier with the spreading vapour.

To the eyes of the dying Poet the creeping mist was as a shadowy castle. Arose the tall turrets and the frowning keep. The gateway with its cavernous recesses and its beetling towers took shape as a skull. The distant battlements towered aloft into the silent air. From the very ground whereon the stricken Poet lay, grew, dim and dark, a vast causeway leading into the gloom of the Castle gate.

The dying Poet raised his head and looked. His fast failing eyes, quickened by the love and hope of his spirit, pierced through the dark walls of the keep and the gloomy terrors of the gateway.

There, within the great Hall where the grim King of Terrors himself holds his court, he saw her whom he sought. She was standing in the ranks of those who wait in patience for their Beloved to follow them into the Land of Death.

The Poet knew that he had but a little while to wait, and he was patient—stricken though he lay, amongst the Eternal Solitudes.

Afar off, beyond the distant horizon, came a faint light as of the dawn of a coming day.

As it grew brighter the Castle stood out more and more clearly; till in the quickening dawn it stood revealed in all its cold expanse.

The dying Poet knew that the end was at hand. With a last effort he raised himself to his feet, that standing erect and bold, as is the right of manhood, he might so meet face to face the grim King of Death before the eyes of his Beloved One.

The distant sun of the coming day rose over the horizon's edge.

A ray of light shot upward.

As it struck the summit of the Castle keep the Poet's Spirit in an instant of time swept along the causeway. Through the ghostly portal of the Castle it swept, and met with joy the kindred Spirit that it loved before the very face of the King of Death.

Quicker then than the lightning's flash the whole Castle melted into nothingness; and the sun of the coming day shone calmly down upon the Eternal Solitudes.

In the Land within the Portal rose the sun of the coming day. It shone calmly and brightly on a fair garden, where, among the long summer grass lay the Poet, colder than the marble statues around him.

Atmosphere and the evidence of the senses are powerful tools when crafting a ghost myth, and "Blind Man's Buff" takes great advantage of both— though through most of its short length, the author ignores the sense of vision entirely . . . an astonishing tour de force *from a modern master of weird tales, H. R. WAKEFIELD, a Briton who wrote most of his supernatural tales between 1928 and 1935.*

Blind Man's Buff
by H. R. Wakefield

"Well, thank heavens that yokel seemed to know the place," said Mr. Cort to himself. " 'First to the right, second to the left, black gates.' I hope the oaf in Wendover who sent me six miles out of my way will freeze to death. It's not often like this in England—cold as the penny in a dead man's eye." He'd barely reach the place before dusk. He let the car out over the rasping, frozen roads. " 'First to the right' "—must be this—second to the left, must be this—and there were the black gates. He got out, swung them open, and drove cautiously up a narrow, twisting drive, his headlights peering suspiciously round the bends. Those hedges wanted clipping, he thought, and this lane would have to be remetaled— full of holes. Nasty drive up on a bad night; would cost some money, though.

The car began to climb steeply and swing to the right, and presently the high hedges ended abruptly, and Mr. Cort pulled up in front of Lorn Manor. He got out of the car, rubbed his hands, stamped his feet, and looked about him.

Lorn Manor was embedded halfway up a Chiltern spur and, as the agent had observed, "commanded extensive vistas." The place looked its age, Mr. Cort decided, or rather ages, for the double Georgian brick chimneys warred with the Queen Anne left front. He could just make out the date, 1703, at the base of the nearest chimney. All that wing must have been added later. "Big place, marvellous bargain at seven thousand, can't understand it. How those windows with their little curved eyebrows seem to frown down on one!" And then he turned and examined the "vistas." The trees were tinted exquisitely to an uncertain glory as the great red sinking sun flashed its rays on their crystal mantle. The vale of Aylesbury was drowsing beneath a slowly deepening shroud of mist. Above it the hills, their crests rounded and shaded by silver and rose coppices, seemed to have set in them great smoky eyes of flame where the last rays burned in them.

"It is like some dream world," thought Mr. Cort. "It is curious how, wherever the sun strikes, it seems to make an eye, and each one fixed on me; those hills, even those windows. But, judging from that mist, I shall have a slow journey home; I'd better have a quick look inside, though I have already taken a prejudice against the place—I hardly know why. Too lonely and isolated, perhaps." And then the eyes blinked and closed, and it was dark. He took a key from his pocket and went up three steps and thrust it into the key-hole of the massive oak door. The next moment he looked forward into absolute blackness, and the door swung to and closed behind him. This, of course, must be the "palatial panelled hall" which the agent described. He must strike a match and find the light-switch. He fumbled in his pockets without success, and then he went through them again. He thought for a moment, "I must have left them on the seat in the car," he decided; "I'll go and fetch them. The door must be just behind me here."

He turned and groped his way back, and then drew himself up sharply, for it had seemed that something had slipped past him, and then he put out his hands—to touch the back of a chair, brocaded, he judged. He moved to the left of it and walked into a wall, changed his direction, went back past the chair, and found the wall again. He went back to the chair, sat down, and went through his pockets again, more thoroughly and carefully this time. Well, there was nothing to get fussed about; he was bound to find the door sooner or later. Now let him think. When he came in he had gone straight back, because he'd stumbled into this chair. The door must be a little to the left or the right of it. He'd try each in turn. He turned to the left first, and found himself going down a little narrow passage; he could feel its sides when he stretched out his hands. Well, then, he'd try his right. He did so, and walked into a wall. He groped his way along it, and again it seemed as if something slipped past him. "I wonder if there's a bat in here?" he asked himself, and then found himself back at the chair.

How Rachel would laugh if she could see him now. Surely he had a stray match somewhere. He took off his overcoat and ran his hands round the seam of every pocket, and then he did the same to the coat of his suit. And then he put them on again. Well, he'd try again. He'd follow the wall along. He did so, and found himself in a little narrow passage. Suddenly he shot out his right hand, for he had the impression that something had brushed his face very lightly. "I'm beginning to get a little bored with that bat, and with this blasted room generally," he said to himself. "I could imagine a more nervous person than myself getting a little fussed and panicky; but that's the one thing not to do." Ah, here was that chair again. "Now, I'll try the wall the other side." Well, that seemed to go on forever, so he retraced his steps till he found the chair, and sat down again. He whistled a little snatch resignedly. What an echo! The little tune had been flung back at him so fiercely, almost menacingly. Menacingly: that was just the feeble, panicky word a nervous person would use. Well, he'd go to the left again this time.

As he got up, a quick spurt of cold air fanned his face. "Is anyone there?" he said. He had purposely not raised his voice—there was no need to shout. Of course, no one answered. Who could there have been to answer since the caretaker was away? Now let him think it out. When he came in he must have gone straight forward and then swerved slightly on the way back; therefore—no, he was getting confused. At that moment he heard the whistle of a train, and felt reassured. The line from Wendover to Aylesbury ran half-left from the front door, so it should be about there—he pointed with his finger, got up, groped his way forward, and found himself in a little narrow passage. Well, he must turn back and go to the right this time. He did so, and something seemed to slip just past him, and then he scratched his finger slightly on the brocade of the chair. "Talk about a maze," he thought to himself; "it's nothing to this." And then he said to himself, under his breath: "Curse this vile, godforsaken place!" A silly, panicky thing to do he realised—almost as bad as shouting aloud. Well, it was obviously no use trying to find the door, he *couldn't* find it—*couldn't*. He'd sit in the chair till the light came. He sat down.

How very silent it was; his hands began searching in his pockets once more. Except for that sort of whispering sound over on the left somewhere—except for that, it was absolutely silent—except for that. What could it be? The caretaker was away. He turned his head slightly and listened intently. It was almost as if there were several people whispering together. One got curious sounds in old houses. How absurd it was! The chair couldn't be more than three or four yards from the door. There was no doubt about that. It must be slightly to one side or the other. He'd try the left once more. He got up, and something lightly brushed his face. "Is anyone there?" he said, and this time he knew he had shouted. "Who touched me? Who's whispering? Where's the door?" What a nervous fool he was to shout like that; yet someone outside might have heard him. He went groping forward again, and touched a wall. He followed along it, touching it with his fingertips, and there was an opening.

The door, the door, it must be! And he found himself going down a little narrow passage. He turned and ran back. And then he remembered! He had put a match-booklet in his note-case! What a fool to have forgotten it, and make such an exhibition of himself. Yes, there it was; but his hands were trembling, and the booklet slipped through his fingers. He fell to his knees, and began searching about on the floor. "It must be just here, it can't be far"—and then something icy-cold and damp was pressed against his forehead. He flung himself forward to seize it, but there was nothing there. And then he leapt to his feet, and with tears streaming down his face cried: "Who is there? Save me! Save me!" And then he began to run round and round, his arms outstretched. At last he stumbled against something, the chair—and something touched him as it slipped past. And then he ran screaming round the room; and suddenly his screams slashed back at him, for he was in a little narrow passage.

*   *   *

"Now, Mr. Runt," said the coroner, "you say you heard screaming coming from the direction of the Manor. Why didn't you go to find out what was the matter?"

"None of us chaps goes to Manor after sundown," said Mr. Runt.

"Oh, I know there's some absurd superstition about the house; but you haven't answered the question. There were screams, obviously coming from someone who wanted help. Why didn't you go to see what was the matter, instead of running away?"

"None of us chaps goes to Manor after sundown," said Mr. Runt.

"Don't fence with the question. Let me remind you that the doctor said Mr. Cort must have had a seizure of some kind, but that had help been quickly forthcoming, his life might have been saved. Do you mean to tell me that, even if you had known this, you would still have acted in so cowardly a way?"

Mr. Runt fixed his eyes on the ground and fingered his cap.

"None of us chaps goes to Manor after sundown," he repeated.

Little data is available on ROBERT HUGH BENSON, *other than the fact that he is an older brother of the better-known E. F. Benson* (Q.V.). *Robert rose to the position of Monsignor in the Catholic archdiocese of Westminster and wrote a small number of rare books on the supernatural from a Catholic viewpoint.* "Father Stein's Tale" *is taken from one of those,* A Mirror of Shalott.

Father Stein's Tale
by Robert Hugh Benson

Old Father Stein was a figure that greatly fascinated me during my first weeks in Rome, after I had got over the slight impatience that his personality roused in me. He was slow of speech and thought and movement, and had that distressing grip of the obvious that is characteristic of the German mind. I soon rejoiced to look at his heavy face, generally unshaven, his deep twinkling eyes, and the ponderous body that had such an air of eternal immovability, and to watch his mind, as through a glass case, laboring like an engine over a fact that he had begun to assimilate. He took a kind of paternal interest in me, too, and would thrust his thick hand under my arm as he stood by me, or clap me heavily on the shoulder as we met. But he was excellently educated, had seen much of the world, although always through a haze of the Fatherland that accompanied him everywhere, and had acquired an exceptional knowledge of English during his labors in a London mission. He used his large vocabulary with a good deal of skill.

I was pleased then when Monsignor announced on the following evening that Father Stein was prepared to contribute a story. But the German, knowing that he was master of the situation, would utter nothing at first but hoarse ejaculations at the thought of his reminiscences, and it was not until we had been seated for nearly half an hour before the fire that he consented to begin.

*   *   *

"It is of a dream," he said; "no more than that; and yet dreams, too, are under the hand of the good God, so I hold. Some, I know, are just folly, and tell us nothing but the confusion of our own nature when the controlling will is withdrawn; but some, I hold, are the whispers of God, and tell us of what we are too dull to hear in our waking life. You do not believe me? Very well; then listen.

"I knew a man in Germany, thirty years ago, who had lived many years away from God. He had been a Catholic, and was well educated in religion till he grew to be a lad. Then he fell into sin, and dared not confess it; and he lied, and made bad confessions, and approached the altar so. He once went to a strange priest to tell his sin, and dared not when the time came; and so added sin to sin, and lost his faith. It is ever so. We know it well. The soul dare not go on in that state, believing in God, and so by an inner act of the will renounces Him. It is not true, it is not true, she cries; and at last the voice of faith is silent and her eyes blind."

The priest stopped and looked round him, and the old Rector nodded once or twice and murmured assent.

"For twenty years he had lived so, without God, and he was not unhappy; for the powers of his soul died one by one, and he could no longer feel. Once or twice they struggled, in their death agony, and he stamped on them again. Once, when his mother died, he nearly lived again; and his soul cried once more within him, and stirred herself; but he would not hear her; it is useless, he said to her; there is no hope for you; lie still; there is nothing for you; you are dreaming; there is no life such as you think; and he trampled her again, and she lay still."

We were all very quiet now. I certainly had not suspected such passion in this old priest; he had seemed to me slow and dull and not capable of any sort of delicate thought or phrase, far less of tragedy; but somehow now his great face was lighted up, his eyebrows twitched as he talked, and it seemed as if we were hearing of a murder that this man had seen for himself. Monsignor sat perfectly motionless, staring intently into the fire, and Father Brent was watching the German sideways; Father Stein took a deliberate pinch of snuff, snapped his box, and put it away, and went on.

"This man had lived on the sea coast as a child, but was now in business in a town on the Rhine, and had never visited his old home since he left it with his mother on his father's death. He was now about thirty-five years of age, when God was gracious to him. He was living in a cousin's house, with whom he was partner.

"One night he dreamed he was a child, and walking with one whom he knew was his sister who had died before he was born, but he could not see her face. They were on a white, dusty road, and it was the noon of a hot summer day. There was nothing to be seen round him but great slopes of a dusty country with dry grass, and the burning sky overhead, and the sun. He was tired, and his feet ached, and he was crying as he walked, but he dared not cry loud for fear that his sister would turn and look at him, and he knew she was a—a *revenant,* and did not wish to see her eyes. There was no wind and no birds and no clouds; only the grasshoppers sawed in the dry grass, and the blood drummed in his ears until he thought he would go mad with the noise. And so they walked, the boy behind his sister, up a long hill. It seemed to him that they had been walking so for hours, for a lifetime, and that there would be no end to it. His feet sank to the ankles in dust, the sun beat on to his brain from above, the white road glared from below, and the tears ran down his cheeks.

"Then there was a breath of salt wind in his face, and his sister began to go faster, noiselessly; and he tried, too, to go faster, but could not; his heart beat like a hammer in his throat, and his feet lagged more and more, and little by little his sister was far in front, and he dared not cry out to her not to leave him for fear she should turn and look at him; and at last he was walking alone, and he dared not lie down or rest.

"The road passed up a slope, and when he reached the top of it at last he saw her again, far away, a little figure that turned to him and waved its hand, and behind her was the blue sea, very faint and in a mist of heat, and then he knew that the end of the bitter journey was very near.

"As he passed up the last slope the sea-line rose higher against the sky, but the line was only as the fine mark of a pencil where sea and sky met, and a dazzling white bird or two passed across it and then dropped below the cliff. By the time he came near his sister the dusty road had died away into the grass, and he was walking over the fresh turf that felt cool to his hot feet. He threw himself down on the edge of it by his sister, where she was lying with her head on her hands looking out at the sea where it spread itself out, a thousand feet below; and still he had not seen her face.

"At the foot of the cliff was a little white beach, and the rocks ran down into deep water on every side of it, and threw a purple shadow across the sand; there were birds here, too, floating out from the cliff and turning and returning; and the sea beneath them was a clear blue, like a Cardinal's ring that I saw once, and the breeze blew up from the water and made him happy again."

Father Stein stopped again, with something of a sob in his old heavy voice, and then he turned to us.

"You know such dreams," he said; "I cannot tell it as—as he told me;

but he said it was like the bliss of the redeemed to look down on the sea and feel the breeze in his hair, and taste its saltness.

"He did not wish his sister to speak, though he was afraid of her no more; and yet he knew that there was some secret to be told that would explain all—why they were here, and why she had come back to him, and why the sea was here, and the little beach below them, and the wind and the birds. But he was content to wait until it was time for her to tell him, as he knew she would. It was enough to lie here, after the dusty journey, beside her, and to wait for the word that should be spoken.

"Now, at first he was so out of breath and his heart beat so in his ears that he could hear nothing but that and his own panting; but it grew quieter soon, and he began to hear something else—the noises of the sea beneath him. It was a still day, but there was movement down below, and the surge heaved itself softly against the cliff and murmured in deep caves below, like the pedal note of the Frankfort organ, solemn and splendid; and the waves leaned over and crashed gently on the sand. It was all so far beneath that he saw the breaking wave before the sound came up to him, and he lay there and watched and listened; and that great sound made him happier even than the light on the water and the coolness and rest; for it was the sea itself that was speaking now.

"Then he saw suddenly that his sister had turned on her elbow and was looking at him; and he looked into her eyes, and knew her, though she had died before he was born. And she, too, was listening, with her lips parted, to the sound of the surge. And now he knew that the secret was to be told; and he watched her eyes, smiling. And she lifted her hand, as if to hold him silent, and waited, and again the sweet murmur and crash rose up from the sea, and she spoke softly.

" 'It is the Precious Blood,' she said."

Father Stein was silent, and we all were silent for a while. As far as I was concerned, at least, the story had somehow held me with an extraordinary fascination, I scarcely knew why.

There was a movement among the others, and presently the Frenchman spoke.

"*Et puis?*" he said.

"The man awoke," said Father Stein, "and found tears on his face."

*   *   *

It was such a short story that there were still a few minutes before the time for night-prayers, and we sat there without speaking again until the clock sounded in the campanile overhead, and the Rector rose and led the way into the west gallery of the church. I saw Father Stein waiting at the door for me to come up, and I knew why he was waiting.

He took my arm in his thick hand and held it a moment as the others passed down the two steps.

"I was that man," he said.

DICK BALDWIN *is a transplanted Long Islander living and working in Mount Vernon, New York. Both vocationally and avocationally involved in the film business, he is an expert on cinematic horror—yet here he delivers, with deadpan slyness, a low blow (that is still absolutely logical) to the vampire tradition. And be it remembered that the undead are technically considered to be reanimated corpses, manipulated by spectres dispatched from Hell. The vampire in "Money Talks" is one of the most enterprising of that breed, and may indeed have been taking lessons over in 'Salem's Lot, but if he did, he hasn't quite got all the bugs out yet.*

Money Talks
by Dick Baldwin

On Wednesday evening, August the fourth, a vampire will visit. Welcome him into your home. It is advisable to remove reflective items (such as mirrors) and all religious icons from your person and the immediate area of reception.

There were no flyers.

Not even a prepaid reply envelope.

Just the single sheet of cream-colored stationery without a letterhead, the message typed dead center of the page, folded neatly in thirds, and tucked squarely into the number-ten envelope.

Boyer reread it, regarding the fact that in this enlightened era, rich with tangible wonders like wafer-thin calculators, kids' toys with electronic brains, and vast computer reliance systems, belief in bogeymen was as antiquated as believing in God. But he reread it anyway, sitting in his sunken living room, leaning back on the comfortable Saporiti Italia sofa. The room was furnished in gold Missoni fabrics, and the late afternoon sunlight coming through the expansive picture window played wonderfully off the material, giving it all a rich, warm glow. Boyer himself was still dressed from work: gray Oscar de la Renta suit, pale blue Yves Saint Laurent shirt with pencil-stripe Pierre Cardin tie. He was a man in his thirties who carried himself well—even at home, reading over the mail.

This particular letter had been at the bottom of a stack of charity-club newsletters and parchment-like store-sale circulars left on the sofa's end table for him. He had examined the locally postmarked envelope and found it to be poor bulk-bought quality, but what piqued

Boyer's curiosity, causing him to open this letter first, was that the familiar addressograph label was in red. Usually the labels were printed in a standard black ink spread so thin that impressions were little more than faint specks. The red ink was a neat angle, he thought, and knew, even before he sliced the flap, that this was an unusual piece of junk mail. The stationery inside had an enjoyable coarse texture: definitely some of the better stuff.

As he finished the second reading, he pictured how Wednesday evening might be: a well-scrubbed young man dressed in a barely afforded three-piece suit, sample case at his side like a trained puppy, pointing out an obscure bit of jargon linking the word *salesman* to the word *vampire*. A thumbmarked page from a volume of some encyclopedia or out-of-print reference tome would pop open in the salesman-cum-vampire's hand, and there would be the exact quotation to back his claim. Handy. The sales pitch would come next.

Boyer grinned, like a child discovering the hidden cookie jar. He knew the sales game; you can't sell a salesman . . . still, the approach was different. Unique, in fact. He admired the technique, the style, because money talks when used on eye-catching devices for tenuous selling ventures.

Wednesday evening would be interesting.

Wednesday afternoon was hot. When Boyer came home from the office at four, he noticed first his refreshing central air conditioning, and then the blank space on the landing wall where, up to that afternoon, the gilt-edged mirror had been firmly hooked. Both contingencies were quite agreeable to him. Still standing inside the front door, he accepted his wife's melodious hello and cursory kiss. She was thirty-four, had glossy good looks, a designer's figure, and there was a fluidity of movement when she walked that was nothing short of elegant.

They dined, as usual, at seven. At eight they freshened the living room to receive a visitor. By nine o'clock they doubted a salesman would call and settled for the evening in the stillness of the house.

Mrs. Boyer sat reading a best seller, her long legs curled up on the sofa under her, and Boyer pored over the final draft of a contract, perched in his easy chair. At ten-thirty there was a knock at their door. Mrs. Boyer was so startled by its suddenness she nearly bit her tongue.

Boyer stepped authoritatively up the riser onto the landing, straightening his tie automatically in the spot where the mirror should be. Mrs. Boyer slipped into her shoes and stayed behind primping her hair as Boyer opened the door.

Outside, in the pale moonlight, stood a tall figure. Boyer could see the streetlamp across the way outlined through the long and loose coat the caller wore. A balaclava covered both head and lower portion of face so that only red eyes, flecked with silver, shone out of sockets set deep in cold, white skin. There wasn't a doubt in Boyer's mind that this was not a salesman. He stepped back into the protection of the house.

The caller did not move, but silently stood in the doorway.

"Hello!" Mrs. Boyer called brightly from the living room. She started up the landing. "Do come in and—" There was a catch in her smooth voice as the visitor entered.

Still without a word, the newcomer took his hand from his pocket. It was a pasty-looking, clawlike thing with which he effortlessly pushed closed the door behind him, effecting a force that made the picture window rattle. He unfastened his coat, which then slid down to the floor. Underneath, his clothes were stale and of a style indescribably old. The headgear followed, to rest on top of the coat. There were no eyebrows or hair on his mounded head, although there were remnants of what might have been hair hanging down over ears that were lupine. His nose was beaked; his mouth, canine. He was extraordinarily thin and looked cold and hungry.

"Good evening," he said, finally, his voice deep and vapory. He gestured toward the living room with a cordial wave of hand. The Boyers edged in, pressed together, their hands lightly touching. The guest followed. They backed to the sofa and stood, unsure of what to do.

"You are the Boyers," he said, rather than asked, drawing a notepad from inside his decrepit jacket.

Their attention was riveted on the gaunt figure at the foot of their coffee table. Boyer nodded.

"Sit down," he invited them.

They sat.

To Boyer, this was inconceivable: it could not be true that a vampire was in his house—*checking his name off a list!* Yet . . . He tried to speak, but seemed as if he were talking inside a vacuum. He asked about the mailing list.

The guest smiled. "Oh, yes. Mass communication. It benefits everyone. Don't you agree? Progress is very important to survival, and is especially helpful to me when coupled with your mortal's desire to believe only what your puny intellects dictate as truth. A simple letter of introduction opens wide the door of your skepticism and drops what remains of your protective shield of belief. You ask yourself why *I* would bother with exchange of remuneration for paper and postage: I have lackeys to handle that. My hands are never soiled. What concerns me are the host of names at my disposal." He replaced the well-used notepad inside his pocket.

"But . . . why?" Boyer managed to ask.

"A reasonable question. For countless years—centuries—I have done little more than beg and use devious methods of mind control to gain entrance into hovels such as this for the purpose of fulfilling my hunger. I have been at the mercy of the dawn and those of your kind knowledgeable enough to destroy me. I have survived, at times poorly, finding sustenance only on crude animal life—inferior by anyone's standard.

"Thirty years ago the last descendant of the last vampire hunter left your plane and with him took the remaining link of belief in my race. This loss of belief has become chief bastion of my power and the sole reason I have flourished. But I weary of the demeaning devices I must employ for fresh pap. I wish to retire to an easy existence. And what could be easier, more trouble-free, and more fulfilling than the method I have chosen? Once invited, I am free to return as often as I need, and offsetting my calls with other hosts assures time between visits for replenishing supplies. I would not want my visits to be too draining."

Eyes downcast to the coffee table, Boyer saw a grim future reflected back in fear-filled eyes. He sensed once the vampire took possession they would be lost. There must be a way to rid his house of this unwanted guest . . . or at least buy time until dawn . . .

. . . and tomorrow. Cash bonds. Empty bank accounts. Sell the house and leave no forwarding address. Perhaps settle in Mexico.

There were three things he knew about the vampire: one was the warning to remove reflective objects before the visit. This connoted a fear or weakness. Then there was the caution about religious items. Another fear? The third was the vampire's stated dread of dawn—which brought Boyer back to the problem of delaying the monster. The landing mirror was, of course, taken down to humor the expected salesman, and the only religious artifact in the house was a cross his wife hadn't worn for years. It was probably lost now in a drawer upstairs, useless as the oak-leaf mirror in the hall closet.

It suddenly occurred to him that he might be looking the solution in the eye: the highly polished coffee table.

He stood quickly, fighting a strange lethargy. The vampire eyed him with suspicion. Using strength from some untapped source, Boyer upended the heavy mahogany table to face the adversary. Magazines, cut-glass bowls and ashtrays, as well as an oversize art book slid down the slick wood to lay at the vampire's feet.

Mrs. Boyer reacted with horror when she saw that the finish reflected no trace of the gaunt figure. She shuddered back against the sofa, then pushed further, curling protectively as a flash of white, clawing flesh sliced through the air. The table was now nothing more than a pile of rubble.

"That was exceptionally rude, Boyer." Fury glazed the marmoreal face. "You annoy me."

Boyer, stunned, turned to his wife and noticed the pendant which had tumbled outside her blouse. It was the tiny cross, hanging on a thin gold chain. He knew instantly she must have worn it in the same attitude that prompted him to have the mirror removed. He felt a surge of hope. Boyer snatched the chain from around her neck, breaking the delicate clasp, and, holding the ridiculously small crucifix outstretched, rushed toward the vampire.

Air thickened and lights hazed. Time stood stock-still and there was a pure soundlessness not even the beat of two human hearts could penetrate. Blazing cold radiated from the figure in the Boyers' living room.

The vampire reached out his hand and the cross seemed to twist from Boyer's grasp into it.

"Besides loss of belief in my race, another stronghold I possess is the complete disintegration of mortal's religious faith." He closed his hand, then released a lump of jagged metal to the floor. "It was never crosses or stars of David or sacred cows, you see. It was the faith behind them which held power over me. And because you have faith in *nothing,* they are nothing more than detested objects, irritating baubles which disgust me.

"Now I hunger for rich, male blood."

Boyer searched his brain for a ploy or weapon. A way out. The vampire advanced, grinning: an eternity of hell with glazed fangs. Boyer backed recklessly into his stereo unit.

"Look," he said wildly. "Leave me alone. I can make it worth your while—I have money!" Insanely, he tore bills from his wallet. The vampire halted.

"Lots of money!" Boyer cried, thrusting twenties and tens and fives forward, pushing them into a clammy hand.

There arose a shriek so laden with pain and rage that Boyer felt his hair hackle. The living room was swept with an explosion of mouldy frigid wind, sucking books from pine shelves and house plants from quaint wooden buckets. The picture window shattered outward.

It happened so suddenly, Mr. and Mrs. Boyer did not immediately realize they were alone.

Spirits walk the earth for a relatively small number of reasons. In this anonymous first-person narrative, one of the classic reasons for a haunting is set forth.

The Ghost of the Count
Anonymous

Not far from the Alameda, in the City of Mexico, there is a great old stone building, in which once lived a very wealthy and wicked Spanish count. The house has about four floors, and ninety rooms, more or less. The entire fourth floor is rented and occupied by a big American firm, and their bookkeeper, an American girl, has given us the following true account of the ghost that for years haunted the building. The second floor is unoccupied, as no one cares to live there for obvious reasons. And the bottom floor is also unoccupied, save for lumber rooms, empty boxes and crates and barrels. And last of all is the great patio with its tiled floor, where secretly in the night a duel was fought to the death by the wicked count and a famous Austrian prince, who was one of Maximilian's men. The count was killed.

No one knows why the duel was fought; some say it was because of a beautiful Spanish woman; some say that it was because of treasure that the two jointly "conveyed," and which the count refused to divide with his princely *"socio,"* and more people—Mexicans—shrug their shoulders if you ask about it, and say, *"Quien sabe?"*

"I saw a ghost here last night, Miss James," announces our cashier with much eclat and evident pride.

So great is the shock that I gasp, and my pen drops, spattering red ink on my nice fresh cuffs, and (worse luck!) on the ledger page that I had just totted up. It is ruined, and I will have to erase it, or—something! Wretched man!

"I wish to goodness it had taken you off," I cry, wrathfully, as I look at the bespattered work. "Now will you just look here and see what you have done? I wish you and your ghosts were in——"

"Gehenna?" he inquires, sweetly; "I'll fix that—it won't take half a minute. And don't look so stern, else I won't tell you about the *espanto*. And you will be sorry if you don't hear about it—it would make such a good story." (Insinuatingly.)

"Then go ahead with it." (Ungraciously.)

"Well, last night I was waiting for West. He was to meet me here, after which it was our intention to hit the—that is, I mean we were going out together. (I nod scornfully.) And it seems that while I was patiently waiting here, in my usual sweet-tempered way, the blank idiot had his supper. and then lay down to rest himself for a while. You know how delicate he is? (Another contemptuous nod.) Unfortunately he forgot the engagement, and slept on. He says he never awoke until three o'clock, and so didn't come, thinking I wouldn't be there. Meantime I also went to sleep, and might have snoozed on until three, likewise, but for the fact that the ghost woke me——"

"Well? Do go on," I urge.

"The ghost woke me, as I said," proceeds the simpleton, slowly. "It was passing its cold fingers over my face and groaning. Really, it was most extraordinary. At first I didn't know what it was; then, as I felt the icy fingers stroking my face and heard blood-curdling groans issuing from the darkness, I knew what it was. And I remembered the story of the prince and his little duel down in the patio, and knew it was the ghost of the prince's victim. By the way, you don't know what a funny sensation it is to have a ghost pat your face, Miss James——"

"Pat nothing," I retort, indignantly. "I wonder you are not ashamed to tell me such fibs. Such a ta-ra-diddle! And as for the man that the prince killed downstairs, you know as well as I do that he was taken home to Spain and buried there. Why, then, should he come back here into our offices, and pat your face?"

"Ah, that I can't say," with a supercilious drawl. "I can only account for it by thinking that the ghost has good taste—better than that of some people I know," meaningly. "But honestly, I swear that I am telling you the truth—cross my heart and hope to die if I am not! And you don't know how brave I was—I never screamed; in fact, I never made a sound; oh, I was brave!"

"Then what did you do?" sternly.

"I ran. *Por Dios,* how I ran! You remember with what alacrity we got down the stairs during the November earthquake? (I remember only too distinctly.) Well, last night's run wasn't a run, in comparison—it was a disappearance, a flight, a sprint! I went down the four flights of stairs like a streak of blue lightning, and the ghost flew with me. I heard the pattering of its steps and its groans clean down to the patio door, and I assure you I quite thought I had made such an impression that it was actually going on home with me. And the thought made me feel so weak that I felt perforce obliged to take a—have a—that is, strengthen myself with a cocktail. After which I felt stronger and went home quite peacefully. But it was an uncanny experience, wasn't it?"

"Was it before or after taking that cocktail?" I ask, incredulously. "And did you take one only or eleven?"

I am hard on the man, but he really deserves it. Ghosts! Spirits, perhaps, but not ghosts. Whereat his feelings are quite "hurted"—so much so that he vows he will never tell me anything again; I had better read about Doubting Thomas; he never has seen such an unbelieving woman in all his life, and if I were only a man he would be tempted to pray that I might see the ghost; it would serve me right. Then, wrathfully departs, to notice me no more that day.

Not believing the least bit in ghosts I gave the matter no more thought. In fact, when you fall heir to a set of books that haven't been posted for nineteen days, and you have to do it all, and get up your trial balance, too, or else give up your Christmas holidays, you haven't much time to think about ghosts, or anything else, except entries. And though I had been working fourteen hours per day, the 24th of December, noon hour, found me with a difference of $13.89. The which I, of course, must locate and straighten out before departing next morning on my week's holiday. *Por supuesto,* it meant night work. Nothing else would do; and besides, our plans had all been made to leave on the eight o'clock train next morning. So I would just sit up all night, if need be, and find the wretched balance and be done with it.

Behold me settled for work that night at seven o'clock in my own office, with three lamps burning to keep it from looking dismal and lonely, and books and ledgers and journals piled up two feet high around me. If hard work would locate that nasty, hateful $13.89 it would surely be found. I had told the *portero* downstairs on the ground floor to try and keep awake for a time, but if I didn't soon finish the work I would come down and call him when I was ready to go home.

He lived in a little room, all shut off from the rest of the building, so that it was rather difficult to get at him. Besides, he was the very laziest and sleepiest peon possible, and though he was supposed to take care of the big building at night, patrolling it so as to keep off *ladrones,* he in reality slept so soundly that the last trumpet, much less Mexican robbers, would not have roused him.

And for this very reason, before settling to my work I was careful to go around and look to locks and bolts myself; everything was secure, and the doors safely fastened. So that if *ladrones* did break through they would have to be in shape to pass through keyholes or possess false keys.

With never a thought of spirits or *porteros,* or anything else, beyond the thirteen dollars and eighty-nine cents, I worked and added and re-added and footed up. And at eleven o'clock, *grazia a Dios,* I had the thirteen dollars all safe, and would have whooped for joy, had I the time. However, I wasn't out of the woods yet, the sum of eighty-nine dollars being often more easy of location than eighty-nine cents. The latter must be found, also, before I could have the pleasure of shouting in celebration thereof.

At it I went again. After brain cudgeling and more adding and prayerful thought I at last had under my thumb that abominable eighty cents. Eureka! Only nine cents out. I could get it all straight and have some sleep, after all! Inspired by which thought I smothered my yawns and again began to add. I looked at my watch—ten minutes to twelve. Perhaps I could get it fixed before one.

I suppose I had worked at the nine cents for about twenty minutes. One of the cash entries looked to me to be in error. I compared it with the voucher—yes, that was just where the trouble lay! Eleven cents—ten —nine—

S-t-t! Out went the lights in the twinkling of an eye—as I sat, gaping in my astonishment, from out of the pitchy darkness of the room came the most dreary, horrible, blood-curdling groan imaginable. As I sat paralyzed, not daring to breathe, doubting my senses for a moment, and then thinking indignantly that it was some trick of that wretched cashier, I felt long, thin, icy fingers passing gently over my face. *Malgame Dios!* what a sensation! At first I was afraid to move. Then I nervously tried to brush the icy, bony things away. As fast as I brushed, with my heart beating like a steam-hammer, and gasping with deadly fear, the fingers would come back again; a cold wind was blowing over me. Again came that dreadful groan, and too frightened to move or scream, I tumbled in a heap on the floor, among the books and ledgers. Then I suppose I fainted.

When I regained my senses I was still in a heap with the ledgers; still it was dark and still I felt the cold fingers caressing my face. At which I became thoroughly desperate. No ghost should own me! I had laughed at the poor cashier and hinted darkly at cocktails. Pray, what better was I?

I scrambled to my feet, the fingers still stroking my face. I must address them—what language—did they understand English or Spanish, I wondered? Spanish would doubtless be most suitable, if indeed, it was the ghost of the murdered count——.

"Will you do me the favor, Señor Ghost," I started out bravely, in my best Spanish, but with a very trembling voice, "to inform me what it is that you desire? Is there anything I can do for you? Because, if not, I would like very much to be allowed to finish my work, which I cannot do (if you will pardon my abruptness) if I am not alone."

(Being the ghost of a gentleman and a diplomat, surely he would take the hint and vanish. *Ojala!*)

Perhaps the ghost did not understand my Spanish; at any rate there was no articulate reply; there was another groan—again the fingers touched me, and then there was such a mournful sigh that I felt sorry for the poor thing—what could be the matter with it? With my pity, all fear was lost for a moment, and I said to the darkness all about me:

"What is it that you wish, *pobre señor?* Can I not aid you? I am not afraid—let me help you!"

The fingers moved uncertainly for a moment; then the ledgers all fell down, with a loud bang; a cold hand caught mine, very gently—I tried not to feel frightened, but it was difficult—and I was led off blindly, through the offices. I could not see a thing—not a glimmer of light showed; not a sound was heard except my own footsteps, and the faint sound of the invisible something that was leading me along—there were no more groans, thank goodness, else I should have shrieked and fainted, without a doubt. Only the pattering footsteps and the cold hand that led me on and on.

We—the fingers and I—were somehow in the great hall, then on the second floor, and at last on the stairs, going on down, flight after flight. Then I knew that I was being led about by the fingers on the tiled floor of the patio, and close to the *portero's* lodge. Simpleton that he was! Sleeping like a log, no doubt, while I was being led about in the black darkness by an invisible hand, and no one to save me! I would have yelled, of course, but for one fact—I found it utterly impossible to speak or move my tongue, being a rare and uncomfortable sensation.

But where were we going? Back into the unused lumber rooms, joining onto the patio? Nothing there, except barrels and slabs and empty boxes. What could the ghost mean? He must be utterly demented, surely.

In the middle of the first room we paused. I had an idea of rushing out and screaming for the *portero,* but abandoned it when I found that my feet wouldn't go. I heard steps passing to and fro about the floor, and waited, cold and trembling. They approached me; again my hand was taken, and I was led over near the corner of the room. Obedient to the unseen will, I bent down and groped about the floor, guided by the cold fingers holding mine, until I felt something like a tiny ring, set firmly in the floor. I pulled at it faintly, but it did not move, at which the ghost gave a faint sigh. For a second the cold fingers pressed mine, quite affectionately, then released me, and I heard steps passing slowly into the patio, then dying away. Where was it going, and what on earth did it all mean?

But I was so tired and wrought up I tried to find the door, but couldn't (the cashier would have been revenged could he have seen me stupidly fumbling at a barrel, thinking it was the door), and at last, too fatigued and sleepy to stand, I dropped down on the cold stone floor and went to sleep.

I must have slept for some hours, for when I awoke the light of dawn was coming in at the window, and I sat up and wondered if I had taken leave of my senses during the night. What on earth could I be doing here in the lumber room? Then, like a flash, I remembered, and, half unconsciously, crept about on the floor seeking the small ring. There it was! I caught it and jerked at it hard. Hey, presto, change! For it seemed to me that the entire floor was giving way. There was a sliding, crashing sound, and I found myself hanging on for dear life to a barrel that, fortunately, retained its equilibrium, and with my feet dangling into space. Down below me was a small, stone-floored room, with big boxes and small ones ranged about the walls. Treasure! Like a flash the thought struck me, and with one leap I was down in the secret room gazing about at the boxes.

But, alas! upon investigation, the biggest chests proved empty. The bad, wicked count! No wonder he couldn't rest in his Spanish grave, but must come back to the scene of his wickedness and deceit to make reparation! But the smaller chests were literally crammed with all sorts of things—big heavy Spanish coins, in gold and silver—gold and silver dinner services, with the crest of the unfortunate emperor; magnificent pieces of jeweled armor and weapons, beautiful jewelry and loose precious stones. I deliberately selected handfuls of the latter, giving my preference to the diamonds and pearls—I had always had a taste for them, which I had never before been able to gratify!—and packed them in a wooden box that I found in the lumber room. The gold and dinner services and armor, etc., I left as they were, being rather cumbersome, and carried off, rejoicing, my big box of diamonds and pearls and other jewelry.

Needless to say we didn't go away for the holidays on the eight-o'clock train. But I did come down to the office and proceeded to locate my missing nine cents. After which I unfolded the tale of the ghost and the treasure—only keeping quiet the matter of my private loot. Of which I was heartily glad afterwards. For when the government learned of the find, what do you suppose they offered me for going about with the ghost and discovering the secret room and treasure? Ten thousand dollars! When I refused, stating that I would take merely, as my reward, one of the gold dinner services, the greedy things objected at first, but I finally had my way. And to this very day they have no idea that I—even I—have all the beautiful jewels. Wouldn't they be furious if they knew it? But they aren't apt to, unless they learn English and read this story. Which isn't likely.

"Tusitala," the teller of tales, was what the natives affectionately called ROB-
ERT LOUIS STEVENSON *when he retired to Samoa late in his short, disease-
racked life. Born in Edinburgh in 1850, son of a lighthouse engineer,
Stevenson wanted to take up his father's occupation but proved too sickly
for it. Instead, he penned some of our best-beloved adventure stories, including* Kidnapped, The Master of Ballantrae *and, of course,* Treasure Island.
He wrote many tales of suspense and horror, the most famous of which are
The Strange Case of Dr. Jekyll and Mr. Hyde, The Suicide Club, A Lodging
for the Night *and* "The Body Snatcher," *one of the literary byproducts of
the murderous cadaver-dealing of the ghoulish team, Burke and Hare.* "The
Body Snatcher" *was turned into one of the two or three greatest ghost-terror
films in the history of cinema.*

The Body Snatcher
by Robert Louis Stevenson

Every night in the year, four of us sat in the small parlour of the *George*
at Debenham—the undertaker, and the landlord, and Fettes, and myself.
Sometimes there would be more; but blow high, blow low, come rain or
snow or frost, we four would be each planted in his own particular arm-
chair. Fettes was an old drunken Scotsman, a man of education obviously, and a man of some property, since he lived in idleness. He had
come to Debenham years ago, while still young, and by a mere continuance of living had grown to be an adopted townsman. His blue
camlet cloak was a local antiquity, like the church-spire. His place in
the parlour at the *George,* his absence from church, his old, crapulous,
disreputable vices, were all things of course in Debenham. He had some
vague Radical opinions and some fleeting infidelities, which he would
now and again set forth and emphasize with tottering slaps upon the
table. He drank rum—five glasses regularly every evening; and for the
greater portion of his nightly visit to the *George* sat, with his glass in
his right hand, in a state of melancholy alcoholic saturation. We called
him the Doctor, for he was supposed to have some special knowledge
of medicine and had been known, upon a pinch, to set a fracture or re-
duce a dislocation; but beyond these slight particulars, we had no
knowledge of his character and antecedents.

One dark winter night—it had struck nine some time before the landlord joined us—there was a sick man in the *George,* a great neighbour-

ing proprietor suddenly struck down with apoplexy on his way to Parliament; and the great man's still greater London doctor had been telegraphed to his bedside. It was the first time that such a thing had happened in Debenham, for the railway was but newly open, and we were all proportionately moved by the occurrence.

"He's come," said the landlord, after he had filled and lighted his pipe.

"He?" said I. "Who?—not the doctor?"

"Himself," replied our host.

"What is his name?"

"Dr. Macfarlane," said the landlord.

Fettes was far through his third tumbler, stupidly fuddled, now nodding over, now staring mazily around him; but at the last word he seemed to awaken and repeated the name "Macfarlane" twice, quietly enough the first time, but with sudden emotion at the second.

"Yes," said the landlord, "that's his name, Doctor Wolfe Macfarlane."

Fettes became instantly sober; his eyes awoke, his voice became clear, loud and steady, his language forcible and earnest. We were all startled by the transformation, as if a man had risen from the dead.

"I beg your pardon," he said, "I am afraid I have not been paying much attention to your talk. Who is this Wolfe Macfarlane?" And then, when he had heard the landlord out, "It cannot be, it cannot be," he added; "and yet I would like well to see him face to face."

"Do you know him, Doctor?" asked the undertaker, with a gasp.

"God forbid!" was the reply. "And yet the name is a strange one; it were too much to fancy two. Tell me, landlord, is he old?"

"Well," said the host, "he's not a young man, to be sure, and his hair is white; but he looks younger than you."

"He is older, though; years older. But," with a slap upon the table, "it's the rum you see in my face—rum and sin. This man, perhaps, may have an easy conscience and a good digestion. Conscience! Hear me speak. You would think I was some good, old, decent Christian, would you not? But no, not I; I never canted. Voltaire might have canted if he'd stood in my shoes; but the brains"—with a rattling fillip on his bald head—"the brains were clear and active and I saw and made no deductions."

"If you know this doctor," I ventured to remark, after a somewhat awful pause, "I should gather that you do not share the landlord's good opinion."

Fettes paid no regard to me.

"Yes," he said, with sudden decision, "I must see him face to face."

There was another pause and then a door was closed rather sharply on the first floor and a step was heard upon the stair.

"That's the doctor," cried the landlord. "Look sharp and you can catch him."

It was but two steps from the small parlour to the door of the old *George* inn; the wide oak staircase landed almost in the street; there was room for a Turkey rug and nothing more between the threshold and the last round of the descent; but this little space was every evening brilliantly lit up, not only by the light upon the stair and the great signal-lamp below the sign, but by the warm radiance of the bar-room window. The *George* thus brightly advertised itself to passers-by in the cold street. Fettes walked steadily to the spot and we, who were hanging behind, beheld the two men meet, as one of them had phrased it, face to face. Dr. Macfarlane was alert and vigorous. His white hair set off his pale and placid, although energetic, countenance. He was richly dressed in the finest of broadcloth and the whitest of linen, with a great gold watchchain, and studs and spectacles of the same precious material. He wore a broad-folded tie, white and speckled with lilac, and he carried on his arm a comfortable driving-coat of fur. There was no doubt but he became his years, breathing, as he did, of wealth and consideration; and it was a surprising contrast to see our parlour sot—bald, dirty, pimpled and robed in his old camlet cloak—confront him at the bottom of the stairs.

"Macfarlane!" he said somewhat loudly, more like a herald than a friend.

The great doctor pulled up short on the fourth step, as though the familiarity of the address surprised and somewhat shocked his dignity.

"Toddy Macfarlane!" repeated Fettes.

The London man almost staggered. He stared for the swiftest of seconds at the man before him, glanced behind him with a sort of scare, and then in a startled whisper, "Fettes!" he said, "you!"

"Ay," said the other, "me! Did you think I was dead too? We are not so easy shut of our acquaintance."

"Hush, hush!" exclaimed the doctor. "Hush, hush! this meeting is so unexpected—I can see you are unmanned. I hardly knew you, I confess, at first, but I am overjoyed—overjoyed to have this opportunity. For the present it must be how-d'ye-do and goodbye in one, for my fly is waiting and I must not fail the train; but you shall—let me see—yes—you shall give me your address and you can count on early news of me. We must do something for you, Fettes. I fear you are out at elbows; but we must see to that for auld lang syne, as once we sang at suppers."

"Money!" cried Fettes; "money from you! The money that I had from you is lying where I cast it in the rain."

Dr. Macfarlane had talked himself into some measure of superiority and confidence, but the uncommon energy of this refusal cast him back into his first confusion.

A horrible, ugly look came and went across his almost venerable countenance. "My dear fellow," he said, "be it as you please; my last thought is to offend you. I would intrude on none. I will leave you my address, however—"

"I do not wish it—I do not wish to know the roof that shelters you," interrupted the other. "I heard your name; I feared it might be you; I wished to know if, after all, there were a God; I know now that there is none. Begone!"

He still stood in the middle of the rug, between the stair and the doorway; and the great London physician, in order to escape, would be forced to step to one side. It was plain that he hesitated before the thought of this humiliation. White as he was, there was a dangerous glitter in his spectacles; but while he still paused uncertain, he became aware that the driver of his fly was peering in from the street at this unusual scene and caught a glimpse at the same time of our little body from the parlour, huddled by the corner of the bar. The presence of so many witnesses decided him at once to flee. He crouched together, brushing on the wainscot, and made a dart like a serpent, striking for the door. But his tribulation was not yet entirely at an end, for even as he was passing Fettes clutched him by the arm and these words came in a whisper, and yet painfully distinct, "Have you seen it again?"

The great rich London doctor cried out aloud with a sharp, throttling cry; he dashed his questioner across the open space, and, with his hands over his head, fled out of the door like a detected thief. Before it had occurred to one of us to make a movement, the fly was already rattling towards the station. The scene was over like a dream, but the dream had left proofs and traces of its passage. Next day the servant found the fine gold spectacles broken on the threshold, and that very night we were all standing breathless by the bar-room window, and Fettes at our side, sober, pale, and resolute in look.

"God protect us, Mr. Fettes!" said the landlord, coming first into possession of his customary senses. "What in the universe is all this? These are strange things you have been saying."

Fettes turned towards us; he looked us each in succession in the face. "See if you can hold your tongues," said he. "That man Macfarlane is not safe to cross; those that have done so already have repented it too late."

And then, without so much as finishing his third glass, far less waiting for the other two, he bade us goodbye and went forth, under the lamp of the hotel, into the black night.

We three turned to our places in the parlour, with the big red fire and four clear candles; and as we recapitulated what had passed, the first chill of our surprise soon changed into a glow of curiosity. We sat late; it was the latest session I have known in the old *George*. Each man, before we parted, had his theory that he was bound to prove; and none of us had any nearer business in this world than to track out the past of our condemned companion, and surprise the secret that he shared with the great London doctor. It was no great boast, but I believe I was a better hand at worming out a story than either of my fellows at the *George;* and perhaps there is now no other man alive who could narrate to you the following foul and unnatural events.

In his young days Fettes studied medicine in the schools of Edinburgh. He had talent of a kind, the talent that picks up swiftly what it hears and readily retails it for its own. He worked little at home; but he was civil, attentive, and intelligent in the presence of his masters. They soon picked him out as a lad who listened closely and remembered well; nay, strange as it seemed to me when I first heard it, he was in those days well favoured, and pleased by his exterior. There was, at that period, a certain extramural teacher of anatomy, whom I shall here designate by the letter K. His name was subsequently too well known. The man who bore it skulked through the streets of Edinburgh in disguise, while the mob that applauded at the execution of Burke called loudly for the blood of his employer. But Mr. K—— was then at the top of his vogue; he enjoyed a popularity due partly to his own talent and address, partly to the incapacity of his rival, the university professor. The students, at least, swore by his name, and Fettes believed himself, and was believed by others, to have laid the foundations of success when he had acquired the favour of this meteorically famous man. Mr. K—— was a *bon vivant* as well as an accomplished teacher; he liked a sly allusion no less than a careful preparation. In both capacities Fettes enjoyed and deserved his notice, and by the second year of his attendance he held the half-regular position of second demonstrator or sub-assistant in his class.

In this capacity, the charge of the theatre and lecture-room devolved in particular upon his shoulders. He had to answer for the cleanliness of the premises and the conduct of the other students, and it was a part of his duty to supply, receive, and divide the various subjects. It was with a view to this last—at that time very delicate—affair that he was lodged by Mr. K— in the same wynd, and at last in the same building, with the dissecting-rooms. Here, after a night of turbulent pleasures, his hand still tottering, his sight still misty and confused, he would be called out of bed in the black hours before the winter dawn by the unclean and desperate interlopers who supplied the table. He would open the door to these men, since infamous throughout the land. He would help them with their tragic burthen, pay them their sordid price, and remain alone, when they were gone, with the unfriendly relics of humanity. From such a scene he would return to snatch another hour or two of slumber, to repair the abuses of the night, and refresh himself for the labours of the day.

Few lads could have been more insensible to the impressions of a life thus passed among the ensigns of mortality. His mind was closed against all general considerations. He was incapable of interest in the fate and fortunes of another, the slave of his own desires and low ambitions. Cold, light, and selfish in the last resort, he had that modicum of prudence, miscalled morality, which keeps a man from inconvenient drunkenness or punishable theft. He coveted, besides, a measure of consideration from his masters and his fellow-pupils, and he had no desire to fail conspicuously in the external parts of life. Thus he made it his pleasure to gain some distinction in his studies, and day after day rendered unimpeachable eye-service to his employer, Mr. K—. For his day of work he indemnified himself by nights of roaring, blackguardly enjoyment; and when that balance had been struck, the organ that he called his conscience declared itself content.

The supply of subjects was a continual trouble to him as well as to his master. In that large and busy class, the raw material of the anatomists kept perpetually running out; and the business thus rendered necessary was not only unpleasant in itself, but threatened dangerous consequences to all who were concerned. It was the policy of Mr. K— to ask no questions in his dealings with the trade. "They bring the body, and we pay the price," he used to say, dwelling on the alliteration—"*quid pro quo*." And again, and somewhat profanely, "Ask no questions," he

would tell his assistants, "for conscience' sake." There was no understanding that the subjects were provided by the crime of murder. Had
that idea been broached to him in words, he would have recoiled in horror; but the lightness of his speech upon so grave a matter was, in itself,
an offence against good manners, and a temptation to the men with
whom he dealt. Fettes, for instance, had often remarked to himself
upon the singular freshness of the bodies. He had been struck again and
again by the hang-dog, abominable looks of the ruffians who came to
him before the dawn; and, putting things together clearly in his private
thoughts, he perhaps attributed a meaning too immoral and too cate-
gorical to the unguarded counsels of his master. He understood his
duty, in short, to have three branches: to take what was brought, to pay
the price, and to avert the eye from any evidence of crime.

One November morning this policy of silence was put sharply to the
test. He had been awake all night with a racking toothache—pacing his
room like a caged beast or throwing himself in fury on his bed—and
had fallen at last into that profound, uneasy slumber that so often follows on a night of pain, when he was awakened by the third or fourth
angry repetition of the concerted signal. There was a thin, bright
moonshine: it was bitter cold, windy, and frosty; the town had not yet
awakened, but an indefinable stir already preluded the noise and business of the day. The ghouls had come later than usual, and they seemed
more than usually eager to be gone. Fettes, sick with sleep, lighted them
upstairs. He heard their grumbling Irish voices through a dream; and as
they stripped the sack from their sad merchandise he leaned dozing with
his shoulder propped against the wall; he had to shake himself to find
the men their money. As he did so his eyes lighted on the dead face. He
started; he took two steps nearer, with the candle raised.

"God Almighty!" he cried. "That is Jane Galbraith!"

The men answered nothing, but they shuffled nearer the door.

"I know her, I tell you," he continued. "She was alive and hearty
yesterday. It's impossible she can be dead; it's impossible you should
have got this body fairly."

"Sure, sir, you're mistaken entirely," asserted one of the men.

But the other looked Fettes darkly in the eyes, and demanded the
money on the spot.

It was impossible to misconceive the threat or to exaggerate the danger. The lad's heart failed him. He stammered some excuses, counted
out the sum, and saw his hateful visitors depart. No sooner were they
gone than he hastened to confirm his doubts. By a dozen unques-

tionable marks he identified the girl he had jested with the day before. He saw, with horror, marks upon her body that might well betoken violence. A panic seized him, and he took refuge in his room. There he reflected at length over the discovery that he had made; considered soberly the bearing of Mr. K——'s instructions and the danger to himself of interference in so serious a business, and at last, in sore perplexity, determined to wait for the advice of his immediate superior, the class assistant.

This was a young doctor, Wolfe Macfarlane, a high favourite among all the restless students, clever, dissipated, and unscrupulous to the last degree. He had travelled and studied abroad. His manners were agreeable and a little forward. He was an authority on the stage, skilful on the ice or the links with skate or golf-club; he dressed with nice audacity, and, to put the finishing touch upon his glory, he kept a gig and a strong trotting-horse. With Fettes he was on terms of intimacy; indeed their relative positions called for some community of life; and when subjects were scarce the pair would drive far into the country in Macfarlane's gig, visit and desecrate some lonely graveyard, and return before dawn with their booty to the door of the dissecting-room.

On that particular morning Macfarlane arrived somewhat earlier than his wont. Fettes heard him, and met him on the stairs, told him his story, and showed him the cause of his alarm. Macfarlane examined the. marks on her body.

"Yes," he said with a nod, "it looks fishy."

"Well, what should I do?" asked Fettes.

"Do?" repeated the other. "Do you want to do anything? Least said soonest mended, I should say."

"Someone else might recognize her," objected Fettes. "She was as well known as the Castle Rock."

"We'll hope not," said Macfarlane, "and if anybody does—well you didn't, don't you see, and there's an end. The fact is, this has been going on too long. Stir up the mud, and you'll get K—— into the most unholy trouble; you'll be in a shocking box yourself. So will I, if you come to that. I should like to know how any one of us would look, or what the devil we should have to say for ourselves, in any Christian witness-box. For me, you know there's one thing certain—that, practically speaking, all our subjects have been murdered."

"Macfarlane!" cried Fettes.

"Come now!" sneered the other. "As if you hadn't suspected it yourself!"

"Suspecting is one thing—"

"And proof another. Yes, I know; and I'm as sorry as you are this should have come here," tapping the body with his cane. "The next best thing for me is not to recognize it; and," he added coolly, "I don't. You may, if you please. I don't dictate, but I think a man of the world would do as I do; and I may add, I fancy that is what K—— would look for at our hands. The question is, why did he choose us two for his assistants? And I answer, because he didn't want old wives."

This was the tone of all others to affect the mind of a lad like Fettes. He agreed to imitate Macfarlane. The body of the unfortunate girl was duly dissected, and no one remarked or appeared to recognize her.

One afternoon, when his day's work was over, Fettes dropped into a popular tavern and found Macfarlane sitting with a stranger. This was a small man, very pale and dark, with coal-black eyes. The cut of his features gave a promise of intellect and refinement which was but feebly realized in his manners, for he proved, upon a nearer acquaintance, coarse, vulgar, and stupid. He exercised, however, a very remarkable control over Macfarlane; issued orders like the Great Bashaw; became inflamed at the least discussion or delay, and commented rudely on the servility with which he was obeyed. This most offensive person took a fancy to Fettes on the spot, plied him with drinks, and honoured him with unusual confidences on his past career. If a tenth part of what he confessed were true, he was a very loathsome rogue; and the lad's vanity was tickled by the attention of so experienced a man.

"I'm a pretty bad fellow myself," the stranger remarked, "but Macfarlane is the boy—Toddy Macfarlane I call him. Toddy, order your friend another glass." Or it might be, "Toddy, you jump up and shut the door." "Toddy hates me," he said again. "Oh, yes, Toddy, you do!"

"Don't call me that confounded name," growled Macfarlane.

"Hear him! Did you ever see the lads play knife? He would like to do that all over my body," remarked the stranger.

"We medicals have a better way than that," said Fettes. "When we dislike a dead friend of ours, we dissect him."

Macfarlane looked up sharply, as though this jest was scarcely to his mind.

The afternoon passed. Gray, for that was the stranger's name, invited Fettes to join them at dinner, ordered a feast so sumptuous that the tavern was thrown in commotion, and when all was done commanded Macfarlane to settle the bill. It was late before they separated; the man Gray was incapably drunk. Macfarlane, sobered by his fury, chewed the cud of the money he had been forced to squander and the slights he had been obliged to swallow. Fettes, with various liquors singing in his head, returned home with devious footsteps and a mind entirely in abeyance. Next day Macfarlane was absent from the class, and Fettes smiled to himself as he imagined him still squiring the intolerable Gray from tavern to tavern. As soon as the hour of liberty had struck he posted from place to place in quest of his last night's companions. He could find them, however, nowhere; so returned early to his rooms, went early to bed, and slept the sleep of the just.

At four in the morning he was awakened by the well-known signal. Descending to the door, he was filled with astonishment to find Macfarlane with his gig, and in the gig one of those long and ghastly packages with which he was so well acquainted.

"What?" he cried. "Have you been out alone? How did you manage?"

But Macfarlane silenced him roughly, bidding him turn to business. When they had got the body upstairs and laid it on the table, Macfarlane made at first as if he were going away. Then he paused and seemed to hesitate; and then, "You had better look at the face," said he, in tones of some constraint. "You had better," he repeated, as Fettes only stared at him in wonder.

"But where, and how, and when did you come by it?" cried the other.

"Look at the face," was the only answer.

Fettes was staggered; strange doubts assailed him. He looked from the young doctor to the body, and then back again. At last, with a start, he did as he was bidden. He had almost expected the sight that met his eyes, and yet the shock was cruel. To see, fixed in the rigidity of death and naked on that coarse layer of sackcloth, the man whom he had left well-clad and full of meat and sin upon the threshold of a tavern, awoke, even in the thoughtless Fettes, some of the terrors of the conscience. It was a *cras tibi* which re-echoed in his soul, that two whom he had known should have come to lie upon these icy tables. Yet these were only secondary thoughts. His first concern regarded Wolfe. Unprepared for a challenge so momentous, he knew not how to look his comrade in the face. He durst not meet his eye, and he had neither words nor voice at his command.

It was Macfarlane himself who made the first advance. He came up quietly behind and laid his hand gently but firmly on the other's shoulder.

"Richardson," said he, "may have the head."

Now Richardson was a student who had long been anxious for that portion of the human subject to dissect. There was no answer, and the murderer resumed: "Talking of business, you must pay me; your accounts, you see, must tally."

Fettes found a voice, the ghost of his own: "Pay you!" he cried. "Pay you for that?"

"Why, yes, of course you must. By all means and on every possible account, you must," returned the other. "I dare not give it for nothing, you dare not take it for nothing; it would compromise us both. This is another case like Jane Galbraith's. The more things are wrong the more we must act as if all were right. Where does old K—— keep his money—"

"There," answered Fettes hoarsely, pointing to a cupboard in the corner.

"Give me the key, then," said the other, calmly, holding out his hand.

There was an instant's hesitation, and the die was cast. Macfarlane could not suppress a nervous twitch, the infinitesimal mark of an immense relief, as he felt the key turn between his fingers. He opened the cupboard, brought out pen and ink and a paper-book that stood in one compartment, and separated from the funds in a drawer a sum suitable to the occasion.

"Now, look here," he said, "there is the payment made—first proof of your good faith: first step to your security. You have now to clinch it by a second. Enter the payment in your book, and then you for your part may defy the devil."

The next few seconds were for Fettes an agony of thought; but in balancing his terrors it was the most immediate that triumphed. Any future difficulty seemed almost welcome if he could avoid a present quarrel with Macfarlane. He sat down the candle which he had been carrying all the time, and with a steady hand entered the date, the nature, and the amount of the transaction.

"And now," said Macfarlane, "it's only fair that you should pocket the lucre. I've had my share already. By-the-by, when a man of the world falls into a bit of luck, has a few shillings extra in his pocket—I'm ashamed to speak of it, but there's a rule of conduct in the case. No treating, no purchase of expensive class-books, no squaring of old debts; borrow, don't lend."

"Macfarlane," began Fettes, still somewhat hoarsely. "I have put my neck in a halter to oblige you."

"To oblige me?" cried Wolfe. "Oh, come! You did, as near as I can see the matter, what you downright had to do in self defence. Suppose I got into trouble, where would you be? This second little matter flows clearly from the first. Mr. Gray is the continuation of Miss Galbraith. You can't begin and then stop. If you begin, you must keep on beginning; that's the truth. No rest for the wicked."

A horrible sense of blackness and the treachery of fate seized hold upon the soul of the unhappy student.

"My God!" he cried, "but what have I done? and when did I begin? To be made a class assistant—in the name of reason, where's the harm in that? Service wanted the position; Service might have got it. Would *he* have been where *I* am now?"

"My dear fellow," said Macfarlane, "what a boy you are! What harm *has* come to you? What harm *can* come to you if you hold your tongue? Why, man, do you know what this life is? There are two squads of us— the lions and the lambs. If you're a lamb, you'll come to lie upon these tables like Gray or Jane Galbraith; if you're a lion, you'll live and drive a horse like me, like K——, like all the world with any wit or courage. You're staggered at the first. But look at K——! My dear fellow, you're clever, you have pluck. I like you, and K—— likes you. You were born to lead the hunt: and I tell you, on my honour and my experience of life, three days from now you'll laugh at all these scarecrows like a high-school boy at a farce."

And with that Macfarlane took his departure and drove off up the wynd in his gig to get under cover before daylight. Fettes was thus left alone with his regrets. He saw the miserable peril in which he stood involved. He saw, with inexpressible dismay, that there was no limit to his weakness, and that, from concession to concession, he had fallen from the arbiter of Macfarlane's destiny to his paid and helpless accomplice. He would have given the world to have been a little braver at the time, but it did not occur to him that he might still be brave. The secret of Jane Galbraith and the cursed entry in the daybook closed his mouth.

Hours passed; the class began to arrive; the members of the unhappy Gray were dealt out to one and to another, and received without remark. Richardson was made happy with the head; and before the hour of freedom rang Fettes trembled with exultation to perceive how far they had already gone towards safety.

For two days he continued to watch, with increasing joy, the dreadful process of disguise.

On the third day Macfarlane made his appearance. He had been ill, he said; but he made up for lost time by the energy with which he directed the students. To Richardson in particular he extended the most valuable assistance and advice, and that student, encouraged by the praise of the demonstrator, burned high with ambitious hopes, and saw the medal already in his grasp.

Before the week was out Macfarlane's prophecy had been fulfilled. Fettes had outlived his terrors and had forgotten his baseness. He began to plume himself upon his courage, and had so arranged the story in his mind that he could look back on these events with an unhealthy pride. Of his accomplice he saw but little. They met, of course, in the business of the class; they received their orders together from Mr. K——. At times they had a word or two in private, and Macfarlane was from first to last particularly kind and jovial. But it was plain that he avoided any reference to their common secret; and even when Fettes whispered to him that he had cast in his lot with the lions and forsworn the lambs, he only signed to him smilingly to hold his peace.

At length an occasion arose which threw the pair once more into a closer union. Mr. K—— was again short of subjects; pupils were eager, and it was a part of this teacher's pretensions to be always well supplied. At the same time there came the news of a burial in the rustic graveyard of Glencorse. Time has little changed the place in question. It stood then, as now, upon the crossroad, out of call of human habitations, and buried fathom deep in the foliage of six cedar trees. The cries of the sheep upon the neighbouring hills, the streamlets upon either hand, one loudly singing among pebbles, the other dripping furtively from pond to pond, the stir of the wind in mountainous old flowering chestnuts, and once in seven days the voice of the bell and the old tunes of the precentor, were the only sounds that disturbed the silence around the rural church. The Resurrection Man—to use a by-name of the period—was not to be deterred by any of the sanctities of customary piety. It was part of his trade to despise and desecrate the scrolls and trumpets of old tombs, the paths worn by the feet of worshippers and mourners, and the offerings and the inscriptions of bereaved affection. To rustic neighbourhoods, where love is more than commonly tenacious, and where some bonds of blood or fellowship unite the entire society of a parish, the body-snatcher, far from being repelled by natural respect, was attracted by the ease and safety of the task. To bodies that had been laid in earth, in joyful expectation of a far different awakening, there came that hasty, lamp-lit, terror-haunted resurrection of the spade and mattock. The coffin was forced, the cerements torn, and the melancholy relics, clad in sackcloth, after being rattled for hours on moonless by-ways, were at length exposed to uttermost indignities before a class of gaping boys.

Somewhat as two vultures may swoop upon a dying lamb, Fettes and Macfarlane were to be let loose upon a grave in that green and quiet resting-place. The wife of a farmer, a woman who had lived for sixty years, and been known for nothing but good butter and a godly conversation, was to be rooted from her grave at midnight and carried, dead and naked, to that far-away city that she had always honoured with her Sunday best; the place beside her family was to be empty till the crack of doom; her innocent and almost venerable members to be exposed to that last curiosity of the anatomist.

Late one afternoon the pair set forth, well wrapped in cloaks and furnished with a formidable bottle. It rained without remission—a cold, dense, lashing rain. Now and again there blew a puff of wind, but these sheets of falling water kept it down. Bottle and all, it was a sad and silent drive as far as Penicuik, where they were to spend the evening. They stopped once, to hide their implements in a thick bush not far from the churchyard, and once again at the Fisher's Tryst, to have a toast before the kitchen fire and vary their nips of whisky with a glass of ale. When they reached their journey's end the gig was housed, the horse was fed and comforted, and the two young doctors in a private room sat down to the best dinner and the best wine the house afforded. The lights, the fire, the beating rain upon the window, the cold, incongruous work that lay before them, added zest to their enjoyment of the meal. With every glass their cordiality increased. Soon Macfarlane handed a little pile of gold to his companion.

"A compliment," he said. "Between friends these little damned accommodations ought to fly like pipe-lights."

Fettes pocketed the money, and applauded the sentiment to the echo. "You are a philosopher," he cried. "I was an ass till I knew you. You and K—— between you, by the Lord Harry! but you'll make a man of me."

"Of course we shall," applauded Macfarlane. "A man? I tell you, it required a man to back me up the other morning. There are some big, brawling, forty-year-old cowards who would have turned sick at the look of the damned thing; but not you—you kept your head. I watched you."

"Well, and why not?" Fettes thus vaunted himself. "It was no affair of mine. There was nothing to gain on the one side but disturbance, and on the other I could count on your gratitude, don't you see?" And he slapped his pocket till the gold pieces rang.

Macfarlane somehow felt a certain touch of alarm at these unpleasant words. He may have regretted that he had taught his young companion so successfully, but he had no time to interfere, for the other noisily continued in this boastful strain:

"The great thing is not to be afraid. Now, between you and me, I don't want to hang—that's practical; but for all cant, Macfarlane, I was born with a contempt. Hell, God, Devil, right, wrong, sin, crime, and all the old gallery of curiosities—they may frighten boys, but men of the world, like you and me, despise them. Here's to the memory of Gray!"

It was by this time growing somewhat late. The gig, according to order, was brought round to the door with both lamps brightly shining, and the young men had to pay their bill and take the road. They announced that they were bound for Peebles, and drove in that direction till they were clear of the last houses of the town; then, extinguishing the lamps, returned upon their course, and followed a by-road towards Glencorse. There was no sound but that of their own passage, and the incessant, strident pouring of the rain. It was pitch dark; here and there a white gate or a white stone in the wall guided them for a short space across the night; but for the most part it was at a foot pace, and almost groping, that they picked their way through that resonant blackness to their solemn and isolated destination. In the sunken woods that traverse the neighbourhood of the burying-ground the last glimmer failed them, and it became necessary to kindle a match and re-illumine one of the lanterns of the gig. Thus, under the dripping trees, and environed by huge and moving shadows, they reached the scene of their unhallowed labours.

They were both experienced in such affairs, and powerful with the spade; and they had scarce been twenty minutes at their task before they were rewarded by a dull rattle on the coffin lid. At the same moment Macfarlane, having hurt his hand upon a stone, flung it carelessly above his head. The grave, in which they now stood almost to the shoulders, was close to the edge of the plateau of the graveyard; and the gig lamp had been propped, the better to illuminate their labours, against a tree, and on the immediate verge of the steep bank descending to the stream. Chance had taken a sure aim with the stone. Then came a clang of broken glass; night fell upon them; sounds alternately dull and ringing announced the bounding of the lantern down the bank, and its occasional collision with the trees. A stone or two, which it had dislodged in its descent rattled behind it into the profundities of the glen; and then silence, like night, resumed its sway; and they might bend their hearing to its utmost pitch, but naught was to be heard except the rain, now marching to the wind, now steadily falling over miles of open country.

They were so nearly at an end of their abhorred task that they judged it wisest to complete it in the dark. The coffin was exhumed and broken open; the body inserted in the dripping sack and carried between them to the gig; one mounted to keep it in its place, and the other, taking the horse by the mouth, groped along by the wall and bush until they reached the wider road by the Fisher's Tryst. Here was a faint disused radiancy, which they hailed like daylight; by that they pushed the horse to a good pace and began to rattle along merrily in the direction of the town.

They had both been wetted to the skin during their operations, and now, as the gig jumped among the deep ruts, the thing that stood propped between them fell now upon one and now upon the other. At every repetition of the horrid contact each instinctively repelled it with greater haste; and the process, natural although it was, began to tell upon the nerves of the companions. Macfarlane made some ill-favoured jest about the farmer's wife, but it came hollowly from his lips, and was allowed to drop in silence. Still their unnatural burthen bumped from side to side; and now the head would be laid, as if in confidence, upon their shoulders, and now the drenching sackcloth would flap icily about their faces. A creeping chill began to possess the soul of Fettes. He peered at the bundle, and it seemed somehow larger than at first. All over the countryside, and from every degree of distance, the farm dogs accompanied their passage with tragic ululations; and it grew and grew upon his mind that some unnatural miracle had been achieved, that some nameless change had befallen the dead body, and that it was in fear of their unholy burthen that the dogs were howling.

"For God's sake," said he, making a great effort to arrive at speech, "for God's sake, let's have a light!"

Seemingly Macfarlane was affected in the same direction; for though he made no reply, he stopped the horse, passed the reins to his companion, got down, and proceeded to kindle the remaining lamp. They had by that time got no farther than the crossroad down to Auchendinny. The rain still poured as though the deluge were returning, and it was no easy matter to make a light in such a world of wet and darkness. When at last the flickering blue flame had been transferred to the wick and began to expand and clarify, and shed a wide circle of misty brightness round the gig, it became possible for the two young men to see each other and the thing they had along with them. The rain had moulded the rough sacking to the outlines of the body underneath; the head was distinct from the trunk, the shoulders plainly modelled; something at once spectral and human riveted their eyes upon the ghastly comrade of their drive.

For some time Macfarlane stood motionless, holding up the lamp. A nameless dread was swathed, like a wet sheet, about the body, and tightened the white skin upon the face of Fettes; a fear that was meaningless, a horror of what could not be, kept mounting to his brain. Another beat of the watch, and he had spoken. But his comrade forestalled him.

"That is not a woman," said Macfarlane, in a hushed voice.

"It was a woman when we put her in," whispered Fettes.

"Hold that lamp," said the other. "I must see her face."

And as Fettes took the lamp his companion untied the fastenings of the sack and drew down the cover from the head. The light fell very clear upon the dark, well-moulded features and smooth-shaven cheeks of a too familiar countenance, often beheld in dreams of both of these young men. A wild yell rang up into the night; each leaped from his own side into the roadway; the lamp fell, broke, and was extinguished; and the horse, terrified by this unusual commotion, bounded and went off towards Edinburgh at a gallop, bearing along with it, sole occupant of the gig, the body of the dead and long-dissected Gray.

"The Penhale Broadcast" *is surely the most remarkable idea for a ghost story I have ever encountered. It is eerie, beautiful and unforgettable.* JACK SNOW *was a native of Piqua, Ohio, where he was born in 1907. His career in radio eventually led him to New York and a position with NBC. In his spare time, he wrote a handful of fantastic stories, collected in a scarce edition,* Dark Music. *But he is probably best known for his lifelong love of the wonderful Oz tales created by L. Frank Baum. Snow wrote two Oz novels himself:* Magical Mimics in Oz *and* The Shaggy Man of Oz . . . *as well as the indispensable guide to that fairyland,* Who's Who in Oz.

"*The Penhale Broadcast*"
by Jack Snow

All arrangements were completed for the strangest and most unusual radio broadcast ever conceived.

WXAT, New York key station of a coast-to-coast chain of ninety some radio stations, was ready to broadcast the voice of a woman, dead for fifteen years.

Sonya Parrish had died at the height of an operatic career without parallel in musical annals. Her path of glory had led her to the thrones of European monarchs. It had brought her the laudations of the severest music critics. And, most important of all, it had showered her with the adulation of the general public. When she died in 1919, she was an international favorite. Every civilized nation in the world had mourned her passing with a sincerity that was in itself a remarkable tribute to her art and personal charm. Dignified, lovely and gifted, Sonya Parrish was one of the few to whom the word, genius, was correctly applied.

And now, after fifteen years of silence—a silence that was sealed by the grave—it was said that Sonya Parrish would sing again; that her lovely voice would rise sweet and clear in Gounod's inspired "Ave Maria," and mourn plaintively through the haunting beauty of Wagner's "Traume."

WXAT and its affiliated stations publicized the broadcast months previous to the memorable night when it was scheduled to go on the air. It was an experiment, the network officials admitted. There was a possibility that it might not be a success. But they believed it would be. Sonya Parrish—living or dead—was not the sort of artist to disappoint an audience. And this would be an audience of entire nations—uncounted millions—waiting to hear the long-stilled voice of the great soprano. Short wave broadcast would carry the program to South America and European stations for re-broadcast. The whole world would be a world of ears, a world of hushed voices, waiting for that one voice from the beyond. And Sonya Parrish, station officials believed, would not fail to sing for those hushed, awed listeners.

A brief newspaper clipping from Penhale, an obscure Connecticut town, was the first in the series of incidents which led to the plans for the incredible broadcast. By the merest chance, the clipping had come to the attention of a high official of WXAT. The item told, half-humorously in a self-consciously reportorial style, of the strange singing which had been heard recently in the graveyard at Penhale. The clipping proceeded to link the ghostly singing with the grave of Sonya Parrish, whose body had been interred in the humble cemetery fifteen years ago. Penhale had been Sonya's early home and now she lay buried there, beside her father and mother. It was her voice that had been heard.

The WXAT official put the notice aside with mild curiosity. Several weeks passed. Then this same official's attention had been caught by an article in a New York tabloid. It was the Penhale reporter's story retold more ambitiously and lavishly illustrated with photographs of the late Sonya Parrish. The article was further embellished with the work of an imaginative artist who pictured Sonya, radiantly lovely and sad, singing triumphantly against the gruesome background of the Penhale graveyard. It was this vivid picture, stirring his imagination, which sent the WXAT official off on an investigation which was eventually to lead to plans for the broadcast.

Slipping quietly away from New York, the official motored to Penhale and spent some time questioning the villagers. He found it to be an established and accepted belief that Sonya Parrish sang almost nightly in the graveyard. He had been invited to hear her. And he had gone, half-amused at his own credulity, to the graveyard. At midnight, the hour when Sonya was said to sing, he had heard it himself. He had started violently at the first note. It was Sonya Parrish's voice! There was no denying it! There was no other voice in the world—or out of it— like that one. He had listened, enraptured, the first tremor of fear quickly displaced by the magical beauty of the voice that held him spellbound. It was Sonya Parrish! No one could deny it! The radio official hadn't slept the rest of the night. Early in the morning he motored back to New York in record time. In a few weeks plans for the amazing broadcast were announced.

At first the public laughed at the announcements. It was some publicity stunt to introduce a new singer. It was merely a scheme to gain the public's attention and columns of priceless publicity for WXAT and its stations. Of course they could broadcast the voice of Sonya Parrish— hadn't she made scores of phonograph records? But the network officials vigorously denied these charges. No records would be used. This was no stunt. In an effort to convince the public of the sincerity of the venture, the radio officials invited the co-operation of several celebrated psychologists and investigators of psychical phenomena. With the names of these well known men of science back of it, the venture assumed solemnity and dignity in the layman's mind, and much of the public jeering and ridiculing of the proposed broadcast subsided. Thus, the almost magical power of the mere mention of the name of Science to render logical in the public mind the most extravagant project.

The broadcast was set for the night of August 30th. At five minutes before midnight, the remote control line from Penhale would be plugged into the key station WXAT in New York, and the announcer would open the broadcast. Five minutes later—at midnight—it was hoped that the voice of Sonya Parrish would bridge the gap of fifteen years of death and sing again.

Adrian Ramsey, gifted young announcer of WXAT and winner of the coveted gold medal diction award from the Academy of Arts and Letters for two successive years, was assigned to handle the broadcast. It was arranged that Ramsey would be alone in the graveyard beside the great monolith which marked the hallowed ground in which the body of Sonya Parrish lay resting.

A slender cable, extending from Ramsey's microphone to a point just outside the graveyard gate, connected the microphone with an amplifying system, operated by WXAT engineers. Telephone wires would then carry the broadcast to the local telephone exchange in Penhale, from which point it would be dispatched by long distance telephone lines to WXAT in New York, and thence by radio to the listening world.

It was decided that no one was to be in the graveyard but Ramsey, as it had been found that the singing was always clearest when the cemetery was nearly deserted. On several evenings, following the wide-spread publicizing of the phenomena, curious crowds had collected in the graveyard, and as a result there had been no singing. Upon formulating its plans for the broadcast, WXAT had secured permission from the

Penhale authorities to station a strict guard about the cemetery after nightfall. On the night of the broadcast, it was planned to double the guard.

At last the great night arrived. Long before midnight, practically every radio receiver in the United States was tuned to WXAT and its network of stations. Foreign listeners awaited the short wave rebroadcast, which would reach them through their local stations. Heretofore neglected radios suddenly loomed as instruments of the utmost importance, and became the center of interest of excited groups of listeners.

Adrian Ramsey stood just outside the gate of the gloomy little Penhale graveyard. It was 11:30. In just twenty-five minutes he would walk into the shadows of those trees—alone—and take his solitary position before the microphone, which had been set up hours previous beside the grave of Sonya Parrish, the greatest singer the world had ever known.

In spite of his training in the commercial world of radio, Adrian was an artist with an artist's temperament. While he was possessed of a naturally keen and vivid imagination, he wasn't the nervous type, nor likely to become easily excited—radio announcers can't afford to—yet he was conscious of a mounting tenseness and an eerie sense of the unreal. Certainly no man had ever been assigned to a stranger duty—to announce to an audience of uncounted millions the singing of a woman, fifteen years dead!

Adrian glanced at the slender gold watch on his wrist. Ten minutes till twelve. It was time he took his place at the microphone. A small group of WXAT officials and technicians stood about, talking in lowered tones.

"Everything's ready, Ramsey," said a tall dark man. He was Turner, program director of WXAT. "We have men stationed every few feet about the place. You won't be disturbed." The program director paused. Then, placing his hand on Adrian's shoulder, he added quietly, "It's got to work." In those four words he expressed the fear that haunted every member of the WXAT staff.

"It's got to work!" If it didn't, there would be no choice but to return the control to New York and proceed with the blaring of a night club orchestra. WXAT and its great nation-wide network of stations would be the laughing stock of the world. It didn't matter that every item of publicity had carried a clause stating that the broadcast was an experiment—a great experiment—and there was a possibility, through no default of the network, that the experiment would fail. All that and the fact that the chain officials were courageous enough to attempt so unusual a broadcast would quickly be lost sight of in the torrent of jeering and ridicule which would follow the unsuccessful venture. The rival network would see to that!

And so, there is small wonder that misgivings and last minute doubts crowded into Adrian Ramsey's mind, as he walked silently through the Penhale graveyard to the tomb of Sonya Parrish.

There was the microphone. He could see it gleaming in the moonlight. Cold, polished steel—an electric ear—insensible to the drama of the moment, waiting only to pick up and record with mechanical precision whatever sounds chanced to strike and agitate its sensitive diaphragm.

Arriving at the microphone, Adrian looked about him. He might be the only human being within miles—so silent, so lonely was the spot. He felt as if he were the only person on earth—save Sonya Parrish. There was her grave, a rounded mound of sod, silver-black in the moonlight, and at its head—the monolith, whitely gleaming and drenched with the rays of the moon that filtered through the leaves of a great elm tree. On either side of the imposing monument were the humble stones marking the resting places of Sonya Parrish's New England forebears.

Adrian Ramsey consulted his watch again. One minute more. Then he would be on the air. During the first few minutes, he would picture the eerie scene about him, and tell something of the greatness that had been Sonya Parish's. Then at midnight—

Now that the actual moment for action had arrived, Adrian was cool and collected. He forgot his doubts. He thought only of his part of the broadcast. Intently his eyes followed his stop watch. Slowly it neared the sixty mark—fifteen seconds—ten seconds—five seconds—11:55. A tiny amber signal light on the microphone stand glowed dully.

"Good evening, Ladies and Gentlemen of the radio audience." It was the cultured and flawlessly correct voice of Adrian Ramsey. He might have been speaking from the luxurious studios in New York, announcing a routine program, surrounded by every refinement of modern civilization. His diction was perfect. His carefully modulated voice was calm and controlled.

For five minutes Adrian talked. He pictured in vivid simple phrases the humble little village graveyard, where this first broadcast of its kind ever attempted was taking place. He read the inscription from the monolith that surmounted Sonya Parrish's resting place. He spoke of the hardy New England forebears of this great woman, all of whom lay buried here. He recalled Sonya's early life, her singing as a child in the village choir, and later her great gift of artistry which had carried her across the ocean to study under the tutelage of European masters. He pictured her triumphs in Continental capitals, the multitudes of Berlin, Paris, Vienna, London, worshipping at her feet. His voice rose as he graphically portrayed her triumphal return to her native shores and her sensational debut with the Metropolitan Opera Company. Then followed her long and full years of glorious singing, her concert tours in which she had swept over the land like a great wave of melody and song —this had been before the days of radio.

Then in lowered tones, Adrian spoke compassionately of the lingering illness which had stricken the singer, when she was at the heights of her powers and fame. He told of her death and of how every nation of the world had paid sorrowful homage to the memory of the great woman whose voice was stilled. Adrian paused. Then in a few words he told of the singing in the graveyard and of the plans of WXAT which had culminated in this memorable experiment. In closing, he expressed the hope that the radio audience would be considerate of the spirit in which the experiment had been attempted, and, if it failed, would think rather of the noble motives which had inspired the venture, than of its failure.

It was intensely moving. Millions heard Adrian's voice. Millions were thrilled by it. The glowing tones—the dramatic phrasing—the supreme significance of the moment.

Again Adrian paused. He himself had been carried away. He trembled slightly. Even as he paused, a sound rose above the night silence and the monotonous chirruping of the crickets. It was the bell of the village church of Penhale tolling the hour of midnight. The vibrations carried clear and pure through the summer night. The microphone was hearing it, even as he was, Adrian knew. What better introduction to what was to follow than the eerie tolling of that distant bell?

Adrian listened, himself spellbound. Eight—nine—ten—eleven—twelve. Breathlessly Adrian counted them off. Then he moved closer to the microphone.

"It is midnight, Ladies and Gentlemen," he spoke in a subdued voice, little more than a whisper. "If Sonya Parrish can hear my voice, she will come now, and sing for the millions who are listening throughout the world." Adrian stepped back from the microphone and waited. Tiny beads of perspiration appeared on his forehead. There was nothing more he could do. His part was finished.

In New York excited groups of apartment dwellers clustered about loudspeakers. The ticking of millions of Gotham's clocks was suddenly, and perhaps for the first time, audible. In restaurants and places of entertainment, all music and talking stopped. No one stirred. New York was an ear.

Across the Middle West there were lights in the living rooms of farm homes at an hour when the occupants were customarily long abed. Hard-working farmers and their wives and families grouped tensely about loudspeakers—waiting. The bass of frogs sounded from nearby pools and streams, and the faint night wind set home-fashioned draperies fluttering in windows that looked out onto spreading fields and well-tended farm lands.

In the South, the moon shone down on wide acres of cotton, white and rolling, like the foam-crested waves of the sea. In humble cabins, far back from the deserted highways, cheap radio receivers inspired a reverent silence. A silence, breathless with the mingled emotions born in the superstitious hearts of the colored folk to whom all this was as a miracle that had passed so many long centuries ago in ancient Jerusalem, pervaded the tiny dwellings. In the mansions of the South, the fine old aristocratic families—last of the Barons of the soil—gathered in the ancestral halls to listen and wait.

On the plains of the West, cattle herders and ranchers sat on their rude bunks, their eyes mesmerized by illuminated dials. Occasionally the stillness was broken by the lonely cry of a coyote.

And in the Far West, up and down the great Pacific coast line with its string of thriving cities, millions more listened and waited, silently enduring the emptiness of those few moments that was like the emptiness that stretches into eternity.

In foreign lands, encircling the globe, the picture was the same. The world was an ear—a vast, multitudinous ear, an ear that listened tensely, hoping for a merest shred of the assurance that had been sought since the birth of the race—the assurance that death holds something more than the grave.

And then, into that ear, softly at first, softly and with incredible sweetness, flowed the unforgettable voice of Sonya Parrish. The world's heart stopped beating for a moment, as it listened. The voice sounded on. It was "Solvejg's Song" from the "Peer Gynt Suite." Delicately lovely, rising at one moment to rich crescendoes of warm beauty, and descending the next to notes of minor plaintiveness that pierced the heart with wistful beauty, the melody wavered and waned across the night air.

This was no hoax. This was Parrish—Sonya Parrish, the incomparable! Many older listeners, recalling the occasions when they had been thrilled by this sublime voice in concert halls and opera houses, listened awe-struck. Tears welled to their eyes.

A warm note of thanks swept through hearts separated by thousands of miles, linking them in a common tide of thanksgiving. There was no more distance—no more space—no more loneliness—even no more death —the impossible had happened—Sonya Parrish was singing again!

The last note of the incredible singing wavered into silence. Then came the voice of Adrian Ramsey. But it was a different Adrian Ramsey who spoke. He, too, had been touched and exalted by the magic that had happened. His voice was vibrant and rich with the strange heady excitement of the moment. He was speaking:

"Sonya Parrish has sung," a slight tremble in his voice betrayed his emotion. "Sonya Parrish has sung for the greatest audience ever assembled. As I look about me, I bow my head in humility. Never was mortal man favored with such a sight. I see the world's immortals gathered in this little graveyard to pay homage to the divine artistry of Sonya Parrish. There—not twenty paces from me—stands great Cæsar with his Roman court. And there—resplendent in the many-colored robes of the Orient—Marco Polo, the dreamer and adventurer. And there—kindly-visaged Shakespeare, mightiest of all the men of letters. His keen eyes gleam with heart-felt appreciation of the artistry he has just witnessed. And there is another divine woman, whose memory the world cherishes—the great Bernhardt, more magnetic and lovely than words can tell. Her eyes are moist with tears, a beautiful tribute to Sonya Parrish's art."

In New York, the WXAT official, who had conceived the broadcast, started. This was carrying the thing a little too far! Even he had been moved by the almost unbelievable success of the weird venture, but Ramsey was going too far. What did he mean? There was no way to stop him now. The official listened again. Ah, Sonya Parrish was singing once more! He listened, enchanted. God! Never had there been such singing as this! The beauty was heart-wringing. It was almost a relief when it wavered into silence.

Ramsey was speaking again. The official listened. "Sonya Parrish has sung again," came the voice from the loudspeaker. "She will sing no more tonight. For those who have assembled here she has displayed the magic of her great art. I bow my head in the glory of the moment in which I am permitted to speak. Such glory has never before come to man. I am humble before the multitude that is Sonya Parrish's audience." Ramsey paused, then continued in a voice that was curiously subdued. "And reverently, worshipfully I speak of One who has lately joined the multitude. For Him the great ones made way as for a King. He is garbed simply in a white robe that falls from His shoulders. A circlet of thorns crowns His head. His eyes are kind and gentle and more wise than—"

There was silence. Quickly the announcer in the New York studios stepped to the microphone and made the customary station identification and the concluding announcement for the program.

The broadcast had been a superb success! It was perfect—save for Ramsey's odd behavior. The man had obviously broken down, a prey to a bad attack of nerves. But even the official of WXAT couldn't find it in his heart to censure him. He was much too elated with the amazing success of the broadcast. And Ramsey's position had undoubtedly been a difficult one. An iron man might have faltered.

At the Penhale graveyard, the little group of station officials and technicians, who had listened breathlessly, just outside the cemetery, with ear-phones clasped to their heads, turned from their equipment and gazed at one another. They breathed a sigh of relief. It was over. It had been a success—more of a success than they had dared hope for. And Ramsey—what an ordeal it must have been for him! Alone there in the graveyard with that singing!

They started along the white-pebbled path of the graveyard to meet Ramsey and congratulate him on the splendid broadcast. But Ramsey wasn't in sight. They could distinguish the gleaming white marble that marked the grave of Sonya Parrish. Still, Ramsey was nowhere to be seen. Then one of the engineers, who was in the lead, shouted and broke into a run. In a few moments they were all standing before the grave of Sonya Parrish. There was the microphone with the familiar call letters, WXAT, across its top. At the base of the instrument, lay the body of Adrian Ramsey. He was dead.

In his eyes shone the light of a greater glory than any living man had ever before looked upon.

No ghost story has ever approached the mundane horrors of one's daily newspaper, particularly in times of war. JAMES GRANT, *born in 1822 of the family of Sir Walter Scott, was the son of a military captain—a fact which surely must have influenced the following grisly narrative.*

The Phantom Regiment
by James Grant

Though the continued march of intellect and education have nearly obliterated from the mind of the Scots a belief in the marvellous, still a love of the supernatural lingers among the more mountainous districts of the northern kingdom; for "the Schoolmaster" finds it no easy task, even when aided by all the light of science, to uproot the prejudices of more than two thousand years.

I was born in Strathnairn, about the year 1802, and, on the death of my mother, was given, when an infant, to the wife of a cotter to nurse. With these good people I remained for some years, and thus became cognizant of the facts I am about to relate.

There was a little romance connected with my old nurse Meinie and her gudeman.

In their younger days they had been lovers—lovers as a boy and girl—but were separated by poverty, and then Ewen Mac Ewen enlisted as a soldier, in the 26th or Cameronian Regiment, with which he saw some sharp service in the West Indies and America. The light-hearted young highlander became, in time, a grave, stern, and morose soldier, with the most rigid ideas of religious deportment and propriety: for this distinguished Scottish regiment was of Puritan origin, being one of those raised among the Westland Covenanters, after the deposition of King James VII by the Estates of Scotland. England surrendered to William of Orange without striking a blow; but the defence of Dunkeld, and the victorious battle of Killycrankie, ended the northern campaign, in which the noble Dundee was slain, and the army of the cavaliers dispersed. The Cameronian Regiment introduced their sectarian forms, their rigorous discipline, and plain mode of public worship into their own ranks, and so strict was their code of morals, that even the Non-jurors and Jacobins admitted the excellence and stern propriety of their bearing. They left the Scottish Service for the British, at the Union, in 1707, but still wear on their appointments the five-pointed star, which was the armorial bearing of the colonel who embodied them; and, moreover, retain the privilege of supplying their own regimental Bibles.

After many years of hard fighting in the old 26th, and after carrying a halbert in the kilted regiment of the Isles, Ewen Mac Ewen returned home to his native place, the great plain of Moray, a graver, and, in bearing, a sadder man than when he left it.

His first inquiry was for Meinie.

She had married a rival of his, twenty years ago.

"God's will be done," sighed Ewen, as he lifted his bonnet, and looked upwards.

He built himself a little cottage, in the old highland fashion, in his native strath, at a sunny spot, where the Uise Nairn—the Water of Alders —flowed in front, and a wooded hill arose behind. He hung his knapsack above the fireplace; deposited his old and sorely thumbed regimental Bible (with the Cameronian star on its boards), and the tin case containing his colonel's letter recommending him to the minister, and the discharge, which gave sixpence per diem as the reward of sixteen battles—all on the shelf of the little window, which contained three panes of glass, with a yoke in the centre of each, and there he settled himself down in peace, to plant his own kail, knit his own hose, and to make his own kilts, a grave and thoughtful but contented old fellow, awaiting the time, as he said, "when the Lord would call him away."

Now it chanced that a poor widow, with several children, built herself a little thatched house on the opposite side of the drove road—an old Fingalian path—which ascended the pastoral glen; and the ready-handed veteran lent his aid to thatch it, and to sling her kail-pot on the cruicks, and was wont thereafter to drop in of an evening to smoke his pipe, to tell old stories of the storming of Ticonderoga, and to ask her little ones the catechism and biblical questions. Within a week or so, he discovered that the widow was Meinie—the ripe, blooming Meinie of other years—an old, a faded, and a sad-eyed woman now; and poor Ewen's lonely heart swelled within him, as he thought of all that had passed since last they met, and as he spake of what they were, and what they might have been, had fate been kind, or fortune proved more true.

We have heard much about the hidden and mysterious principle of affinity, and more about the sympathy and sacredness that belong to a first and early love; well, the heart of the tough old Cameronian felt these gentle impulses, and Meinie was no stranger to them. They were married, and for fifteen years, there was no happier couple on the banks of the Nairn. Strange to say, they died on the same day, and were interred in the ancient burying-ground of Dalcross, where now they lie, near the ruined walls of the old vicarage kirk of the Catholic times. God rest them in their humble highland graves! My father, who was the minister of Croy, acted as chief mourner, and gave the customary funeral prayer. But I am somewhat anticipating, and losing the thread of my own story in telling theirs.

In process of time the influx of French and English tourists who came to visit the country of the clans, and to view the plain of Culloden, after the publication of "Waverley" gave to all Britain that which we name in Scotland "the tartan fever," and caused the old path which passed the cot of Ewen to become a turnpike road; a tollbar—that most obnoxious of all impositions to a Celt—was placed across the mouth of the little glen, barring the way directly to the battlefield; and of this gate the old pensioner Ewen naturally became keeper; and during the summer season, when, perhaps, a hundred carriages per day rolled through, it became a source of revenue alike to him, and to the Lord of Cawdor and the Laird of Kilravock, the road trustees. And the chief pleasure of Ewen's existence was to sit on a thatched seat by the gate, for then he felt conscious of being in office—on duty—a species of sentinel; and it smacked of the old time when the Generale was beaten in the morning, and the drums rolled tattoo at night; when he had belts to pipe-clay, and boots to blackball; when there were wigs to frizzle and queues to tie, and to be all trim and in order to meet Monseigneur le Marquis de Montcalm, or General Washington "right early in the morning"; and there by the new barrier of the glen Ewen sat the live-long day, with spectacles on nose, and the Cameronian Bible on his knee, as he spelled his way through Deuteronomy and the tribes of Judah.

Slates in due time replaced the green thatch of his little cottage; then a diminutive additional story, with two small dormer windows, was added thereto, and the thrifty Meinie placed a paper in her window informing shepherds, the chance wayfarers, and the wandering deerstalkers that she had a room to let; but summer passed away, the sportsman forsook the brown scorched mountains, the gay tourist ceased to come north, and the advertisement turned from white to yellow, and from yellow to flyblown green in her window; the winter snows descended on the hills, the pines stood in long and solemn ranks by the white frozen Nairn, but "the room upstairs" still remained without a tenant.

Anon the snow passed away; the river again flowed free, the flowers began to bloom; the young grass to sprout by the hedgerows, and the mavis to sing on the fauld-dykes, for spring was come again, and joyous summer soon would follow; and one night—it was the 26th of April—Ewen was exhibiting his penmanship in large text-hand by preparing the new announcement of "a room to let," when he paused, and looked up as a peal of thunder rumbled across the sky; a red gleam of lightning flashed in the darkness without, and then they heard the roar of the deep broad Nairn, as its waters, usually so sombre and so slow, swept down from the wilds of Badenoch, flooded with the melting snows of the past winter.

A dreadful storm of thunder, rain, and wind came on, and the little cottage rocked on its foundations; frequently the turf-fire upon the hearth was almost blown about the clay-floor, by the downward gusts that bellowed in the chimney. The lightning gleamed incessantly, and seemed to play about the hill of Urchany and the ruins of Caistel Fionlah; the woods groaned and creaked, and the trees seemed to shriek as their strong limbs were torn asunder by the gusts which in some places laid side by side the green sapling of last summer, and the old oak that had stood for a thousand years—that had seen Macbeth and Duncan ride from Nairn, and had outlived the wars of the Comyns and the Clanehattan.

The swollen Nairn tore down its banks, and swept trees, rocks, and stones in wild confusion to the sea, mingling the pines of Abererder with the old oaks of Cawdor; while the salt spray from the Moray Firth was swept seven miles inland, where it encrusted with salt the trees, the houses, and windows, and whatever it fell on as it mingled with the ceaseless rain, while deep, hoarse, and loud the incessant thunder rattled across the sky, "as if all the cannon on earth," according to Ewen, "were exchanging salvoes between Urchany and the Hill of Geddes."

Meinie grew pale, and sat with a finger on her mouth, and a startled expression in her eyes, listening to the uproar without; four children, two of whom were Ewen's, and her last addition to the clan, clung to her skirts.

Ewen had just completed the invariable prayer and chapter for the night, and was solemnly depositing his old regimental companion, with "Baxter's Saints' Rest," in a place of security, when a tremendous knock—a knock that rang above the storm—shook the door of the cottage.

"Who can this be, and in such a night?" said Meinie.

"The Lord knoweth," responded Ewen, gravely; "but he knocks both loud and late."

"Inquire before you open," urged Meinie, seizing her husband's arm, as the impatient knock was renewed with treble violence.

"Who comes there?" demanded Ewen, in a soldierly tone.

"A friend," replied a strange voice without, and in the same manner.

"What do you want?"

"Fire and smoke!" cried the other, giving the door a tremendous kick; "do you ask that in such a devil of a night as this? You have a room to let, have you not?"

"Yes."

"Well; open the door, or blood and 'oons I'll bite your nose off!"

Ewen hastened to undo the door; and then, all wet and dripping as if he had just been fished up from the Moray Firth, there entered a strange-looking old fellow in a red coat; he stumped vigorously on a wooden leg, and carried on his shoulders a box, which he flung down with a crash that shook the dwelling, saying,—

"There—damn you—I have made good my billet at last."

"So it seems," said Ewen, reclosing the door in haste to exclude the tempest, lest his house should be unroofed and torn asunder.

"Harkee, comrade, what garrison or fortress is this," asked the visitor, "that peaceable folks are to be challenged in this fashion, and forced to give parole and countersign before they march in—eh?"

"It is my house, comrade; and so you had better keep a civil tongue in your head."

"Civil tongue? Fire and smoke, you mangy cur! I can be as civil as my neighbours; but get me a glass of grog, for I am as wet as we were the night before Minden."

"Where have you come from in such a storm as this?"

"Where you'd not like to go—so never mind; but, grog, I tell you—get me some grog, and a bit of tobacco; it is long since I tasted either."

Ewen hastened to get a large quaighful of stiff Glenlivat, which the veteran drained to his health, and that of Meinie; but first he gave them a most diabolical grin, and threw into the liquor some black stuff, saying,—

"I always mix my grog with gunpowder—it's a good tonic; I learned that of a comrade who fell at Minden on the glorious 1st of August, '59."

"You have been a soldier, then?"

"Right! I was one of the 25th, or old Edinburgh Regiment; they enlisted me, though an Englishman, I believe; for my good old dam was a follower of the camp."

"Our number was the 26th—the old Cameronian Regiment—so we were near each other, you see, comrade."

"Nearer than you would quite like, mayhap," said Wooden-leg, with another grin and a dreadful oath.

"And you have served in Germany?" asked Ewen.

"Germany—aye, and marched over every foot of it, from Hanover to Hell, and back again. I have fought in Flanders, too."

"I wish you had come a wee while sooner," said Ewen gravely, for this discourse startled his sense of propriety.

"Sooner," snarled this shocking old fellow, who must have belonged to that army "which swore so terribly in Flanders," as good Uncle Toby says; "sooner—for what?"

"To have heard me read a chapter, and to have joined us in prayer."

"Prayers be d——ned!" cried the other, with a shout of laughter, and a face expressive of fiendish mockery, as he gave his wooden leg a thundering blow on the floor; "fire and smoke—another glass of grog—and then we'll settle about my billet upstairs."

While getting another dram, which hospitality prevented him from refusing, Ewen scrutinised this strange visitor, whose aspect and attire were very remarkable; but wholly careless of what any one thought, he sat by the hearth, wringing his wet wig, and drying it at the fire.

He was a little man, of a spare, but strong and active figure, which indicated great age; his face resembled that of a rat; behind it hung a long queue that waved about like a pendulum when he moved his head, which was quite bald, and smooth as a cricket-ball, save where a long and livid scar—evidently a sword cut—traversed it. This was visible while he sat drying his wig; but as that process was somewhat protracted, he uttered an oath, and thrust his cocked hat on one side of his head, and very much over his left eye, which was covered by a patch. This head-dress was the old military triple-cocked hat, bound with yellow braid, and having on one side the hideous black leather cockade of the House of Hanover, now happily disused in the British army, and retained as a badge of service by liverymen alone. His attire was an old threadbare red coat, faced with yellow, having square tails and deep cuffs, with braided holes; he wore knee-breeches on his spindle shanks, one of which terminated, as I have said, in a wooden pin; he carried a large knotted stick; and, in outline and aspect, very much resembled, as Ewen thought, Frederick the Great of Prussia, or an old Chelsea pensioner, or the soldiers he had seen delineated in antique prints of the Flemish wars. His solitary orb possessed a most diabolical leer, and, whichever way you turned, it seemed to regard you with the fixed glare of a basilisk.

"You are a stranger hereabout, I presume?" said Ewen drily.

"A stranger now, certainly; but I was pretty well known in this locality once. There are some bones buried hereabout that may remember me," he replied, with a grin that showed his fangless jaws.

"Bones!" reiterated Ewen, aghast.

"Yes, bones—Culloden Muir lies close by here, does it not?"

"It does—then you have travelled this road before?"

"Death and the Devil! I should think so, comrade; on this very night sixty years ago I marched along this road, from Nairn to Culloden, with the army of His Royal Highness, the Great Duke of Cumberland, Captain-General of the British troops, in pursuit of the rebels under the Popish Pretender—"

"Under His Royal Highness Prince Charles, you mean, comrade," said Ewen, in whose breast—Cameronian though he was—a tempest of Highland wrath and loyalty swelled up at these words.

"Prince—ha! ha! ha!" laughed the other; "had you said as much then, the gallows had been your doom. Many a man I have shot, and many a boy I have brained with the butt end of my musket, for no other crime than wearing the tartan, even as you this night wear it."

Ewen made a forward stride as if he would have taken the wicked boaster by the throat; his anger was kindled to find himself in presence of a veritable soldier of the infamous "German Butcher," whose merciless massacre of the wounded clansmen and their defenceless families will never be forgotten in Scotland while oral tradition and written record exist; but Ewen paused, and said in his quiet way,—

"Blessed be the Lord! these times and things have passed away from the land, to return to it no more. We are both old men now; by your own reckoning, you must at least have numbered four-score years, and in that, you are by twenty my better man. You are my guest tonight, moreover, so we must not quarrel, comrade. My father was killed at Culloden."

"On which side?"

"The right one—for he fell by the side of old Keppoch, and his last words were, 'Righ Hamish gu Bragh!' "

"Fire and smoke!" laughed the old fellow, "I remember these things as if they only happened yesterday—mix me some more grog and put it in the bill—I was the company's butcher in those days—it suited my taste —so when I was not stabbing and slashing the sheep and cattle of the rascally commissary, I was cutting the throats of the Scots and French, for there were plenty of them, and Irish too, who fought against the king's troops in Flanders. We had hot work, that day at Culloden—hotter than at Minden, where we fought in heavy marching order, with our blankets, kettles, and provisions, on a broiling noon, when the battlefield was cracking under a blazing sun, and the whole country was sweltering like the oven of the Great Baker."

"Who is he?"

"What! you don't know him? Ha! ha! ha! Ho! ho! ho! come, that is good."

Ewen expostulated with the boisterous old fellow on this style of conversation, which, as you may easily conceive, was very revolting to the prejudices of a well-regulated Cameronian soldier.

"Come, come, you old devilskin," cried the other, stirring up the fire with his wooden leg, till the sparks flashed and gleamed like his solitary eye; "you may as well sing psalms to a dead horse, as preach to me. Hark how the thunder roars, like the great guns at Carthagena! More grog—put it in the bill—or, halt, d——me! pay yourself," and he dashed on the table a handful of silver of the reigns of George II, and the Glencoe assassin, William of Orange.

He obtained more whiskey, and drank it raw, seasoning it from time to time with gunpowder, just as an Arab does his cold water with ginger.

"Where did you lose your eye, comrade?"

"At Culloden; but I found the fellow who pinked me, next day, as he lay bleeding on the field; he was a Cameron, in a green velvet jacket, all covered with silver; so I stripped off his lace, as I had seen my mother do, and then I brained him with the butt-end of brown-bess—and before his wife's eyes, too! What the deuce do you growl at, comrade? Such things will happen in war, and you know that orders must be obeyed. My eye was gone—but it was the left one, and I was saved the trouble of closing it when taking aim. This slash on the sconce I got at the battle of Preston Pans, from the Celt who slew Colonel Gardiner."

"That Celt was my father—the Miller of Invernahyle," said Meinie, proudly.

"Your father! fire and smoke! do you say so? His hand was a heavy one!" cried Wooden-leg, while his eye glowed like the orb of a hyaena.

"And your leg?"

"I lost at Minden, in Kingsley's Brigade, comrade; aye, my leg—d——n!—that was indeed a loss."

"A warning to repentance, I would say."

"Then you would say wrong. Ugh! I remember when the shot—a twelve-pounder—took me just as we were rushing with charged bayonets on the French cannoniers. Smash! my leg was gone, and I lay sprawling and bleeding in a ploughed field near the Weser, while my comrades swept over me with a wild hurrah! the colours waving, and drums beating a charge."

"And what did you do?"

"I lay there and swore, believe me."

"That would not restore your limb again."

"No; but a few hearty oaths relieve the mind; and the mind relieves the body; you understand me, comrade; so there I lay all night under a storm of rain like this, bleeding and sinking; afraid of the knives of the plundering death-hunters, for my mother had been one, and I remembered well how she looked after the wounded, and cured them of their agony."

"Was your mother one of those infer——" began Mac Ewen.

"Don't call her hard names now, comrade; she died on the day after the defeat at Val; with the Provost Marshal's cord round her neck—a cordon less ornamental than that of St. Louis."

"And your father?"

"Was one of Howard's Regiment; but which the devil only knows, for it was a point on which the old lady, honest woman, had serious doubts herself."

"After the loss of your leg, of course you left the service?"

"No, I became the company's butcher; but, fire and smoke, get me another glass of grog; take a share yourself, and don't sit staring at me like a Dutch Souterkin conceived of a winter night over a 'pot de feu,' as all the world knows King William was. Dam! let us be merry together—ha, ha, ha! ho, ho, ho! and I'll sing you a song of the old whig times."

> " 'O, brother Sandie, hear ye the news,
>   Lillibulero, bullen a la!
> An army is coming sans breeches and shoes,
>   Lillibulero, bullen a la!
>
> " 'To arms! to arms! brave boys to arms!
>   A true British cause for your courage doth ca';
> Country and city against a kilted banditti,
>   Lillibulero, bullen a la!' "

And while he continued to rant and sing the song (once so obnoxious to the Scottish Cavaliers), he beat time with his wooden leg, and endeavoured to outroar the stormy wind and the hiss of the drenching rain. Even Mac Ewen, though he was an old soldier, felt some uneasiness, and Meinie trembled in her heart, while the children clung to her skirts and hid their little faces, as if this singing, riot, and jollity were impious at such a time, when the awful thunder was ringing its solemn peals across the midnight sky.

Although this strange old man baffled or parried every inquiry of Ewen as to whence he had come, and how and why he wore that antiquated uniform, on his making a lucrative offer to take the upper room of the little toll-house for a year—exactly a year—when Ewen thought of his poor pension of sixpence per diem, of their numerous family, and Meinie now becoming old and requiring many little comforts, all scruples were overcome by the pressure of necessity, and the mysterious old soldier was duly installed in the attic, with his corded chest, scratch-wig, and wooden leg; moreover, he paid the first six months' rent in advance, dashing the money—which was all coin of the first and second Georges, on the table with a bang and an oath, swearing that he disliked being indebted to any man.

The next morning was calm and serene; the green hills lifted their heads into the blue and placid sky. There was no mist on the mountains, nor rain in the valley. The flood in the Nairn had subsided, though its waters were still muddy and perturbed; but save this, and the broken branches that strewed the wayside—with an uprooted tree, or a paling laid flat on the ground, there was no trace of yesterday's hurricane, and Ewen heard Wooden-leg (he had no other name for his new lodger) stumping about overhead, as the old fellow left his bed betimes, and after trimming his queue and wig, pipeclaying his yellow facings, and beating them well with the brush, in a soldier-like way, he descended to breakfast, but, disdaining porridge and milk, broiled salmon and bannocks of barley-meal, he called for a can of stiff grog, mixed it with powder from his wide waistcoat pocket, and drank it off at a draught. Then he imperiously desired Ewen to take his bonnet and staff, and accompany him so far as Culloden, "because," said he, "I have come a long, long way to see the old place again."

Wooden-leg seemed to gather—what was quite unnecessary to him—new life, vigour, and energy—as they traversed the road that led to the battlefield, and felt the pure breeze of the spring morning blowing on their old and wrinkled faces.

The atmosphere was charmingly clear and serene. In the distance lay the spires of Inverness, and the shining waters of the Moray Firth, studded with sails, and the ramparts of Fort George were seen jutting out at the termination of a long and green peninsula. In the foreground stood the castle of Dalcross, raising its square outline above a wood, which terminates the eastern side of the landscape. The pine-clad summit of Dun Daviot incloses the west, while on every hand between, stretched the dreary moor of Drummossie—the Plain of Culloden—whilom drenched in the blood of Scotland's bravest hearts.

Amid the purple heath lie two or three grass-covered mounds.

These are the graves of the dead—the graves of the loyal Highlanders, who fell on that disastrous field, and of the wounded, who were so mercilessly murdered next day by an order of Cumberland, which he pencilled on the back of a card (the Nine of Diamonds); thus they were dispatched by platoons, stabbed by bayonets, slashed by swords and spontoons, or brained by the butt-end of musket and carbine; officers and men were to be seen emulating each other in this scene of cowardice and cold-blooded atrocity, which filled every camp and barrack in Continental Europe with scorn at the name of an English soldier.

Ewen was a Highlander, and his heart filled with such thoughts as these, when he stood by the grassy tombs where the fallen brave are buried with the hopes of the house they died for; he took off his bonnet and stood bare-headed, full of sad and silent contemplation; while his garrulous companion viewed the field with his single eye, that glowed like a hot coal, and pirouetted on his wooden pin in a very remarkable manner, as he surveyed on every side the scene of that terrible encounter, where, after enduring a long cannonade of round shot and grape, the Highland swordsmen, chief and gillie, the noble and the nameless, flung themselves with reckless valour on the ranks of those whom they had already routed in two pitched battles.

"It was an awful day," said Ewen, in a low voice, but with a gleam in his grey Celtic eye; "yonder my father fell wounded; the bullet went through his shield and pierced him here, just above the belt; he was living next day, when my mother—a poor wailing woman with a babe at her breast—found him; but an officer of Barrel's Regiment ran a sword twice through his body and killed him; for the orders of the German Duke were, 'that no quarter should be given.' This spring is named MacGillivray's Well, because here they butchered the dying chieftain who led the MacIntoshes—aye bayonetted him, next day at noon, in the arms of his bonnie young wife and his puir auld mother! The inhuman monsters! I have been a soldier," continued Ewen, "and I have fought for my country; but had I stood, that day on this Moor of Culloden, I would have shot the German Butcher, the coward who fled from Flanders—I would, by the God who hears me, though that moment had been my last!"

"Ha, ha, ha! Ho, ho, ho!" rejoined his queer companion. "It seems like yesterday since I was here; I don't see many changes, except that the dead are all buried, wheras we left them to the crows, and a carriage-road has been cut across the field, just where we seized some women, who were looking among the dead for their husbands, and who—"

"Well?"

Wooden-leg whistled, and gave Ewen a diabolical leer with his snaky eye, as he resumed,—

"I see the ridge where the clans formed line—every tribe with its chief in front, and his colours in the centre, when we, hopeless of victory, and thinking only of defeat, approached them; and I can yet see standing the old stone wall which covered their right flank. Fire and smoke! It was against that wall we placed the wounded, when we fired at them by platoons next day. I finished some twenty rebels there myself."

Ewen's hand almost caught the haft of his skene-dhu, as he said, hoarsely—

"Old man, do not call them rebels in my hearing, and least of all by the graves where they lie; they were good men and true; if they were in error, they have long since answered to God for it, even as we one day must answer; therefore let us treat their memory with respect, as soldiers should ever treat their brothers in arms who fall in war."

But Wooden-leg laughed with his strange eldritch yell, and then they returned together to the toll-house in the glen; but Ewen felt strongly dissatisfied with his lodger, whose conversation was so calculated to shock alike his Jacobitical and his religious prejudices. Every day this sentiment grew stronger, and he soon learned to deplore in his inmost heart having ever accepted the rent, and longed for the time when he should be rid of him; but, at the end of the six months, Wooden-leg produced the rent for the remainder of the year, still in old silver of the two first Georges, with a few Spanish dollars, and swore he would set the house on fire, if Ewen made any more apologies about their inability to make him sufficiently comfortable and so forth; for his host and hostess had resorted to every pretence and expedient to rid themselves of him handsomely.

But Wooden-leg was inexorable.

He had bargained for his billet for a year; he had paid for it; and a year he would stay, though the Lord Justice General of Scotland himself should say nay!

Boisterous and authoritative, he awed every one by his terrible gimlet eye and the volleys of oaths with which he overwhelmed them on suffering the smallest contradiction; thus he became the terror of all; and shepherds crossed the hills by the most unfrequented routes rather than pass the toll-bar, where they vowed that his eye bewitched their sheep and cattle. To every whispered and stealthy inquiry as to where his lodger had come from, and how or why he had thrust himself upon this lonely toll-house, Ewen could only groan and shrug his shoulders, or reply,—

"He came on the night of the hurricane, like a bird of evil omen; but on the twenty-sixth of April we will be rid of him, please Heaven! It is close at hand, and he shall march then, sure as my name is Ewen Mac Ewen!"

He seemed to be troubled in his conscience, too, or to have strange visitors; for often in stormy nights he was heard swearing or threatening, and expostulating; and once or twice, when listening at the foot of the stair, Ewen heard him shouting and conversing from his window with persons on the road, although the bar was shut, locked, and there was no one visible there.

On another windy night, Ewen and his wife were scared by hearing Wooden-leg engaged in a furious altercation with some one overhead.

"Dog, I'll blow out your brains!" yelled a strange voice.

"Fire and smoke! blow out the candle first—ha, ha, ha! ho, ho, ho!" cried Wooden-leg; then there ensued the explosion of a pistol, a dreadful stamping of feet, with the sound of several men swearing and fighting. To all this Ewen and his wife hearkened in fear and perplexity; at last something fell heavily on the floor, and then all became still, and not a sound was heard but the night wind sighing down the glen.

Betimes in the morning Ewen, weary and unslept, left his bed and ascended to the door of this terrible lodger and tapped gently.

"Come in; why the devil this fuss and ceremony, eh, comrade?" cried a hoarse voice, and there was old Wooden-leg, not lying dead on the floor as Ewen expected, or perhaps hoped; but stumping about in his shirt sleeves, pipeclaying his facings, and whistling the "Point of War."

On being questioned about the most unearthly "row" of last night, he only bade Ewen mind his own affairs, or uttered a volley of oaths, some of which were Spanish, and mixing a can of gunpowder grog drained it at a draught.

He was very quarrelsome, dictatorial, and scandalously irreligious; thus his military reminiscences were of so ferocious and blood-thirsty a nature, that they were sufficient to scare any quiet man out of his seven senses. But it was more particularly in relating the butcheries, murders, and ravages of Cumberland in the highlands, that he exulted, and there was always a terrible air of probability in all he said. On Ewen once asking of him if he had ever been punished for the many irregularities and cruelties he so freely acknowledged having committed,—

"Punished? Fire and smoke, comrade, I should think so; I have been flogged till the bones of my back stood through the quivering flesh; I have been picquetted, tied neck and heels, or sent to ride the wooden horse, and to endure other punishments which are now abolished in the king's service. An officer once tied me neck and heels for eight and forty hours—ay, damme, till I lost my senses; but he lost his life soon after, a shot from the rear killed him; you understand me, comrade: ha, ha, ha! ho, ho, ho! a shot from the rear."

"You murdered him?" said Ewen, in a tone of horror.

"I did not say so," cried Wooden-leg with an oath, as he dealt his landlord a thwack across the shins with his stump; "but I'll tell you how it happened. I was on the Carthagena expedition in '41, and served amid all the horrors of that bombardment, which was rendered unsuccessful by the quarrels of the general and admiral; then the yellow fever broke out among the troops, who were crammed on board the ships of war like figs in a cask, or like the cargo of a slaver, so they died in scores—and in scores their putrid corpses lay round the hawsers of the shipping, which raked them up every day as they swung round with the tide; and from all the open gunports, where their hammocks were hung, our sick men saw the ground sharks gorging themselves on the dead, while they daily expected to follow. The air was black with flies, and the scorching sun seemed to have leagued with the infernal Spaniards against us. But, fire and smoke, mix me some more grog, I am forgetting my story!

"Our Grenadiers, with those of other regiments, under Colonel James Grant of Carron, were landed on the Island of Tierrabomba, which lies at the entrance of the harbour of Carthagena, where we stormed two small forts which our ships had cannonaded on the previous day.

" 'Grenadiers—open your pouches—handle grenades—blow your fuses!' cried Grant, 'forward.'

"And then we bayonetted the dons, or with the clubbed musket smashed their heads like ripe pumpkins, while our fleet, anchored with broadsides to the shore, threw shot and shell, grape, cannister, carcasses, and hand-grenades in showers among the batteries, booms, cables, chains, ships of war, gunboats, and the devil only knows what more.

"It was evening when we landed, and as the ramparts of San Luiz de Bocca Chica were within musket shot of our left flank, the lieutenant of our company was left with twelve grenadiers (of whom I was one) as a species of out-picquet to watch the Spaniards there, and to acquaint the officer in the captured forts if anything was essayed by way of sortie.

"About midnight I was posted as an advanced sentinel, and ordered to face La Bocca Chica with all my ears and eyes open. The night was close and sultry; there was not a breath of wind stirring on the land or waveless sea; and all was still save the cries of the wild animals that preyed upon the unburied dead, or the sullen splash caused by some half-shrouded corpse, as it was launched from a gun-port, for our ships were moored within pistol-shot of the place where I stood.

"Towards the west the sky was a deep and lurid red, as if the midnight sea was in flames at the horizon; and between me and this fiery glow, I could see the black and opaque outline of the masts, the yards, and the gigantic hulls of those floating charnel-houses our line-of-battle ships, and the dark solid ramparts of San Luiz de Bocca Chica.

"Suddenly I saw before me the head of a Spanish column!

"I cocked my musket, they seemed to be halted in close order, for I could see the white coats and black hats of a single company only. So I fired at them point blank, and fell back on the picquet, which stood to arms.

"The lieutenant of our grenadiers came hurrying towards me.

" 'Where are the dons?' said he.

" 'In our front, sir,' said I, pointing to the white line which seemed to waver before us in the gloom under the walls of San Luiz, and then it disappeared.

" 'They are advancing,' said I.

" 'They have vanished, fellow,' said the lieutenant, angrily.

" 'Because they have marched down into a hollow.'

"In a moment after they reappeared, upon which the lieutenant brought up the picquet, and after firing three volleys retired towards the principal fort where Colonel Grant had all the troops under arms; but not a Spaniard approached us, and what, think you, deceived me and caused this alarm? Only a grove of trees, fire and smoke! yes, it was a grove of manchineel trees, which the Spaniards had cut down or burned to within five feet of the ground; and as their bark is white it resembled the Spanish uniform, while the black burned tops easily passed for their grenadier caps to the overstrained eyes of a poor anxious lad, who found himself under the heavy responsibility of an advanced sentinel for the first time in his life."

"And was this the end of it?" asked Ewen.

"Hell and Tommy?" roared Wooden-leg, "no—but you shall hear. I was batooned by the lieutenant; then I was tried at the drumhead for causing a false alarm, and sentenced to be tied neck and heels, and lest you may not know the fashion of this punishment I shall tell you of it. I was placed on the ground; my firelock was put under my hams, and another was placed over my neck; then the two were drawn close together by two cartouch-box straps; and in this situation, doubled up as round as a ball, I remained with my chin wedged between my knees until the blood spouted out of my mouth, nose, and ears, and I became insensible. When I recovered my senses the troops were forming in column, preparatory to assaulting Fort San Lazare; and though almost blind, and both weak and trembling, I was forced to take my place in the ranks; and I ground my teeth as I handled my musket and saw the lieutenant of our company, in lace-ruffles and powdered wig, prepare to join the forlorn hope, which was composed of six hundred chosen grenadiers, under Colonel Grant, a brave Scottish officer. I loaded my piece with a charmed bullet, cast in a mould given to me by an Indian warrior, and marched on with my section. The assault failed. Of the forlorn hope I alone escaped, for Grant and his Grenadiers perished to a man in the breach. There, too, lay our lieutenant. A shot had pierced his head behind, just at the queue. Queer, was it not? when I was his covering file?"

As he said this, Wooden-leg gave Ewen another of those diabolical leers, which always made his blood run cold, and continued,—

"I passed him as he lay dead, with his sword in his hand, his fine ruffled shirt and silk waistcoat drenched with blood—by the bye, there was a pretty girl's miniature, with powdered hair peeping out of it too. 'Ho, ho!' thought I, as I gave him a hearty kick; 'you will never again have me tied neck-and-heels for not wearing spectacles on sentry, or get me a hundred lashes, for not having my queue dressed straight to the seam of my coat.' "

"Horrible!" said Ewen.

"I will wager my wooden leg against your two of flesh and bone, that your officer would have been served in the same way, if he had given you the same provocation."

"Heaven forbid!" said Ewen.

"Ha, ha, ha! Ho, ho, ho!" cried Wooden-leg.

"You spoke of an Indian warrior," said Ewen, uneasily, as the atrocious anecdotes of this hideous old man excited his anger and repugnance; "then you have served, like myself, in the New World?"

"Fire and smoke! I should think so; but long before your day."

"Then you fought against the Cherokees?"

"Yes."

"At Warwomans Creek?"

"Yes; I was killed there."

"You were—what?" stammered Ewen.

"Killed there."

"Killed?"

"Yes, scalped by the Cherokees; dam! don't I speak plain enough?"

"He is mad," thought Ewen.

"I am not mad," said Wooden-leg gruffly.

"I never said so," urged Ewen.

"Thunder and blazes! but you thought it, which is all the same."

Ewen was petrified by this remark, and then Wooden-leg, while fixing his hyaena-like eye upon him, and mixing a fresh can of his peculiar grog, continued thus,—

"Yes, I served in the Warwomans Creek expedition in '60. In the preceding year I had been taken prisoner at Fort Ninety-six, and was carried off by the Indians. They took me into the heart of their own country, where an old Sachem protected me, and adopted me in place of a son he had lost in battle. Now this old devil of a Sachem had a daughter—a graceful, pretty and gentle Indian girl, whom her tribe named the Queen of the Beaver dams. She was kind to me, and loved to call me her pale-faced brother. Ha, ha, ha! Ho, ho, ho! Fire and smoke! Do I now look like a man that could once attract a pretty girl's eye— now, with my wooden-leg, patched face and riddled carcase? Well, she loved me, and I pretended to be in love too, though I did not care for her the value of an old snapper. She was graceful and round in every limb, as a beautiful statue. Her features were almost regular—her eyes black and soft; her hair hung nearly to her knees, while her smooth glossy skin, was no darker than a Spanish brunette's. Her words were like notes of music, for the language of the Cherokees, like that of the Iroquois, is full of the softest vowels. This Indian girl treated me with love and kindness, and I promised to become a Cherokee warrior, a thundering turtle and scalp-hunter for her sake—just as I would have promised anything to any other woman, and had done so a score of times before. I studied her gentle character in all its weak and delicate points, as a general views a fortress he is about to besiege, and I soon knew every avenue to the heart of the place. I made my approaches with modesty, for the mind of the Indian virgin was timid, and as pure as the new fallen snow. I drew my parallels and pushed on the trenches whenever the old Sachem was absent, smoking his pipe and drinking firewater at the council of the tribe; I soon reached the base of the glacis and stormed the breast-works—dam! I did, comrade.

"I promised her everything, if she would continue to love me, and swore by the Great Spirit to lay at her feet the scalp-lock of the white chief, General the Lord Amherst, K.C.B., and all that, with every other protestation that occurred to me at the time; and so she soon loved me—and me alone—as we wandered on the green slopes of Tennessee, when the flowering forest-trees, and the magnolias, the crimson strawberries, and the flaming azalea made the scenery beautiful; and where the shrill cry of the hawk, and the carol of the merry mocking-bird, filled the air with sounds of life and happiness.

"We were married in the fantastic fashion of the tribe, and the Indian girl was the happiest squaw in the Beaver dams. I hoed cotton and planted rice; I cut rushes that she might plait mats and baskets; I helped her to weave wampum, and built her a wig-wam, but I longed to be gone, for in six months I was wearied of her and the Cherokees too. In short, one night, I knocked the old Sachem on the head, and without perceiving that he still breathed, pocketed his valuables, such as they were, two necklaces of amber beads and two of Spanish dollars, and without informing my squaw of what I had done, I prevailed upon her to guide me far into the forest, on the skirts of which lay a British out-post, near the lower end of the vale, through which flows the Tennessee River. She was unable to accompany me more than a few miles, for she was weak, weary, and soon to become a mother; so I gave her the slip in the forest, and, leaving her to shift for herself, reached headquarters, just as the celebrated expedition from South Carolina was preparing to march against the Cherokees.

"Knowing well the localities, I offered myself as a guide, and was at once accepted—"

"Cruel and infamous!" exclaimed honest Ewen, whose chivalric Highland spirit fired with indignation at these heartless avowals; "and the poor girl you deceived—"

"Bah! I thought the wild beasts would soon dispose of her."

"But then the infamy of being a guide, even for your comrades, against those who had fed and fostered, loved and protected you! By my soul, this atrocity were worthy of King William and his Glencoe assassins!"

"Ho, ho, ho! fire and smoke! you shall hear.

"Well, we marched from New York in the early part of 1760. There were our regiment, with four hundred of the Scots Royals, and Montgomery's Highlanders. We landed at Charleston, and marched up the country to Fort Ninety-six on the frontier of the Cherokees. Our route was long and arduous, for the ways were wild and rough, so it was the first of June before we reached Twelve-mile River. I had been so long unaccustomed to carry my knapsack, that its weight rendered me savage and ferocious, and I cursed the service and my own existence; for in addition to our muskets and accoutrements, our sixty rounds of ball cartridge per man, we carried our own tents, poles, pegs, and cooking utensils. Thunder and blazes! when we halted, which we did in a pleasant valley, where the great shady chestnuts and the flowering hickory made our camp alike cool and beautiful, my back and shoulders were nearly skinned; for as you must know well, comrade, the knapsack straps are passed so tightly under the armpits, that they stop the circulation of the blood, and press upon the lungs almost to suffocation. Scores of our men left the ranks on the march, threw themselves down in despair, and were soon tomahawked and scalped by the Indians.

"We marched forward next day, but without perceiving the smallest vestige of an Indian trail; thus we began to surmise that the Cherokees knew not that we were among them; but just as the sun was sinking behind the blue hills, we came upon a cluster of wig-wams, which I knew well; they were the Beaver dams, situated on a river, among wild woods that never before had echoed to the drum or bugle.

"Bad and wicked as I was, some strange emotions rose within me at this moment. I thought of the Sachem's daughter—her beauty—her love for me, and the child that was under her bosom when I abandoned her in the vast forest through which we had just penetrated; but I stifled all regret, and heard with pleasure the order to 'examine flints and priming.'

"Then the Cherokee warwhoop pierced the echoing sky; a scattered fire was poured upon us from behind the rocks and trees; the sharp steel tomahawks came flashing and whirling through the air; bullets and arrows whistled, and rifles rung, and in a moment we found ourselves surrounded by a living sea of dark-skinned and yelling Cherokees, with plumes on their scalp locks, their fierce visages streaked with war paint, and all their moccasins rattling.

"Fire and fury, such a time it was!

"We all fought like devils, but our men fell fast on every side; the Royals lost two lieutenants, and several soldiers whose scalps were torn from their bleeding skulls in a moment. Our regiment, though steady under fire as a battalion of stone statues, now fell into disorder, and the brown warriors, like fiends in aspect and activity, pressed on with musket and war-club brandished, and with such yells as never rang in mortal ears elsewhere. The day was lost, until the Highlanders came up, and then the savages were routed in an instant, and cut to pieces. 'Shoot and slash' was the order; and there ensued such a scene of carnage as I had not witnessed since Culloden, where His Royal Highness, the fat Duke of Cumberland, galloped about the field, overseeing the wholesale butchery of the wounded.

"We destroyed their magazines of powder and provisions; we laid the wig-wams in ashes, and shot or bayonetted every living thing, from the babe on its mother's breast, to the hen that sat on the roost; for as I had made our commander aware of all the avenues, there was no escape for the poor devils of Cherokees. Had the pious, glorious, and immortal King William been there, he would have thought we had modelled the whole affair after his own exploit at Glencoe.

"All was nearly over, and among the ashes of the smoking wig-wams and the gashed corpses of king's soldiers and Indian warriors, I sat down beneath a great chestnut to wipe my musket, for butt, barrel, and bayonet were clotted with blood and human hair—ouf, man, why do you shudder? it was only Cherokee wool;—all was nearly over, I have said, when a low fierce cry, like the hoarse hiss of a serpent, rang in my ear; a brown and bony hand clutched my throat as the fangs of a wolf would have done, and hurled me to the earth! A tomahawk flashed above me, and an aged Indian's face, whose expression, was like that of a fiend, came close to mine, and I felt his breath upon my cheek. It was the visage of the sachem, but hollow with suffering and almost green with fury, and he laughed like a hyaena, as he poised the uplifted axe.

"Another form intervened for a moment; it was that of the poor Indian girl I had so heartlessly deceived; she sought to stay the avenging hand of the frantic sachem; but he thrust her furiously aside, and in the next moment the glittering tomahawk was quivering in my brain—a knife swept round my head—my scalp was torn off, and I remember no more."

"A fortunate thing for you," said Ewen, drily; "memory such as yours were worse than a knapsack to carry; and so you were killed there?"

"Don't sneer, comrade," said Wooden-leg, with a diabolical gleam in his eye; "prithee, don't sneer; I was killed there, and, moreover, buried too, by the Scots Royals, when they interred the dead next day."

"Then how came you to be here?" said Ewen, not very much at ease, to find himself in company with one he deemed a lunatic.

"Here? that is my business—not yours," was the surly rejoinder.

Ewen was silent, but reckoned over that now there were but thirty days to run until the 26th of April, when the stipulated year would expire.

"Yes, comrade, just thirty days," said Wooden-leg, with an affirmative nod, divining the thoughts of Ewen; "and then I shall be off, bag and baggage, if my friends come."

"If not?"

"Then I shall remain where I am."

"The Lord forbid!" thought Ewen; "but I can apply to the sheriff."

"Death and fury! Thunder and blazes! I should like to see the rascal of a sheriff who would dare to meddle with me!" growled the old fellow, as his one eye shot fire, and, limping away, he ascended the stairs grumbling and swearing, leaving poor Ewen terrified even to think, on finding that his thoughts, although only half conceived, were at once divined and responded to by this strange inmate of his house.

"His friends," thought Ewen, "who may they be?"

Three heavy knocks rang on the floor overhead, as a reply.

It was the wooden leg of the Cherokee invader.

This queer old fellow (continued the quarter-master) was always in a state of great excitement, and used an extra number of oaths, and mixed his grog more thickly with gunpowder, when a stray red coat appeared far down the long green glen, which was crossed by Ewen's lonely toll-bar. Then he would get into a prodigious fuss and bustle, and was wont

to pack and cord his trunk, to brush up his well-worn and antique regi-
mentals, and to adjust his queue and the black cockade of his triple-cor-
nered hat, as if preparing to depart.

As the time of that person's wished-for departure drew nigh, Ewen
took courage, and shaking off the timidity with which the swearing and
boisterous fury of Wooden-leg had impressed him, he ventured to ex-
postulate a little on the folly and sin of his unmeaning oaths, and the
atrocity of the crimes he boasted of having committed.

But the wicked old Wooden-leg laughed and swore more than ever,
saying that a "true soldier was never a religious one."

"You are wrong, comrade," retorted the old Cameronian, taking fire
at such an assertion; "religion is the lightest burden a poor soldier can
carry; and, moreover, it hath upheld me on many a long day's march,
when almost sinking under hunger and fatigue, with my pack, kettle,
and sixty rounds of ball ammunition on my back. The duties of a good
and brave soldier are no way incompatible with those of a Christian
man; and I never lay down to rest on the wet bivouac or bloody field,
with my knapsack, or it might be a dead comrade, for a pillow, without
thanking God—"

"Ha, ha, ha!"

"—The God of Scotland's covenanted Kirk for the mercies he vouch-
safed to Ewen Mac Ewen, a poor grenadier of the 26th Regiment."

"Ho, ho, ho!"

The old Cameronian took off his bonnet and lifted up his eyes, as he
spoke fervently, and with the simple reverence of the olden time; but
Wooden-leg grinned and chuckled and gnashed his teeth as Ewen resumed.

"A brave soldier may rush to the cannon's mouth, though it be
loaded with grape and cannister; or at a line of levelled bayonets—and
rush fearlessly too—and yet he may tremble without shame, at the
thought of hell, or of offended Heaven. Is it not so, comrade? I shall
never forget the words of our chaplain before we stormed the Isles of
Saba and St. Martin from the Dutch, with Admiral Rodney, in '81."

"Bah—that was after I was killed by the Cherokees. Well?"

"The Cameronians were formed in line, mid leg in the salt water,
with bayonets fixed, the colours flying, the pipes playing and drums
beating 'Britons strike home,' and our chaplain, a reverend minister of
God's word, stood beside the colonel with the shot and shell from the
Dutch batteries flying about his old white head, but he was cool and

calm, for he was the grandson of Richard Cameron, the glorious martyr of Airdsmoss.

" 'Fear not, my bairns,' cried he (he aye called us his bairns, having ministered unto us for fifty years and more)— 'fear not; but remember that the eyes of the Lord are on every righteous soldier, and that His hand will shield him in the day of battle!'

" 'Forward, my lads,' cried the colonel, waving his broad sword, while the musket shot shaved the curls of his old brigadier wig; 'forward, and at them with your bayonets'; and bravely we fell on—eight hundred Scotsmen, shoulder to shoulder—and in half an hour the British flag was waving over the Dutchman's Jack on the ramparts of St. Martin.''

But to all Ewen's exordiums, the Wooden-leg replied by oaths, or mockery, or his incessant laugh,—

"Ha, ha, ha! Ho, ho, ho!"

At last came the long-wished for twenty-sixth of April!

The day was dark and louring. The pine woods looked black, and the slopes of the distant hills seemed close and near, and yet gloomy withal. The sky was veiled by masses of hurrying clouds, which seemed to chase each other across the Moray Firth. That estuary was flecked with foam, and the ships were riding close under the lee of the Highland shore, with topmasts struck, their boats secured, and both anchors out, for everything betokened a coming storm.

And with night it came in all its fury;—a storm similar to that of the preceding year.

The fierce and howling wind swept through the mountain gorges, and levelled the lonely shielings, whirling their fragile roofs into the air, and uprooting strong pines and sturdy beeches; the water was swept up from the Loch of the Clans, and mingled with the rain which drenched the woods around it. The green and yellow lightning played in ghastly gleams about the black summit of Dun Daviot, and again the rolling thunder bellowed over the graves of the dead on the bleak, dark moor of Culloden. Attracted by the light in the windows of the toll-house, the red deer came down from the hills in herds and cowered near the little dwelling; while the cries of the affrighted partridges, blackcocks, and even those of the gannets from the Moray Firth were heard at times, as they were swept past, with branches, leaves, and stones, on the skirts of the hurrying blast.

"It is just such a storm as we had this night twelvemonths ago," said Meinie, whose cheek grew pale at the elemental uproar.

"There will be no one coming up the glen tonight," replied Ewen; "so I may as well secure the toll-bar, lest a gust should dash it to pieces."

It required no little skill or strength to achieve this in such a tempest; the gate was strong and heavy, but it was fastened at last, and Ewen retreated to his own fireside. Meanwhile, during all this frightful storm without, Wooden-leg was heard singing and carolling upstairs, stumping about in the lulls of the tempest, and rolling, pushing, and tumbling his chest from side to side; then he descended to get a fresh can of grog—for "grog, grog, grog," was ever his cry. His old withered face was flushed, and his excited eye shone like a baleful star. He was conscious that a great event would ensue.

Ewen felt happy in his soul that his humble home should no longer be the resting-place of this evil bird whom the last tempest had blown hither.

"So you leave us tomorrow, comrade?" said he.

"I'll march before daybreak," growled the other; "'twas our old fashion in the days of Minden. Huske and Hawley always marched off in the dark."

"Before daybreak?"

"Fire and smoke, I have said so, and you shall see; for my friends are on the march already; but good night, for I shall have to parade betimes. They come; though far, far off as yet."

He retired with one of his diabolical leers, and Ewen and his wife ensconced themselves in the recesses of their warm box-bed; Meinie soon fell into a sound sleep, though the wind continued to howl, the rain to lash against the trembling walls of the little mansion, and the thunder to hurl peal after peal across the sky of that dark and tempestuous night.

The din of the elements and his own thoughts kept Ewen long awake; but though the gleams of electric light came frequent as ever through the little window, the glow of the "gathering peat" sank lower on the hearth of hard-beaten clay, and the dull measured tick-tack of the drowsy clock as it fell on the drum of his ear, about midnight, was sending him to sleep, by the weariness of its intense monotony, when from a dream that the fierce hawk eye of his malevolent lodger was fixed upon him, he started suddenly to full consciousness. An uproar of tongue now rose and fell upon the gusts of wind without; and he heard an authoritative voice requiring the toll-bar to be opened.

Overhead rang the stumping of the Wooden-leg, whose hoarse voice was heard bellowing in reply from the upper window.

"The Lord have a care of us!" muttered Mac Ewen, as he threw his kilt and plaid round him, thrust on his bonnet and brogues, and hastened to the door, which was almost blown in by the tempest as he opened it.

The night was as dark, and the hurricane as furious as ever; but how great was Ewen's surprise to see the advanced guard of a corps of Grenadiers, halted at the toll-bar gate, which he hastened to unlock, and the moment he did so, it was torn off its iron hooks and swept up the glen like a leaf from a book, or a lady's handkerchief; as with an unearthly howling the wind came tearing along in fitful and tremendous gusts, which made the strongest forests stoop, and dashed the struggling coasters on the rocks of the Firth—the Æstuarium Vararis of the olden time.

As the levin brands burst in lurid fury overhead, they seemed to strike fire from the drenched rocks, the dripping trees, and the long line of flooded roadway, that wound through the pastoral glen towards Culloden.

The advanced guard marched on in silence with arms slung; and Ewen, to prevent himself from being swept away by the wind, clung with both hands to a stone pillar of the bar gate, that he might behold the passage of this midnight regiment, which approached in firm and silent order in sections of twelve files abreast, all with muskets slung. The pioneers were in front, with their leather aprons, axes, saws, bill-hooks, and hammers; the band was at the head of the column; the drums, fifes, and colours were in the centre; the captains were at the head of their companies; the subalterns on the reverse flank, and the field-officers were all mounted on black chargers, that curvetted and pranced like shadows, without a sound.

Slowly they marched, but erect and upright, not a man of them seeming to stoop against the wind or rain, while overhead the flashes of the broad and blinding lightning were blazing like a ghastly torch, and making every musket-barrel, every belt-plate, sword-blade, and buckle, gleam as this mysterious corps filed through the barrier, with who? Wooden-leg among them!

By the incessant gleams Ewen could perceive that they were Grenadiers, and wore the quaint old uniform of George II's time; the sugar-loaf-shaped cap of red cloth embroidered with worsted; the great square-tailed red coat with its heavy cuffs and close-cut collar; the stockings rolled above the knee, and enormous shoe-buckles. They carried grenado-pouches; the officers had espontoons; the sergeants shouldered heavy halberds, and the coats of the little drum-boys were covered with fantastic lace.

It was not the quaint and antique aspect of this solemn battalion that terrified Ewen, or chilled his heart; but the ghastly expression of their faces, which were pale and hollow-eyed, being, to all appearance, the visages of spectres; and they marched past like a long and wavering panorama, without a sound; for though the wind was loud, and the rain was drenching, neither could have concealed the measured tread of so many mortal feet; but there was no footfall heard on the roadway, nor the tramp of a charger's hoof; the regiment defiled past, noiseless as a wreath of smoke.

The pallor of their faces, and the stillness which accompanied their march, were out of the course of nature; and the soul of Mac Ewen died away within him; but his eyes were riveted upon the marching phantoms —if phantoms, indeed, they were—as if by fascination; and, like one in a terrible dream, he continued to gaze until the last files were past; and with them rode a fat and full-faced officer, wearing a three-cocked hat, and having a star and blue ribbon on his breast. His face was ghastly like the rest, and dreadfully distorted, as if by mental agony and remorse. Two aides-de-camps accompanied him, and he rode a wild-looking black horse, whose eyes shot fire. At the neck of the fat spectre—for a spectre he really seemed—hung a card.

It was the Nine of Diamonds!

The whole of this silent and mysterious battalion passed in line of march up the glen, with the gleams of lightning flashing about them. One bolt more brilliant than the rest brought back the sudden flash of steel.

They had fixed bayonets, and shouldered arms!

And on, and on they marched, diminishing in the darkness and the distance, those ghastly Grenadiers, towards the flat bleak moor of Culloden, with the green lightning playing about them, and gleaming on the storm-swept waste.

The Wooden-leg—Ewen's unco' guest—disappeared with them, and was never heard of more in Strathnairn.

He had come with a tempest, and gone with one. Neither was any trace ever seen or heard of those strange and silent soldiers. No regiment had left Nairn that night, and no regiment reached Inverness in the morning; so unto this day the whole affair remains a mystery, and a

subject for ridicule with some, although Ewen, whose story of the midnight march of a corps in time of war—caused his examination by the
authorities in the Castle of Inverness—stuck manfully to his assertions,
which were further corroborated by the evidence of his wife and children. He made a solemn affidavit of the circumstances I have related
before the sheriff, whose court books will be found to confirm them in
every particular; if not, it is the aforesaid sheriff's fault, and not mine.

There were not a few (but these were generally old Jacobite ladies of
decayed Highland families, who form the gossiping tabbies and wall-
flowers of the Northern Meeting) who asserted that in their young days
they had heard of such a regiment marching by night, once a year to the
field of Culloden; for it is currently believed by the most learned on
such subjects in the vicinity of the "Clach na Cudden," that on the anni-
versary of the sorrowful battle, a *certain place,* which shall be nameless,
opens, and that the restless souls of the murderers of the wounded
clansmen march in military array to the green graves upon the purple
heath, in yearly penance; and this story was thought to receive full cor-
roboration by the apparition of a fat lubberly spectre with the nine of
diamonds chained to his neck; as it was on that card—since named the
Curse of Scotland—the Duke of Cumberland hastily pencilled the savage order to "show no quarter to the wounded, but to slaughter all."

The year 1812 was famous for yet another bloody war, but it also saw the birth of CHARLES DICKENS, *who, in spite of critical backlash, may well endure as England's greatest novelist. His deprived childhood and difficult mature years found echoes in his darker pages, many of which were devoted to the ghostly. But "The Tale of the Bagman's Uncle" is a thoroughly high-spirited romp, a dashing tale of swashbuckling ghosts that ends in a devastating punchline.*

The Tale of the Bagman's Uncle
by Charles Dickens

"My uncle, gentlemen," said the bagman, "was one of the merriest, pleasantest, cleverest fellows that ever lived. I wish you had known him, gentlemen. On second thoughts, gentlemen, I *don't* wish you had known him, for if you had, you would have been all, by this time, in the ordinary course of nature, if not dead, at all events so near it, as to have taken to stopping at home and giving up company: which would have deprived me of the inestimable pleasure of addressing you at this moment. Gentlemen, I wish your fathers and mothers had known my uncle. They would have been amazingly fond of him, especially your respectable mothers; I know they would. If any two of his numerous virtues predominated over the many that adorned his character, I should say they were his mixed punch and his after supper song. Excuse my dwelling on these melancholy recollections of departed worth; you won't see a man like my uncle every day in the week.

"I have always considered it a great point in my uncle's character, gentlemen, that he was the intimate friend and companion of Tom Smart, of the great house of Bilson and Slum, Cateaton Street, City. My uncle collected for Tiggin and Welps, but for a long time he went pretty near the same journey as Tom; and the very first night they met, my uncle took a fancy for Tom, and Tom took a fancy for my uncle. They made a bet of a new hat before they had known each other half an hour, who should brew the best quart of punch and drink it the quickest. My uncle was judged to have won the making, but Tom Smart beat him in the drinking by about half a salt-spoonfull. They took another quart a-piece to drink each other's health in, and were staunch friends ever afterwards. There's a destiny in these things, gentlemen; we can't help it.

"In personal appearance, my uncle was a trifle shorter than the middle size; he was a thought stouter too, than the ordinary run of people, and perhaps his face might be a shade redder. He had the jolliest face you ever saw, gentlemen: something like Punch, with a handsomer nose and chin; his eyes were always twinkling and sparkling with good humour; and a smile—not one of your unmeaning wooden grins, but a real, merry, hearty, good-tempered smile—was perpetually on his countenance. He was pitched out of his gig once, and knocked, head first, against a mile-stone. There he lay, stunned, and so cut about the face with some gravel which had been heaped up alongside it, that, to use my uncle's own strong expression, if his mother could have revisited the earth, she wouldn't have known him. Indeed, when I come to think of the matter, gentlemen, I feel pretty sure she wouldn't, for she died when my uncle was two years and seven months old, and I think it's very likely that, even without the gravel, his top-boots would have puzzled the good lady not a little: to say nothing of his jolly red face. However, there he lay, and I have heard my uncle say, many a time, that the man said who picked him up that he was smiling as merrily as if he had tumbled out for a treat, and that after they had bled him, the first faint glimmerings of returning animation, were, his jumping up in bed, bursting out into a loud laugh, kissing the young woman who held the basin, and demanding a mutton chop and a pickled walnut. He was very fond of pickled walnuts, gentlemen. He said he always found that, taken without vinegar, they relished the beer.

"My uncle's great journey was in the fall of the leaf, at which time he collected debts, and took orders, in the north: going from London to Edinburgh, from Edinburgh to Glasgow, from Glasgow back to Edinburgh, and thence to London by the smack. You are to understand that his second visit to Edinburgh was for his own pleasure. He used to go back for a week, just to look up his old friends; and what with breakfasting with this one, lunching with that, dining with a third, and supping with another, a pretty tight week he used to make of it. I don't know whether any of you, gentlemen, ever partook of a real substantial hospitable Scotch breakfast, and then went out to a slight lunch of a bushel of oysters, a dozen or so of bottled ale, and a noggin or two of whiskey to close up with. If you ever did, you will agree with me that it requires a pretty strong head to go out to dinner and supper afterwards.

"But, bless your hearts and eye-brows, all this sort of thing was nothing to my uncle! He was so well seasoned, that it was mere child's play. I have heard him say that he could see the Dundee people out, any day, and walk home afterwards without staggering; and yet the Dundee people have as strong heads and as strong punch, gentlemen, as you are likely to meet with, between the poles. I have heard of a Glasgow man and a Dundee man drinking against each other for fifteen hours at a sitting. They were both suffocated, as nearly as could be ascertained, at the same moment, but with this trifling exception, gentlemen, they were not a bit the worse for it.

"One night, within four-and-twenty hours of the time when he had settled to take shipping for London, my uncle supped at the house of a very old friend of his, a Baillie Mac something and four syllables after it, who lived in the old town of Edinburgh. There were the baillie's wife, and the baillie's three daughters, and the baillie's grown-up son, and three or four stout, bushy eye-browed, canny old Scotch fellows, that the baillie had got together to do honour to my uncle, and help to make merry. It was a glorious supper. There were kippered Salmon, and Finnan haddocks, and a lamb's head, and a haggis—a celebrated Scotch dish, gentlemen, which my uncle used to say always looked to him, when it came to table, very much like a cupid's stomach—and a great many other things besides, that I forget the names of, but very good things notwithstanding. The lassies were pretty and agreeable; the baillie's wife was one of the best creatures that ever lived; and my uncle was in thoroughly good cue. The consequence of which was, that the young ladies tittered and giggled, and the old lady laughed out loud, and the baillie and the other old fellows roared till they were red in the face, the whole mortal time. I don't quite recollect how many tumblers of whiskey toddy each man drank after supper; but this I know, that about one o'clock in the morning, the baillie's grown-up son became insensible while attempting the first verse of 'Willie brewed a peck o' maut'; and he having been, for half an hour before, the only other man visible above the mahogany, it occurred to my uncle that it was almost time to think about going: especially as drinking had set in at seven o'clock, in order that he might get home at a decent hour. But, thinking it might not be quite polite to go just then, my uncle voted himself into the chair, mixed another glass, rose to propose his own health, addressed himself in a neat and complimentary speech, and drank the toast with great enthusiasm. Still nobody woke; so my uncle took a little drop more—neat this time, to prevent the toddy from disagreeing with him—and, laying violent hands on his hat, sallied forth into the street.

"It was a wild gusty night when my uncle closed the baillie's door, and settling his hat firmly on his head, to prevent the wind from taking it, thrust his hands into his pockets, and looking upward, took a short survey of the state of the weather. The clouds were drifting over the moon at their giddiest speed: at one time wholly obscuring her: at another, suffering her to burst forth in full splendour and shed her light on all the objects around; anon, driving over her again, with increased velocity, and shrouding everything in darkness. 'Really, this won't do,' said my uncle, addressing himself to the weather, as if he felt himself personally offended. 'This is not at all the kind of thing for my voyage. It will not do, at any price,' said my uncle very impressively. Having repeated this, several times, he recovered his balance with some difficulty —for he was rather giddy with looking up into the sky so long—and walked merrily on.

"The baillie's house was in the Canongate, and my uncle was going to the other end of Leith Walk, rather better than a mile's journey. On either side of him, there shot up against the dark sky, tall gaunt straggling houses, with time-stained fronts, and windows that seemed to have shared the lot of eyes in mortals, and to have grown dim and sunken with age. Six, seven, eight stories high, were the houses; story piled above story, as children build with cards—throwing their dark shadows over the roughly paved road, and making the dark night darker. A few oil lamps were scattered at long distances, but they only served to mark the dirty entrance to some narrow close, or to show where a common stair communicated, by steep and intricate windings, with the various flats above. Glancing at all these things with the air of a man who had seen them too often before, to think them worthy of much notice now, my uncle walked up the middle of the street, with a thumb in each waistcoat pocket, indulging from time to time in various snatches of song, chaunted forth with such good will and spirit, that the quiet honest folk started from their first sleep and lay trembling in bed till the sound died away in the distance; when, satisfying themselves that it was only some drunken ne'er-do-weel finding his way home, they covered themselves up warm and fell asleep again.

"I am particular in describing how my uncle walked up the middle of the street, with his thumbs in his waistcoat pockets, gentlemen, because, as he often used to say (and with great reason too) there is nothing at all extraordinary in this story, unless you distinctly understand at the beginning that he was not by any means of a marvellous or romantic turn.

"Gentlemen, my uncle walked on with his thumbs in his waistcoat pockets, taking the middle of the street to himself, and singing, now a verse of a love song, and then a verse of a drinking one, and when he was tired of both, whistling melodiously, until he reached the North Bridge, which, at this point, connects the old and new towns of Edinburgh. Here he stopped for a minute, to look at the strange irregular clusters of lights piled one above the other, and twinkling afar off so high, that they looked like stars, gleaming from the castle walls on the one side and the Calton Hill on the other, as if they illuminated veritable castles in the air; while the old picturesque town slept heavily on, in gloom and darkness below: its palace and chapel of Holyrood, guarded day and night, as a friend of my uncle's used to say, by old Arthur's Seat, towering, surly and dark, like some gruff genius over the ancient city he has watched so long. I say, gentlemen, my uncle stopped here, for a minute, to look about him; and then, paying a compliment to the weather which had a little cleared up, though the moon was sinking, walked on again, as royally as before; keeping the middle of the road with great dignity, and looking as if he would very much like to meet with somebody who would dispute possession of it with him. There was nobody at all disposed to contest the point, as it happened; and so, on he went, with his thumbs in his waistcoat pockets, like a lamb.

"When my uncle reached the end of Leith Walk, he had to cross a pretty large piece of waste ground which separated him from a short street which he had to turn down, to go direct to his lodging. Now, in this piece of waste ground, there was, at that time, an enclosure belonging to some wheelwright who contracted with the Post-office for the purchase of old worn-out mail coaches; and my uncle, being very fond of coaches, old, young, or middle-aged, all at once took it into his head to step out of his road for no other purpose than to peep between the palings at these mails—about a dozen of which, he remembered to have seen, crowded together in a very forlorn and dismantled state, inside. My uncle was a very enthusiastic, emphatic sort of person, gentlemen; so, finding that he could not obtain a good peep between the palings, he got over them, and sitting himself quietly down on an old axletree, began to contemplate the mail coaches with a deal of gravity.

"There might be a dozen of them, or there might be more—my uncle was never quite certain on this point, and being a man of very scrupulous veracity about numbers, didn't like to say—but there they stood, all huddled together in the most desolate condition imaginable. The doors had been torn from their hinges and removed; the linings had been stripped off: only a shred hanging here and there by a rusty nail; the lamps were gone, the poles had long since vanished, the iron-work was rusty, the paint was worn away; the wind whistled through the chinks in the bare wood work; and the rain, which had collected on the roofs, fell, drop by drop, into the insides with a hollow and melancholy sound. They were the decaying skeletons of departed mails, and in that lonely place, at that time of night, they looked chill and dismal.

"My uncle rested his head upon his hands, and thought of the busy bustling people who had rattled about, years before, in the old coaches, and were now as silent and changed; he thought of the numbers of people to whom one of those crazy mouldering vehicles had borne, night after night, for many years, and through all weathers, the anxiously expected intelligence, the eagerly looked-for remittance, the promised assurance of health and safety, the sudden announcement of sickness and death. The merchant, the lover, the wife, the widow, the mother, the schoolboy, the very child who tottered to the door at the postman's knock—how had they all looked forward to the arrival of the old coach. And where were they all now!

"Gentlemen, my uncle used to *say* that he thought all this at the time, but I rather suspect he learnt it out of some book afterwards, for he distinctly stated that he fell into a kind of doze, as he sat on the old axletree looking at the decayed mail coaches, and that he was suddenly awakened by some deep church bell striking two. Now, my uncle was never a fast thinker, and if he had thought all these things, I am quite certain it would have taken him till full half-past two o'clock, at the very least. I am, therefore, decidedly of opinion, gentlemen, that my uncle fell into the kind of doze, without having thought about anything at all.

"Be this as it may, a church bell struck two. My uncle woke, rubbed his eyes, and jumped up in astonishment.

"In one instant after the clock struck two, the whole of this deserted and quiet spot had become a scene of most extraordinary life and animation. The mail-coach doors were on their hinges, the lining was replaced, the iron-work was as good as new, the paint was restored, the lamps were alight, cushions and great coats were on every coach box, porters were thrusting parcels into every boot, guards were stowing away letter bags, hostlers were dashing pails of water against the renovated wheels; numbers of men were rushing about, fixing poles into every coach; passengers arrived, portmanteaus were handed up, horses were put to; in short, it was perfectly clear that every mail there was to be off directly. Gentlemen, my uncle opened his eyes so wide at all this, that, to the very last moment of his life, he used to wonder how it fell out that he had ever been able to shut 'em again.

" 'Now then!' said a voice, as my uncle felt a hand on his shoulder, 'You're booked for one inside. You'd better get in.'

" '*I* booked!' said my uncle, turning round.

" 'Yes, certainly.'

"My uncle, gentlemen, could say nothing; he was so very much astonished. The queerest thing of all, was, that although there was such a crowd of persons, and although fresh faces were pouring in, every moment, there was no telling where they came from. They seemed to start up, in some strange manner, from the ground, or the air, and disappear in the same way. When a porter had put his luggage in the coach, and received his fare, he turned round and was gone; and before my uncle had well begun to wonder what had become of him, half-a-dozen fresh ones started up, and staggered along under the weight of parcels which seemed big enough to crush them. The passengers were all dressed so oddly too! Large, broad-skirted laced coats with great cuffs and no collars; and wigs, gentlemen—great formal wigs with a tie behind. My uncle could make nothing of it.

" 'Now, *are* you going to get in?' said the person who had addressed my uncle before. He was dressed as a mail guard, with a wig on his head and most enormous cuffs to his coat, and had a lantern in one hand, and a huge blunderbuss in the other, which he was going to stow away in his little arm-chest. '*Are* you going to get in, Jack Martin?' said the guard, holding the lantern to my uncle's face.

" 'Hallo!' said my uncle, falling back a step or two. 'That's familiar!'

" 'It's so on the way-bill,' replied the guard.

" 'Isn't there a "Mister" before it?' said my uncle. For he felt, gentlemen, that for a guard he didn't know, to call him Jack Martin, was a liberty which the Post-office wouldn't have sanctioned if they had known it.

" 'No, there is not,' rejoined the guard coolly.

" 'Is the fare paid?' inquired my uncle.

" 'Of course it is,' rejoined the guard.

" 'It is, is it?' said my uncle. 'Then here goes! Which coach?'

" 'This,' said the guard, pointing to an old-fashioned Edinburgh and London Mail, which had the steps down, and the door open. 'Stop! Here are the other passengers. Let them get in first.'

"As the guard spoke, there all at once appeared, right in front of my uncle, a young gentleman in a powdered wig, and a sky-blue coat trimmed with silver, made very full and broad in the skirts, which were lined with buckram. Tiggin and Welps were in the printed calico and waistcoat piece line, gentlemen, so my uncle knew all the materials at once. He wore knee breeches, and a kind of leggings rolled up over his silk stockings, and shoes with buckles; he had ruffles at his wrists, a three-cornered hat on his head, and a long taper sword by his side. The flaps of his waistcoat came half way down his thighs, and the end of his cravat reached to his waist. He stalked gravely to the coach-door, pulled off his hat, and held it above his head at arm's length: cocking his little finger in the air at the same time, as some affected people do, when they take a cup of tea. Then he drew his feet together, and made a low grave bow, and then put out his left hand. My uncle was just going to step forward, and shake it heartily, when he perceived that these attentions were directed, not towards him, but to a young lady who just then appeared at the foot of the steps, attired in an old-fashioned green velvet dress with a long waist and stomacher. She had no bonnet on her head, gentlemen, which was muffled in a black silk hood, but she looked round for an instant as she prepared to get into the coach, and such a beautiful face as she disclosed, my uncle had never seen—not even in a picture. She got into the coach, holding up her dress with one hand; and, as my uncle always said with a round oath, when he told the story, he wouldn't have believed it possible that legs and feet could have been brought to such a state of perfection unless he had seen them with his own eyes.

"But, in this one glimpse of the beautiful face, my uncle saw that the young lady cast an imploring look upon him, and that she appeared terrified and distressed. He noticed, too, that the young fellow in the powdered wig, notwithstanding his show of gallantry, which was all very fine and grand, clasped her tight by the wrist when she got in, and followed himself immediately afterwards. An uncommonly ill-looking fellow, in a close brown wig and a plum-coloured suit, wearing a very large sword, and boots up to his hips, belonged to the party; and when he sat himself down next to the young lady, who shrunk into a corner at his approach, my uncle was confirmed in his original impression that something dark and mysterious was going forward, or, as he always said himself, that 'there was a screw loose somewhere.' It's quite surprising how quickly he made up his mind to help the lady at any peril, if she needed help.

" 'Death and lightning!' exclaimed the young gentleman, laying his hand upon his sword as my uncle entered the coach.

" 'Blood and thunder!' roared the other gentleman. With this, he whipped his sword out, and made a lunge at my uncle without further ceremony. My uncle had no weapon about him, but with great dexterity he snatched the ill-looking gentleman's three-cornered hat from his head, and, receiving the point of his sword right through the crown, squeezed the sides together, and held it tight.

" 'Pink him behind!' cried the ill-looking gentleman to his companion, as he struggled to regain his sword.

" 'He had better not,' cried my uncle, displaying the heel of one of his shoes, in a threatening manner. 'I'll kick his brains out, if he has any, or fracture his skull if he hasn't.' Exerting all his strength, at this moment, my uncle wrenched the ill-looking man's sword from his grasp, and flung it clean out of the coach-window: upon which the younger gentleman vociferated 'Death and lightning!' again, and laid his hand upon the hilt of his sword, in a very fierce manner, but didn't draw it. Perhaps, gentlemen, as my uncle used to say with a smile, perhaps he was afraid of alarming the lady.

" 'Now, gentlemen,' said my uncle, taking his seat deliberately, 'I don't want to have any death, with or without lightning, in a lady's presence, and we have had quite blood and thundering enough for one journey; so, if you please, we'll sit in our places like quiet insides. Here, guard, pick up that gentleman's carving-knife.'

"As quickly as my uncle said the words, the guard appeared at the coach-window, with the gentleman's sword in his hand. He held up his lantern, and looked earnestly in my uncle's face, as he handed it in: when, by its light, my uncle saw, to his great surprise, that an immense crowd of mail-coach guards swarmed round the window, every one of whom had his eyes earnestly fixed upon him too. He had never seen such a sea of white faces, red bodies, and earnest eyes, in all his born days.

" 'This is the strangest sort of thing I ever had anything to do with,' thought my uncle; 'allow me to return you your hat, sir.'

"The ill-looking gentleman received his three-cornered hat in silence, looked at the hole in the middle with an inquiring air, and finally stuck it on the top of his wig with a solemnity the effect of which was a trifle impaired by his sneezing violently at the moment, and jerking it off again.

" 'All right!' cried the guard with the lantern, mounting into his little seat behind. Away they went. My uncle peeped out of the coach-window as they emerged from the yard, and observed that the other mails, with coachmen, guards, horses, and passengers, complete, were driving round and round in circles, at a slow trot of about five miles an hour. My uncle burnt with indignation, gentlemen. As a commercial man, he felt that the mail bags were not to be trifled with, and he resolved to memorialise the Post-office on the subject, the very instant he reached London.

"At present, however, his thoughts were occupied with the young lady who sat in the farthest corner of the coach, with her face muffled closely in her hood; the gentleman with the sky-blue coat sitting opposite to her; the other man in the plum-coloured suit, by her side, and both watching her intently. If she so much as rustled the folds of her hood, he could hear the ill-looking man clap his hand upon his sword, and could tell by the other's breathing (it was so dark he couldn't see his face) that he was looking as big as if he were going to devour her at a mouthful. This roused my uncle more and more, and he resolved, come what might, to see the end of it. He had a great admiration for bright eyes, and sweet faces, and pretty legs and feet; in short, he was fond of the whole sex. It runs in our family, gentlemen—so am I.

"Many were the devices which my uncle practised, to attract the lady's attention, or at all events, to engage the mysterious gentlemen in conversation. They were all in vain; the gentlemen wouldn't talk, and the lady didn't dare. He thrust his head out of the coach-window at intervals, and bawled out to know why they didn't go faster? But he called till he was hoarse; nobody paid the least attention to him. He leant back in the coach, and thought of the beautiful face, and the feet and legs. This answered better; it whiled away the time, and kept him from wondering where he was going, and how it was that he found himself in such an odd situation. Not that this would have worried him much, any way—he was a mighty free and easy, roving, devil-may-care sort of person, was my uncle, gentlemen.

"All of a sudden the coach stopped. 'Hallo!' said my uncle, 'what's in the wind now?'

" 'Alight here,' said the guard, letting down the steps.

" 'Here!' cried my uncle.

" 'Here,' rejoined the guard.

" 'I'll do nothing of the sort,' said my uncle.

" 'Very well, then stop where you are,' said the guard.

" 'I will,' said my uncle.

" 'Do,' said the guard.

"The other passengers had regarded this colloquy with great attention, and, finding that my uncle was determined not to alight, the younger man squeezed past him, to hand the lady out. At this moment, the ill-looking man was inspecting the hole in the crown of his three-cornered hat. As the young lady brushed past, she dropped one of her gloves into my uncle's hand, and softly whispered, with her lips so close to his face that he felt her warm breath on his nose, the single word 'Help!' Gentlemen, my uncle leaped out of the coach at once, with such violence that it rocked on the springs again.

" 'Oh! You've thought better of it, have you?' said the guard when he saw my uncle standing on the ground.

"My uncle looked at the guard for a few seconds, in some doubt whether it wouldn't be better to wrench his blunderbuss from him, fire it in the face of the man with the big sword, knock the rest of the company over the head with the stock, snatch up the young lady, and go off in the smoke. On second thoughts, however, he abandoned this plan, as being a shade too melodramatic in the execution, and followed the two mysterious men, who, keeping the lady between them, were now entering an old house in front of which the coach had stopped. They turned into the passage, and my uncle followed.

"Of all the ruinous and desolate places my uncle had ever beheld, this was the most so. It looked as if it had once been a large house of entertainment; but the roof had fallen in, in many places, and the stairs were steep, rugged, and broken. There was a huge fire-place in the room into which they walked, and the chimney was blackened with smoke; but no warm blaze lighted it up now. The white feathery dust of burnt wood was still strewed over the hearth, but the stove was cold, and all was dark and gloomy.

" 'Well,' said my uncle, as he looked about him, 'a mail travelling at the rate of six miles and a half an hour, and stopping for an indefinite time at such a hole as this, is rather an irregular sort of proceeding, I fancy. This shall be made known. I'll write to the papers.'

"My uncle said this in a pretty loud voice, and in an open unreserved sort of manner, with the view of engaging the two strangers in conversation if he could. But, neither of them took any more notice of him than whispering to each other, and scowling at him as they did so. The lady was at the farther end of the room, and once she ventured to wave her hand, as if beseeching my uncle's assistance.

"At length the two strangers advanced a little, and the conversation began in earnest.

" 'You don't know this is a private room, I suppose, fellow?' said the gentleman in sky-blue.

" 'No, I do not, fellow,' rejoined my uncle. 'Only if this is a private room specially ordered for the occasion, I should think the public room must be a *very* comfortable one'; with this my uncle sat himself down in a high-backed chair, and took such an accurate measure of the gentleman, with his eyes, that Tiggin and Welps could have supplied him with printed calico for a suit, and not an inch too much or too little, from that estimate alone.

" 'Quit this room,' said both the men together, grasping their swords.

" 'Eh?' said my uncle, not at all appearing to comprehend their meaning.

" 'Quit the room, or you are a dead man,' said the ill-looking fellow with the large sword, drawing it at the same time and flourishing it in the air.

" 'Down with him!' cried the gentleman in sky-blue, drawing his sword also, and falling back two or three yards. 'Down with him!' The lady gave a loud scream.

"Now, my uncle was always remarkable for great boldness, and great presence of mind. All the time that he had appeared so indifferent to what was going on, he had been looking slyly about, for some missile or weapon of defence, and at the very instant when the swords were drawn, he espied, standing in the chimney corner, an old basket-hilted rapier in a rusty scabbard. At one bound, my uncle caught it in his hand, drew it, flourished it gallantly above his head, called aloud to the lady to keep out of the way, hurled the chair at the man in sky-blue, and the scabbard at the man in plum-colour, and taking advantage of the confusion, fell upon them both, pell-mell.

"Gentleman, there is an old story—none the worse for being true—regarding a fine young Irish gentleman, who being asked if he could play the fiddle, replied he had no doubt he could, but he couldn't exactly say, for certain, because he had never tried. This is not inapplicable to my uncle and his fencing. He had never had a sword in his hand before, except once when he played Richard the Third at a private theatre: upon which occasion it was arranged with Richmond that he was to be run through, from behind, without showing fight at all. But here he was, cutting and slashing with two experienced swordsmen: thrusting and guarding and poking and slicing, and acquitting himself in the most manful and dexterous manner possible, although up to that time he had never been aware that he had the least notion of the science. It only shows how true the old saying is, that a man never knows what he can do till he tries, gentlemen.

"The noise of the combat was terrific; each of the three combatants swearing like troopers, and their swords clashing with as much noise as if all the knives and steels in Newport market were rattling together, at the same time. When it was at its very height, the lady (to encourage my uncle most probably) withdrew her hood entirely from her face, and disclosed a countenance of such dazzling beauty, that he would have fought against fifty men, to win one smile from it, and die. He had done wonders before, but now he began to powder away like a raving mad giant.

"At this very moment, the gentleman in sky-blue turning round, and seeing the young lady with her face uncovered, vented an exclamation of rage and jealousy, and, turning his weapon against her beautiful bosom, pointed a thrust at her heart, which caused my uncle to utter a cry of apprehension that made the building ring. The lady stepped lightly aside, and snatching the young man's sword from his hand, before he had recovered his balance, drove him to the wall, and running it through him, and the panelling, up to the very hilt, pinned him there, hard and fast. It was a splendid example. My uncle, with a loud shout of triumph, and a strength that was irresistible, made his adversary retreat in the same direction, and plunging the old rapier into the very centre of a large red flower in the pattern of his waistcoat, nailed him beside his friend; there they both stood, gentlemen, jerking their arms and legs about, in agony, like the toy-shop figures that are moved by a piece of packthread. My uncle always said, afterwards, that this was one of the surest means he knew of, for disposing of an enemy; but it was liable to one objection on the ground of expense, inasmuch as it involved the loss of a sword for every man disabled.

"'The mail, the mail!' cried the lady, running up to my uncle and throwing her beautiful arms round his neck; 'we may yet escape.'

"'*May!*' cried my uncle; 'why, my dear, there's nobody else to kill, is there?' My uncle was rather disappointed, gentlemen, for he thought a little quiet bit of love-making would be agreeable after the slaughtering, if it were only to change the subject.

"'We have not an instant to lose here,' said the young lady. 'He (pointing to the young gentleman in sky-blue) is the only son of the powerful Marquess of Filletoville.'

"'Well, then, my dear, I'm afraid he'll never come to the title,' said my uncle, looking coolly at the young gentleman as he stood fixed up against the wall, in the cockchafer fashion I have described. You have cut off the entail, my love.'

" 'I have been torn from my home and friends by these villains,' said the young lady, her features glowing with indignation. 'That wretch would have married me by violence in another hour.'

" 'Confound his impudence!' said my uncle, bestowing a very contemptuous look on the dying heir of Filletoville.

" 'As you may guess from what you have seen,' said the young lady, 'the party were prepared to murder me if I appealed to any one for assistance. If their accomplices find us here, we are lost. Two minutes hence may be too late. The mail!' With these words, overpowered by her feelings, and the exertion of sticking the young Marquess of Filletoville, she sunk into my uncle's arms. My uncle caught her up, and bore her to the house-door. There stood the mail, with four long-tailed, flowing-maned, black horses, ready harnessed; but no coachman, no guard, no hostler even, at the horses' heads.

"Gentlemen, I hope I do no injustice to my uncle's memory, when I express my opinion, that although he was a bachelor, he *had* held some ladies in his arms, before this time; I believe indeed, that he had rather a habit of kissing barmaids; and I know, that in one or two instances, he had been seen by credible witnesses, to hug a landlady in a very perceptible manner. I mention the circumstance, to show what a very uncommon sort of person this beautiful young lady must have been, to have affected my uncle in the way she did; he used to say, that as her long dark hair trailed over his arm, and her beautiful dark eyes fixed themselves upon his face when she recovered, he felt so strange and nervous that his legs trembled beneath him. But, who can look in a sweet soft pair of dark eyes, without feeling queer? *I* can't, gentlemen. I am afraid to look at some eyes I know, and that's the truth of it.

" 'You will never leave me,' murmured the young lady.

" 'Never,' said my uncle. And he meant it too.

" 'My dear preserver!' exclaimed the young lady. 'My dear, kind, brave preserver!'

" 'Don't,' said my uncle, interrupting her.

" 'Why?' inquired the young lady.

" 'Because your mouth looks so beautiful when you speak,' rejoined my uncle, 'that I'm afraid I shall be rude enough to kiss it.'

"The young lady put up her hand as if to caution my uncle not to do so, and said—no, she didn't say anything—she smiled. When you are looking at a pair of the most delicious lips in the world, and see them gently break into a roguish smile—if you are very near them, and nobody else by—you cannot better testify your admiration of their beautiful form and colour than by kissing them at once. My uncle did so, and I honour him for it.

"'Hark!' cried the young lady, starting. 'The noise of wheels and horses!'

"'So it is,' said my uncle, listening. He had a good ear for wheels, and the trampling of hoofs; but there appeared to be so many horses and carriages rattling towards them, from a distance, that it was impossible to form a guess at their number. The sound was like that of fifty breaks, with six blood cattle in each.

"'We are pursued!' cried the young lady, clasping her hands. 'We are pursued. I have no hope but in you!'

"There was such an expression of terror in her beautiful face, that my uncle made up his mind at once. He lifted her into the coach, told her not to be frightened, pressed his lips to hers once more, and then advising her to draw up the window to keep the cold air out, mounted to the box.

"'Stay, love,' cried the young lady.

"'What's the matter?' said my uncle, from the coach-box.

"'I want to speak to you,' said the young lady: 'only a word. Only one word, dearest.'

"'Must I get down?' inquired my uncle. The lady made no answer, but she smiled again. Such a smile, gentlemen! It beat the other one, all to nothing. My uncle descended from his perch in a twinkling.

"'What is it, my dear?' said my uncle, looking in at the coach-window. The lady happened to bend forward at the same time, and my uncle thought she looked more beautiful than she had done yet. He was very close to her just then, gentlemen, so he really ought to know.

"'What is it, my dear?' said my uncle.

"'Will you never love any one but me; never marry any one beside?' said the young lady.

"My uncle swore a great oath that he never would marry anybody else, and the young lady drew in her head, and pulled up the window. He jumped upon the box, squared his elbows, adjusted the ribands, seized the whip which lay on the roof, gave one flick to the off leader, and away went the four long-tailed flowing-maned black horses, at fifteen good English miles an hour, with the old mail coach behind them. Whew! How they tore along!

"The noise behind grew louder. The faster the old mail went, the faster came the pursuers—men, horses, dogs, were leagued in the pursuit. The noise was frightful, but, above all, rose the voice of the young lady, urging my uncle on, and shrieking, 'Faster! Faster!'

"They whirled past the dark trees, as feathers would be swept before a hurricane. Houses, gates, churches, haystacks, objects of every kind they shot by, with a velocity and noise like roaring waters suddenly let loose. Still the noise of pursuit grew louder, and still my uncle could hear the young lady wildly screaming, 'Faster! Faster!'

"My uncle plied whip and rein, and the horses flew onward till they were white with foam; and yet the noise behind increased; and yet the young lady cried 'Faster! Faster!' My uncle gave a loud stamp on the boot in the energy of the moment, and—found that it was grey morning, and he was sitting in the wheelwright's yard, on the box of an old Edinburgh mail, shivering with the cold and wet and stamping his feet to warm them! He got down, and looked eagerly inside for the beautiful young lady. Alas! There was neither door nor seat to the coach. It was a mere shell.

"Of course my uncle knew very well that there was some mystery in the matter, and that everything had passed exactly as he used to relate it. He remained staunch to the great oath he had sworn to the beautiful young lady: refusing several eligible landladies on her account, and dying a bachelor at last. He always said, what a curious thing it was that he should have found out, by such a mere accident as his clambering over the palings, that the ghosts of mail coaches and horses, guards, coachmen, and passengers, were in the habit of making journeys regularly every night. He used to add, that he believed he was the only living person who had ever been taken as a passenger on one of these excursions. And I think he was right, gentlemen—at least I never heard of any other."

"I wonder what these ghosts of mail coaches carry in their bags," said the landlord, who had listened to the whole story with profound attention.

"The dead letters, of course," said the bagman.

"Oh, ah! to be sure," rejoined the landlord. "I never thought of that."

In the preceding story, CHARLES DICKENS *showed us what high adventure might be found in the company of ghostly passengers of antique coaches. But there is another side to the question, as the following dreadful tale shows.* AMELIA B. EDWARDS *was born in 1831 and showed literary tendencies as early as age seven.*

The North Mail

by Amelia B. Edwards

The circumstances I am about to relate to you have truth to recommend them. They happened to myself, and my recollection of them is as vivid as if they had taken place only yesterday. Twenty years, however, have gone by since that night. During those twenty years I have told the story to but one other person. I tell it now with a reluctance which I find it difficult to overcome. All I entreat, meanwhile, is that you will abstain from forcing your own conclusions upon me. I want nothing explained away. I desire no arguments. My mind on this subject is quite made up; and, having the testimony of my own senses to rely upon, I prefer to abide by it.

Well! It was just twenty years ago, and within a day or two of the end of the grouse season. I had been out all day with my gun, and had had no sport to speak of. The wind was due east; the month, December; the place, a bleak wide moor in the far north of England. And I had lost my way. It was not a pleasant place in which to lose one's way, with the first feathery flakes of a coming snow-storm just fluttering down upon the heather, and the leaden evening closing in all around. I shaded my eyes with my hand, and stared anxiously into the gathering darkness, where the purple moorland melted into a range of low hills, some ten or twelve miles distant. Not the faintest smoke-wreath, not the tiniest cultivated patch, or fence, or sheep-track, met my eyes in any direction. There was nothing for it but to walk on, and take my chance of finding what shelter I could, by the way. So I shouldered my gun again, and pushed wearily forward; for I had been on foot since an hour after daybreak, and had eaten nothing since breakfast.

Meanwhile, the snow began to come down with ominous steadiness, and the wind fell. After this, the cold grew more intense, and the night came rapidly up. As for me, my prospects darkened with the darkening sky, and my heart grew heavy as I thought how my young wife was already watching for me through the window of our little inn parlour, and imagined all the suffering in store for her throughout this weary night. We had been married four months, and, having spent our autumn in the Highlands, were now lodging in a remote little village situated just on the verge of the great English moorlands. We were very much in love, and, of course, very happy. This morning, when we parted, she had implored me to return before dusk, and I had promised her that I would. What would I not have given to keep my word!

Even now, weary as I was, I felt that with a supper, an hour's rest, and a guide, I might still get back to her before midnight, if only guide and shelter could be found.

And all this time the snow fell, and the night thickened. I stopped and shouted every now and then, but my shouts seemed only to make the silence deeper. Then a vague sense of uneasiness came upon me, and I began to remember stories of travellers who had walked on and on in the falling snow until, wearied out, they were fain to lie down and sleep their lives away. Would it be possible, I asked myself, to keep on thus through all the long dark night? Would there not come a time when my limbs must fail, and my resolution give way? When I, too, must sleep the sleep of death. Death! I shuddered. How hard to die just now, when life lay all so bright before me! How hard for my darling, whose whole loving heart . . . but that thought was not to be borne! To banish it, I shouted again, louder and longer, and then listened eagerly. Was my shout answered, or did I only fancy that I heard a far-off cry? I hallooed again, and again the echo followed. Then a wavering speck of light came suddenly out of the dark, shifting, disappearing, growing momentarily nearer and brighter. Running towards it at full speed, I found myself, to my great joy, face to face with an old man and a lantern.

"Thank God!" was the exclamation that burst involuntarily from my lips.

Blinking and frowning, he lifted the lantern and peered into my face. "What for?" growled he, sulkily.

"Well—for you. I began to fear I should be lost in the snow."

"Eh, then, folks do get cast away hereabouts fra' time to time, an' what's to hinder you from bein' cast away likewise, if the Lord's so minded?"

"If the Lord is so minded that you and I shall be lost together, friend, we must submit," I replied; "but I don't mean to be lost without you. How far am I now from Dwolding?"

"A gude twenty mile, more or less."

"And the nearest village?"

"The nearest village is Wyke, an' that's twelve mile t'other side."

"Where do you live, then?"

"Out yonder," said he, with a vague jerk of the lantern.

"You're going home, I presume?"

"Maybe I am."

"Then I'm going with you."

The old man shook his head, and rubbed his nose reflectively with the handle of the lantern.

"It ain't o' no use," growled he. "He 'ont let you in—not he."

"We'll see about that," I replied, briskly. "Who is He?"

"The master."

"Who is the master?"

"That's now't to you," was the unceremonious reply.

"Well, well; you lead the way, and I'll engage that the master shall give me shelter and a supper tonight."

"Eh, you can try him!" muttered my reluctant guide; and, still shaking his head, he hobbled, gnome-like, away through the falling snow.

A large mass loomed up presently out of the darkness, and a huge dog rushed out barking furiously.

"Is this the house?" I asked.

"Ay, it's the house. Down, Bey!" And he fumbled in his pocket for the key.

I drew up close behind him, prepared to lose no chance of entrance, and saw in the little circle of light shed by the lantern that the door was heavily studded with iron nails, like the door of a prison. In another minute he had turned the key, and I had pushed past him into the house.

Once inside, I looked round with curiosity, and found myself in a great raftered hall, which served, apparently, a variety of uses. One end was piled to the roof with corn, like a barn. The other was stored with flour-sacks, agricultural implements, casks, and all kinds of miscellaneous lumber; while from the beams overhead hung rows of hams, flitches, and bunches of dried herbs for winter use. In the centre of the floor stood some huge object gauntly dressed in a dingy wrapping-cloth, and reaching halfway to the rafters. Lifting a corner of this cloth, I saw, to my surprise, a telescope of very considerable size, mounted on a rude moveable platform with four small wheels. The tube was made of painted wood, bound round with bands of metal rudely fashioned; the speculum, so far as I could estimate its size by the dim light, measured at least fifteen inches in diameter. While I was yet examining the instrument, and asking myself whether it was not the work of some self-taught optician, a bell rang sharply.

"That's for you," said my guide, with a malicious grin. "Yonder's his room."

He pointed to a low black door at the opposite side of the hall. I crossed over, rapped somewhat loudly, and went in, without waiting for an invitation. A huge, white-haired old man rose from a table covered with books and papers, and confronted me sternly.

"Who are you?" said he. "How came you here? What do you want?"

"James Murray, barrister-at-law. On foot across the moor. Meat, drink, and sleep."

He bent his bushy brows in a portentous frown.

"Mine is not a house of entertainment," he said, haughtily. "Jacob, how dared you admit this stranger?"

"I didn't admit him," grumbled the old man. "He followed me over the muir, and shouldered his way in before me. I'm no match for six foot two."

"And pray, sir, by what right have you forced an entrance into my house?"

"The same by which I should have clung to your boat, if I were drowning. The right of self-preservation."

"Self-preservation?"

"There's an inch of snow on the ground already," I replied briefly; "and it will be deep enough to cover my body before daybreak."

He strode to the window, pulled aside a heavy black curtain, and looked out.

"It is true," he said. "You can stay, if you choose, till morning. Jacob, serve the supper."

With this he waved me to a seat, resumed his own, and became at once absorbed in the studies at which I had disturbed him.

I placed my gun in a corner, drew a chair to the hearth, and examined my quarters at leisure. Smaller and less incongruous in its arrangements than the hall, this room contained, nevertheless, much to awaken my curiosity. The floor was carpetless. The whitewashed walls were in parts scrawled over with strange diagrams, and in others covered with shelves crowded with philosophical instruments, the uses of many of which were unknown to me. On one side of the fireplace stood a bookcase filled with dingy folios; on the other, a small organ, fantastically decorated with painted carvings of mediaeval saints and devils.

Through the half-opened door of a cupboard at the further end of the room, I saw a long array of geological specimens, surgical preparations, crucibles, retorts, and jars of chemicals; while on the mantelshelf beside me, amid a number of small objects, stood a model of the solar system, a small galvanic battery, and a microscope. Every chair had its burden. Every corner was heaped high with books. The very floor was littered over with maps, casts, papers, tracings, and learned lumber of all conceivable kinds.

I stared about me with an amazement increased by every fresh object upon which my eyes chanced to rest. So strange a room I had never seen; yet seemed it stranger still to find such a room in a lone farmhouse, amid these wild and solitary moors! Over and over again, I looked from my host to his surroundings, and from his surroundings back to my host, asking myself who and what he could be? His head was singularly fine; but it was more the head of a poet than a philosopher. Broad in the temples, prominent over the eyes, and clothed with a rough profusion of perfectly white hair, it had all the ideality and much of the ruggedness that characterises the head of Louis von Beethoven. There were the same deep lines about the mouth, and the same stern furrows in the brow. There was the same concentration of expression. While I was yet observing him, the door opened, and Jacob brought in the supper. His master then closed his book, rose, and with more courtesy of manner than he had yet shown, invited me to the table.

A dish of ham and eggs, a loaf of brown bread, and a bottle of admirable sherry, were placed before me.

"I have but the homeliest farmhouse fare to offer you, sir," said my entertainer. "Your appetite, I trust, will make up for the deficiencies of our larder."

I had already fallen upon the viands, and now protested, with the enthusiasm of a starving sportsman, that I had never eaten anything so delicious.

He bowed stiffly, and sat down to his own supper, which consisted, primitively, of a jug of milk and a basin of porridge. We ate in silence, and, when we had done, Jacob removed the tray. I then drew my chair back to the fireside. My host, somewhat to my surprise, did the same, and turning abruptly towards me said:—

"Sir, I have lived here in strict retirement for three-and-twenty years. During that time, I have not seen as many strange faces, and I have not read a single newspaper. You are the first stranger who has crossed my threshold for more than four years. Will you favour me with a few words of information respecting that outer world from which I have parted company so long?"

"Pray interrogate me," I replied. "I am heartily at your service."

He bent his head in acknowledgement; leaned forward, with his elbows resting on his knees, and his chin supported in the palms of his hands; stared fixedly into the fire, and proceeded to question me.

His inquiries related chiefly to scientific matters, with the later progress of which, as applied to the practical purposes of life, he was almost wholly unacquainted. No student of science myself, I replied as well as my slight information permitted; but the task was far from easy, and I was much relieved when, passing from interrogation to discussion, he began pouring forth his own conclusions upon the facts which I had been attempting to place before him. He talked, and I listened spellbound. He talked till I believe he almost forgot my presence, and only thought aloud. I had never heard anything like it then; I have never heard anything like it since. Familiar with all systems of all philosophies, subtle in analysis, bold in generalisation, he poured forth his thoughts in an uninterrupted stream, and, still leaning forward in the same moody attitude with his eyes fixed upon the fire, wandered from topic to topic, from speculation to speculation, like an inspired dreamer. From practical science to mental philosophy; from electricity in the wire to electricity in the nerve; from Watts to Mesmer, from Mesmer to Reichenbach, from Reichenbach to Swedenborg, Spinoza, Condillac, Descartes, Berkeley, Aristotle, Plato, and the Magi and Mystics of the East, were transitions which, however bewildering in their variety and scope, seemed easy and harmonious upon his lips as sequences in music. By-and-by—I forget now by what link of conjecture or illustration—he passed on to that field which lies beyond the boundary line of even conjectural philosophy, and reaches no man knows whither. He spoke of the soul and its aspirations; of the spirit and its powers; of second sight; of prophecy; of those phenomena which, under the names of ghosts, spectres, and supernatural appearances, have been denied by the sceptics and attested by the credulous, of all ages.

"The world," he said, "grows hourly more and more sceptical of all that lies beyond its own narrow radius; and our men of science foster the fatal tendency. They condemn as fable all that resists experiment. They reject as false all that cannot be brought to the test of the laboratory or the dissecting-room. Against what superstition have they waged so long and obstinate a war, as against the belief in apparitions? And yet what superstition has maintained its hold upon the minds of men so long and so firmly? Show me any fact in physics, in history, in archaeology, which is supported by testimony so wide and so various. Attested by all races of men, in all ages, and in all climates, by the soberest sages of antiquity, by the rudest savages of today, by the Christian, the Pagan, the Pantheist, the Materialist, this phenomenon is treated as a nursery tale by the philosophers of our century. Circumstantial evidence weighs with them as a feather in the balance. The comparison of causes with effects, however valuable in physical science, is put aside as worthless and unreliable. The evidence of competent witnesses, however conclusive in a court of justice, counts for nothing. He who pauses before he pronounces, is condemned as a trifler. He who believes, is a dreamer or a fool."

He spoke with bitterness, and, having said thus, relapsed for some minutes into silence. Presently he raised his head from his hands, and added, with an altered voice and manner—

"I, sir, paused, investigated, believed, and was not ashamed to state my convictions to the world. I, too, was branded as a visionary, held up to ridicule by my contemporaries, and hooted from that field of science in which I had laboured with honour during all the best years of my life. These things happened just three-and-twenty years ago. Since then, I have lived as you see me living now, and the world has forgotten me, as I have forgotten the world. You have my history."

"It is a very sad one," I murmured, scarcely knowing what to answer.

"It is a very common one," he replied. "I have only suffered for the truth, as many a better and wiser man has suffered before me."

He rose, as if desirous of ending the conversation, and went over to the window.

"It has ceased snowing," he observed, as he dropped the curtain, and came back to the fireside.

"Ceased!" I exclaimed, starting eagerly to my feet. "Oh, if it were only possible—but no! it is hopeless. Even if I could find my way across the moor, I could not walk twenty miles tonight."

"Walk twenty miles tonight!" repeated my host. "What are you thinking of?"

"Of my wife," I replied, impatiently. "Of my young wife, who does not know that I have lost my way, and who is at this moment breaking her heart with suspense and terror."

"Where is she?"

"At Dwolding, twenty miles away."

"At Dwolding," he echoed, thoughtfully. "Yes, the distance, it is true, is twenty miles; but—are you so anxious to save the next six or eight hours?"

"So anxious, that I would give ten guineas at this moment for a guide and a horse."

"Your wish can be gratified at a less costly rate," said he, smiling. "The night mail from the north, which changes horses at Dwolding, passes within five miles of this spot, and will be due at a certain cross-road in about an hour and a quarter. If Jacob were to go with you across the moor, and put you into the old coach road, you could find your way, I suppose, to where it joins the new one?"

"Easily—gladly."

He smiled again, rang the bell, gave the old servant his directions, and, taking a bottle of whiskey and a wine-glass from the cupboard in which he kept his chemicals, said—

"The snow lies deep, and it will be difficult walking tonight on the moor. A glass of usquebaugh before you start."

I would have declined the spirit, but he pressed it on me, and I drank it. It went down my throat like liquid flame, and almost took my breath away.

"It is strong," he said; "but it will help to keep out the cold. And now you have no moments to spare. Good night!"

I thanked him for his hospitality, and would have shaken hands, but that he had turned away before I could finish my sentence. In another minute I had traversed the hall, Jacob had locked the outer door behind me, and we were out on the wide white moor.

Although the wind had fallen, it was still bitterly cold. Not a star glimmered in the black vault overhead. Not a sound, save the rapid crunching of the snow beneath our feet, disturbed the heavy stillness of the night. Jacob, not too well pleased with his mission, shambled on before in sullen silence, his lantern in his hand, and his shadow at his feet. I followed, with my gun over my shoulder, as little inclined for conversation as himself. My thoughts were full of my late host. His voice yet rang in my ears. His eloquence yet held my imagination captive. I remember to this day, with surprise, how my over-excited brain retained whole sentences and parts of sentences, troops of brilliant images, and fragments of splendid reasoning, in the very words in which he had uttered them. Musing thus over what I had heard, and striving to recall a lost link here and there, I strode on at the heels of my guide, absorbed and unobservant. Presently—at the end, as it seemed to me, of only a few minutes—he came to a sudden halt, and said:

"Yon's your road. Keep the stone fence to your right hand, and you can't fail of the way."

"This, then, is the old coach-road?"

"Ay, 'tis the old coach-road."

"And how far do I go, before I reach the cross-roads?"

"Nigh upon three miles."

I pulled out my purse, and he became more communicative.

"The road's a fair road enough," said he, "for foot passengers; but 'twas over steep and narrow for the northern traffic. You'll mind where the parapet's broken away, close again the sign-post. It's never been mended since the accident."

"What accident?"

"Eh, the night mail pitched right over into the valley below—a gude sixty feet an' more—just at the worst bit o' road in the whole county."

"Horrible! Were many lives lost?"

"All. Four were found dead, and t'other two died next morning."

"How long is it since this happened?"

"Just nine year."

"Near the sign-post, you say? I will bear it in mind. Good night."

"Gude night, sir, and thankee."

Jacob pocketed his half-crown, made a faint pretence of touching his hat, and trudged back by the way he had come.

I watched the light of his lantern till it quite disappeared, and then turned to pursue my way alone. This was no longer a matter of the slightest difficulty, for, despite the dead darkness overhead, the line of stone fence showed distinctly enough against the pale gleam of the snow. How silent it seemed now, with only my own footsteps to listen to; how silent and how solitary! A strange disagreeable sense of loneliness stole over me. I walked faster. I hummed a fragment of a tune. I cast up enormous sums in my head, and accumulated them at compound interest. I did my best, in short, to forget the startling speculations to which I had but just been listening and to some extent, I succeeded.

Meanwhile the night air seemed to become colder and colder, and though I walked fast, I found it impossible to keep myself warm. My feet were like ice. I lost sensation in my hands, and grasped my gun mechanically. I even breathed with difficulty, as though, instead of traversing a quiet north country highway, I were sealing the uppermost heights of some gigantic Alp. This last symptom became presently so distressing, that I was forced to stop for a few minutes, and lean against the stone fence. As I did so, I chanced to look back up the road, and there, to my infinite relief, I saw a distant point of light, like the gleam of an approaching lantern. I at first concluded that Jacob had retraced his steps and followed me; but even as the conjecture presented itself, a second light flashed into sight—a light evidently parallel with the first, and approaching at the same rate of motion. It needed no second thought to show me that these must be the carriage-lamps of some private vehicle; though it seemed strange that any private vehicle should take a road professedly disused and dangerous.

There could be no doubt, however, of the fact, for the lamps grew larger and brighter every moment, and I even fancied I could already see the dark outline of the carriage between them. It was coming up very fast, and quite noiselessly; the snow being nearly a foot deep under the wheels.

And now the body of the vehicle became distinctly visible behind the lamps. It looked strangely lofty. A sudden suspicion flashed upon me. Was it possible that I had passed the cross-roads in the dark without observing the sign-post, and could this be the very coach which I had come to meet?

No need to ask myself that question a second time, for here it came round the bend of the road, guard and driver, one outside passenger, and four steaming greys, all wrapped in a soft haze of light, through which the lamps blazed out like a pair of fiery meteors.

I jumped forward, waved my hat, and shouted. The mail came down at full speed, and passed me. For a moment I feared that I had not been seen or heard, but it was only for a moment. The coachman pulled up; the guard, muffled to the eyes in capes and comforters, and apparently sound asleep in the rumble, neither answered my hail nor made the slightest effort to dismount; the outside passenger did not even turn his head. I opened the door for myself, and looked in. There were but three travellers inside, so I stepped in, shut the door, slipped into the vacant corner, and congratulated myself on my good fortune.

The atmosphere of the coach seemed, if possible, colder than that of the outer air, and was pervaded by a singularly damp and disagreeable smell. I looked round at my fellow passengers. They were all three men; and all silent. They did not seem to be asleep, but each leaned back in his corner of the vehicle, as if absorbed in his own reflections. I attempted to open a conversation.

"How intensely cold it is tonight," I said, addressing my opposite neighbour.

He lifted his head, looked at me, but made no reply.

"The winter," I added, "seems to have begun in earnest."

Although the corner in which he sat was so dim that I could distinguish none of his features very clearly, I saw that his eyes were still turned full upon me. And yet he answered never a word.

At any other time I should have felt, and perhaps expressed, some annoyance; but at that moment I felt too ill to do either. The icy coldness of the night air had struck a chill to my very marrow, and the strange smell inside the coach was affecting me with an intolerable nausea. I shivered from head to foot, and, turning to my left-hand neighbour, asked if he had any objection to an open window.

He neither spoke nor stirred.

I repeated the question somewhat more loudly, but with the same result. Then I lost patience, and let the sash down. As I did so, the leather strap broke in my hand, and I observed that the glass was covered with a thick coat of mildew, the accumulation, apparently, of years. My attention being thus drawn to the condition of the coach, I examined it more narrowly, and saw by the uncertain light of the outer lamps that it was in the last state of dilapidation. Every part of it was not only out of repair, but in a state of actual decay. The sashes splintered at a touch. The leather fittings were crusted over with mould, and literally rotting from the woodwork. The floor was almost breaking away beneath my feet. The whole machine, in short, was foul with damp, and had evidently been dragged from some outhouse in which it had been mouldering away for years, to do another day of two of duty on the road.

I turned to the third passenger, whom I had not yet addressed, and hazarded one more remark.

"This coach," I said, "is in a deplorable condition. The regular mail, I suppose, is under repair?"

He moved his head slowly, and looked me in the face, without speaking a word. I shall never forget that look while I live. I turned cold at heart under it. I turn cold at heart even now when I recall it. His eyes glowed with a fiery unnatural lustre. His face was livid as the face of a corpse. His bloodless lips were drawn back as if in the agony of death, and showed the gleaming teeth between.

The words that I was about to utter died upon my lips, and a strange horror came upon me. My sight had by this time become used to the gloom of the coach, and I could see with tolerable distinctness. I turned to my opposite neighbour. He, too, was looking at me, with the same startling pallor in his face, and the same stony glitter in his eyes. I passed my hand across my brow. I turned to the passenger on the seat beside my own, and saw—oh Heaven! how shall I describe what I saw? I saw that he was no living man—that none of them were living men, like myself! A pale phosphorescent light—the light of putrefaction—played upon their awful faces; upon their hair, dank with the dews of the grave; upon their clothes, earth-stained and dropping to pieces; upon their hands, which were as the hands of corpses long buried. Only their eyes, their terrible eyes, were living; and those eyes were all turned menacingly upon me!

A shriek of terror, a wild unintelligible cry for help and mercy, burst from my lips as I flung myself against the door, and strove in vain to open it.

In that single instant, brief and vivid as a landscape beheld in the flash of summer lightning, I saw the moon shining down through a rift of stormy cloud—the ghastly sign-post rearing its warning finger by the wayside—the broken parapet—the plunging horses—the black gulf below. Then the coach reeled like a ship at sea. Then came a mighty crash—a sense of crushing pain—and then, darkness.

It seemed as if years had gone by, when I awoke one morning from a deep sleep, and found my wife watching by my bedside. I will pass over the scene that ensued, and give you, in half a dozen words, the tale she told me with tears of thanksgiving. I had fallen over a precipice, close against the junction of the old coach-road and the new, and had only been saved from certain death by lighting upon a deep snowdrift that had accumulated at the foot of the rock beneath. In this snowdrift I was discovered at daybreak by a couple of shepherds, who carried me to the nearest shelter, and brought a surgeon to my aid. The surgeon found me in a state of raving delirium, with a broken arm and a compound fracture of the skull. The letters in my pocket-book showed my name and address; my wife was summoned to nurse me; and, thanks to youth and a fine constitution, I came out of danger at last. The place of my fall, I need scarcely say, was precisely that at which a frightful accident had happened to the north mail nine years before.

I never told my wife the fearful events which I have just related to you. I told the surgeon who attended me; but he treated the whole adventure as a mere dream born of the fever in my brain. We discussed the question over and over again, until we found that we could discuss it with temper no longer, and then we dropped it. Others may form what conclusions they please—I *know* that twenty years ago I was the fourth inside passenger in that Phantom Coach.

The supernatural stories of EDWARD FREDERICK BENSON *are some of the most effective and frightening in all supernatural literature. "The Room in the Tower" is my personal nominee for the most chilling tale I've ever read. Less familiar is the wonderful story that follows. Benson, born in 1867, was the youngest of three sons of a former archbishop of Canterbury. He wrote many recently revived comedic novels of manners, and a very few ghostly tales. "How Fear Departed from the Long Gallery" creates a surprising variety of moods: beginning with drollness, it passes through several pages of disquieting prologue leading to the final episode, which is dreadful and terrifying, yet unexpectedly . . . but that would spoil the ending. I have given this tale the last position because I do not believe it can be bettered.*

How Fear Departed from the Long Gallery

by E. F. Benson

Church-Peveril is a house so beset and frequented by spectres, both visible and audible, that none of the family which it shelters under its acre and a half of green copper roofs takes psychical phenomena with any seriousness. For to the Peverils the appearance of a ghost is a matter of hardly greater significance than the appearance of the post to those who live in more ordinary houses. It arrives, that is to say, practically every day, it knocks (or makes other noises), it is observed coming up the drive (or in other places). I myself, when staying there have seen the present Mrs. Peveril, who is rather short-sighted, peer into the dusk, while we were taking our coffee on the terrace after dinner, and say to her daughter:

"My dear, was not that the Blue Lady who has just gone into the shrubbery? I hope she won't frighten Flo. Whistle for Flo, dear."

(Flo, it may be remarked, is the youngest and most precious of many dachshunds.)

Blanche Peveril gave a cursory whistle, and crunched the sugar left unmelted at the bottom of her coffee-cup between her very white teeth.

"Oh, darling, Flo isn't so silly as to mind," she said. "Poor blue Aunt Barbara is such a bore! Whenever I meet her she always looks as if she wanted to speak to me, but when I say, 'What is it, Aunt Barbara?' she never speaks, but only points somewhere toward the house, which is so vague. I believe there was something she wanted to confess about two hundred years ago, but she has forgotten what it is."

Here Flo gave two or three short pleased barks, and came out of the shrubbery wagging her tail, and capering round what appeared to me to be a perfectly empty space on the lawn.

"There! Flo has made friends with her," said Mrs. Peveril. "I wonder why she dresses in that very stupid shade of blue."

From this it may be gathered that even with regard to psychic phenomena there is some truth in the proverb that speaks of familiarity. But the Peverils do not exactly treat their ghosts with contempt, since most of that delightful family never despised anybody except such people as avowedly did not care for hunting or shooting, or golf or skating. And as all of their ghosts are of their family, it seems reasonable to suppose that they all, even the poor Blue Lady, excelled at one time in field-sports. So far then they harbor no such unkindness or contempt, but only pity. Of one Peveril, indeed, who broke his neck in vainly attempting to ride up the main staircase on a thoroughbred mare after some monstrous and violent deed in the back-garden, they are very fond, and Blanche comes downstairs in the morning with an eye unusually bright when she can announce that Master Anthony was "very loud" last night. He (apart from the fact of his having been so foul a ruffian) was a tremendous fellow across country, and they like these indications of the continuance of his superb vitality. In fact, it is supposed to be a compliment, when you go to stay at Church-Peveril, to be assigned a bedroom which is frequented by defunct members of the family. It means that you are worthy to look on the august and villainous dead, and you will find yourself shown into some vaulted or tapestried chamber, without benefit of electric light, and are told that great-great-grandmamma Bridget occasionally has vague business by the fire-place, but it is better not to talk to her, and that you will hear Master Anthony "awfully well" if he attempts the front staircase any time before morning. There you are left for your night's repose, and, having quakingly undressed, begin reluctantly to put out your candles. It is draughty in these great chambers, and the solemn tapestry swings and bellows and subsides, and the firelight dances on the forms of huntsmen and warriors and stern pursuits. Then you climb into your bed, a bed so huge that you feel as if the desert of Sahara was spread for you, and pray, like the mariners who sailed with St. Paul, for day. And, all the time, you are aware that Freddy and Harry and Blanche and possibly even

Mrs. Peveril are quite capable of dressing up and making disquieting tappings outside your door, so that when you open it some inconjecturable horror fronts you. For myself, I stick steadily to the assertion that I have an obscure valvular disease of the heart, and so sleep undisturbed in the new wing of the house, where Aunt Barbara and great-great-grandmamma Bridget and Master Anthony never penetrate. I forget the details of great-great-grandmamma Bridget, but she certainly cut the throat of some distant relation before she disembowelled herself with the axe that had been used at Agincourt. Before that she had led a very sultry life, crammed with amazing incidents.

But there is one ghost at Church-Peveril at which the family never laugh, in which they feel no friendly and amused interest, and of which they only speak just as much as is necessary for the safety of their guests. More properly it should be described as two ghosts, for the "haunt" in question is that of two very young children, who were twins. These, not without reason, the family take very seriously indeed. The story of them, as told me by Mrs. Peveril, is as follows:

In the year 1602, the same being the last of Queen Elizabeth's reign, a certain Dick Peveril was greatly in favor at Court. He was brother to Master Joseph Peveril, then owner of the family house and lands, who two years previously, at the respectable age of seventy-four, became father of twin-boys, first-born of his progeny. It is known that the royal and ancient virgin had said to handsome Dick, who was nearly forty years his brother's junior, " 'Tis pity that you are not master of Church-Peveril," and these words probably suggested to him a sinister design. Be that as it may, handsome Dick, who very adequately sustained the family reputation for wickedness, set off to ride down to Yorkshire, and found that, very conveniently, his brother Joseph had just been seized with an apoplexy, which appeared to be the result of a continued spell of hot weather combined with the necessity of quenching his thirst with an augmented amount of sack, and had actually died while handsome Dick, with God knows what thoughts in his mind, was journeying northwards. Thus it came about that he arrived at Church-Peveril just in time for his brother's funeral. It was with great propriety that he attended the obsequies, and returned to spend a sympathetic day or two of mourning with his widowed sister-in-law, who was but a faint-hearted dame, little fit to be mated with such hawks as these. On the second night of his stay, he did that which the Peverils regret to this day. He entered the room where the twins slept with their nurse and quietly strangled the latter as she slept. Then he took the twins and put them into the fire which warms the long gallery. The weather, which up to the day of Joseph's death had been so hot, had changed suddenly to bitter cold, and the fire was heaped high with burning logs and was exultant with flame. In the core of this conflagration he struck out a cremation-chamber, and into that he threw the two children, stamping them down with his riding-boots. They could just walk, but they could not walk out of that ardent place. It is said that he laughed as he added more logs. Thus he became master of Church-Peveril.

The crime was never brought home to him, but he lived no longer than a year in the enjoyment of his blood-stained inheritance. When he lay adying he made his confession to the priest who attended him, but his spirit struggled forth from its fleshly coil before Absolution could be given him. On that very night there began in Church-Peveril the haunting which to this day is but seldom spoken of by the family, and then only in low tones with serious mien. For, only an hour or two after handsome Dick's death, one of the servants passing the door of the long gallery heard from within peals of the loud laughter so jovial and yet so sinister, which he had thought would never be heard in the house again. In a moment of that cold courage which is so nearly akin to mortal terror, he opened the door and entered, expecting to see he knew not what manifestation of him who lay dead in the room below. Instead he saw two little white-robed figures toddling towards him hand in hand across the moonlit floor.

The watchers in the room below ran upstairs startled by the crash of his fallen body, and found him lying in the grip of some dread convulsion. Just before morning he regained consciousness and told his tale. Then pointing with trembling and ash-grey finger towards the door, he screamed aloud, and so fell back dead.

During the next fifty years this strange and terrible legend of the twin-babies became fixed and consolidated. Their appearance, luckily for those who inhabited the house, was exceedingly rare, and during these years they seem to have been seen four or five times only. On each occasion they appeared at night, between sunset and sunrise, always in the same long gallery, and always as two toddling children scarcely able to walk. And on each occasion the luckless individual who saw them died either speedily or terribly, or with both speed and terror, after the accursed vision had appeared to him. Sometimes he might live for a few months: he was lucky if he died, as did the servant who first saw them, in a few hours. Vastly more awful was the fate of a certain

Mrs. Canning, who had the ill-luck to see them in the middle of the next century, or to be quite accurate, in the year 1760. By this time the hours and the place of their appearance were well-known, and, as up till a year ago, visitors were warned not to go between sunset and sunrise into the long gallery.

But Mrs. Canning, a brilliantly clever and beautiful woman, admirer also and friend of the notorious sceptic M. Voltaire, wilfully went and sat night after night in spite of all protestations, in the haunted place. For four evenings she saw nothing, but on the fifth she had her will, for the door in the middle of the gallery opened, and there came toddling towards her the ill-omened, innocent little pair. It seemed that even then she was not frightened, but she thought good, poor wretch, to mock at them, telling them it was time for them to get back into the fire. They gave no word in answer, but turned away from her, crying and sobbing. Immediately after they disappeared from her vision, she rustled downstairs to where the family and guests in the house were waiting for her, with the triumphant announcement that she had seen them both, and must needs write to M. Voltaire, saying that she had spoken to spirits made manifest. It would make him laugh. But when some months later the whole news reached him he did not laugh at all.

Mrs. Canning was one of the great beauties of her day, and in the year 1760 she was at the height and zenith of her blossoming. The chief beauty, if it is possible to single out one point where all was so exquisite, lay in the dazzling color and incomparable brilliance of her complexion. She was now just thirty years of age, but in spite of the excesses of her life, retained the snow and roses of girlhood, and she courted the bright light of day which other women shunned, for it but showed to greater advantage the splendor of her skin. In consequence she was very considerably dismayed one morning, about a fortnight after her strange experience in the long gallery, to observe on her left cheek an inch or two below her turquoise-colored eyes, a little greyish patch of skin, about as big as a threepenny piece. It was in vain that she applied her accustomed washes and unguents; vain, too, were the arts of her *fardeuse* and of her medical adviser. For a week she kept herself secluded, martyring herself with solitude and unaccustomed physics, and for result at the end of the week she had no amelioration to comfort herself with: instead, this woeful grey patch had doubled itself in size. Thereafter the nameless disease, whatever it was, developed in new and terrible ways. From the center of the discolored place there sprouted forth little lichen-like tendrils of greenish-grey, and another patch appeared on her lower lip. This, too, soon vegetated, and one morning on opening her eyes to the horror of the new day, she found that her vision was strangely blurred. She sprang to her looking-glass, and what she saw caused her to shriek aloud with horror. From under her upper eyelid a fresh growth had sprung up, mushroom-like, in the night, and its filaments extended downwards, screening the pupil of her eye. Soon after her tongue and throat were attacked: the air passages became obstructed, and death by suffocation was merciful after such suffering.

More terrible yet was the case of a certain Colonel Blantyre who fired at the children with his revolver. What he went through is not to be recorded here.

It is this haunting, then, that the Peverils take quite seriously, and every guest on his arrival in the house is told that the long gallery must not be entered after nightfall on any pretext whatever. By day, however, it is a delightful room and intrinsically merits description, apart from the fact that the due understanding of its geography is necessary for the account that here follows. It is full eighty feet in length, and is lit by a row of six tall windows looking over the gardens at the back of the house. A door communicates with the landing at the top of the main staircase, and about halfway down the gallery in the wall facing the windows is another door communicating with the back staircase and servants' quarters, and thus the gallery forms a constant place of passage for them in going to the rooms on the first landing. It was through this door that the baby-figures came when they appeared to Mrs. Canning, and on several other occasions they have been known to make their entry here, for the room out of which handsome Dick took them lies just beyond at the top of the back stairs. Further on again in the gallery is the fireplace into which he thrust them, and at the far end a large box-window looks straight down the avenue. Above this fireplace, there hangs with grim significance a portrait of handsome Dick, in the insolent beauty of early manhood, attributed to Holbein, and a dozen other portraits of great merit face the windows. During the day this is the most frequented sitting-room in the house, for its other visitors never appear there then, nor does it then ever resound with the harsh jovial laugh of handsome Dick, which sometimes, after dark has fallen, is heard by passers-by on the landing outside. But Blanche does not grow bright-eyed when she hears it: she shuts her ears and hastens to put a greater distance between her and the sound of that atrocious mirth.

But during the day the long gallery is frequented by many occupants, and much laughter in no wise sinister or saturnine resounds there. When summer lies hot over the land, those occupants lounge in the deep window-seats, and when winter spreads his icy fingers and blows shrilly between his frozen palms, congregate around the fireplace at the far end, and perch, in companies of cheerful chatterers, upon sofa and chair, and chair-back and floor. Often have I sat there on long August evenings up till dressing-time, but never have I been there when anyone has seemed disposed to linger over-late without hearing the warning: "It is close on sunset: shall we go?" Later on in the shorter autumn days they often have tea laid there, and sometimes it has happened that, even while merriment was most uproarious, Mrs. Peveril has suddenly looked out of the window and said, "My dears, it is getting so late: let us finish our nonsense downstairs in the hall." And then for a moment a curious hush always falls on loquacious family and guests alike, and as if some bad news had just been known, we all make our silent way out of the place. But the spirits of the Peverils (of the living ones, that is to say) are the most mercurial imaginable, and the blight which the thought of handsome Dick and his doings casts over them passes away again with amazing rapidity.

A typical party, large, young, and peculiarly cheerful, was staying at Church-Peveril shortly after Christmas last year, and as usual on December 31, Mrs. Peveril was giving her annual New Year's Eve ball. The house was quite full, and she had commandeered as well the greater part of the Peveril Arms to provide sleeping-quarters for the overflow from the house. For some days past a black and windless frost had stopped all hunting, but it is an ill windlessness that blows no good (if so mixed a metaphor may be forgiven), and the lake below the house had for the last day or two been covered with an adequate and admirable sheet of ice. Everyone in the house had been occupied all the morning of that day in performing swift and violent manoeuvres on the elusive surface, and as soon as lunch was over we all, with one exception, hurried out again. This one exception was Madge Dalrymple, who had had the misfortune to fall rather badly earlier in the day, but hoped, by resting her injured knee, instead of joining the skaters again, to be able to dance that evening. The hope, it is true, was of the most sanguine sort, for she could but hobble ignobly back to the house, but with the breezy optimism which characterizes the Peverils (she is Blanche's first cousin), she remarked that it would be but tepid enjoyment that she could, in her present state, derive from further skating, and thus she sacrificed little, but might gain much.

Accordingly after a rapid cup of coffee which was served in the long gallery, we left Madge comfortably reclined on the big sofa at right-angles to the fireplace, with an attractive book to beguile the tedium till tea. Being of the family, she knew all about handsome Dick and the babies, and the fate of Mrs. Canning and Colonel Blantyre, but as we went out I heard Blanche say to her, "Don't run it too fine, dear," and Madge had replied, "No, I'll go away well before sunset." And so we left her alone in the long gallery.

Madge read her attractive book for some minutes, but failing to get absorbed in it, put it down and limped across to the window. Though it was still but little after two, it was but a dim and uncertain light that entered, for the crystalline brightness of the morning had given place to a veiled obscurity produced by flocks of thick clouds which were coming sluggishly up from the northeast. Already the whole sky was overcast with them, and occasionally a few snowflakes fluttered waveringly down past the long windows. From the darkness and bitter cold of the afternoon, it seemed to her that there was like to be a heavy snowfall before long, and these outward signs were echoed inwardly in her by that muffled drowsiness of the brain, which to those who are sensitive to the pressures and lightness of weather portends storm. Madge was peculiarly the prey of such external influences: to her a brisk morning gave an ineffable brightness and briskness of spirit, and correspondingly the approach of heavy weather produced a somnolence in sensation that both drowsed and depressed her.

It was in such mood as this that she limped back again to the sofa beside the log-fire. The whole house was comfortably heated by water-pipes, and though the fire of logs and peat, an adorable mixture, had been allowed to burn low, the room was very warm. Idly she watched the dwindling flames, not opening her book again, but lying on the sofa with face towards the fireplace, intending drowsily and not immediately to go to her own room and spend the hours, until the return of the skaters made gaiety in the house again, in writing one or two neglected letters. Still drowsily she began thinking over what she had to communicate: one letter several days overdue should go to her mother, who was immensely interested in the psychical affairs of the family. She would tell her how Master Anthony had been prodigiously active on the staircase a night or two ago, and how the Blue Lady, regardless of the severity of the weather, had been seen by Mrs. Peveril that morning, strolling about. It was rather interesting: the Blue Lady had gone down the laurel walk and had been seen by her to enter the stables, where, at the moment, Freddy Peveril was inspecting the frost-bound hunters. Identically then, a sudden panic had spread through the stables, and the horses had whinnied and kicked, and shied, and sweated. Of the fatal twins nothing had been seen for many years past, but, as her mother knew, the Peverils never used the long gallery after dark.

Then for a moment she sat up, remembering that she was in the long gallery now. But it was still but a little after half-past two, and if she went to her room in half an hour, she would have ample time to write this and another letter before tea. Till then she would read her book. But she found she had left it on the window-sill, and it seemed scarcely worth while to get it. She felt exceedingly drowsy.

The sofa where she lay had been lately re-covered, in a greyish green shade of velvet, somewhat the color of lichen. It was of very thick, soft texture, and she luxuriously stretched her arms out, one on each side of her body, and pressed her fingers into the nap. How horrible that story of Mrs. Canning was: the growth on her face was of the color of lichen. And then without further transition or blurring of thought Madge fell asleep.

She dreamed. She dreamed that she awoke and found herself exactly where she had gone to sleep, and in exactly the same attitude. The flames from the logs had burned up again, and leaped on the walls, fitfully illuminating the picture of handsome Dick above the fireplace. In her dream she knew exactly what she had done today, and for what reason she was lying here now instead of being out with the rest of the skaters. She remembered also (still dreaming), that she was going to write a letter or two before tea, and prepared to get up in order to go to her room. As she half-rose she caught sight of her own arms lying out on each side of her on the grey velvet sofa. But she could not see where her hands ended, and where the grey velvet began: her fingers seemed to have melted into the stuff. She could see her wrists quite clearly, and a blue vein on the backs of her hands, and here and there a knuckle. Then, in her dream she remembered the last thought which had been in her mind before she fell asleep, namely the growth of the lichen-colored vegetation on the face and the eyes and the throat of Mrs. Canning. At that thought the strangling terror of real nightmare began: she knew that she was being transformed into this grey stuff, and she was absolutely unable to move. Soon the grey would spread up her arms, and over her feet; when they came in from skating they would find here nothing but a huge misshapen cushion of lichen-colored velvet, and that would be she. The horror grew more acute, and then by a violent effort she shook herself free of the clutches of this very evil dream, and she awoke.

For a minute or two she lay there, conscious only of the tremendous relief at finding herself awake. She felt again with her fingers the pleasant touch of the velvet, and drew them backwards and forwards, assuring herself that she was not, as her dream had suggested, melting into greyness and softness. But she was still, in spite of the violence of her awakening, very sleepy, and lay there till, looking down, she was aware that she could not see her hands at all. It was very nearly dark.

At that moment a sudden flicker of flame came from the dying fire, and a flare of burning gas from the peat flooded the room. The portrait of handsome Dick looked evilly down on her, and her hands were visible again. And then a panic worse than the panic of her dreams seized her. Daylight had altogether faded, and she knew that she was alone in the dark and terrible gallery. The panic was of the nature of nightmare, for she felt unable to move for terror. But it was worse than nightmare because she knew she was awake. And then the full cause of this frozen fear dawned on her; she knew with the certainty of absolute conviction that she was about to see the twin-babies.

She felt a sudden moisture break out on her face, and within her mouth her tongue and throat went suddenly dry, and she felt her tongue grate along the inner surface of her teeth. All power of movement had slipped from her limbs, leaving them dead and inert, and she stared with wide eyes into the blackness. The spurt of flame from the peat had burned itself out again, and darkness encompassed her.

Then on the wall opposite her, facing the windows, there grew a faint light of dusky crimson. For a moment she thought it but heralded the approach of the awful vision, then hope revived in her heart, and she remembered that thick clouds had overcast the sky before she went to sleep, and guessed that this light came from the sun not yet quite sunk and set. This sudden revival of hope gave her the necessary stimulus, and she sprang off the sofa where she lay. She looked out of the window and saw the dull glow on the horizon. But before she could take a step forward it was obscured again. A tiny sparkle of light came from the hearth which did not more than illuminate the tiles of the fireplace, and snow falling heavily tapped at the window panes. There was neither light nor sound except these.

But the courage that had come to her, giving her the power of movement, had not quite deserted her, and she began feeling her way down
the gallery. And then she found that she was lost. She stumbled against
a chair, and, recovering herself, stumbled against another. Then a table
barred her way, and, turning swiftly aside, she found herself up against
the back of the sofa. Once more she turned and saw the dim gleam of
the firelight on the side opposite to that on which she expected it. In her
blind gropings she must have reversed her direction. But which way was
she to go now? She seemed blocked in by furniture. And all the time in-
sistent and imminent was the fact that the two innocent terrible ghosts
were about to appear to her.

Then she began to pray, "Lighten our darkness, O Lord," she said to
herself. But she could not remember how the prayer continued, and she
had sore need of it. There was something about the perils of the night.
All this time she felt about her with groping, fluttering hands. The fire-
glimmer which should have been on her left was on her right again;
therefore she must turn herself round again. "Lighten our darkness,"
she whispered, and then aloud she repeated, "Lighten our darkness."

She stumbled up against a screen, and could not remember the existence of any such screen. Hastily she felt beside it with blind hands, and
touched something soft and velvety. Was it the sofa on which she had
lain? If so, where was the head of it? It had a head and a back and feet
—it was like a person, all covered with grey lichen. Then she lost her
head completely. All that remained to her was to pray; she was lost,
lost in this awful place, where no one came in the dark except the babies that cried. And she heard her voice rising from whisper to speech,
and speech to scream. She shrieked out the holy words, she yelled them
as if blaspheming as she groped among tables and chairs and the pleasant things of ordinary life which had become so terrible.

Then came a sudden and awful answer to her screamed prayer. Once
more a pocket of inflammable gas in the peat on the hearth was reached
by the smouldering embers, and the room started into light. She saw the
evil eyes of handsome Dick, she saw the little ghostly snowflakes falling
thickly outside. And she saw where she was, just opposite the door
through which the terrible twins made their entrance. Then the flame
went out again, and left her in blackness once more. But she had gained
something, for she had her geography now. The center of the room was
bare of furniture, and one swift dart would take her to the door of the
landing above the main staircase and into safety. In that gleam she had
been able to see the handle of the door, bright-brassed, luminous like a

star. She would go straight for it; it was but a matter of a few seconds now.

She took a long breath, partly of relief, partly to satisfy the demands of her galloping heart. But the breath was only half-taken when she was stricken once more into the immobility of nightmare.

There came a little whisper, it was no more than that, from the door opposite which she stood, and through which the twin-babies entered. It was not quite dark outside, for she could see that the door was opening. And there stood in the opening two little white figures, side by side. They came towards her slowly, shufflingly. She could not see face or form at all distinctly, but the two little white figures were advancing. She knew them to be the ghosts of terror, innocent of the awful doom they were bound to bring, even as she was innocent. With the inconceivable rapidity of thought, she made up her mind what to do. She had not hurt them or laughed at them, and they, they were but babies when the wicked and bloody deed had sent them to their burning death. Surely the spirits of these children would not be inaccessible to the cry of one who was of the same blood as they, who had committed no fault that merited the doom they brought. If she entreated them they might have mercy, they might forbear to bring the curse upon her, they might allow her to pass out of the place without blight, without the sentence of death, or the shadow of things worse than death upon her.

It was but for the space of a moment that she hesitated, then she sank down on to her knees, and stretched out her hands towards them.

"Oh, my dears," she said, "I only fell asleep. I have done no more wrong than that——"

She paused a moment, and her tender girl's heart thought no more of herself, but only of them, those little innocent spirits on whom so awful a doom was laid, that they should bring death where other children bring laughter, and doom for delight. But all those who had seen them before had dreaded and feared them, or had mocked at them.

Then, as the enlightenment of pity dawned on her, her fear fell from her like the wrinkled sheath that holds the sweet folded buds of spring.

"Dears, I am so sorry for you," she said. "It is not your fault that you must bring me what you must bring, but I am not afraid any longer. I am only sorry for you. God bless you, you poor darlings."

She raised her head and looked at them. Though it was so dark, she could now see their faces, though all was dim and wavering, like the light of pale flames shaken by a draught. But the faces were not miserable or fierce—they smiled at her with shy little baby smiles. And as she looked they grew faint, fading slowly away like wreaths of vapor in frosty air.

Madge did not at once move when they had vanished, for instead of fear there was wrapped round her a wonderful sense of peace, so happy and serene that she would not willingly stir, and so perhaps disturb it. But before long she got up, and feeling her way, but without any sense of nightmare pressing her on, or frenzy of fear to spur her, she went out of the long gallery, to find Blanche just coming upstairs whistling and swinging her skates.

"How's the leg, dear?" she asked. "You're not limping any more."

Till that moment Madge had not thought of it.

"I think it must be all right," she said. "I had forgotten it anyhow. Blanche, dear, you won't be frightened for me, will you, but—I have seen the twins."

For a moment Blanche's face whitened with terror.

"What?" she said in a whisper.

"Yes, I saw them just now. But they were kind, they smiled at me, and I was so sorry for them. And somehow I am sure I have nothing to fear."

It seems that Madge was right, for nothing untoward has come to her. Something, her attitude to them, we must suppose, her pity, her sympathy, touched and dissolved and annihilated the curse. Indeed, I was at Church-Peveril only last week, arriving there after dark. Just as I passed the gallery door, Blanche came out.

"Ah, there you are," she said. "I've just been seeing the twins. They looked too sweet and stopped nearly ten minutes. Let us have tea at once."